ROYALS

For Their Royal Heir

CW00953648

ROYALS

COLLECTION

ROYALS

For Their Royal Heir

Abby
GREEN

Ann Marie
WINSTON

Christine
RIMMER

Published in Great Britain 2017
By Mills & Boon, an imprint of HarperCollins*Publishers*
1 London Bridge Street, London, SE1 9GF

ROYALS: FOR THEIR ROYAL HEIR © 2017 Harlequin Books S.A.

An Heir Fit for a King © 2015 Abby Green
The Pregnant Princess © 2000 by Harlequin Books S.A
Special thanks and acknowledgement are given to Anne Marie Winston for her contribution to the Royally Wed series.
The Prince's Secret Baby © 2012 Christine Rimmer

ISBN: 978-0-263-93251-5

09-0318

Our policy is to use papers that are natural, renewable and recyclable products and made from wood grown in sustainable forests.
The logging and manufacturing processes conform to the legal environmental regulations of the country of origin.

Printed and bound in Spain
by CPI, Barcelona

AN HEIR FIT
FOR A KING

ABBY GREEN

This is for Sheila Hodgson...thanks for your support and calming influence while life got seriously in the way of this book!

I'd also like to thank the beautiful stranger working in the perfume shop in the Westbury Mall in Dublin, who sparked the original idea for this story and a very special thanks to Penny Ellis of Floris, London, who gave me my first experience in how to build a perfume. Any glaring errors are purely my own!

Irish author **Abby Green** threw in a very glamorous career in film and TV – which really consisted of a lot of standing in the rain outside actors' trailers – to pursue her love of romance. After she'd bombarded Mills & Boon with manuscripts they kindly accepted one, and an author was born. She lives in Dublin, Ireland, and loves any excuse for distraction. Visit www.abby-green.com or e-mail abbygreenauthor@gmail.com

CHAPTER ONE

LEILA VERUGHESE WAS just wondering morosely to herself what would happen when her dwindling supplies of perfume ran out completely when out of the corner of her eye she spotted something and turned to look, glad of the distraction to her maudlin thoughts.

It was a sleek black car, pulled up outside her small House of Leila perfume shop. The shop she'd inherited from her mother, on the Place Vendôme in Paris. When she took a closer look she saw a veritable *fleet* of sleek black cars. The lead one had flags flying on the bonnet, but Leila couldn't make out what country they were from—even though she'd spent most of her life identifying the glamorous comings and goings from the exclusive Ritz Hotel across the square.

A man hopped out of the front of the car, clearly a bodyguard of some sort, with an earpiece in his ear. He looked around before opening the back door and Leila's eyes widened when she saw who emerged. As if they had to widen purely to be able to take him in better.

It was a man—unmistakably and unashamedly a man. Which was a ridiculous thing to think… One was either a man or a woman, after all. But it was as if his very masculinity reached out before him like a crackling energy. He uncoiled to a height well over six feet, towering over the smaller, blockier man beside him. Powerfully built, with broad shoulders in a long black overcoat.

He looked as if he was about to come towards Leila's shop when he stopped suddenly, and Leila saw a moment of irritation cross his face before he turned back to talk to someone who had to be in the back of the car. A wife? A girlfriend? He went and put a big hand on the roof of the car as he consulted the person inside.

Leila caught a glimpse of a long length of bare toned thigh and a flash of blonde hair and then the man straightened again and began striding towards the shop, flanked by his minders.

It was only now that Leila even registered his face. She'd never seen anything so boldly beautiful in all her life. Dark olive skin—dark enough to be Arabic? High cheekbones and a sensual mouth. It might have been pretty if it hadn't been for the deep-set eyes, strong brows and even stronger jaw, which had clenched now, along with that look of irritation.

He had short hair—dark, cut close to his skull. Which had that same beautiful masculine shape as his face.

Shock held Leila still for a long moment as he got closer and closer. For a second, just before the shop door opened, his eyes caught hers and she had the strangest notion of a huge sleek bird of prey, swooping down to pick her up in his talons and carry her away.

The dark-haired shop assistant behind the glass of the shop barely impinged on Alix Saint Croix's consciousness as he strode to the door. *Surprise me.* His mouth tightened. If he'd been able to say that the previous night had been… pleasurable, he might have been more inclined to 'surprise' his lover. He was a man who was not used to obeying the demands of anyone else, and the only reason he was indulging Carmen's sudden whim for perfume was because he was all too eager to get away from her.

She'd arrived in his suite the previous evening, and their subsequent lovemaking had been…*adequate*. Alix had found himself wondering when was the last time he'd been so consumed with lust or by a woman that he'd lost his mind in pleasure? *Never*, a little voice had whispered as his lover had sauntered from the bed to the bathroom, making sure all her assets were displayed to best advantage.

Alix had been bored. And, because women seemed to have a seventh sense designed purely to detect that, his lover had become very uncharacteristically compliant and sweet. So much so that it had set Alix's teeth on edge. And after a day of watching waif-thin models prancing up and down a catwalk he was even more on edge.

But, as his advisor had pointed out when he'd grumbled to him on the phone earlier, 'This is good, Alix. It's helping us lull them into a false sense of security: they believe you have nothing on your agenda but the usual round of socialising and modelising.'

Alix did not like being considered a *modeliser*, and he pushed open the door to the shop with more force than was necessary, finally registering the shop assistant who was looking at him with a mixture of shock and awe on her face.

He also registered within the same nanosecond that she was the most beautiful woman he'd ever seen in his life.

The door shut behind him, a small bell tinkling melodically, but he didn't notice. She had pale olive skin, a straight nose and full soft lips. *Sexy*. A firm, yet delicate jaw. High cheekbones. Her hair was a sleek fall of black satin behind her shoulders and Alix had the bizarre compulsion to reach out and see if it would slip through his fingers like silk.

But it was her eyes that floored him... They were huge light emerald gems with the longest black lashes, framed by gracefully arched black brows. She looked like a Far Eastern princess.

'Who are you?'

Was that his voice? It sounded like a croak. Stunned. There was an instant fire kindling in his belly and his blood. The fire he'd lamented the lack of last night. It was as if his body was ahead of his brain in terms of absorbing her beauty.

She blinked and those long lashes veiled her stunning eyes for a moment.

'I'm the owner of the shop, Leila Verughese.'

The name suited her. Exotic. Alix somehow found the necessary motor skills to put out his hand. 'Alix Saint Croix.'

Recognition flashed in her eyes, unmistakable. She flushed, her cheeks going a pretty shade of pink and Alix surmised cynically that of *course* she'd heard of him. Who hadn't?

Her hand slipped into his then, small and delicate, cool, and the effect was like a rocket launching deep inside Alix. His blood boiled and his hand tightened reflexively around hers.

He struggled to make sense of this immediate and extreme physical and mental reaction. He was used to seeing a woman and assessing her from a distance, his desires firmly under control. This woman...*Leila*...was undeniably beautiful, yes. But she was dressed like a pharmacist, with a white coat over a very plain blue shirt and black trousers. Even in flat shoes, though, she was relatively tall, reaching his shoulder. He found himself imagining her in spindly high heels, how close her mouth would be if he wanted to just bend down slightly...

She took her hand back and Alix blinked.

'You are looking for a perfume?'

Alix's brain felt sluggish. Perfume? Why was he looking for perfume? *Carmen*. Waiting for him in the car. Immediately he scowled again, and the woman in front of him took a step back.

He put out a hand. 'Sorry, no...' He cursed silently—what was wrong with him? 'That is, *yes*, I'm looking for a perfume. For someone.'

The woman looked at him. 'Do you have any particular scent in mind?'

Alix dragged his gaze from her with an effort and looked around the small shop for the first time. Each wall was mirrored glass, with glass shelves and counters. Glass and gold perfume bottles covered the surfaces, giving the space a golden hue.

The decor was opulent without being stifling. And there wasn't the stench of overpowering perfume that Alix would normally associate with a shop like this. The ambience was cool, calm. Serene. Like her. He realised that she exuded a sense of calm and that he was reacting to that as well.

Almost absently he said, 'I'm looking for a scent for my mistress.'

When there was no immediate reaction such as Alix was used to—he said what he wanted and people jumped—he looked at the woman. Her mouth was pursed and an unmistakable air of disapproval was being directed at him. Intriguing. No one ever showed Alix their true reactions.

He arched a brow. 'You have a problem with that?'

To his further fascination her cheeks coloured and she looked away. Then she said stiffly, 'It's not for me to say what's an appropriate term for your…partner.'

Leila cursed herself for showing her reaction and moved away to one of the walls of shelves, as if to seek out some perfume samples.

Her father had once offered the role of mistress to Leila's mother—*after* she'd given birth to their illegitimate daughter. He'd seduced Deepika Verughese when he'd been doing business in India with Leila's grandfather, but had then turned his back on her when she'd arrived in Paris, disgraced and pregnant, all the way from Jaipur.

Her mother had declined his offer to become his kept woman, too proud and bitter after his initial rejection, and had told Leila the story while pointing out all the kept women of the various famous people and dignitaries who'd come into the shop over the years, as a salutary lesson in what women were prepared to do to feather their nests.

Leila's mind cleared of the painful memory. She hated it that she'd reacted so unprofessionally just now, but before she could say anything else she heard the man move and looked up into the glass to see him coming closer. He looked even larger reflected in the mirror, with his dark image being sent back a hundred times.

She realised that his eyes were a very dark grey.

'You know who I am?'

She nodded. She'd known who he was as soon as he'd said his name. He was the infamous exiled King of a small island kingdom off the coast of North Africa, near Southern Spain. He was a renowned financial genius, with fingers in almost every business one could think of—including most recently an astronomical investment in the new oil fields of Burquat in the Middle East.

There were rumours that he was going to make a claim on his throne, but if this visit was anything to go by he was concerned with nothing more than buying trinkets for his lover. And she had no idea why that made her feel so irritable.

Alix Saint Croix continued. 'So you'll know that a man like me doesn't have girlfriends or partners. I take mistresses. Women who know what to expect and don't expect anything more.'

Something hardened inside her. She knew all about men like him. Unfortunately. And the evidence of this man's single-minded, cynical nature made her see red. It made her sick, because it reminded her of her own naivety in the face of overwhelming evidence that what she sought didn't exist.

Nevertheless she was determined not to let this man draw her down another painful memory lane. She crossed her arms over her chest. 'Not all women are as cynical as you make out.'

Something hard crossed his face. 'The women who move in my circles are.'

'Well, maybe your circles are too small?'

She couldn't believe the words tripping out of her mouth, but he'd pushed a button—a very sensitive button. She almost expected him to storm out of her shop, but to her surprise Alix Saint Croix's mouth quirked on one side, making him look even sexier. Dangerous.

'Perhaps they are, indeed.'

Leila suddenly felt hot and claustrophobic. He was looking at her too intensely, and then his gaze dropped to where the swells of her breasts were pushed up by her crossed arms. She took them down hurriedly and reached for the nearest bottle of perfume, only half registering the label.

She thrust it towards him. 'This is one of our most popular scents. It's floral-based with a hint of citrus. It's light and zesty—perfect for casual wear.'

Alix Saint Croix shook his head. 'No, I don't think that'll do. I want something much earthier. Sensuous.'

Leila put down the bottle with a clatter and reached for another bottle. 'This might be more appropriate, then. It's got fruity top notes, but a woody, musky base.'

He cocked his head and said consideringly, 'It's so hard to know unless you can smell it.'

Leila's shirt felt too tight. She wanted to undo a top button. What was wrong with her?

She turned back to the counter and took a smelling strip out of a jar, ready to spray it so that he could smell it. And go. She wanted him gone. He was too disturbing to her usually very placid equilibrium.

But before she could spray, a large hand wrapped around her arm, stopping her.

Heat zinged straight to her belly. She looked up at him.

'Not on a piece of paper. I think you'd agree that a scent has to be on the skin to be best presented?'

Feeling slightly drugged and stupid, Leila said, 'It's a woman's scent.'

He cocked a brow again. 'So spray some on your wrist and I'll smell it.'

The shock that reverberated through Leila was as if he'd just said *Take off all your clothes, please*.

She had to struggle to compose herself, get a grip. She'd often sprayed perfume on her own skin so that someone could get a fuller sense of it. But this man had made the request sound almost indecent.

Praying that her hand wouldn't shake, Leila took the top off the bottle and pulled up her sleeve to spray some of the scent. When the liquid hit the underside of her wrist she shivered slightly. It felt absurdly sensual all of a sudden.

Alix Saint Croix still had a hand wrapped around her arm and now he moved it down to take the back of her hand in his, wrapping long fingers around hers. He moved his head down to smell the perfume, his dark head coming close to her breast.

But he kept his eyes on her, and from this close she could see lighter flecks of grey, like silver mercury. Leila's breath stopped when she felt his breath feather along her skin. Those lips were far too close to the centre of her palm, which was clammy.

He seemed to consider the scent until Leila's nerves twanged painfully. Her belly was a contracted ball of nerves.

A movement over his head caught her eye and she saw a sleek, tall blonde emerge from the back of the car with a phone clamped to her ear. She was wearing an indecently tight, slinky dress and a ridiculously ineffectual jacket for the cool autumn weather.

He must have picked up on her distraction and straightened to look out of the window too. Leila noticed a tension come into his body as his girlfriend—*mistress*—saw him and gesticulated with clear irritation, all while still talking on the phone.

'Your…er…mistress is waiting for you.' Leila's voice felt scratchy.

He still had his hand wrapped around hers and now let her go. Leila tucked it well out of reach.

He morphed before her eyes into someone much cooler, indecipherable. Perversely, it didn't comfort her.

'I'll take it.'

Leila blinked at him.

'The perfume,' he expanded, and for a moment a glint of what they'd just shared made his eyes flash.

Leila jerked into action. 'Of course. It'll only take me a moment to package it up.'

She moved to get a bag and paper and quickly and inexpertly packaged up the perfume, losing all of her customary cool. When she had it ready she handed it over and avoided his eye. A wad of cash landed on the counter but Leila wasn't about to check it.

And then, without another word, he turned around and strode out again, catching his…whatever she was…by the arm and hustling her back into the car.

His scent lingered on the air behind him, and in a very delayed reaction Leila assimilated the various components with an expertise that was like a sixth sense—along with the realisation that his scent had impacted on her as soon as he'd walked in, on a level that wasn't rational. Someplace else. Somewhere she wasn't used to scents impacting.

It was a visceral reaction. Primal. His scent was clean, with a hint of something very *male* that most certainly hadn't come out of a bottle. The kind of evocative scent that would make someone a fortune if they could bottle it: the pure essence of a virile male in his prime. Earthy. Musky.

A pulse between Leila's legs throbbed and she pressed her thighs together, horrified.

What was wrong with her? The man was a *king*, for God's sake, and he had a mistress that he was unashamed about. She should be thinking *good riddance*, but what she was thinking was much more confused.

It made alarm bells ring. It reminded her of another man who had come into the shop and who had very skilfully set about wooing her—only to turn into a nasty stranger when he'd realised that Leila had no intention of giving him what he wanted...which had been very far removed from what *Leila* had wanted.

She looked stupidly at the money on the counter for a moment, before realising that he'd vastly overpaid her for the perfume, but all she could think about was that last enigmatic look he'd shot her, just before he'd ducked into the car—a look that had seemed to say he'd be back. And soon.

And in light of their conversation, and the way he'd made her feel, Leila knew she shouldn't be remotely intrigued. But she was. And not even the ghost of memories past could stop it.

A little later, after Leila had locked up and gone upstairs to the small flat she'd shared with her mother all her life, she found herself gravitating to the window, which looked out over the Place Vendôme. The opera glasses that her mother had used for years to check out the comings and goings at the Ritz were sitting nearby, and for a second Leila felt an intense pang of grief for her mother.

Leila pushed aside the past and picked up the glasses and looked through them, seeing the usual flurry of activity when someone arrived at the hotel in a flash car. She tilted the glasses upwards to where the rooms were—and her whole body froze when she caught a glimpse of a familiar masculine figure against a brightly lit opulent room.

She trained the glasses on the sight, hating herself for

it but unable to look away. It was him. Alix Saint Croix.
The overcoat was gone. And the jacket. He had his back
to her and was dressed in a waistcoat and shirt and trousers. Hands in his pockets were drawing the material of his
trousers over his very taut and muscular backside.

Instantly Leila felt damp heat coil down below and
squeezed her legs together.

He was looking at something in front of him, and Leila
tensed even more when the woman he'd been with came
into her line of vision. She'd taken off the jacket and the
flimsy dress was now all she wore. Her body was as sleek
and toned as a throughbred horse. Leila vaguely recognised
her as a world-famous lingerie model.

She could see that she held something in her hand, and
when it glinted she realised it was the bottle of perfume.
The woman sprayed it on her wrist and lifted it to smell,
a sexy smile curling her wide mouth upwards.

She sprayed more over herself and Leila winced slightly.
The trick with perfume was always *less is more*. And then
she threw the bottle aside, presumably to a nearby chair
or couch, and proceeded to pull down the skinny straps of
her dress. Then she peeled the top half of her dress down,
exposing small but perfect breasts.

Leila gasped at the woman's confidence. She'd never
have the nerve to strip in that way in front of a man.

And then Alix Saint Croix moved. He turned away from
the woman and walked to the window. For a second he
loomed large in Leila's glasses, filling them with that hard-
boned face. He looked intent. And then he pulled a drape
across, obscuring the view, almost as if he'd known Leila
was watching from across the square like a Peeping Tom.

Disgusted with herself, Leila threw the glasses down
and got up to pace in her small apartment. She berated herself. *How* could a man like that even capture her attention?
He was exactly what her mother had warned her about:

rich and arrogant. Not even prepared to see women as
anything other than mistresses, undoubtedly interchanged
with alarming frequency once the novelty with each one
had worn off.

Leila had already refused to take her mother's warnings to heart once, and had suffered a painful blow to her
confidence and pride because of it.

Full of pent-up energy, she dragged on a jacket and
went outside for a brisk walk around the nearby Tuileries
gardens, telling herself over and over again first of all that
nothing had happened with Alix Saint Croix in her shop
that day, secondly that she'd never see him again, and
thirdly that she didn't care.

The following evening dusk was falling as Leila went to
lock the front door of her shop. It had been a long day, with
only a trickle of customers and two measly sales. Thanks
to the recession, niche businesses everywhere had taken
a nosedive, and since the factory that manufactured the
House of Leila scents had closed down she hadn't had the
funds to seek out a new factory.

She'd been reduced to selling off the stock she had left
in the hope that enough sales would give her the funds to
start making perfumes again.

She was just about to turn the lock when she looked up
through the glass to see a familiar tall dark figure, flanked
by a couple of other men, approaching her door. The almost violent effect on her body of seeing him in the flesh
again mocked her for fooling herself that she'd managed
not to think about him all day.

The exiled King with the tragic past.

Leila had looked him up on the Internet last night in a
moment of weakness and had read about how his parents
and younger brother had been slaughtered during a mili-

tary coup. The fact that he'd escaped to live in exile had become something of a legend.

Her immediate instinct was to lock the door and pull the blind down—fast. But he was right outside now and looking at her. The faintest glimmer of a smile touched his mouth. She could see a day's worth of stubble shadowing his jaw.

Obeying professional reflexes rather than her instincts, Leila opened the door and stepped back. He came in and once again it was as if her brain was slowing to a halt. It was consumed with taking note of his sheer masculine beauty.

Determined not to let him rattle her again, Leila assumed a polite, professional mask. 'How did your mistress like the perfume?'

A lurid image of the woman putting on that striptease threatened to undo Leila's composure but she pushed it out of her head with effort.

Alix Saint Croix made an almost dismissive gesture with his hand. 'She liked it fine. That's not why I'm here.'

Leila found it hard to draw in a breath. Suddenly terrified of why he *was* there, she gabbled, 'By the way, you left far too much money for the perfume.'

She turned and went to the counter and took out an envelope containing the excess he'd paid. She'd been intending to drop it to the hotel for him, but hadn't had the nerve all day. She held it out now.

Alix barely looked at it. He speared her with that grey gaze and said, 'I want to take you out to dinner.'

Panic fluttered in Leila's gut and her hand tightened on the envelope, crushing it. 'What did you say?'

He pushed open his light overcoat to put his hands in his pockets, drawing attention to another pristine three-piece suit, lovingly moulded to muscles that did not belong to an urban civilised man, more to a warrior.

'I said I would like you to join me for dinner.'

Leila frowned. 'But you have a mistress.'

Something stern crossed Alix Saint Croix's face and the grey in his eyes turned to steel. 'She is no longer my mistress.'

Leila recalled what she'd seen the previous night and blurted out, 'But I saw you—you were together—' She stopped and couldn't curb the heat rising. The last thing she wanted was for him to know she'd been spying, and she said quickly, 'She certainly seemed to be under the impression that you were together.'

She hoped he'd assume she was referring to when she'd seen the woman waiting for him outside the shop.

Alix's face was indecipherable. 'As I said, we are no longer together.'

Leila felt desperate. And disgusted. And disappointed, which was even worse. Of course a man like him would interchange his women without breaking a sweat.

'But I don't even know you—you're a total stranger.'

His mouth twitched slightly. 'Which could be helped by sharing conversation over dinner, *non*?'

Leila had a very strong urge to back away, but forced herself to stand her ground. She was in *her* shop. *Her* space. And everything in her screamed at her to resist this man. He was too gorgeous, too big, too smooth, too famous...too much.

Something reckless gripped her and she blurted out, 'I saw you. The two of you... I didn't intend to, but when I looked out of my window last night I saw you in your room. With her. She was taking off her clothes...'

Leila willed down the embarrassed heat and tilted up her chin defiantly. She didn't care if he thought she was some kind of stalker.

His gaze narrowed on her. 'I saw you too...across the square, silhouetted in your window.'

Now she blanched. 'You did?'

He nodded. 'It merely confirmed that I wanted you. And not her.'

Leila was caught, trapped in his gaze and in his own confession. 'You pulled the curtain across. For privacy.'

His mouth firmed. 'Yes. For privacy while I asked her to put her dress back on and get out, because the relationship was over.'

Leila shivered at his coolness. 'But that's so cruel. You'd just bought her a gift.'

Something infinitely cynical lit those grey eyes and Leila hated it.

'Believe me, a woman like Carmen is no soft-centred fool with notions of where the relationship was going. She knew it was finite. The relationship was ending whether I'd met you or not.'

Leila balked. She definitely veered more towards the *soft-centred fool* end of the scale.

She folded her arms and fought the pull from her gut to follow him blindly. She'd done that with a man once before, with her stupid, vulnerable heart on her sleeve. It made her hard now. 'Thank you for the invitation, but I'm afraid I must say no.'

His brows snapped together in a frown. 'Are you married?'

His gaze dropped to her left hand as if to look for a ring, and something flashed in his eyes when he took in her ringless fingers. Leila's hands curled tight. Too late.

The personal question told her she was doing the right thing and she said frostily, 'That is none of your business, sir. I'd like you to leave.'

For a tiny moment Alix Saint Croix's eyes widened on her, and then he said coolly, 'Very well, I'm sorry for disturbing you. Good evening, Miss Verughese.'

CHAPTER TWO

ALIX WAS HALFWAY across the quiet square, fuelled by a surge of angry disbelief, before the thought managed to break through: no woman, *ever*, had turned him down like that. So summarily. Coldly. As if he'd overstepped some invisible mark on the ground. As if he was...*beneath* her.

He dismissed his security detail with a flick of his hand as he walked into the hotel, with staff scurrying in his wake, the elevator attendant jumping to attention. Alix ignored them all, his mind filled with incredulity that she had said *no*.

He'd ended his liaison with Carmen specifically to pursue Leila Verughese.

When Carmen had undressed in front of him in his suite he'd felt nothing but impatience to see her gone. And then, when he'd gone to his window and seen the light shining from a small window above the perfume shop and that slim figure, all he'd seen was *her* alluring body in his mind's eye. The hint of generous curves told of a very classic feminine shape—not exactly fashion-forward, like Carmen, with tiny breasts and an almost androgynous figure, but all the more alluring for that.

He wanted her with a hunger he hadn't allowed himself to feel in a long time. And that impatience to see Carmen gone had become a compelling need.

When Alix got to his suite of rooms he threw off his coat and prowled like a restless animal. He felt animalistic.

How *dared* she turn him down? He wanted her. The exotic princess who sold perfume.

Why did he want her so badly?

The question pricked at him like a tiny barb and he couldn't ignore it. He'd only ever wanted one other woman in a similar way. A woman who had made him think she was different from all the others. When she'd been even worse.

Alix, young and far more naive than he'd ever wanted to admit at the age of eighteen, had been seduced by a beautiful body and an act of innocence honed to perfection.

Until he'd walked into her college rooms one day and seen one of his own bodyguards thrusting between her pale legs. The image was clear enough to mock him. Years later.

As if his own parents' toxic marriage hadn't already drummed it into him that men and women together brought pain and disharmony.

Ever since then Alix had excised all emotion where women were concerned. They were mistresses—who pleasured him and accompanied him to social events. Until the time came for him to choose a wife who would be his Queen. And then his marriage would be different. It wouldn't be toxic. It would be harmonious and respectful.

Alix thought about that now. Because that time would be coming soon. He was already being presented with prospective wives to choose from. Princesses from different principalities who all looked dismayingly like horses. But Alix didn't care. His wife would be his consort, adept at dealing with the social aspects of her role and providing him with heirs.

So why is this woman getting under your skin?

She's not, he affirmed to himself.

She was just a stunningly beautiful woman who'd connected with him on some very base level and he wasn't used to that.

Alix didn't like to recall that first meeting, when just seeing her had been like a defibrillator shocking him back to life.

His was a life that needed no major distractions right

now. He had enough going on with the very real prospect that in a couple of weeks he was going to regain control of his throne. Something he'd been working towards all his life.

And yet this woman was lingering in his mind, compelling him to make impetuous decisions. And despite that Alix found himself drawn once again to the massive window through which he'd seen Leila across the square last night. The shop was in darkness now, the blind pulled firmly down.

A sense of impotent frustration gripped him even more fiercely now. The upstairs was in darkness too. Was she out? With another man? Saying yes to him? Alix tensed all over at that thought and had to relax consciously. He did not *do* jealousy. Not since he'd kicked his naked bodyguard out of his traitorous lover's bed. And had that even been jealousy? Or just young injured male pride?

He emitted a sound of irritation and plucked a phone out of his pocket. He was connected in seconds and said curtly, 'I want you to find out everything you can about a woman called Leila Verughese. She owns a perfume shop on the Place Vendôme in Paris.'

Alix terminated the connection. He told himself that she was most likely playing a game. Hard to get. But he didn't really care—because he was no woman's fool any more and, game or no game, he *would* have her and sate this burning urge before his life changed irrevocably and became one of duty and responsibility.

She didn't have the power to derail him. No woman did.

For two days Leila stood in her shop, acutely aware of Alix Saint Croix's cavalcade sweeping in and out of the square. Every time his sleek car drove past she tensed inwardly— as if waiting for him to stop and get out and come in again. To ask her to dinner again.

She hated it that she knew when his cars were parked outside the hotel. It made her feel jittery, on edge.

Just then her phone rang, and she jumped and cursed softly before answering it. It was the hotel. They wanted Leila to bring over an assortment of perfumes for one of their guests.

She agreed and put the phone down, immediately feeling nervous. Which was ridiculous. This wasn't an unusual request—hotel guests often spotted the shop and asked for a personal service. At one time Leila had gone over with perfumes for a foreign president's wife.

Even though she would be venturing far too near to the lion in his lair, she welcomed the diversion and set about gathering as many diverse samples of perfumes as she could.

On arrival at the hotel, dressed smartly in a dark trouser suit and white shirt, hair up, and with her specially fortified and protective wheelie suitcase, Leila was shown to the top floor by a duty manager.

The same floor as Alix Saint Croix's suite.

She felt a flutter of panic, but pushed it down as the lift doors opened and she stepped into the opulent luxury of one of the hotel's most sumptuous floors.

To her vast relief they were heading in the opposite direction from the suite she'd watched so closely the other night.

The duty manager opened the door to the suite and ushered Leila in, saying, 'Your clients will be here shortly—they said to go ahead and set up while you're waiting.'

Leila smiled. 'Okay, thank you.'

When she was alone she set about opening her case and taking out some bottles, glad to have the distraction of what she did best. No time to think about—

She heard the door open behind her and stood up and turned around with a smile on her face, expecting to see a woman.

The smile promptly slid off her face when she saw Alix Saint Croix and the door closing softly behind him. *Client*, not clients. For a long moment Leila was only aware of her heartbeat, fast and hard. He was dressed in a white shirt and dark trousers. Sleeves rolled up, top button open. Hands in his pockets. He was looking at her with a gleam in his eyes that told her the predator had tracked down his prey.

So why was she suddenly feeling a thrum of excitement?

He took a step further into the room and inclined his head towards her suitcase, which was open on an ottoman. 'Do you supply men's scents also?'

Leila was determined not to appear as ruffled as she felt. She said coolly, 'First of all, I don't appreciate being ambushed, Mr Saint Croix. But, as I'm here now—yes, I do men's scents also.'

Alix Saint Croix looked at her with that enigmatic gaze, a small smile playing around his mouth. 'The hotel told me that you regularly come to do personal consultations. Do you regard *all* clients as ambushing you?'

Leila's face coloured. 'Of course not.' She felt flustered now. 'Look, why don't we get on with it? I'm sure you're a busy man.'

He came closer, rolling his sleeves up further as he said, with a definite glint in his grey eyes, 'On the contrary, I have all the time in the world.'

Leila's hands clenched into fists at her sides. She boiled inside at the way he'd so neatly caught her and longed to be able to storm out...but to where? Back to an empty shop? To polish the endless glass shelves? He'd just suggested a lucrative personal consultation—even if his actions were nefarious. Not to mention the wad of cash he'd left her the other day...

Swallowing her ire, and not liking the way he was getting under her skin so easily, she forced a smile and said, 'Of course. Then, please, sit down.'

Leila was careful to take a chair at a right angle to the couch. Briskly she took out some of her sample bottles containing pure oils and a separate mixer bottle.

As he passed her to sit down she unconsciously found herself searching for his scent again, and it hit her as powerfully as it had the first time. Leila had a sudden and fantastical image of herself having access to this man's naked body and being allowed to spend as much time as she liked discovering the secret scents of his very essence, so that she could try to analyse them and distil them into a perfume.

She cursed her wayward imagination and said, without looking at him, 'Had you any particular scent in mind? What do you usually like?'

She was aware of strong thighs in her peripheral vision, his trousers doing little to hide their length or muscularity.

'I have no idea,' he said dryly. 'I get sent new perfumes all the time and usually just pick whatever appeals to me in the moment. But generally I don't like anything too heavy.'

Leila glanced at him sharply. His face was expressionless, but there was an intensity in his eyes that made her nervous. For a moment she could almost believe he wasn't talking about scents at all, and felt like telling him to save his breath if he was warning her obliquely that he wasn't into commitment—because she had no intention of getting to know him any better.

She couldn't deny, though, how her very body seemed to hum in his presence.

Instinctively she reached for a bottle and pulled it out, undoing the stopper. She sniffed for a moment and then dipped a smelling strip into the bottle and extracted it and held it out towards him. 'What do you think of this, Monsieur Saint Croix?'

'Please...' he purred. 'Call me Alix.'

Leila tensed, her hand held out, refusing to give in to

his unashamed flirtation. Eventually, eyes sparkling as he registered her obvious struggle against him, he took the sliver of paper and Leila snatched her hand back.

He kept his eyes on her as he smelled it carefully, passing it over and back under his nose. She saw something flare in his eyes, briefly, and felt an answering rush of heat under her skin.

Consideringly, he said, 'I like it—what is it?'

'It's fougère—a blend of notes based on lavender, oakmoss and coumarin: a derivative of the tonka bean. It's a good base on which to build a scent if you like it.'

He handed her back the tester and lifted a brow. 'The tonka bean?'

Leila nodded as she pulled out another bottle. 'It's a soft, woody note. We extract ingredients for a scent from anything and everything.'

She was beginning to feel more relaxed, concentrating on her work as if there *wasn't* a whole subtext going on between her and this man. Maybe she could just ignore it.

'It was developed in the late eighteen-hundreds by Houbigant and I find it evocative of a woody, ferny environment.'

Leila handed him another smelling strip.

'Try this.'

He took it and looked at her again. She found it hard to take her eyes away as he breathed deep. Every move this man made was so boldly sensual. Sexy. It made Leila want to curl in on herself and try not to be noticed.

'This is more...exotic?'

Leila answered, 'It's oudh—quite rare. From agarwood. A very distinctive scent—people either love it or hate it.'

He looked at her, his mouth quirking slightly. 'I like it. What does that say about me?'

Leila shrugged minutely as she reached for another bottle, trying to affect nothing but professionalism. 'Just that you respond to the more complex make-up of the scent. It's perhaps no surprise that a king should favour such a rare specimen.'

Immediately tension sprang up between them, and Leila busied herself opening another bottle.

Alix Saint Croix's voice was sharper this time. 'A king in exile, to be more accurate. Does that make a difference?'

Leila looked at him as she handed him another sample and said, equally coolly, 'I'm sure it doesn't. You're still a king, after all, are you not?'

He made a dissenting sound as he took the new tester. Leila wondered how much more patience he would have for this game they were playing. As if someone like him *really* had time for a personal perfume consultation...

She looked to see him sniff the strip and saw how he immediately recoiled from the smell. He grimaced, and Leila had to bite back a smile.

'What is *that*?'

She reached across and took the paper back. 'It's extracted from the narcissus flower.'

His mouth curled up slightly. 'Should I take that as a compliment? That I don't immediately resonate with the narcissus?'

Leila avoided looking at him and started packing up her bottles, eager to get away from this man. 'If you like any of those scents we tested I can make something up for you.'

'I'd like that. But I want you to add something I haven't considered...something you think would uniquely suit me.'

Leila tightened inwardly at the prospect of choosing something unique to him. She closed the case and looked at him. 'I'm afraid I will be bound to disappoint you. Perfume is such a personal—'

'And I'd like you to deliver it personally this evening.' He cut her off as if she hadn't even been talking.

Leila stood up abruptly and looked down at him. 'Monsieur Saint Croix, while I appreciate the custom you've given me today, I'm afraid I...'

He stood up then too, and the words dried in her throat as his tall body towered over hers. They were too close.

His voice was low, with a thread of steel. 'Are you seriously telling me that you're turning down the opportunity to custom make a scent for the royal house of Isle Saint Croix?'

When he said it like that Leila could hear her mother's voice in her head, shrill and panicked, *Are you completely crazy?* What was she doing? In her bid to escape from this disturbing tension was she prepared to jeopardise the most potentially lucrative sale she'd had in years? The merest hint of a professional association with a *king*, no less, and her sales would go through the roof.

In a small voice she finally said, 'No, of course I wouldn't turn down such an opportunity. I can put a couple of sample fragrances together and deliver them to the hotel later. You can let me know which you prefer.'

His eyes were a mesmerising shade of pewter. 'One scent, Leila, and I want you to bring it to me personally. Say seven p.m.?'

Her name on his lips felt absurdly intimate, as if he'd just touched her. She glared at him but had no room to manoeuvre. And then she told herself to get a grip. Alix Saint Croix might be disturbing her on all sorts of levels but he was hardly going to kidnap her. *He wouldn't need to.* That was the problem. Leila was afraid that if she had much more contact with him, her defences would start to feel very flimsy.

Hiding her irritation at how easily he was sweeping aside her reservations, she bent down and closed her suitcase—but before she could lift it off the ottoman he brushed her hand aside and took it, wrapped a big hand firmly around the handle.

Leila straightened, face flushed. He extended a hand and lifted a brow. 'After you.'

Much to her embarrassment, he insisted on escorting her all the way down to the lobby and seemed to be oblivious to the way everyone jumped to attention—not least his security guards. He called one of them over and handed the thickset man the case, instructing him to carry it back to the shop for Leila. Her protests fell on deaf ears.

And then, before she could leave, he said, 'What time shall I send Ricardo to escort you to the hotel?'

Leila turned and looked up. She was about to assert that she'd had no problem crossing the square on her own for some two decades, but as soon as she saw the look in his eye she said with a resigned sigh, 'Five to seven.'

He dipped his head. 'Till then, Leila.'

Once back in his own suite, Alix stood looking across the square for a long time. Leila's reluctance to acquiesce to him intrigued him. Anticipation tightened his gut. Even though he knew this was likely just a game on her part, he was prepared to indulge it because he wanted her. And he had time on his hands.

He felt a mild pang of guilt now when he thought of what his security team had reported to him about her.

The Verughese family were wealthy and respectable in India. A long line of perfumers, supplying scents to maharajas and the richest in society. There were a scant few lines about Deepika Verughese, who had been Leila's mother. She'd come to France after breaking off relations with her family, where she'd proceeded to have one daughter: Leila. No mention of a father.

In all other respects she was squeaky clean. No headlines had ever appeared about her.

He felt something vibrate in his pocket and extracted a small, sleek mobile phone. Without checking to see who it was, and not taking his eyes off his quarry across the square, he answered, 'Yes?'

It was his chief advisor, and Alix welcomed the distraction, reminded of the bigger picture.

He turned his back to the view. 'How are the plans for the referendum coming along?'

Isle Saint Croix was due to vote within two weeks on whether or not they wanted Alix to return as King. It was still too volatile for Alix to be in the country himself, so he was depending on loyal politicians and his people, who had campaigned long and hard to restore the monarchy. Finally the end goal was in sight. But it was a very delicate balancing act that could all come tumbling down at any moment.

The ruling party in Isle Saint Croix were ruthless, and only the fact that they'd had to reluctantly agree to let international observers into the country had saved the process from falling apart already.

Andres was excited. 'The polls are showing in your favour, but not so much that it's unduly worrying the military government. They're still arrogant enough to believe they're in control.'

Alix listened to him reiterate what he already knew, but it was still reassuring. Something bittersweet pierced his heart. When he regained the throne he would finally have a chance to avenge his younger brother's brutal death.

Alix tuned back into the conversation when the other man cleared his voice awkwardly and said, 'Is it true that your affair with Carmen Desanto is over? It was in the papers today.'

Alix's mouth tightened. Only because of the fact that Andres was one of his oldest and most trusted friends did he even contemplate answering the question. 'What of it?'

'Well, it's unfortunate timing. The busier you can look with very *un*political concerns the better—to lull the re-

gime on Isle Saint Croix into a false sense of security. Even
if they hear rumours of you gaining support from abroad,
when they see pictures in the papers…'

He didn't need to finish. Alix would appear to be the
louche and unthreatening King in exile he'd always been.
Still, he didn't like to be dictated to like this.

'Well,' he said with a steely undertone, 'I'm afraid that,
as convenient a front as Carmen might have proved to be,
I wasn't prepared to put up with her inane chatter for any
longer.'

An image popped into Alix's head of another woman.
Someone whose chatter he wouldn't mind listening to.
And he very much doubted that *she* ever chattered inanely.
Those beautiful eyes were far too intelligent.

On the other end of the phone Andres sighed theatri-
cally. 'Look, all I'm saying is that now would be a really
good time to be living up to your reputation as an eligi-
ble bachelor, cutting a swathe through the beauties of the
world.'

Alix had only been interested in a very personal con-
quest before now, but suddenly the thought of pursuing
Leila Verughese took on a whole new dimension. It was,
in fact, completely justifiable.

A small smile curled his lips. 'Don't worry, Andres. I'm
sure I can think of something to keep the media hounds
happy.'

When the knock came on Alix's door at about one minute past seven that evening he didn't like to acknowledge
the anticipation rushing through his blood. The reminder
that Leila was getting to him on a level that was unprec-
edented was not welcome. He told himself it was just lust.
Chemical. Controllable.

He strode forward and opened the door to see Leila
with a vaguely mutinous look on her beautiful face and

Ricardo behind her. Alix nodded to his bodyguard and the man melted away.

Alix stood back and held the door open. 'Please, come in.'

He noted that Leila hadn't changed outfits since earlier. She was still wearing the smart dark trouser suit and her hair was pulled back into a low, sleek ponytail. She wore not a scrap of make-up, yet her features stood out as if someone had lovingly painted her.

The pale olive skin, straight nose, lush mouth and startling green eyes combined together to such an effect that Alix could only mentally shake his head as he followed her into his suite... How did such a woman as this work quietly in a perfume shop, going largely unnoticed?

She turned to face him in the palatial living room and held up a glossy House of Leila bag. 'Your fragrance, Monsieur Saint Croix.'

Alix bit back the urge to curse and said smoothly, 'Leila, I've asked you to call me Alix.'

Her eyes glittered. 'Well, I don't think it's appropriate. You're a client—'

'A client who,' he inserted smoothly, 'has just paid a significant sum of money for a customised fragrance.'

Her mouth shut and remorse lit her eyes. Alix was fascinated again by the play of unguarded emotions. God knew he certainly hadn't revealed emotion himself for years. And the women he dealt with probably wouldn't know a real emotion if it jumped up and bit them on the ass.

She looked at him and he felt short of breath, acutely aware of the thrust of her perfect breasts against the silk of her shirt.

'Very well. Alix.'

Her mouth and tongue wrapping around his name had an effect similar to that if she'd put her mouth on his body intimately. Blood rushed south and he hardened.

Gritting his jaw against the onset of a fierce arousal that

made a mockery of any illusion of control, Alix responded, 'That wasn't so hard, was it?' He groaned inwardly at his unfortunate choice of words and reached for the bag she still held out in a bid to distract her from seeing her seismic effect in his body.

With the bag in his hand he gestured for her to sit down. 'Please, make yourself comfortable. Would you like a drink?'

Leila's hands twisted in front of her. 'No, thank you. I really should be getting back—'

'Don't you want to know if I like the scent or not?'

Her mouth stayed open and eventually she said, 'Of course I do... But you could send word if you don't like it.'

Alix frowned minutely and moved closer to Leila, cocking his head to one side. 'Why are you so nervous with me?'

She swallowed. He could see the long slim column of her throat, the pulse beating near the base. Hectic.

'I'm not nervous.'

He came closer and a warm seeping of colour made her skin flush.

'Liar. You're ready to jump out of that window to get away from me right now.'

One graceful brow arched. 'Not a reaction you're used to?'

Alix's mouth quirked. The tension was diffused a little. 'No, not usually.'

He indicated again for Leila to sit down and after a moment, when he really wasn't sure if she'd just walk out, she moved over to the couch and sat down. Something relaxed inside him.

He put down the bag containing the scent while he poured himself a drink and glanced at her over his shoulder. 'Are you sure I can't get you anything?'

She'd been taking in the room, eyes wide, and suddenly all its opulence felt garish to Alix.

Those eyes clashed with his. 'Okay,' she said huskily. 'I'll have a little of whatever you're having.'

It was crazy. Alix wanted to howl in triumph at this concession. At the fact that she was still here, when usually he was batting women away.

'Bourbon?'

She half nodded and shrugged. 'I've never tried it before.'

There was something incredibly disarming about her easy admission. Like watching the play of emotion on her face and in her eyes. Alix brought the drinks over and was careful to take a seat at right angles to the couch, knowing for certain that she'd bolt if he sat near her.

He handed her the glass and she took it. He held his out. '*Santé*, Leila.'

She tipped her glass towards his and took a careful sip, as he took a sip of his own. He watched her reaction, saw her eyes watering slightly, her cheeks warming again. His own drink slipped down his throat, making his already warm body even hotter.

'What do you think?'

She considered for a moment and then gave a tiny smile. 'It's like fire… I like it.'

'Yes,' Alix said faintly, transfixed by Leila's mouth, 'It's like fire.'

A moment stretched between them, and then she dropped her gaze from his and put her glass down on the table to indicate the bag she'd brought. 'You should see if you like the scent.'

Alix put down his own glass and took the bag, extracting a gold box embossed with a black line around the edges. It had a panel on the front with a label that said simply *Alix Saint Croix*.

Alix opened the box and took out the heavy and beautifully cut glass bottle, with its black lid and distinctive gold piping. It was masculine—solid.

'It's quite strong,' Leila said, as he took off the lid and looked at her. 'You only need a small amount. Try it on the back of your hand.'

Alix sprayed and then bent his head. He wasn't ready for the immediate effect on his senses. It impacted deep down in his gut—so many layers of scent, filtering through his brain and throwing up images like a slideshow going too fast for him to analyse.

He was thrown back in time to his home on the island, with the sharp, tangy smell of the sea in the air, and yet he could smell the earth too, and the scent of the exotic flowers that bloomed on Isle Saint Croix. He could even smell something oriental, spicy, that made him think of his Moorish ancestors who had given the island its distinctive architecture.

He wasn't prepared for the sharp pang of emotion that gripped him as a memory surged: him and his younger brother, playing, carefree, near the sea.

'What's in it?' he managed to get out.

Leila was looking concerned. 'You don't like it?'

'Like' was too flimsy a word for what this scent was doing to him. Alix stood up abruptly, feeling acutely exposed. *Dieu.* Was she a witch? He strode over to the window and kept his back to her, brought his hand up to smell again.

The initial shock of the impact was lessening as the scent opened out and mellowed. It was *him*. The scent was everything that was deep inside him, where no one could see his true self. Yet this woman had got it—after only a couple of meetings and a few hours.

CHAPTER THREE

LEILA STOOD UP, not sure how to respond. She'd never seen someone react so forcefully to a scent before.

'I researched a little about the island, to find out what its native flowers were, and I approximated them as closely as I could with what I have available in the shop. And I added citrus and calone, which has always reminded me of a sea breeze.'

Alix Saint Croix looked huge, formidable, against the window and the autumnal darkness outside. Her first reaction when she'd met this man had been fascination, a feeling of being dazzled, and since then her instinct had been to run away—fast. But now her feet were glued to the floor.

'If you don't like it—'

'I like it.'

His response was short, sharp. He sounded almost... *angry*. Leila was completely confused.

Hesitantly she said, 'Are you sure? You don't sound very pleased.'

He turned around then and thrust both hands into his pockets. His chest was broad, the darkness of his skin visible under his shirt. He looked at her closely and shook his head, as if trying to clear it.

Finally he said, 'I'm just a little surprised. The fragrance is not what I was expecting.'

Leila shrugged. 'A customised scent has a bigger impact than a generic designer scent...'

His mouth quirked sexily and he came back over to the couch. Leila couldn't take her eyes off him.

'It certainly has an impact.'

'If it's too strong I can—'

'No.' Alix's voice cut her off. 'I don't want you to change it.'

A knock came on the door then, and Leila flinched a little. She was so caught up in this man's reaction and his charisma that she'd almost forgotten where she was. The seductive warmth of the bourbon in her belly didn't help.

Alix said, 'That's dinner. I took the liberty of ordering for two, if you'd care to join me?'

Leila just looked at him and felt again that urge to run—but also a stronger urge to stay. *Rebel*. Even though she wasn't exactly sure who she was rebelling against. Herself and every instinct screaming at her to run? Or the ghost of her mother's disappointment?

She justified her weakness to herself: this man had thrown more business her way than she'd see in the next month. She should be polite. *Ha!* said a snide inner voice. *There's nothing polite about the way you feel around him.*

She ignored that and said, as coolly as she could, 'Only if it's not too much of an imposition.'

He had a very definite mocking glint to his eye. 'It's no imposition…really.'

Alix went to the door and opened it to reveal obsequious staff who proceeded straight towards a room off the main reception area. Within minutes they were leaving again, and Alix was waiting for Leila to precede him into the dining room—which was as sumptuously decorated as the rest of the suite.

She caught a glimpse of a bedroom through an open door and almost tripped over her feet to avoid looking that way again. It brought to mind too easily the way that woman had stripped so nonchalantly for her lover. And how Alix had maintained that nothing had happened in spite of appearances.

Why should she even care, when he was probably lying?

Leila almost balked at that point, but as if sensing her trepidation, Alix pulled out a chair and looked at her pointedly. No escape. She moved forward and sat down, looking at the array of food laid out on the table. There was enough for a small army.

Alix must have seen something on her face, because he grimaced a little and said, 'I wasn't sure if you were vegetarian or not, so I ordered a selection.'

Leila couldn't help a wry smile. 'I *am* vegetarian, actually—mostly my mother's influence. Though I do sometimes eat fish.'

Alix started to put some food on a plate for her: a mixture of tapas-type starters, including what looked like balls of rice infused with herbs and spices. The smells had her mouth watering, and she realised that she hadn't eaten since earlier that day, her stomach having been too much in knots after seeing Alix Saint Croix again, and then thinking about him all afternoon as she'd worked on his fragrance.

She could smell it now, faintly—exotic and spicy, with that tantalising hint of citrus—and her insides quivered. It suited him: light, but with much darker undertones.

He handed her the plate and then plucked a chilled bottle of white wine out of an ice bucket. Leila wasn't used to drinking, and could still feel the effects of the bourbon, so she held up a hand when Alix went to pour her some wine.

'I'll stick to water, thanks.'

As he poured himself some wine he asked casually, 'Where are your parents from?'

Leila tensed inevitably as the tall, shadowy and indistinct shape of her father came into her mind's eye. She'd only ever seen him in photos in the newspaper. Tightly she answered, 'My mother was a single parent. She was from India.'

'Was?'

Leila nodded and concentrated on spearing some food with her fork. 'She died a few years ago.'

'I'm sorry. That must have been hard if it was just the two of you.'

Leila was a little taken aback at the sincerity she heard in his voice and said quietly, 'It was the hardest thing.'

She avoided his eyes and put a forkful of food in her mouth, not expecting the explosion of flavours from the spice-infused rice ball. She looked at him and he smiled at her reaction, chewing his own food.

When he could speak he said, 'My personal chef is here. He's from Isle Saint Croix, so he sticks to the local cuisine. It's a mixture of North African and Mediterranean.'

Relieved to be moving away from personal areas, Leila said, 'I've never tasted anything like it.' Then she admitted ruefully, 'I haven't travelled much, though.'

'You were born here?'

Leila reached for her water, as much to cool herself down as anything else. 'Yes, my mother travelled over when she was pregnant. My father was French.'

'Was?'

Leila immediately regretted letting that slip out. But her mother was no longer alive. Surely the secret didn't have to be such a secret any more? But then she thought of how easily her father had turned his back on them and repeated her mother's words, used whenever anyone had asked a similar question. 'He died a long time ago. I never knew him.'

To her relief, Alix didn't say anything to that, just looked at her consideringly. They ate in companionable silence for a few minutes, and Leila tried not to think too hard about where she was and who she was with.

When she'd cleared half her plate she sneaked a look at

Alix. He was sitting back, cradling his glass of wine, looking at her. And just like that her skin prickled with heat.

'I hope I didn't lose you too much custom by taking up your attention today?'

He looked entirely unrepentant, and in spite of herself Leila had to allow herself a small wry smile. 'No—the opposite. The business has been struggling to get back on track since the recession...niche industries like mine were the worst hit.'

Alix frowned. 'Yet you kept hold of your shop?'

Leila nodded, tensing a little at the thought of the uphill battle to restore sales. 'I've owned it outright since my mother died.'

'That's good—but you *could* sell. You don't need me to tell you what that shop and flat must be worth in this part of Paris.'

Leila's insides clenched hard. 'I won't *ever* sell,' she said in a low voice. The shop and the flat were her mother's legacy to her—a safe haven. Security. She barely knew this man...she wasn't about to confide in him.

Feeling self-conscious again, she took her napkin from her lap and put it on the table. That silver gaze narrowed on her.

'I should go. Thank you for dinner—you really didn't have to.'

She saw a muscle twitch in Alix's jaw and half-expected—*wanted?*—him to stop her from going.

But he just stood up smoothly and said, 'Thank you for joining me.'

Much to Leila's sense of disorientation, Alix made no effort to detain her with offers of tea or coffee. He picked up the bag that she'd had with her when she'd arrived and handed it to her in the main reception room.

Feeling at a loss, and not liking the sense of disappointment that he was letting her go so easily, Leila said again, 'Thank you.'

Alix bowed slightly towards her and once again she was struck by his sheer beauty and all that potent masculinity. He looked as if he was about to speak some platitude, then he stopped and said, 'Actually... I have tickets to the opera for tomorrow evening. I wonder if you'd like to join me?'

Leila didn't trust his all-too-innocent façade for a second—as if he'd just thought of it. But she couldn't think straight because giddy relief was mocking her for the disappointment she'd felt just seconds ago because he was letting her go so easily.

She was dealing with a master here.

This was not the first time a man had asked her out but it still hit her in the solar plexus like a blow. Her last disastrous dating experience rose like a dark spectre in her memory—except this man in front of her eclipsed Pierre Gascon a hundred times over. Enough to give her a little frisson of satisfaction.

As if *any* man could compete with this tall, dark specimen before her. *Sexy.* Leila had never been overtly aware of sexual longing before. But now she was—she could feel the awareness throbbing in her blood, between her legs.

And it was that awareness of how out of her depth Alix Saint Croix made her feel that had Leila blurting out, 'I really don't think it would be a good idea.' *Coward*, whispered a voice.

He lifted a brow in lazy enquiry. 'And why would that be? You're single...I'm single. We're two consenting adults. I'm offering a pleasant way to spend the evening. That's all.'

Now she felt gauche. She was thinking of sex when he certainly wasn't. 'I'm just...not exactly in your league, Monsieur Saint Croix—'

'It's Alix,' he growled, coming closer. 'Call me Alix.'

Leila swallowed, caught in the beam of those incredible eyes. 'Alix...'

'That's better. Now, tell me again exactly why this is not a good idea?'

Feeling cornered and angry now—with herself as much as him—Leila flung out a hand. 'I own a shop and you're a king. We're not exactly on a level footing.'

Alix cocked his head to one side. 'You're a perfumer, are you not? A very commendable career.'

Unable to keep the bitterness out of her voice, Leila said, 'To be a perfumer one needs to be making perfumes.'

'Something I've no doubt you'll do when your business recovers its equilibrium.'

His quiet and yet firm encouragement made something glow in Leila's chest. She ruthlessly pushed it down. This man could charm the devil over to the light side.

'Don't you have more important things to be doing?'

A curious expression she couldn't decipher crossed his hard-boned face before his mouth twitched and he said,'Not right now, no.'

Leila's stubborn refusal to accede to his wishes was having a bizarre effect on Alix. He could quite happily stay here for hours and spar with her, watching those expressions cross her face and her gorgeous eyes spark and glow.

'Don't you know,' he said carefully, watching her reaction with interest, 'that feigning uninterest is one sure way to get a man interested in you?'

Immediately her cheeks were suffused with colour and her back went poker straight with indignation. Eyes glittering, she said, 'I am *not* feigning uninterest, Mr Saint Croix, I am genuinely mystified as to why you are persisting like this—and to be perfectly frank I think I'd prefer it if you just left me alone.'

He took a step closer. 'Really, Leila? I could let you walk out of this suite right now and you'll never see me again.' He waited a beat and then said softly, 'If that's *really* what you want. But I don't think it is.'

Oh, God. He'd seen her disappointment. She'd never been any good at hiding her emotions. She'd also never felt so hot with the need to break out of some confinement holding her back.

She hadn't felt this hungry urgency with Pierre. He'd been far more subtle—and ultimately manipulative. Alix was direct. And there was something absurdly comforting about that. There were no games. He wasn't dressing his words up with illusions of more being involved. It made her breathless.

Her extended silence had made something go hard in Alix's eyes and Leila felt a dart of panic go through her. She sensed that he would stop pursuing her if she asked him to. If he did indeed believe she was stringing him along. Which she wasn't. Or was she? Unconsciously?

She hated to think that she might be capable of such a thing, but she couldn't deny the thrilling rush of something illicit every time she saw him. The rush of sparring with him. The rush each time he came back even though she'd said no.

Leila felt as if she was skirting around the edges of a very large and angry fire that mesmerised her as much as it made her fear its heat. She'd shut down after her experience with Pierre, dismayed at coming to terms with the fact that she'd made such a huge misjudgement. But now she could feel a part of her expanding inside again, demanding to be heard. To be set free. Another chance.

She'd never been to the opera. Pierre's most exciting invitation had been to a trip down the Seine, which Leila had done a million times with her mother. The sense of yearning got stronger.

She heard herself asking, 'It's *just* a trip to the opera?'

The hardness in Alix's eyes softened, but he was careful enough not to show that he'd gained a point.

'Yes, Leila, it's just a simple trip to the opera. If you can close a little early tomorrow I'll pick you up at five.'

Closing a little early would hardly damage her already dented business. She took a deep breath and tried not to let this moment feel bigger than it should. 'Very well. I'll accept your invitation.'

Alix took up her hand and raised it to his mouth before brushing a very light, almost imperceptible kiss across the back of it. Even so, his breath burned her skin.

'I look forward to it, Leila. *A bientôt.*'

At about three o'clock the next day Leila found herself dealing with an unusual flurry of customers, and it took her a couple of seconds to notice the thickset man waiting just inside the door. When she finally registered that it was Ricardo, Alix's bodyguard, she noticed that he had a big white box in his hands.

She went over and he handed it to her, saying gruffly, 'A gift from Mr Saint Croix.'

Leila took the box warily and glanced at her customers, who were all engrossed in trying out the samples she'd been showing them. She looked back to Ricardo and felt a trickle of foreboding. 'Can you wait for a second?'

He nodded, and if Leila had had the time to appreciate how out of place he looked against the backdrop of delicate perfume bottles she might have smiled.

She suspected that she knew what was in the box.

She ducked into a small anteroom behind the counter and opened it to reveal layers of expensive-looking silver tissue paper. Underneath the paper she saw a glimmer of silk, and gasped as she pulled out the most beautiful dress she'd ever seen.

It was a very light green, with one simple shoulder strap and a ruched bodice. The skirt fell to the floor from under the bust in layers of delicate chiffon. On further investigation Leila saw that there were matching shoes and even underwear. Her face burned at that. It burned even more when she realised that Alix had got her size spot-on.

She felt tempted to march right across the square and tell him to shove his date, but she held on to her temper. This was how he must operate with *all* his women. And he was arrogant enough to think that Leila was just like them?

'What do you mean, she wouldn't accept it?'

Ricardo looked exceedingly uncomfortable and shifted from foot to foot, before saying *sotto voce*, mindful of the other men in the room, 'She left a note inside the box.'

'Did she now?' Alix curbed his irritation and said curtly, 'Thank you, Ricardo, that will be all.'

Alix had been holding a meeting in his suite, and the other men around the table started to move a little, clearly anticipating a break from the customarily intense sessions Alix conducted. He dismissed them too, with a look that changed their expressions of relief to ones of meek servitude.

When they were all gone Alix flicked open the lid of the box and saw the plain piece of white paper lying on the silver paper with its succinct message:

Thank you, but I can dress myself.
Leila.

Alix couldn't help his mouth quirking in a smile. Had any woman ever handed him back a gift? Not in his memory.

He let the lid drop down and stood up to walk over to the window of his suite, which looked out over the square below.

For a large portion of his life, ever since his dramatic escape from Isle Saint Croix all those years ago, he'd felt like a caged animal—forced into this role of pretending that he *wasn't* engaged in an all-out battle to regain his throne. The prospect of being on his island again, with the salty tang of the sea in the hot air... Sometimes the yearning for home was almost unbearable.

Alix sighed and let his gaze narrow on the small shop that glinted across the square in the late-afternoon sunlight. He could see the familiar slim white-coated shape moving back and forth. The caged animal within him got even more restless. The yearning was replaced with sharp anticipation.

It would be no hardship to pursue Miss Verughese and let the world think nothing untoward was going on behind the scenes. No hardship at all.

Leila looked at herself in the mirror and had a sudden attack of nerves. Maybe she'd been really stupid to send Alix's gift back to him? She'd never been to the opera—she wasn't even sure what the dress code was, except posh.

The scent she'd put on so sparingly drifted up, and for a moment she wanted to run and wash it off. It wasn't her usual scent, which was light and floral. This was a scent that had always fascinated her: one of her mother's most sensual creations. It had called to Leila from the shelf just after she'd locked up before coming upstairs to get ready.

It was called *Dark Desiring*. Her mother had had a penchant for giving their perfumes enigmatic names. As soon as Leila had sprayed a little on her wrist she'd heard her mother's voice in her head: *'This scent is for a woman, Leila. The kind of woman who knows what she wants and gets it. You will be that woman someday, and you won't be foolish like your mother.'*

She felt the scent now, deep in the pit of her belly. Felt its dark sensuality, earthy musky notes and exotic floral arrangement. It was so unlike her...and yet it resonated with her. But she felt exposed wearing it—as if it would be obvious to everyone that she was trying to be something she wasn't.

The doorbell sounded... Too late to remove it now, even if she wanted to.

She made her way downstairs, her heart palpitating in her chest. She thrust aside memories of another man she'd let too close. It had been as if as soon as her mother's influence had been removed Leila had automatically sought out proof that not all men weren't to be trusted. But that had spectacularly backfired and proved her *very* wrong.

Walking through the darkened shop, Leila forced the clamouring memories down. She'd learnt her lesson. She was no fool any more. She still wanted something different from her mother's experience, but Alix Saint Croix was the last man to offer such a thing. So, if anything, she couldn't be safer than with this man.

She sucked in a big breath and opened the door. The sky was dusky outside and Alix blocked most of it with his broad shoulders. He was dressed in a classic black tuxedo and white bow tie under his overcoat. Leila's mouth went dry. That assurance of safety suddenly felt very flimsy.

She wasn't even aware that Alix's eyes had widened on her when she'd appeared.

'You look beautiful.'

She stopped gawking at him long enough to meet his eyes. And those nerves gripped her again as she gestured shyly to her outfit. 'I wasn't sure... I hope it's appropriate?'

Alix lifted his eyes to hers. 'It's stunning. You look like a princess.'

Leila blushed and busied herself pulling the door behind her and locking it to deflect his scrutiny.

The outfit was a traditional Indian *salwar kameez* with a bit of a modern twist. The tunic was made out of green and gold silk, with slim-fitting trousers in the same shade of green. She had on gold strappy sandals that she'd bought one day on a whim but never worn. A loose chiffon throw was draped over her shoulders and she'd put her hair up in a high bun. She wore ornate earrings that had belonged to her mother—like a talisman that might protect her from falling into the vortex that this man created whenever he was near.

The driver of the sleek car parked nearby was holding the door open, and Leila slid into the luxurious confines as Alix joined her from the other side. She plucked nervously at the material of her tunic as they pulled away.

Alix took her hand and she looked at him.

'You look amazing. No other woman will be dressed the same.'

Leila quirked a wry smile, liking the feel of Alix's hand around hers far too much. 'That's what I'm suddenly afraid of.'

He shook his head. 'You'll stand out like a bird of paradise—they'll be insanely jealous.'

Leila gave a small dissenting sound and went to pull her hand back, but Alix gripped it tighter and lifted it up, turning her wrist. He frowned slightly and bent to smell. Leila's heart thumped, hard.

He looked at her. 'This isn't your usual scent?'

Damn him for noticing. Leila cursed her impetuosity and felt as if that scarlet letter was on her forehead for all to see. She pulled her hand back. 'No, it's a different scent—one more suitable for evenings.'

'I like it.'

Leila could smell his scent too. The one she'd made him. She knew that it lingered on his skin from when he'd put it on much earlier that day—it didn't have the sharp tang of having been recently applied. She thought of their scents now, mingling and wrapping around one another. It made her feel unbearably aware of the fact that they were so close. Aware of the warm blood pumping just under their skin, making those scents mellow and change subtly.

It was an alchemy that happened to everyone in a totally different way, as the perfume responded uniquely to each individual.

She finally looked away from Alix to see that they were leaving the confines of the city and heading towards the grittier outskirts. Nowhere near the Paris opera house.

She frowned and looked back at him. 'I thought we were going to the opera?'

'We are.'

'But we're leaving Paris.'

Alix smiled. 'I said we were going to the opera. I didn't say where.'

Flutters of panic made her tense. 'I don't appreciate surprises. Tell me where we're going, please.'

His eyes narrowed on her and Leila bit back the urge to lambast him for assuming she was just some wittering dolly bird, only too happy to let him whisk her off to some unknown location.

Alix's voice had an edge of steel to it when he said, 'We're going to Venice.'

'Venice?' Leila squeaked. 'But I don't have my passport. I mean, how can we just—?'

Alix took her hand again and spoke as if he was soothing a nervous horse. 'You don't need your passport. I have diplomatic immunity and you're with me. The flight will take an hour and forty minutes. I'll have you back in Paris and home by midnight. I promise.'

Leila reeled. 'You said flight?'

Alix nodded warily, as if expecting another explosion.

'I've never been on a plane before,' she admitted somewhat warily. As if Alix might be so disgusted with her lack of sophistication that he'd turn around and deliver her home right now.

He just frowned slightly. 'But…how is that possible?'

Leila shrugged, finding to her consternation that once again she was loath to take her hand out of Alix's much bigger one. 'My mother and I…we didn't travel much. Apart from to other parts of France. We went to England once, to visit a factory outside London, but we took the train. My mother was terrified of flying.'

'Well, then,' said Alix throatily, 'do you want to go home? Or do you want to take your first flight? We can turn around right now if you want.'

That was like asking if she wanted to keep moving forward in life or backwards. Leila felt that fire reaching out to lick at her with a tantalising flash of heat. Alix's thumb was rubbing the underside of her wrist, making the flash of heat more intense. Leila thought of the car turning around, of returning to that square and her shop. She felt nauseous.

She shook her head. 'I'd like to fly with you.'

Alix brought her hand to his mouth and kissed it lightly before saying, 'Then let's fly.'

Leila might not be half as sophisticated as his usual women, but even she knew that they were talking about something else entirely—just as the flames of that fire reached out to consume her completely and Alix moved close enough to slant his hard sensual mouth over hers.

She'd been kissed before—by Pierre. But his kiss had been insistent and invasive. Too wet, with no finesse. This was…

Leila lost any sense of being able to string a rational thought together when her mouth opened of its own volition under Alix's and she felt the first electrifying contact of his tongue to hers. She was lost.

CHAPTER FOUR

THE ONLY THING stopping Alix exploding into orbit at the feel of Leila's lush soft mouth under his and the shy touch of her tongue was the hand he'd clamped around her waist. He was rock-hard almost instantaneously. He'd never tasted such sweetness. Her mouth trembled under his and he had to use extreme restraint to go slowly, coaxing her to open up to him.

He felt the hitch in her breathing as their kiss deepened and he gathered her closer to feel the swell of her breasts against his chest. Right at that moment Alix couldn't have remembered his own name. He was drowning in heat and lust and an urgent desire to haul Leila over his lap, so that he could seat her against where he ached most.

She pulled back suddenly and he cracked open his eyes to look down into wide green ones. Leila had her hands on his chest and was pushing at him.

'Please—don't do that again.'

Alix was on unsure ground. Another first. He wasn't used to women pushing him away. And he knew Leila had been enjoying it. She'd been melting into him like his hottest teenage fantasy, and he felt about as suave as a teenager right then. All raging hormones and no control.

Drawing on what little control he *did* still have, Alix moved back, putting space between them. He looked at her. Cheeks flushed, chest rising and falling rapidly, eyes avoiding his. Mouth pink and wet. It made him think of other parts of her that might be wet. He cursed himself silently. Where was his finesse?

He reached out and cupped her jaw, seeing how she tensed. He tipped her chin up so that she had no choice but to look at him. Her eyes were huge and wary. There was an edge of something in her eyes that he couldn't read. He felt a spike of recrimination. Had he been too forceful? But he knew he hadn't. It had nearly killed him to rein himself in.

'Did you have a bad experience with a previous lover?'

She pulled his hand down. 'That's none of your business.'

She avoided his eyes again and he wanted to growl his frustration. But they were pulling into the small private airport now, and staff were rushing to meet the car.

Alix got out and pulled his coat around his body, not liking that he had to conceal his arousal. He glared at the driver who was about to help Leila out of the car and the man ducked back to let Alix take her hand. When she stood up beside him, the breeze blowing a loose tendril of dark hair across one cheek, he had to forcibly stop himself from kissing her again.

Gripping her hand, when he usually avoided public displays of affection like the plague, he led her over to the waiting plane: a small sleek private jet that he used for short hops around Europe. He realised then how much he took things like this for granted. Leila had never even flown before.

He stopped and turned to her. 'You're not frightened, are you?'

She glanced from the plane to him and admitted warily, 'It looks a bit small.'

He grinned and felt the dense band of cynicism around his heart loosen a little. 'It's as safe as houses—I promise.'

He urged her forward and up the steps, past a steward in uniform. He chose two seats opposite each other so he could see Leila's expression. He buckled them both in, and then the plane was taxiing down the runway. With a roar of the throttle, it lifted up into the darkening Paris sky. Alix had had a discreet word with the pilot, and watched Leila's face for her reaction as they climbed into the air.

Her hands were gripping the seat's armrests, and when she cast him a quick glance he raised a brow while shrugging off his overcoat. 'Okay?'

She smiled and it was a bit wobbly. 'I think so.' She put a hand to her belly as if to calm it.

Alix was charmed by her reaction. Her expression was avid as the ground was left behind, and her hands gradually relaxed as the plane rose and gained altitude and then found its cruising level. And then her face became suffused with wonder as she took in the fact that they were flying directly over the city of Paris.

It was perfect timing, with all the lights coming on. Alix looked down through his own window and saw the Eiffel Tower flashing. He'd taken this for granted for so long it was a novelty to see it through someone else's eyes.

Leila felt as if she was in a dream. Her stomach had been churning slightly with the motion of the plane, but it was calming now. To be so high above the city and all its glittering lights...the sheer beauty of it almost moved her to tears. And it was distracting enough to help her block out how amazing that kiss had been. How hard it had been to pull away.

What had finally made her come to her senses had been the realisation that she was being kissed by an expert—who'd kissed scores of far more beautiful women than her.

'Why did your mother hate flying so much?'

Leila composed herself before she looked at Alix, where he was lounging in the chair opposite, long legs stretched out and crossed at the ankle, effectively caging her in. Despite her best efforts, one look at his hard, sensual mouth was bringing their kiss back in glorious Technicolor...the way it had burnt her up.

She forced her gaze up to his eyes and tried to remember his question. 'My mother flew only once in her life, when she came to France from India. It was a traumatic journey for her… She was in disgrace, pregnant and unwed, and was suffering badly from morning sickness.' Leila shrugged lightly, knowing she was leaving so much out of that explanation. 'She always associated flying with that trauma and never wanted to get on a plane again.'

'Aren't you curious about your Indian roots and family?'

An innocuous enough question, but one that had a familiar resentment rising up within Leila. Her mother's family had all but left her for dead—they'd never once contacted her or Leila. Not even when a newspaper had reported that some of them were in Paris for a massive perfume fair.

Leila hid her true emotions under a bland mask. She forced a smile. 'I'm afraid my mother's family cut all ties with us… But perhaps one day I'll go back and visit the country of my ancestors.'

She took refuge in looking at the view again, hoping that Alix wouldn't ask any more personal questions. The lights of the city were becoming sparser. They must be flying further away from Paris now.

But it was as if Alix could read her mind and was deliberately thwarting her. He asked softly, 'Why did you pull back when I kissed you, Leila? I know it wasn't because you really wanted me to stop.'

She froze. She hadn't expected Alix to notice that fleeting moment when she'd felt so insecure. She hadn't wanted it to stop at all…she'd never felt such exquisite pleasure. And the thought of him kissing her again—she knew she wouldn't be able to pull back the next time.

An urgent self-protective need rose up inside her. She had to try and repel Alix on some level—surely a man of a blue-blooded royal line wouldn't want anything to do with the illegitimate daughter of a disgraced Indian woman?

She looked at him, and he was regarding her from under hooded lids.

'You asked before if I'd had a bad experience with a lover...'

Alix sat up straighter. 'You told me it was none of my business.'

'And it's not,' Leila reiterated. 'But, yes, I had a negative encounter with someone, and I don't really wish to repeat the experience.'

Alix went very still, and Leila could see the innate male pride in his expression. He couldn't believe that she would compare him to another man.

'I'm sorry you had to experience that, but you can't damn all men because of one.'

Leila took a breath. Alix wasn't being dissuaded. In spite of the flutters in her belly she went on. 'In fact, if you must know, my mother was rather overprotective.' The flutters increased under Alix's steady regard. 'The truth is that I'm not as experienced as you might—'

'Are you ready for supper, Your Majesty?'

They both looked to see the steward holding out some menus. Relief flooded Leila that she'd been cut off from revealing the ignominious truth of just how inexperienced she was. She welcomed the diversion of taking the menu being proffered.

She imagined that Alix would believe she was still a virgin as much as he'd believe in unicorns. But thankfully, when they were alone again, he didn't seem inclined to continue the discussion.

When she glanced at him, he just sent her an enigmatic glance and said, 'I recommend the risotto—it's vegetarian.'

Leila smiled. 'That sounds good.'

When the young man came back, moments later, Alix

ordered. Then he poured them both some champagne. When the flutes were filled and a table had been set between them, Alix lifted his glass and said, with a very definite glint in his eye, 'To new experiences, Leila.'

She cringed inwardly. He didn't have to pursue the discussion. He'd guessed her secret. She lifted her glass too, but said nothing. She got the distinct impression that he still wasn't put off. And, as much as she'd like to tell Alix that flying in a plane was the *only* new experience she was interested in sharing with him, she couldn't formulate the words. Traitorously.

'Why is everyone looking at us?'

Alix looked at Leila incredulously. She had no idea what a sensation she was causing—*had* caused as soon as they'd stepped from his boat and into the ancient *palazzo* on the Grand Canal where the opera was being staged. Leila stood out effortlessly—like a jewel amongst much duller stones. Now it was the interval, and they were seated in a private area to the right of the stage. Private, yet visible.

His mouth quirked. 'They're not looking at us—they're looking at *you*.'

She looked at him and blushed. 'Oh…it's the clothes, isn't it? I should have—'

Alix shook his head, cutting her off. 'It's not the clothes…well, it *is*. But that's because you are more beautiful than any other woman here and you're putting them to shame with your sense of style. Every woman is looking at you and wondering why their finger is not on the pulse.'

Leila's blush deepened, and it had a direct effect on Alix's arousal levels.

'I'm sure that's not it at all. I've never seen so many beautiful people in one place in my entire life. I've never seen anywhere so breathtaking—the canal, this *palazzo*…'

She ducked her head for a moment before looking back at him. 'Thank you…this evening has been magical.'

Alix had to school his features. He couldn't remember the last time a woman had thanked him for taking her out.

'You're glad you overcame your reluctance to spend time with me?' he queried innocently.

Her green gaze held his and Alix felt breathless for a second. *Crazy.* Women didn't make him breathless.

Her mouth twitched minutely. 'Yes, I'm glad—but don't let it go to your head.'

An unfortunate choice of words when it made him aware of the part of his anatomy that refused to obey his efforts to control it.

Leila looked so incandescent in that moment—a small smile playing around her mouth, eyes sparkling—that Alix had to curl his hands into fists to stop himself from kissing her again.

The lights dimmed and the cast resumed their places. Alix tore his gaze from her, questioning his sanity and praying that he'd have enough control not to ravish her like a wild animal in the darkened surroundings.

After the opera had finished Alix took Leila out of the *palazzo* and along the Grand Canal in his boat, to a small rustic Italian restaurant where he was greeted like an old friend by the owner. They ate a selection of small starters and drank wine, and to Leila's surprise the conversation flowed as easily as if they'd known each other for months, not days.

Something had happened—either as soon as she'd agreed to this date or on the plane, when events had become a dizzying spectacle. Or maybe it had been when she'd chosen a different perfume for herself…

She'd stepped over a line—irrevocably. She felt as if she was a different person, inhabiting the same skin. As if she'd thrown off some kind of shackle holding her to the past. She was a little drunk. She knew that. But she'd never felt so light, so…effervescent. So open to new possibilities, experiences.

She wasn't naive enough to think that it would be anything more than transient. Especially with a man like Alix. And that was okay. If anything it was a form of protection. He was practically emblazoned with *Warning!* And *Hazardous!* signs.

She must have giggled a little, because Alix said dryly, 'Something I said was funny?'

Leila shook her head and looked at him, all of a sudden stone-cold sober again. He was beautiful. Their mingled scents wrapped around her. Leila imagined them curling around her brain's synapses, rendering them weak. Making her want what he was offering with those slate-grey eyes— hot with a decadent promise she could only imagine.

Leila realised with a sense of desperation that she *wanted* whatever he was offering. She wanted to lose herself and be broken apart. She wanted to know what it was like. She wanted to taste the forbidden.

She didn't want to go back to her small poky apartment above her failing shop and be the same person. Looking at life passing by across the square. She wanted life to be happening *to her*. She'd never felt it this strongly before. It was his persistent seduction, the perfume, the wine, the opera…leaving her country for the first time. It was his kiss. It was *him*.

Impetuously she leaned forward. 'Do we have to go back to Paris tonight?'

Immediately his gaze narrowed on her. She was acutely conscious of the fact that his jacket and bow tie were gone and his shirt was open at the throat, revealing the strong bronzed column of his neck.

'What are you suggesting?'

Feeling bold for the first time in her life, Leila said, 'I'm suggesting…not going back to Paris. Staying here… in Venice.'

'For the night?'

She nodded. The enormity of what she was doing was dizzying, but she couldn't turn back now. Her heart was thumping.

Alix cocked his head slightly. 'I think you might be a little drunk, Miss Verughese.'

'Perhaps,' she agreed huskily. 'But I know what I'm saying.'

'Do you now…?' Alix looked at her consideringly.

For a second something cold touched Leila's spine. Maybe she had this all wrong. Maybe Alix was just toying with this gauche girl from a shop until a more suitable woman came along? No doubt he was getting a kick out of her untutored reactions to flying and seeing the opera.

And now this… Maybe the thought of bedding a virgin wasn't palatable to a man of his undoubted experience and sophisticated tastes? She thought of how that woman had undressed in front of him and her insides contracted painfully. She could never do that.

She looked away, searching for her bag and wrap. 'Forget I said anything. I'm sure you have meetings—'

Suddenly her hand was clasped in his and reluctantly she looked at him. He was intense.

'Are you saying you want to stay in Venice for the night to share my bed, Leila?'

She hated it that he was making her spell it out, but she lifted her chin and said, 'If you're not interested—'

His hand tightened on hers. 'Oh, I'm interested. I just want to make sure you're not going to regret this in the morning and blame it on too much wine.'

Leila stared back, suppressing an urge to say *I'm blam-*

ing it on much more than that. He wouldn't understand. 'I want this—even if it's just one night.'

Alix interlaced his fingers with hers. It felt like a shockingly intimate caress.

'It won't be one night, Leila, I can guarantee that.'

She shivered lightly. The way he said that sounded like a vow. Or a promise.

'Signor Alix…?'

He didn't even look at his friend. He just said, 'We're finished, Giorgio, thank you.'

But it was a long moment before Alix broke his gaze from hers and let go of her hand to stand up.

Leila couldn't remember much of leaving the restaurant, or of the boat ride along the magical Grand Canal at night. She was only aware of Alix's strong thighs beside hers on the seat, his arm tight around her shoulders, his hand resting disturbingly close to the curve of her breast.

She was only aware that she was finally leaving a part of her life behind and stepping into the unknown.

She couldn't believe she'd been so forward, and yet she knew that even if given a choice she wouldn't turn back now. This man had unlocked some deep secret part of her and she wanted to explore it. She didn't care about the fact that Alix Saint Croix was famous or rich or royalty. She was interested in the man. He called to her on a very basic level that no one had ever touched before.

And as the boat scythed through the choppy waters she reassured herself that she was going into this with eyes wide open. No romantic illusions. She was *not* starry-eyed any more. Pierre had seen to that when she'd let him woo her. That had been just after the death of her mother, when she'd been at her most vulnerable. She wasn't vulnerable any more. And Leila had no intention of shutting herself away like a nun for the rest of her life.

They were approaching a building now—another grand

palazzo. A man stood on the small landing dock and threw a rope to the driver. They came alongside the wooden jetty and Alix jumped nimbly out of the boat before turning back to lift Leila out as easily as if she weighed nothing.

As he let her down on the jetty he kept her close to his body, and her eyes widened when she felt her belly brush against a very hard part of him. Her pulse quickened and between her legs she felt damp.

Then he turned, and held her hand as he strode through the open doors. Leila had to almost run to keep up and she tugged at his hand. He looked back, something stark etched onto his face. She refused to let it intimidate her.

'What is this place?'

'It belongs to a friend—he's away.'

'Oh…'

A petite older woman dressed in black approached them and Alix exchanged some words with her in fluent Italian. It was only then that Leila looked around and took in the grandeur of the reception hall. The floor was marble, and there were massive stone columns stretching all the way up to a ceiling that was covered in very old-looking frescoes.

Then Alix was tugging her hand again and they were following the woman up the main staircase. The eyes from numerous huge stern portraits followed their progress and Leila superstitiously avoided looking at them, sensing a judgment she wasn't really blasé enough to ignore in spite of her bravado.

The corridor they walked into had thick carpet, muffling their footsteps. Massive ornate wooden doors were closed on each side. At the end of the corridor the woman came to some double doors and opened them wide, standing aside so they could go in.

Leila's breath stopped. It was the most stunningly sumptuous suite of rooms she'd ever seen. She let go of Alix's hand and walked over to where the glass French doors were open, leading out to a stone balcony overlooking a smaller canal.

She heard the door close softly and looked behind her to see Alix standing in the centre of the room, hands in his pockets, legs wide. Chest broad.

He took a hand out of his pocket and held it out. Silently Leila went to him, kicking off her sandals as she did so.

When she got to Alix, he drew her chiffon wrap off her shoulders and it drifted to the floor beside them. Then he reached around to the back of her head and removed the pin holding her hair up. It fell around her shoulders in a heavy silken curtain and he ran his hand through the strands.

'I wanted to do this the moment I saw you,' he said.

Feeling suddenly vulnerable, she blurted out, 'Did you really not sleep with that woman after you pulled the curtains that night?'

His grey gaze bored into hers. 'No, I did not sleep with Carmen that night. I wouldn't lie to you about that, Leila.'

She found that she believed him, but she still had to battle the insidious suspicion that he would say whatever he wanted to get her into bed. Not that he'd had to say much—she'd all but begged him!

Furiously she blocked out the raising clamour of voices and reached up, touching her mouth to his. 'Take me to bed, Alix,' she whispered.

CHAPTER FIVE

AGAINST THE MUTED lighting of the opulent suite Alix looked every inch the powerful man he was. He took up so much space, and a sudden flutter of fear clutched at Leila's belly. Could she really handle a man like this?

But then he took her hand and led her into another room. The bedroom.

Its furnishings were ridiculously, gloriously lush. A four-poster, canopied bed stood in the centre of the room, surrounded by thick velvet drapes held back by decorative rings. Through the windows Leila could see the Grand Canal, and boats moving up and down. The curtains fluttered in the breeze and yet she was hot. Burning up.

Alix came and stood in front of her. Leila was at eye level with the middle of his chest. Never more than now had she been so aware of his sheer masculinity and strength. She wished she had the nerve to reach out and touch him, but she didn't. The boldness that had led her here seemed to be fleeing in the face of the stark reality facing her.

Alix tipped up her chin with a curled forefinger and Leila couldn't escape his gaze.

'We'll take this slow.'

Leila swallowed. So much for trying to repel him with her inexperience. His eyes burned. And something melted inside her at his consideration. He pulled her forward then, until her breasts were touching his body, her nipples tightening in reaction. Both his hands went to her jaw, caressing the delicate bone structure before tilting her face upwards. And then his head dipped and his mouth was over hers.

Leila made a soft sound in the back of her throat. His tongue explored along the seam of her mouth until she opened up to him, and then he was stroking her tongue intimately, teeth nipping at her full lower lip. Her hands curled into his shirt, clutching. He was all hard muscle and heat and he tasted of wine.

When Alix drew back after long, drugging moments, Leila followed him, opening her eyes slowly, all her senses colliding and melting into one throbbing beat of desire. She'd never imagined it could be like this. After just a kiss.

Alix brought his hands to the small buttons running down the front of her tunic. His skin was dark against the silk and Leila watched as slowly the front of her tunic fell open to reveal her lacy bra underneath.

'So beautiful...' breathed Alix as he saw her breasts revealed, more voluptuous than Leila had ever been comfortable with.

He slid a hand inside her tunic and cupped one, testing its shape, its firm weight. The effect on her body was so intensely pleasurable that Leila was too embarrassed to look at Alix. She ducked her head forward and her hair slipped over her shoulders, the ends touching his hand.

She gave a little gasp when Alix's other hand caught her hair at the back of her head and tugged gently. His fingers were squeezing her breast now, and her nipple was pinched tight with need. Leila wanted something but she wasn't sure what. *More.*

When he bent to take her mouth again she whimpered. And then his hand was pulling down the silk cup of her bra and he was palming her naked breast, fingers trapping her nipple, squeezing gently.

Alix's kiss was rougher than before, but Leila met it full-on, already feeling more confident, sucking his tongue deep, nipping his mouth. He was pushing her bra up now, over her breasts, freeing them. Pulling the top part of her tunic wide open.

When he eventually broke the kiss he was breathing harshly, eyes glittering like molten mercury.

There was something raw in his expression that made excitement mixed with sheer terror spike inside Leila. Alix moved back, tugging her with him, until he sat down on the edge of the massive bed.

Leila's breasts were exposed—framed by her pushed-up bra and the tunic. She should have felt self-conscious, but she didn't. Alix's gaze rested there and then he cupped one breast and brought his mouth to it, teasing the hard tip with his tongue before pulling it into his mouth and suckling.

Leila thought she might die. Right there and then. She'd never experienced anything so decadent, so delicious, as this hot, sucking heat. When he administered the same attention to her other breast her legs buckled and she landed on Alix's lap, his mouth and tongue lapping at her engorged flesh, making her squirm and writhe as a coil of tension wound higher and higher between her legs.

He broke away suddenly, his voice gruff. 'I need to see you.'

He carefully stood Leila up again and she felt momentarily dizzy, holding on to his arm to steady herself. He stood in front of her and slowly started to peel her tunic up and over her head. After a moment's hesitation Leila lifted her arms and it came all the way off, landing on the floor at their feet.

Then Alix deftly removed her twisted bra, and that disappeared too. Now she was naked apart from her trousers and underwear.

He was looking at her, eyes dark and unreadable. His hands were tracing her contours as reverently as if she was a piece of sculpted marble.

'I want to see you too.' Leila heard the words coming from her mouth and wasn't even aware of thinking them. *Dangerous*.

He dropped his hands and stood before her, silently inviting her to undress him. Leila lifted her hands to his shirt and slowly undid his buttons, his shirt falling open as she moved down his massive chest.

When she got to where his shirt was tucked into his trousers she hesitated for a moment, before pulling it free and undoing the last buttons. Soon it was open completely, and she pushed it wide open and off his shoulders. Alix opened his cufflinks, and then the shirt slid off completely.

Leila was in awe. The sleek strength of his muscles under the dark olive skin was fascinating to her. There was a little hair around his pectorals and a dark line down through his muscle-packed abdomen, disappearing enticingly into his trousers.

She reached out and put her hands on him, spread her fingers wide. His scent was hypnotising her...earthy and musky and *male*. The scent she'd made for him mixed with his own unique essence. She bent forward to press her lips against his hot skin, her mouth exploring and finding the small hard point of his nipple. She licked it experimentally and Alix jerked.

She pulled back, looked up. 'Did I hurt you?'

He shook his head and smiled. 'No, you didn't hurt me...*sorcière*. Lie down on the bed,' he instructed.

Leila was only too happy to comply. She felt shaky. The taste of his skin was addictive. She collapsed onto the bed and Alix moved over her before pressing a kiss to her mouth and moving down, trailing his lips over her jaw and neck, down to her breasts, anointing one and then the other.

He pulled back slightly and looked at her before saying, 'I'm going to take your trousers off...'

Leila bit her lip and then nodded. Her belly contracted

when Alix's fingers came to her button and zip, undoing them both, and then he put his hands to the sides of her silk trousers to slide them down.

She lifted her hips to help. When they were off Alix's hands went to his own trousers, and with a swift economy of movement they were off too. Along with his underwear. He was now gloriously and unashamedly naked. Leila came up on her elbows, her eyes going wide at the sight of him.

His body was a honed mass of hard muscles and masculine contours. She'd never seen anything like it. All the way from his shoulders and chest, down to slim hips and strong muscled thighs. Between his thighs and lower belly was a thicket of dark hair, out of which rose the very core of his virility. Long and thick and hard. Proud.

As Leila watched he brought a hand to himself, stroking gently. It was so unbelievably sensual that her mouth dried even as other parts of her felt as if they were gushing with wet heat.

When he took his hand from himself Leila fell back against the soft covers of the bed. Alix reached forward and gently pulled her panties free of her hips and legs. Dropping them to the floor.

Now they were both naked, and Alix came alongside her on the bed. She could feel his bold erection against her thigh. A potent invitation. But she was too shy to explore him there.

Instead, he kissed her—long, drugging kisses that sent her out of her mind completely as his hands explored her body, squeezing her buttocks, her breasts, following the contours of her waist and hips. And then he was pushing her legs apart and long fingers were exploring her *there*, where no one had ever touched her. Not even herself.

In a moment of panic at this intimate exploration she

reached down and put a hand on his, stopping him. She looked at him, breath laboured, feeling hot.

One of Alix's thighs was between her legs and she could feel the heat of him there, very close to the apex of her legs, where his hand was. And as suddenly as she'd felt panic she felt an urgency she couldn't understand. She took her hand away again.

'I won't hurt you, Leila.' Alix promised. 'Any moment you want to stop, just say and I will.'

She nodded her head. 'Thank you…'

His hand started moving again, and when she felt him push one finger and then two inside her she let out a gasp, her head going back, eyes shut tight, as if that could control the almost violent reactions happening in her body.

He was moving his fingers in and out and she could feel how wet she was. His movements got faster and the heel of his hand pressed against a part of her that needed more friction. Without even realising she was doing it Leila lifted her hips, pushing into him, seeking more.

She was unaware of the smile of pure masculine satisfaction on Alix's face as he watched her.

There was something coiling so tight and deep within her that Leila begged incoherently for it to stop, or break, or do *something*. It was painful, but it was also the most exquisitely pleasurable thing she'd ever felt. And then suddenly her whole body was caught in the grip of a storm and she broke into a million pieces. She felt like the sun, the moon, stardust, pleasure and pain. All at once.

When her body was as lax as if someone had drained every bone out of it, she opened her eyes and blinked.

Alix looked vaguely incredulous. 'That was your first orgasm?'

Leila nodded faintly. She guessed it was. Living in such a small space with her mother hadn't exactly been conducive to normal female exploration. And then she'd been so grief-stricken and busy...

The expression on Alix's face changed from incredulous to intent. He moved so that his body lay between her legs, forcing them apart. Leila still felt sensitive down there, but as Alix moved against her subtly she found that excitement was growing again—a need for more even though *more* surely couldn't be possible...

Alix kissed her, surrounding her in his heat and strength. Leila moved her hands all over him—down his torso to his hips, his muscular buttocks. And all the while he was rocking against her gently, and that urgency was building in her again...for something...for *him*.

He pulled his mouth away from her breast and she could feel the tip of his erection nudging against her opening, sliding in tantalisingly.

'Are you okay?'

She nodded. She wasn't on earth any more. She was on some new and exotic planet where time and space had become immaterial. There was no real world any more.

'Yes,' she said out loud, so that there was no ambiguity.

Alix's jaw tightened. 'This might hurt at first... Stay with me—it'll get better, I promise.'

And with that he thrust in, deep into Leila's untried flesh, stretching her wide. She gasped and arched against him, part in rejection of his invasion and part in awe at how right it felt in spite of the pain—which was blinding and red-hot. But she took a breath and looked into Alix's eyes, trusting him.

He was so big and heavy inside her. And then he moved—slowly, deeper. Pushing against her resistance. And then he pulled out again. Leila could feel sweat break out on her brow, between her breasts. She'd never thought sex would be so gritty, *base*.

Alix was relentless, moving in a little deeper each time,

and as Leila's flesh got used to him, accommodated him better, the awful sting of pain faded, becoming something else. Something much more pleasurable. Even more pleasurable than before.

Something about Alix's urgency was transmitted to her and Leila instinctively wrapped her legs around him. She felt inordinately tender in that moment, cradling this huge man between her legs, feeling the force of him inside her body.

His movements got stronger, more powerful. And Leila's hips were moving, circling. He reached down between them and touched her *there*, close to where he was thrusting. Circling his thumb, making stars explode behind her eyes, making her body tight with need again.

She was gasping, her body arching against him, buttocks tightening as he pushed her to the very limit of her endurance and she fell again, down and down, from an even higher height than the first time.

She was coasting on such a wave of bliss that she was barely aware of Alix's own body, pumping hard into hers, before he too went taut and with a guttural groan exploded in a rush of heat inside her.

Leila came to when she felt herself being lifted out of the bed, pliant and weak. She managed to raise her head and open her eyes to see he was walking them into a dimly lit bathroom…acres of marble and golden fixtures.

Steam was rising from a sunken bath that looked big enough to swim in, and Alix knelt and gently deposited Leila into the pleasantly hot water.

She looked at him, properly awake now. 'What are you doing?'

He grimaced. 'You'll be sore…and you bled a little.'

Leila thought of the bed and the sumptuous sheets. Mortified, she said, 'Oh, no!'

Alix looked stern. 'It was my fault. I should have known to prepare...'

Another expression crossed his face then, something like dawning horror, but it was hard to see in the shadows of the room, and then it was gone, replaced by something indecipherable.

He stood up and Leila saw that he'd wrapped a towel around his waist. It still didn't disguise the healthy bulge underneath, though, and her face flamed as she sank down into the bubbles.

'I'll be back in a minute.'

Alix left the bathroom and Leila moved experimentally, wincing when she felt the sting of something between pleasure and pain between her legs. She ached too—all over. But pleasurably.

Letting her head fall back, she allowed the water to soothe her body. Her brain was foggy but one thing was crystal clear: she was no longer a virgin. She'd allowed Alix Saint Croix to be more intimate with her than anyone else. And it had felt...*amazing*. Stupendous. Transformative.

It was as if this body she'd had all her life was suddenly a new thing. Her hand moved of its own volition up over the flat plane of her belly and cupped her breast. Her nipple was roused to a hard peak under her hand, still slightly sensitive. When Leila brushed it a zing of pleasure went to her groin.

She felt emboldened—empowered. Like a woman for the first time in her life. That perfume she'd chosen earlier...she got it now. She could own a scent like that and wear it with sensual pride. Dreamily, she smiled, her hand over her breast, fingers trapping her nipple, squeezing gently as Alix had done...

Alix felt marginally more under control dressed in his trousers. Up until a couple of minutes ago he had felt as if someone had drugged him and he'd lost any sense of rationale or control. And he *had*. And about something so fundamentally important to him that he was still reeling.

But he was already becoming distracted again, losing focus. He stood in the doorway of the bathroom, watching Leila cup her breast in her hand, a small smile playing around her mouth, and just like that Alix was hard again, ready for her.

That first initial thrust into her body... It had been heaven and hell—because he'd known that while he was experiencing possibly the most exquisitely sensual moment of his life she'd been in pain. Even though he'd been as gentle as he could... And then, when that pain had faded from her eyes and her body had begun to move under his, Alix hadn't had a hope of retaining any sense at all. He'd become a slave to the dictates of his body and hers.

He'd had to push her over the edge—touching her intimately, taking advantage of her inexperience—because he'd known he couldn't wait for her completion.

And then he'd exploded. Inside her. Without any barrier of protection.

Alix curbed the panic. Stepped into the bathroom. 'How are you feeling now?'

Leila immediately dropped her hand from her breast and tensed, opening her eyes, her smile fading. But then it came back...shyly.

'I'm okay. I think.'

Alix reached for a towel and held it out. Leila stood up and Alix couldn't help watching as the water sluiced down her perfect body. Her skin was like silk. She was exquisite. Slim and yet all woman, with full hips and breasts. Alix gritted his jaw to stop thinking about how it had felt to be cradled by her hips and thighs. How right it had felt. Right enough to send him mad—to make him forget important things. Like protection.

Leila rubbed herself dry with the towel, avoiding his eye now, and then Alix offered her a robe. She turned her back to him to put her arms into it and when she turned around again, belting it, she looked worried.

'Is something wrong?'

Alix felt a weight on his chest. Her eyes were so huge, so green. So innocent.

'Come into the bedroom. I asked the housekeeper to send some food and drinks up.'

He took her hand and led her out. A table was set up near the window. A candle flickered in the dim light. The sounds of the canal lapping against the building came faintly from outside.

They sat down and Leila looked even more worried. 'What is it, Alix? You're scaring me... '

'We didn't use protection.' He grimaced. 'That is, *I* didn't think of it. I presume you're not on any form of contraception?'

Leila shook her head, damp tendrils of dark hair slipping over her shoulders. Her cheeks coloured. 'No...I didn't think of it either.'

Alix's voice was harsh. 'It was my responsibility.'

She avoided his eyes for a long moment, and then she looked back at him. 'I think I'm okay, though. It's not a fertile time in my cycle. I've just finished a period.'

Something eased in his chest even as something else pierced him. A sense of loss. *Strange.*

He took her hand. 'I wasn't thinking. Ordinarily I never forget. And I can't *afford* to forget...'

He saw when comprehension dawned in those huge eyes.

Leila pulled her hand back. Her voice was stilted. 'Of course. A man like you has to be more careful than most. I understand.'

Alix felt a bizarre urge to say something to reassure her,

to tell her that it was nothing personal. But he couldn't. Because it was true. He would have to father an heir with his Queen and no one else. His own father had created a storm of controversy by bedding numerous mistresses, who had all come forward at one time or another claiming to have had children by him.

It had been one of the many reasons the people of Isle Saint Croix had become so disillusioned with their King and overthrown him.

'It won't happen again, Leila. I'm sorry.'

Her eyes snapped back to his and Alix quirked a smile. 'I don't mean *that*. We *will* be doing that again, I just won't forget about protection again.'

Food lay on the table between them, unnoticed, and Alix forced himself to try and retain a modicum of civility. He held up a piece of cheese. 'Are you hungry?'

Leila shook her head and then looked away, embarrassed.

Alix reached across and took her chin, tipping it up. He smiled. 'But you *are* hungry for something…?'

It entranced Alix that she seemed to have no sense of guile, or of playing the coquette. And why would she? She'd been a virgin. Her gaze dropped to his mouth and he saw the same insatiable appetite that had been awoken inside himself. His body hummed and soared with it.

She nodded, telling him silently what she was hungry for. Alix wanted to groan. 'But you're going to be too sore…'

Leila shook her head, her eyes on his now. Feminine and full of that innate knowledge that a man couldn't possibly ever fathom. Amazing that she already had it. Alix had never really noticed it before now, because he'd never seen it as a spontaneous thing. The women he was usually with were all too cynical even to attempt it.

'I'm okay. Really.'

Her husky words took him out of his reverie. He needed no further encouragement, so he dropped the food, stood up and led Leila back over to the bed.

When Leila woke up again it was morning. She opened her eyes and saw that the room was bathed in sunlight. She was on her own. But just as she thought that, Alix strolled out of the bathroom, straightening his tie. He was impeccably dressed. Shaved. Cleaned up. When Leila felt utterly wanton.

She sat up and clutched the sheet to her body, thoroughly disorientated. Alix leaned against one of the four posters of the bed and crossed his arms. A sexy smile played around his mouth. 'You look adorable...all mussed up.'

Leila scowled, and then grew hot when she thought of how *mussed up* she'd become when Alix had taken her to bed for the second time. Somehow in the dimly lit bathroom and bedroom last night it had been easier to face this man. Now it was daylight, and a return to reality and sanity was here. And it was not welcome.

Twinges and aches made her wince as she leant out to the side of the bed to look for some clothes.

Alix was there in seconds. 'Are you okay?'

Leila looked at him and couldn't breathe. 'I'm fine... What time is it?'

She had no clue what the etiquette of this kind of morning-after scenario was. A morning-after in *Venice,* after a night of more debauchery than she'd ever known she was capable of. Mortification washed through her in a wave.

Alix glanced at his watch, oblivious to her inner turmoil. 'It's after ten. I'm sorry about this, but I do need to get back to Paris for a lunchtime meeting.'

Leila forced herself to meet his eyes, even though she

wanted to slither down under the covers and all the way to Middle Earth. 'Of course. I need to get back too.'

Alix put his hands either side of her hips, effectively trapping her. 'You're not regretting anything, are you?'

His face was so close she could see the lighter flecks of grey in his eyes. And she knew that no matter how embarrassed she was right now, how gauche she felt, she really didn't regret a thing.

She shook her head and he pressed a firm kiss to her mouth before pulling back.

'Good. The housekeeper has sent up some breakfast, and I had some clothes sent over for both of us.'

'You did?' Leila boggled.

Alix shrugged and stood up. 'Sure—I called my assistant in Paris and she got them sent from a boutique here in Venice.'

Of course, Leila thought wryly to herself. She'd almost forgotten for a moment who Alix was. The power he wielded. The ease with which he clicked his fingers and had his orders obeyed. The ease with which she'd fallen into bed with him...

She had to stop thinking about that.

Galvanising herself, Leila got out of bed and pulled the sheet off the bed, tucking it around her body, all the while acutely aware of Alix's amused gaze.

'I'll have a quick shower,' she said, and walked to the bathroom with as much dignity as she could while trailing a long length of undoubtedly expensive Egyptian cotton behind her.

Once in the bathroom, Leila could hear Alix's phone ring and his deep tones as he answered. It was a welcome reminder that he was itching to move on, to get back to Paris and his life. And she needed to get on too.

As she stepped under the hot spray of the shower she

told herself that if all she had was this night in Venice with a beautiful exiled king then she would be happy with that.

She valiantly ignored the physical pang in the region of her chest that told her otherwise. She was *not* her mother, and she was *not* going to fall for the first man she'd slept with.

An hour later they were back on Alix's private jet, taking off from Venice. Alix was talking in low tones in another guttural language on his phone. She guessed it must be a form of Spanish. It was a relief not to have his attention on her for a moment.

Leila looked out of the window and took a shaky breath. Hard to believe her world had changed so irrevocably within less than twenty-four hours.

She wore the new clothes Alix's staff had sent over. Beautifully cut slim-fitting trousers and a loose long-sleeved silk top, with a wrap-around cashmere cardigan in the most divine sapphire-blue colour.

They'd even sent over fresh underwear and flat shoes. She felt cossetted and looked after. *Dangerous.* Because he did this sort of thing with women all the time.

When they'd been eating breakfast, just a short while before, she'd caught him looking at her intently. 'What?' Leila had asked. 'Have I got something on my face?'

Without make-up she'd felt bare. Exposed.

Alix had shaken his head. 'No. You're beautiful.'

And then he'd reached for her hand and she hadn't been able to look away from him.

'I want to see you again. Today...tonight. Tomorrow.'

Her heart had stopped, and then started again at twice the pace. 'But this was just one night...'

Wasn't it?

That was how she'd justified her outrageous behaviour. It had been a moment out of time.

Alix had looked a little fierce. 'Is one night enough for you?'

Trapped in his steely gaze, she'd asked herself if she could do this. Agree to an affair with this man? Have more of him? *Yes*, a pleading voice had answered.

Would he even let her go after she'd acquiesced so spectacularly? She knew the answer. Slowly she'd shaken her head. It wasn't enough for her either. She wanted more—shamelessly.

Alix's fingers had tightened around hers. 'Well, then...'

And now here she was, hurtling back towards the real world and a liaison she wasn't sure she knew how to navigate. She heard Alix terminate his call and thought of the dress he'd bought for her to go to the opera, and these new clothes.

She turned away from the view and found him looking at her. Before she could lose her nerve she said quickly, 'I don't want to be your mistress. I appreciate the clothes this morning, but I don't want you to buy me anything else.'

He looked at her for a moment, as if he truly couldn't understand what she was saying, and then he shrugged nonchalantly. 'Fine.'

Leila thought of something else and felt the cold hand of panic clutch at her gut. The prospect of press intrusion. Being photographed with Alix. It would inevitably bring scrutiny, and she did not want that under any circumstances.

She said, 'We can't go out in public. I don't want to end up in the papers. I'm not prepared for that kind of intrusion.'

Alix straightened, and something flashed across his face—surprise?—before it was masked and Leila thought she might have imagined it.

'I have an entire team at my disposal. I will make sure you're protected.'

Leila looked at him. She thought of Ricardo…and of the fact that Alix had been in and out of her shop a few times now and no one seemed to have picked up on it. Maybe it would be okay. Maybe the skeletons in her closet wouldn't jump out to bite her.

She forced a smile. 'Okay.'

CHAPTER SIX

'EARTH TO ALIX...HELLO? Anyone home?'

Alix blinked and looked at his friend and chief advisor, Andres, who had flown in from Isle Saint Croix to meet him. Andres was Alix's secret weapon. Devoutly loyal to getting Alix back on the throne, he was also working as a spy, of sorts, in the current regime in Isle Saint Croix. He was the reason Alix was going to get reinstated as King.

'Have you heard a word I've said?'

Alix knew he hadn't. His head had been consumed with soft silky skin. Long dark hair. Huge green eyes like jewels. Soft gasps and moans. The heady rush of pleasure when he— *Damn.* He jerked up out of his chair. This was ridiculous.

Leila was like a fever in his blood. He couldn't concentrate.

He went and stood at the window, and then after a few seconds turned back to his friend and said, 'I've met someone new.'

Andres made a small whistling sound, his boyishly handsome face cracking into a wry grin. 'I know you move fast, Alix, but this is your fastest ever. Usually you leave at least a week between switching partners. This is good, though—when will we see pictures hit the press?'

Alix folded his arms and scowled at his friend's exaggeration. And then he thought of what Leila had said about wanting to avoid press intrusion. And, as much as he needed it right now, suddenly the thought of paparazzi hounding her was very unpalatable. It made him feel almost...*protective.*

There had to be a solution. His brain seized on an idea and it took root. And the more it did so, the more seductive it became.

'Our supporters on the ground are aware that we are conducting a campaign of misdirection, aren't they?'

Andres nodded. 'Absolutely. They know that you're primed and ready to return, no matter what the press says.'

'Then if I was to leave and go to my island in the Caribbean for ten days it could only work in our favour?'

Andres huffed out a breath. 'Well, sure… I mean, you're just as contactable there as here… And if there are photos emerging of you frolicking in the sun with some leggy beauty the opposition will be taken completely by surprise when we pull the rug right out from underneath them.'

Alix smiled, sweet anticipation flooding his blood. 'My thoughts exactly.'

Andres frowned. 'But, Alix, you do know that your island is totally impenetrable by the outside world? No paparazzi have ever caught you there. It's too far—too remote.'

Alix's smile faded as he got serious. 'Which is why you're going to arrange for one of my most trustworthy staff on the island to take long-range grainy photos—I'll let you know when is a good time. Enough to identify me, but not Leila. He can email them to you, and you can send them out to whoever you think should get them for maximum beneficial exposure. I want this controlled.'

Alix felt only the smallest pang of his conscience and told himself he'd still be protecting her identity.

Andres's eyes gleamed with unmistakable interest at the lengths his friend was willing to go to for a woman, but Alix cut him off before he could say anything.

'I don't want to discuss her, Andres, just set it up. We'll fly out tomorrow.'

* * *

'You want to take me *where*?'

The blinds were down in Leila's shop and she'd just closed up for the evening when Alix had appeared, causing a seismic physical response. She hadn't heard from him since that morning, when they'd arrived back from Venice, and she didn't like to admit the way her nerves had stretched tighter and tighter over the day, as she'd wondered if she'd hear from him again. In spite of what he'd said.

And now he was here, and he'd just said—

'I have an island in the Caribbean. It's private...secluded. I've cleared my schedule for the next ten days—I need to take a break. I want you to come with me, Leila. I want to explore this with you...what's going on between us.'

Leila felt sideswiped, bewildered, along with an illicit flutter of excitement. 'But...I can't just *leave*! Who'll look after my shop and business? The last thing I can afford now is to close up.'

Smoothly Alix said, 'I can hire someone to manage the shop in your absence. They won't have your knowledge, obviously, but they'll be able to cover basic sales till you get back.'

Leila opened her mouth to protest, but the truth was she wasn't really in a position to take orders for new perfumes until she found some factory space, so all she was doing in essence was selling what they had. She could mix perfumes on a very small scale, which was what she'd done for Alix. So she was dispensable.

Weakly, she protested. 'But we've only spent one night together. I can't just take off like this.'

Alix raised a brow. 'Can't you? What's stopping you?'

Leila felt irritation rise. 'Not everyone lives in a world where you can just take off to the other side of the earth on a whim. Some of us have to think of the consequences.'

But right then Leila knew she wasn't thinking of financial or economic consequences—she was thinking of more emotional ones. Already.

Then Alix did the one thing guaranteed to scramble her brain completely. He came close and slid his hand around the back of her neck, under her hair, and tugged her towards him.

He said softly, 'I'll show you the consequences.'

His scent reached her brain before she even registered the effect it was having on her. Her blood started fizzing, and between her legs she was still tender but she could feel herself growing damp.

An acute physical reaction to desire. To this man.

Hunger, ravenous and scary, whipped through her so fast she couldn't control it. And when Alix lowered his mouth to hers she was already lost. Already saying yes, throwing caution to the wind. Because the truth was that dealing with him in this environment was scarier—so maybe going to the other side of the world would keep them in fantasy land. And when it was over she'd come back to normality. Whatever normal was...

When the kiss ended they were both breathing heavily, and Leila was pressed between the counter and Alix's very hard body. They looked at each other.

Shakily, Leila said, 'This is just... It won't last.' She didn't even frame it as a question.

Something infinitely hard came into Alix's eyes and he shook his head. He almost looked sad for a moment. 'No, it never lasts.'

Leila drew in a slightly shaky breath. One more step over the line couldn't hurt, could it? She was doing this with her eyes wide open. No illusions. No falling in love. She was not her innocent, naive mother.

'Okay, I'll come with you.'

Alix just smiled.

* * *

'There it is—just down there.'

Leila looked, and couldn't quite believe her eyes. She'd never seen such vivid colours. Lush green and pale white sand, clear azure water. Palm trees. It was like the manifestation of a dream she wasn't even aware she'd had.

She couldn't actually speak. She was dumbfounded. This was the last in a series of flights that had taken them from Paris to Nassau and now in a smaller plane to Alix's private island, which was called Isle de la Paix—Island of Peace.

And it looked peaceful from up here. They were circling lower now, and Leila could see a beautiful colonial-style house, and manicured grounds leading down to a long sliver of beach where foamy waves lapped the pristine shore.

She was glad she'd agreed to come here—because she knew this experience would help her to keep Alix in some fantasy place once their affair was over.

They landed, bouncing gently over a strip cut into the grass in a large open, flat area. Leila could see a couple of staff waiting outside and an open-top Jeep.

When they left the plane the warmth hit Leila like a hot oven opening in her face. It was humid—and delicious. She could already feel the effects sinking through her skin to her bones, making them more fluid, less tense.

The smiling staff greeted them with lilting voices and took their bags into a van. Alix led Leila over to the Jeep, taking her by the hand. When he'd buckled her in, and climbed in at the other side, he looked at her and grinned.

Leila grinned back, her heart light. He suddenly looked more carefree than she'd ever seen him, and she realised that he'd always looked slightly stern. Even when relaxed. But not here.

'Would you like a brief tour of the island, madam?'

'That would be lovely,' Leila responded with another grin.

They took off, and Alix drove them along dirt tracks through the lush forest that skirted along the most beautiful beaches she'd ever seen. The sun hit them and the Jeep with dappled rainbows of light, bathing them in warmth. Leila tipped her head back and closed her eyes, revelling in the sensation.

When the Jeep came to a stop she opened her eyes again and saw that they were on the edge of a small, perfect beach.

Leila leant forward. The smell of the sea was heady, along with the sharper tang of vegetation and dry earth. She itched to analyse the scents but the view competed. It was sensory overload. And the most perfectly hued clear seawater she'd ever seen lapped the shore just yards away.

Alix jumped out of the Jeep and came around, expertly unbuckling her belt and lifting her out before she could object, strong arms under her legs and back. He walked them down to the beach. It was late afternoon, and still hot, but the intense heat of the sun had diminished.

He put her down and looked at her, raising a brow. 'Have you ever skinny-dipped?'

Leila's mouth opened and she blustered, 'No, I certainly have *not*!' even as she felt a very illicit tingle of rebellion.

Alix was already pulling off his clothes. He'd changed on the plane before they'd got to Nassau, into a polo shirt and casual trousers. Leila gaped as his body was revealed, piece by mouthwatering piece.

She'd only seen him naked in the dimly lit confines of the Venetian *palazzo*, and now he stood before her, lit by the glorious sun against a paradise backdrop.

He was stunning. Not an ounce of fat. Hewn from rock. Pure olive-skinned muscular beauty. And one muscle in particular was twitching under her rapt gaze.

Leila's cheeks flamed and she dragged her gaze up.

She sounded strangled. 'I can't—we can't! What if some-one comes along?' She glanced behind her into the trees.

But then Alix was in front of her, his hand turning her chin back to him. She looked at him helplessly and he said, 'Listen. Just listen.'

Leila did—and heard nothing. Not one sound that didn't come directly from the island itself. No sirens or traffic or voices. Just the breeze and the trees and birds, and the water lapping near their feet.

'It's just us, Leila. Apart from a handful of staff at the house, we're completely alone.'

A sense of freedom such as she'd never felt before made her chest swell and lightness pervade her body. She felt young and carefree. It was heady.

'Now, are you coming into the water willingly? Or do I have to throw you in fully clothed?'

Leila started to shrug off her jacket, and said, mock petulantly, 'Fine, Your Majesty.'

Alix watched her, stark naked and completely blasé. 'That's more like it.'

His eyes got darker as Leila self-consciously took off her shirt and trousers, very aware of their chain-store dull-ness.

When she was in her bra and pants she hesitated, and Alix growled softly, 'Keep going.'

Leila fought back the memory of that other woman and reached behind her to undo her bra, letting it fall for-ward and off. The bare skin of her breasts prickled and her nipples tightened. Avoiding Alix's gaze now, she pulled down her pants with an economic movement, stepping out of them and laying them neatly on her pile of clothes.

She was naked on a beach, in a tropical paradise with an equally naked man. The reality was too much to take in, so with a whoop of disbelief and sheer joy Leila ran for the sea, feeling the warm, salty water embrace her. And then she dived deep under an oncoming wave before she exploded into pieces completely.

Leila wandered through Alix's house dressed in nothing but one of his oversized T-shirts, her hair in a tangled knot on top of her head. She'd never been so consistently undressed in her life, and after her initial self-consciousness she'd realised to her shock that she was something of a sensualist, relishing the freedom. Much as she'd exulted in the feel of her naked body in the sea on that first day.

Since they'd arrived at his house after skinny-dipping three days before, damp and salty from the sea, they'd barely left his bedroom. He'd retrieved food from the kitchen at intermittent intervals, and they'd gorged on each other in a feast of the senses. Leila's inexperience was fast becoming a thing of the past under Alix's expert tutelage.

When Leila had woken a short time before it had been the first time Alix hadn't been in bed beside her, or in the shower, or bringing food back to the bedroom. So she'd come to find him.

And now she was taking in the splendour of his house properly for the first time. It was luxurious without being ostentatious. Mostly in tones of soothing off-white and grey. Muslin drapes billowed in the soft island breeze through open windows. It truly was paradise, and Leila felt a pang that her mother was gone and couldn't experience this.

Little *objets d'art* were dotted here and there— tastefully. Leila stopped before a small portrait that hung in the main foyer area and her jaw dropped when she realised she must be looking at an original Picasso.

A soft sound from nearby made Leila whirl around, and her face flamed when she saw an attractive middle-aged, casually dressed woman looking at her with a warm smile on her face.

The woman put out a hand. 'Sorry to startle you, Miss Verughese. I was wondering if you'd like some lunch? I'm Matilde—Alix's roving housekeeper.'

She had an American accent. Leila forced an embarrassed smile. She hadn't seen any staff yet. She gestured to her clothes—or lack of them. 'Sorry, I was just looking for Mr Saint—that is…Alix.'

Matilde smiled wider. 'Don't worry, honey, that's what this island is all about—relaxation. You'll find Alix in his study, just down the hall. Why don't I prepare a nice lunch for you both on the terrace? It'll be ready in about half an hour.'

Leila smiled back at the woman, who was clearly friendly enough with Alix to be on first-name terms. 'Please call me Leila—and that sounds lovely.'

The woman was turning away, and then she turned back suddenly and said, *sotto voce* to Leila, 'You know, he's never brought a woman here before.'

And then, with a wink, she was disappearing down the corridor, leaving Leila with a belly full of butterflies. She hated it that it made her so happy to know this wasn't routine for him.

Leila wandered down the hall, with its gleaming polished wooden floors. She heard a low, deep voice and followed it into a room to see Alix, bare-chested, sitting at a desk with a laptop open before him. He was on the phone. And he was frowning.

The room was as beautiful as the rest of the house, with floor-to-ceiling shelves filled with books. Books that looked well used.

He looked up and saw her, and some indecipherable expression crossed his face before he said something Leila couldn't hear and put down the phone. He closed his laptop.

Leila felt as if she'd intruded on something and put out a hand. 'Sorry. I didn't mean to disturb you.'

Alix stood up and Leila saw that he was wearing only low-slung, faded jeans. Her insides sizzled. He looked amazing in a suit and tuxedo, but like this…he was edible.

'You're not disturbing me. Sorry for leaving you…'

He came and stood before her and Leila imagined she could feel the electricity crackle between them.

'I bumped into Matilde,' she babbled. 'She seems lovely. She's making us lunch and it'll be on the terrace in half an—'

Alix put a finger to Leila's mouth and quirked a sexy smile. 'Half an hour?'

Leila nodded.

Alix took his hand away and scooped Leila up into his arms before she knew what was happening. He was soon climbing up the stairs and Leila hissed, 'She's making lunch, Alix. We can't just disappear—'

They were at the bedroom door by now, and the sight of the tumbled bed made Leila stop talking. Apparently they *could*.

When they finally did make it down to the terrace, much later that day, Matilde was totally discreet and delivered a feast of tapas-like food. Salads and pasta. American-style wings and ribs. Seafood—spicy fish and rice, crab claws with garlic sauce. Lobster. Chilled white wine.

Leila had wondered if they would even make a dent in the feast laid before them, but just when she was licking her fingers after eating spicy fish she caught Alix's amused gaze.

'What?'

He leant forward. 'You have some sauce on the corner of your lip.'

Leila darted out her tongue and encountered Alix's finger, because he'd reached out to scoop it up. Immediately a wanton carnality entered Leila's blood and she moved so that she could suck Alix's finger into her mouth, swirling her tongue around the tip, much as he'd shown her how to—

She let his finger go with an abrupt *pop*, aghast at how easily she was becoming a slave to this man and her desires.

She found herself blurting out the first thing that came into her head to try and diffuse the intensity. 'Is it true that you've never brought a woman here?' She immediately regretted her words. Damn her runaway mouth!

Hurriedly she said, 'It's okay. You don't have to answer that—it doesn't matter.'

Alix's voice was wry. 'I should have known Matilde couldn't resist. She's a romantic at heart after all—as I think are *you*, Leila.'

She looked at Alix, horror flooding her at the thought that he might think— She shook her head. She forced all the boneless, mushy feelings out of her body and head and said firmly, 'No, I'm not. I'm a realist, and I know what this is—a moment in time. And I'm fine with that—believe me.'

Alix looked at Leila in the flickering candlelight. The island was soft and fragrant around them. *Like her.* Apparently he didn't need to be worried that she'd got the wrong idea from Matilde, and he wasn't sure why that thought wasn't giving him more of a sense of comfort. What? Did he *want* her to be falling for him?

She had her profile towards him and he was stunned all over again at her very regal beauty. Totally unadorned and all the more astounding because of it. In the last couple of days her skin had lost its pale glow and become more rich. Her Indian heritage was obvious, giving her that air of exotic mystery. Her green eyes stood out even more.

He felt a pang of guilt when he recalled the conversation he'd had with Andres to set up the photo opportunity.

It would be a far less intrusive photo than most of those he'd had taken with other women, so why did he feel so uncomfortable about it? And guilty...?

It didn't help to ease his conscience when Leila looked at him then and he couldn't read the expression on her face or in her eyes. It irritated him—as if she'd retreated behind a shield.

'Do you think you'll ever regain your throne in Isle Saint Croix?'

Alix blinked, jerked unceremoniously back to reality. Immediately he was suspicious—but then he felt ridiculous. She wasn't some spy from Isle Saint Croix, sent to find out his movements.

Even so, Alix had kept his motivation secret for so long that he wasn't about to bare his soul to anyone—even her.

He shrugged nonchalantly. 'Perhaps some day. If the political situation improves enough for me to make a bid for the throne again... But there is a lot of anger still—at my father.'

Leila had turned more towards him now, and put her elbows on the table, resting her chin on one hand. The diaphanous robe she was wearing made it easy to see the outline of her perfect braless breasts and Alix was immediately distracted. He had to drag his mind out of a very carnal place.

'What was he like?'

The question was softly, innocently asked, and yet it aroused an immediate sense of rage in Alix. He felt restless, and got up to stand at the nearby railing that protected the terrace and looked down over the lawns below.

He heard Leila shift in her seat. 'I'm sorry. If you don't want to talk about it...'

But he found that he did. Here in one of the quietest corners of the earth. With her.

He didn't turn around. Tightly he said, 'My father was

corrupt—pure and simple. He grew up privileged and never had to ask for anything. It ruined him. His own father was a good ruler, but weak. He let my father run amok. By the time my father married my mother—who was an Italian princess from an ancient Venetian family line—he was out of control. The country was falling apart, but he didn't notice the growing poverty or dissent. My mother didn't endear herself to the people either. She spent more time gadding around the world than on the island—in Paris, or London, or New York.'

Alix turned around and leant back against the railing. He looked down into his wine glass and swirled the liquid. When he looked at Leila again she was rapt, eyes huge. It made something in Alix's chest tight.

'My father took mistresses—local girls, famous beauties, it made no difference. He had them in the castle whether my mother was there or not. I think her attitude was that once she'd given him his heir and a spare she could do what she wanted.'

Leila said softly, 'You had a younger brother...?'

Alix nodded. 'Yes—Max.'

He went on.

'One day, both my parents were in residence—which was a rare enough occurrence. A young local girl was trying to see my father, holding a baby, crying. Her baby was ill and she needed help. She was claiming that it was his—which was quite probable. My father had his soldiers throw her and the baby out of the castle...'

Alix's mouth twisted.

'What he didn't realise was that a mob had gathered outside, and when they saw this they attacked. Our own soldiers were soon colluding with the crowd and they turned on my father and mother. They shot my parents and my brother, but I got away.'

Alix deliberately skated over the worst of it—made it sound less horrific than it had been.

He drank the rest of his wine in one gulp.

Leila's eyes shone with what looked suspiciously like tears. It had a profound effect on Alix.

'Your brother...were you close to him?'

He nodded. 'The closest. Everything I do now is to avenge his death and to make sure it's not in vain.'

He knew instantly that he'd said too much when Leila frowned slightly. Clearly she was wondering how his living the life of a louche royal playboy tallied with avenging his brother's untimely death.

She didn't know, of course, of the charitable foundations he headed that supported the families of people who'd lost relatives in traumatic circumstances. Or the amount of times he'd gone on peace and reconciliation missions all over the world, observing how it was done so he'd be qualified to apply it to his own country when he returned.

Leila looked at Alix, so tall and brooding in the moonlight. Her heart ached for him—for the young boy he'd been, helpless, watching his own parents destroy their legacy—and taking his younger brother with them.

She thought of how she'd lied about her father being dead and it made her feel dishonest now, after he'd told her what had happened to him.

'Alix,' she began, 'there's something I should—'

But he cut Leila off as he moved, coming over to the table. He put his glass down. His eyes were blazing and she could see they'd dropped to her breasts, unfettered beneath her thin gown. Instantly heat sizzled in her veins and she forgot what she'd wanted to say.

'I think we've talked enough for one evening. I want you, Leila.' And then, almost as an afterthought, he said, 'I need you.'

I need you. Those three words set Leila's blood alight.

She sensed that he needed to lose himself after telling her what he had. So she stood up, allowing him to see all of her, thinly veiled. He might have said he needed her, but she knew that this was about *this*.

And as Alix led her inside and up to the bedroom she reassured herself once again that that was fine.

'Who would have thought you like to read American *noir* crime novels?' Leila's voice was teasing as she lay draped across Alix's chest on a large sun lounger in his garden.

He lowered his book and looked at her, arching a brow. 'And that *you* would like Matilde's collection of historical romance novels covered with half-naked Neanderthals and long, flowing blonde hair?'

Leila giggled and ducked her head, and then looked up again. 'It was my mother's fault. She devoured them and led me astray from a young age.'

'You must miss her.'

Leila unpeeled herself from Alix and sat up, pulling her knees to her chin and wrapping her arms around them. She looked out over the stunning view from their elevated height in the garden at the back of the house, where the pool was.

Quietly, Leila said, 'I miss her, of course. It was always just the two of us.'

Leila was afraid to look at Alix in case he saw the emotion she was feeling. A mix of grief and happiness. And gratitude to be in this place. To be with this man and yet to know not to expect more. Even if her heart *did* give a little lurch at that.

Alix came up on one elbow beside her, his long half-naked body stretched out in her peripheral vision like a mouthwatering temptation.

'The man you were with before—what did he do to you?'

Leila glanced at him. *Damn.* She'd forgotten that she'd

mentioned Pierre, even in passing. She shrugged. 'He was a mistake. I was naive.'

'How?'

Leila bit her lip, and then said, 'It was just after my mother died—I was vulnerable. He paid me attention. I believed him when he said he just wanted to get to know me, that he wouldn't push me. But one night he came up to my apartment and said he was tired of waiting for me to put out. He tried to force himself on me—'

Alix sprang upright in one fluid move and caught Leila's arm, turning her to face him. Anger was blazing from his eyes. 'Did he hurt you?'

Leila was shocked at this display of emotion. 'No. He... he tried to, but I had some mace. I threatened to use it on him. So he just insulted me and left.'

'*Dieu*...Leila...he could have—'

'I know,' Leila said sharply. 'But he didn't. Thank God. And I was proved a fool for believing that he—'

Alix's hand tightened on her arm. 'No, you weren't a fool. You just wanted reassurance and some attention.'

Words trembled on Leila's lips. Words about how much she'd wanted to believe that love and security did exist. *Could* exist. But she couldn't let them spill. Not here, with this man. He'd made no promises. He was offering her this slice of paradise—that was all and if she'd been foolish before she'd be triply so if she started dreaming about anything more with a man like Alix.

He urged her gently back down onto the lounger and pushed their books aside. Tugging her over his chest again, he cupped the back of her head, fingers threading through her hair. 'The man was an idiot, Leila.'

He brought her mouth down to meet his and they luxuriated in a long and explicit kiss. Leila felt emotional—as if Alix was silently communicating his gratitude to her for trusting enough in him to let him be the one to take her innocence.

The kiss got hotter, more desperate. Alix's free hand deftly untied the strings of her bikini and she felt the flimsy material being pulled from between their bodies. Then his hand was smoothing down her back, cupping her buttock and squeezing gently, and then more firmly, long fingers covering the whole cheek, exploring close to where the seam of her body was wet and hot.

Obeying the clamouring of her blood, Leila moved over Alix so that her legs straddled his hips, breasts pressed to his broad chest. With an expert economy of movement, barely breaking their connection, mouths and body, Alix managed to extricate himself from his shorts and disposed of Leila's bikini bottoms too. Now there were no barriers between them.

Leila had got so used to their privacy being respected that she felt completely uninhibited. Her legs were spread and she could feel him, hard and potent, at her buttocks. Alix moved so that his erection was between them, and Leila luxuriated in moving her body up and down, her juices anointing his shaft, making him groan…making them both want more.

Until she couldn't stand teasing him any more and rose up, biting her lip as Alix donned protection, and then letting her breath out in a long hiss as he joined their bodies and he was deep inside her. Nothing existed in the world except this moment. This exquisite climb to the top of ecstasy.

CHAPTER SEVEN

ALIX HAD HIS HANDS in his pockets and he was looking out over one of the back lawns to where Leila was deep in conversation with his head gardener. He smiled and realised that in spite of the fact that he was standing on the precipice of possibly the most tumultuous period of his life he'd never felt so calm...or content.

The last ten days had been unlike anything he'd ever experienced. He'd never spent so much time alone with a woman. Not even the woman he'd thought he'd lost his heart to all those years ago. That had been youthful lust mixed up with folly and arrogance and hurt pride.

Leila was easy to talk to. *Disturbingly* easy to talk to. He'd told her things that he'd never discussed with anyone else. Not even Andres.

And their chemistry was still white-hot. Alix frowned. He knew he had to let Leila go. Within days the news was going to break that Alix's people had voted for him to return to Isle Saint Croix. His life would not be his own any more. And he couldn't return to the island with a mistress. It would undo all his hard work. He had to return alone, and then find a wife.

He felt heavy inside, all of a sudden. And then Leila looked up and spotted him, a smile spreading across her face. She said something to the gardener and shook his hand. The old man looked comically delighted with himself and Alix shook his head. *The Leila effect.* Yesterday he'd found her in the kitchen, showing Matilde how to make a genuine hot Indian vegetarian curry.

She hurried towards him now with a box in her hand, dressed for travelling in slim-fitting trousers and a sleeveless cashmere top. He drank her in greedily...something elemental inside him growled hungrily. He wasn't ready to let her go—and yet how could he keep her?

'I'm sorry. I didn't mean to keep you waiting.'

Alix smiled even as an audacious idea occurred to him. 'You didn't. Was Lucas helpful?'

Leila smiled. 'Amazingly! He's even given me some flower cuttings to take home in special preservative bags. I've never smelled anything like them. If I can just distil their essences somehow—' She broke off, embarrassed. 'Sorry—we should get going, shouldn't we?'

Alix's chest felt tight. 'Yes, we should. The plane is waiting.'

'I'll just get my handbag.'

Leila moved to go inside, but then stopped beside Alix and looked up at him. Her voice was husky. 'Thank you... this has been truly magical.'

He reached out and cupped her jaw, running his thumb across the fullness of her lower lip. 'Yes, it has,' he agreed.

And right then he knew that he wasn't ready to let Leila go, and that whatever it took to keep that from happening, he would do it.

'Stay with me tonight?'

Leila looked at Alix across the back seat of his chauffeur-driven car. It was very late—after midnight—and the rain-wet streets of Paris were like an alien landscape to Leila. She realised she hadn't even missed it. And she also realised that, in spite of her best intentions, she wasn't ready to say goodbye to Alix.

She nodded jerkily and said, 'Okay.'

The Place Vendôme was empty when they arrived, and they were escorted into the hotel with discreet efficiency. It gave Leila a bit of a jolt to see how the staff fawned over Alix, and how he instantly seemed to morph into someone more aloof, austere. She'd forgotten for a moment who he was.

When they entered his suite, low lamps were burning. Alix took off his jacket and Leila walked over to the window, feeling restless all of a sudden. She could see her shop, dark and empty, and a faint prickle of foreboding caused her to shiver minutely.

Then she saw Alix in the reflection of the window. He was looking at her. She turned around. The air shimmered between them. He came towards her and in a bid to break the intensity Leila glanced away, still a little overwhelmed by how much he made her *feel*.

And then something caught her eye on a nearby table, and when it registered she let out a gasp. 'Oh, *no*!'

Alix had spotted what Leila had spotted just a second afterwards and he cursed silently and vowed to have whoever had left the papers here sacked.

It was a popular French tabloid magazine and there was a picture on the front. A picture of Alix and Leila on a beach. They'd gone there the day before. They were sprawled in the sand, their swimwear leaving little to the imagination, but they were not naked, thankfully. Her face was turned away, up to his, so she wasn't identifiable—but he was.

Leila had already picked it up, but Alix whipped it out of her hands and threw it away. He said urgently, 'They didn't get your face...it's okay.'

She was pale, shocked. She looked up at him. 'You *knew* about this?'

Alix's conscience stung so much it hurt. Funny, he'd never considered himself to have much of a conscience. *Before.*

'My assistant sends me updates on any news coverage.'

Leila looked wounded. 'Why didn't you tell me?'

Alix gritted his jaw. 'Because I was hoping you wouldn't see it.'

Leila waved an arm. 'Well, the whole of France has seen it now.' She looked down to where the magazine was on the floor and read out, *'"Who is the exiled King's latest mystery flame?"'*

Alix caught her chin and moved it towards him. He felt her resistance. When she was looking at him he said, 'They don't know who you are and I'll make sure they won't. Please—trust me.'

Something moved across her face—some expression that Alix didn't like. Eventually she said, 'This has to end after tonight, Alix. I'm not made for your world and I don't want to be dragged through the papers as just another one of your women.'

Alix rejected everything she said, and a sense of desperation rose up inside him—that need to make her *his*. But he couldn't articulate it. So instead he used his mouth, moving it over hers, willing her to respond—and she did, because she was as helpless against this as he was.

The following morning when Leila woke up it took her a long time to orientate herself. She was in a massive bed, with the most luxurious coverings she'd ever felt. She was naked and alone. And her body ached. Between her legs she was tender.

And then it all flooded back. Alix had led her in here last night and stripped her bare, as reverently as if she was something precious. Then he'd laid her down and subjected Leila to what could only be described as a sensual attack.

An attack that had been fully consensual.

It was as if everything he'd taught her had been only the first level, and his lovemaking last night had shown her that there could be so much more. Alix hadn't been tender or gentle. He'd been fierce, bordering on rough, but Leila blushed when she thought of how she'd revelled in it, meeting him every step of the way, exulting in it, spurring him on, raking her nails down his back, begging hoarsely for more, harder, deeper...

Even the fact that her picture had been in that magazine, albeit not identifiable, had faded into the background now.

She had a vague memory of finally falling asleep around dawn, with Alix's arms tight around her. Leila frowned as another memory struggled to break through her sluggish thought processes. Alix had kissed the back of her head and said, 'You're not going anywhere...this isn't over...'

Leila frowned. *Had* she heard that? And what could it mean? The prospect that Alix had decided that something more permanent might come out of what they had made her silly heart speed up.

She needed to talk to him.

Leila got out of bed and made her way to the opulent bathroom that her small apartment could have fitted into twice over. Once showered and dressed, she made her way to find Alix, hearing his low, deep tones before she saw him.

She smiled. Even his voice made heat curl in her belly as she recalled the way he sounded in bed—all earthy and husky and desperate... Maybe, just *maybe*, there was something different between them? The fact that she wasn't like his usual women—

Leila stopped in her tracks outside the door when she heard her name.

Alix spoke again. 'Leila's perfect, Andres. She's beautiful, accomplished, intelligent, refined.'

Leila blushed to find herself eavesdropping like this—and to hear herself being spoken of this way.

But Alix sounded a little angry when he spoke next. 'The very fact that she didn't want to be seen with me is a point in her favour. She's totally different to any other woman I've ever been with.'

Leila frowned minutely. *A point in her favour?* It sounded as if she was being graded.

She went to move forward, to let him know she was there, but when she got to the doorway she saw he was standing with his back to her, looking out of the window. So he didn't see her.

And when he spoke again his tone had the little hairs standing up on the back of her neck.

'To be perfectly honest,' he went on, 'I couldn't have possibly engineered this to go better if I'd planned it to happen. We're on the brink of a referendum that will return me to the throne and the ruling party haven't a clue. They probably think I'm still sunning myself with her on a beach in the Caribbean. Everything is falling into place at just the right time.'

Leila stepped back through the doorway, out of sight, horror coursing through her, her skin going clammy with shock.

Alix laughed and it was harsh. 'Since when has *love* had any relevance when it comes to the wife I will choose? The important thing is that she's falling in love with *me*—I'm sure of it. This will be nothing like my parents' marriage… toxic from the inside out.'

He continued, oblivious to the devastation taking place just outside the door as the full import of what he was saying sank into Leila.

'How do I know? She was a *virgin*, Andres…a woman doesn't give that up easily. To return to power with a fiancée by my side will put me in a much stronger position. Leila will make a great queen, I'm sure of it. She's the right choice.'

He was silent again, and then he spoke in a low voice.

'No, I've no doubt that she'll say yes. If I need to reassure her that I love her too, to achieve my aims, then so be it. It won't be a hardship. And the sooner we have children the better—an heir will be the strongest sign of stability for Isle Saint Croix. A sign of hope and things moving on.'

Leila's heart was pounding so hard she thought she might faint. Sweat was breaking out on her brow.

She was a virgin...a woman doesn't give that up easily. If I need to reassure her that I love her too...then so be it.

For a moment a sharp pain near her heart almost caused her to double over. What Alix was proposing to do made her feel sick. He would embark on a life with her based on lies and falsehoods just so that he could present the whole package to his precious island. An island that he was on the brink of regaining after he'd let her believe that it was a far distant possibility—not imminent. He'd lied to her face! And he would father a child purely to further his own political aims!

The irony was like a slap in the face—her own father had rejected a child for the same reasons. But Leila was in no mood to appreciate that dark humour now.

All their conversations took on a sinister glow now. His questions about her opinions on politics—had that been to make sure she wasn't some kind of raving anarchist? His questions on her opinions on anything had just been an interview.

And the intensity of their lovemaking—had that been to make sure Alix felt she could sustain his interest long enough for him to father an heir?

What broke her out of her shock was the fact that Alix had stopped talking. Feeling sick, Leila walked to the door, silent on the carpet. He was still standing at the window with his hands in his pockets. Master of all he surveyed—including, as he obviously believed, his innocent, gullible lover. A ruthless man who saw her only as a vehicle to help him regain his throne.

Leila felt the slow burn of an anger so intense it made her tremble. She only wanted one thing: to walk away from Alix and forget that she'd ever met him, forget that she'd repeated the sin of her mother: falling for the first man to seduce her.

* * *

Alix's brain was still whirring after the phone call. Had he really told Andres that he was prepared to make Leila his wife? His Queen?

Yes. He waited for a sense of regret, panic or claustrophobia. But even now it felt right. He'd never met anyone like her. She was sweet, innocent…and yet not so innocent any more. His body tightened as he recalled how quickly she'd learned, her shyly erotic, bold moves in bed, how she'd taken him in her mouth and tasted him a few short hours ago.

His body went still. A familiar figure walking quickly across the square came into his line of vision and his breath caught.

It was Leila, and she was carrying her holiday bag— the only woman he'd ever known not to travel with twelve pieces of luggage. Where was she going? His skin prickled uncomfortably when he recalled the phone conversation— was there a chance she'd overheard him?

But if she had why was she walking away? What woman would walk away from the prospect of a man like him making their union permanent?

A small voice whispered: *A woman like Leila.*

Alix was about to follow her when his phone rang again. He picked it up and said curtly, 'Yes?' He could see her now, disappearing into her shop, and he didn't like the flare of panic in his gut. The feeling that if he didn't follow her he'd never see her again.

'Your Majesty, are you there? We need to discuss plans for when the result of the referendum is announced tomorrow.'

Tomorrow. Tomorrow was when his life would change for ever. That reminder was a jolt to Alix. A jolt that told him he was in danger of losing focus when he needed it most. Over a woman. Even if she *was* the woman he'd chosen to be his Queen, she was still just a lover, a woman, peripheral to his life.

Alix pushed the insidious feeling of something slipping out of his grasp out of his head and concentrated on the call. For half an hour. When it was finally over he went to look out of the window again, and when he took in the view, every muscle in his body locked tight.

Leila was across the square, closing the door to her shop. The blinds were down and she was dressed in jeans, sneakers and a jacket. With a wheelie travel bag.

And as he watched she hitched up the handle on her bag and started to walk swiftly away from the shop, the bag trailing behind her.

Leila was almost at the corner of the street when Alix caught up with her, catching her arm. She didn't turn around and he felt the tension in her body.

'How much did you hear?' He directed the question to the back of her head.

She turned around then, and Alix steeled himself for some emotion, but Leila's face was expressionless in a way he'd never seen before. It sent something cold through him—along with a very uncomfortable sense of exposure.

'Enough. I heard enough, Alix.' She pulled her arm free and said, 'Now, if you'll excuse me, I have a train to catch.'

Alix frowned. Just a couple of hours ago he'd left her sated and flushed from their lovemaking in his bed. He'd whispered words to her—words he'd never thought he'd hear himself say to any woman. That sense of exposure amplified.

'Where are you going?'

Leila looked surprised. 'Oh, didn't I tell you? I've got to go to Grasse to discuss sharing new factory space with an old mentor of my mother's.'

Alix felt panic and he didn't like it. 'No, you didn't tell me.'

Leila looked at her watch. 'Well, I must have forgotten to mention it—'

She went to walk around him but he stopped her with a hand on her arm again. It felt slender under his hand.

Leila looked expressively at his hand. 'Let me go, please.'

'You had no plans to go anywhere until you overheard that conversation.'

Her eyes blazed into his. 'Don't you mean your royal decree?'

Alix was aware that they were drawing interest from passers-by and he saw the glint of something in the distance that looked suspiciously like the lens of a paparazzi camera.

He gritted his jaw. 'We need to talk—and not in the street.'

Leila must have seen something on his face, because she looked mutinous for a second and then pulled her arm free again and started back towards her shop.

Alix took her case from her hand, although she held on to it until she obviously realised it would end up in a tug of war. She let him take it and the incongruity of the fact that he, Alix Saint Croix, was tussling over a case in the street with a woman was not lost on him.

When she'd opened the door to her shop they stepped inside and she shut it again. Alix fixed his gaze on her pale face. 'Why were you leaving?' *And without saying goodbye...* He bit back those words. Women didn't say goodbye to him—he said goodbye to *them*.

She folded her arms across her chest. She was mad at him—that much was patently obvious. 'I was leaving because I need to sort my business out. And also because your arrogance is truly astounding.' She unlocked her arms enough to point a finger at herself. 'How dare you assume that I'm falling in love with you? We've only known each other for two weeks. Or did you think that because I was a virgin I had less brain cells than the average woman and would fall for the first man I slept with?'

Alix felt something violent move through him at the implication that there would be more men and that he'd just been the first.

Now she looked even angrier. 'You told someone called Andres I was a virgin. How dare you discuss my private details with anyone else?'

Alix gritted his jaw harder. 'Unfortunately the life of a royal tends to be public property. But it wasn't my right to divulge that information.'

Leila huffed a harsh-sounding laugh. 'Well, that's a life I have no intention of ever knowing anything about, so from now on I'd appreciate it if you kept details of our affair to yourself. You can rest assured, *Your Majesty*, I'm not falling in love with you.'

Alix told himself she wouldn't have run like that if something about overhearing that phone call hadn't affected her emotionally.

His eyes narrowed on her. 'So you say.'

'So I *mean*,' Leila shot back, terrified that he'd seen something else on her face. 'I've saved you the bother of having to pretend that you feel something for me, so I'll save you more time with the undoubtedly fake romantic proposal you had in mind...the answer is no.'

Alix lifted a brow. 'You'd say no to becoming a queen? And a life of unlimited wealth and luxury?'

Leila's stomach roiled. 'I'd say no to a marriage devoid of any real human emotion living in a gilded cage. How can you, of all people, honestly think I'd want to bring a child into the world to live with two parents who are acting out roles?'

Alix's eyes were steely. 'You weren't acting a role this morning.'

Immediately Leila was blasted with memory: her legs wrapped around Alix's waist, fingers digging into his muscular buttocks. What had she turned into? Someone unrecognisable.

She huffed a small unamused laugh. 'Surely you don't mean to confuse lust with love, Alix? I thought you were more sophisticated than that?'

His face flushed at that but it didn't comfort Leila. She felt nauseous.

'Look,' Alix said tersely, 'I know that you're probably a little hurt. The fact is that the woman I choose to be my Queen has to fulfil a certain amount of criteria. We respect each other. We like each other. We have insane chemistry. Those are all good foundations for a marriage. Better than something based on fickle emotions or antipathy from the start.'

Something dangerously like empathy pierced Leila when she thought of what he'd told her about his parents' marriage.

And then she thought of his assessment of her being a *little* hurt, and the empathy dissolved. The hurt was all-encompassing and totally humiliating. The last thing she wanted was for him to suspect for a second how devastating hearing that conversation had been.

'You never even told me you were so close to regaining your throne,' she accused.

Alix's jaw was hard as granite. 'I couldn't. Only my closest aides know of this.'

'So everything—the whole trip to your island—was all an elaborate attempt to throw your opponents off the scent? And what was I? A decorative piece for your charade? A convenient lover in the place of the last one you dumped so summarily?' Leila laughed harshly and started to pace. '*Mon Dieu*, but I was a fool, indeed. Two times in a row now.'

Alix sounded harsh. 'I am *not* like that man, and you were *not* a fool.'

Leila's gaze snapped back to his, but she barely saw him through her anger. 'Yes, I was. To have believed for a second that a trip like that was spontaneous.' She recalled something else about the conversation she'd overheard and gasped. '*You* had someone take those pictures of us, didn't you?'

Alix flushed. He didn't deny it.

Leila shook her head and backed away from him. The tender shoots of something that she'd been frantically trying to ignore finally withered away. She'd thought they'd been sharing intimate moments alone…he'd led her to believe they were alone on the island. She'd bared her body and soul to this man and he'd exploited that. She had to protect herself now.

She needed to drive him away before he saw how fragile she really was underneath her anger.

She affected nonchalance. 'To be perfectly honest, Alix, I used *you*.'

I used you. Alix reacted instantly, with an inward clenching of his gut. Pain.

An echo of the past whispered at him—another woman. '*I used you, Alix. I wanted back into Europe and I saw you as a means to get there and restore my reputation.*'

He went cold and hard inside. 'Used me?'

Leila nodded and shrugged lightly. 'I wanted to lose my virginity but I'd never met anyone with whom it was a palatable prospect…until you walked into the shop.'

Her eyes were like hard emeralds.

'It was only ever about that for me, Alix. And excitement— I won't deny that. My mother was over-protective, but now

I'm finally free and independent, and I'm not about to shackle myself to some marriage of convenience because you deem me a suitable candidate for being your bride and the mother of your precious royal heirs.'

A mocking expression came over her face.

'I'm annoyed that you used me for your own ends, but that's the extent of any *hurt*. And surely you don't think you're the first rich man to invite me up to his suite for a private consultation?'

She didn't wait for a response.

'Well, you weren't the first, and you probably won't be the last.'

Alix's vision blurred for a moment at the thought of Leila going into another suite, smiling at some man, taking out her bottles. *Getting under his skin.* Concocting the perfect scent for him like a sorceress. Sleeping with him.

Darkness reared up inside him. She'd used him. Just as he'd been used before. He'd vowed never to let it happen again. Yet he had. The evidence of such weakness made him feel bilious. He'd been prepared to woo her into becoming his bride. He'd been prepared to take her into his life, parade her as his Queen. Prepared for her to bear his children. The heirs of Isle Saint Croix.

One thing broke through his mounting rage. 'You could be pregnant.'

The thought was repugnant to him now, when a couple of hours ago he'd thought it might be something used to persuade her to agree to marriage.

Leila went a little paler, but then her chin lifted. 'I'm not.'

Alix wanted there to be no doubt. None. 'How do you know?'

'I got my period this morning.'

Alix smiled humourlessly. 'And I suppose you'd have

me believe that if you were pregnant you wouldn't come after me for everything you could?'

Alix was aware of her arms dropping and her hands fisting at her sides. *He* felt nothing, though. Only a desire to lash out.

'Your cynicism really knows no bounds. And now I have that train to catch. Please leave.'

Alix took a step back and forced himself to be civil when he wanted to swipe a hand across the nearest glittering shelf covered in glass bottles and bring them all crashing to the ground. To crush Leila under the burning anger in his gut, forcing her out of this hard obduracy. Force her to be soft and pliant again.

The desire made him feel disgusted with himself.

He turned and walked out of the shop.

It wasn't until Alix reached his suite in the hotel that his brain cleared of its dark haze.

He couldn't even accuse Leila of avariciousness. There were a million other women who would have heard that conversation and used it to inveigle their way into his life, take everything he offered and more. But not her.

The dark irony mocked Alix.

He saw the rumpled sheets on the bed out of the corner of his eye—and something else. He strode into his bedroom and picked up the House of Leila perfume bottle, containing his signature scent.

An image came to him of Leila in the bath, after they'd made love for the first time. He saw it as clearly as if she was in the room right now. The small sensual smile that had played around her mouth, her hand on her breast, a nipple trapped between her fingers. That smile scored his insides now like a knife. She'd looked *satisfied*. Mission accomplished. *I used you.*

Acting on a rising tide of rage, Alix lifted his arm and hurled the bottle at the nearest wall, where it smashed into a million tiny shards and scattered golden liquid every-where. And that smell reached into his gut and clenched hard.

He lifted the phone and gave curt instructions that he and his entire team were to be moved to another hotel. And just after that call he got another one from Andres. The man was excited.

'The polls are in and they're all suggesting a landslide victory. The government is panicking but it's too late. This is it, Alix. It's almost time to go home. When you return with Leila on your arm—'

Alix cut him off coldly. 'Do not mention her name again. Ever.'

There was silence on the other end of the phone before the man recovered with professional aplomb and went on as if nothing had happened.

Alix listened with a grim expression.

When the conversation was finished, staff appeared, scurrying to do his bidding. Alix cursed himself for over-reacting. Leila Verughese was just a woman. A beautiful woman. And it had been lust that had clouded his judg-ment. Just lust. Nothing more. If anything, it was a timely and valuable lesson.

By the time Alix was getting out of his car and entering his new temporary home, Leila Verughese wasn't a recent or even a distant memory. She had been excised from his mind with the kind of clinical precision Alix had used for years to excise anything he didn't want to think about. Women...the death of his brother.

His destiny was about to be resurrected from the ashes like a phoenix, and that was the most important thing in the world.

It was only when the train had left Paris far behind that Leila felt some of the rigid tension seep out of her locked muscles. Her jaw unclenched. The ache in her throat eased slightly.

She sent up silent thanks for the old friend of her mother's who would let her stay for a while with her in Grasse. There was no meeting about sharing factory space, but it would get her out of Paris until Alix was gone.

And then the pain started to seep in from where she'd been blocking it out. The pain that told her it had taken more strength than she'd thought she had to stand in front of Alix and pretend he'd meant nothing to her. That she'd used him.

He'd used her. Thank God the press hadn't discovered her identity.

Her naivety made her want to be sick. And that reminded her of the slightly nauseous feeling she'd had for the last few days—not strong enough to cause concern, but there in the background. She'd put it down to Matilde's rich food.

She'd lied to him about her period. It hadn't come yet. But she'd wanted him gone. If he'd thought there was the slightest chance... Horror swept through her at the prospect.

She put her hand on her belly now and told herself fiercely that she *wouldn't* be pregnant, because the universe wouldn't be so cruel as to inflict the sins of the mother on the daughter. It couldn't.

If she *was* pregnant she didn't want to contemplate Alix Saint Croix's reaction. After their last conversation he would advocate only one thing to protect his precious ascent to power: termination. Because Leila Verughese had just comprehensively ruled herself out of the suitable bride stakes.

CHAPTER EIGHT

Seven weeks later

ALIX LOOKED OUT over the view from where his office was situated in the fortress castle of Isle Saint Croix. It was at the back, where the insurmountable wall of the castle dropped precipitously to the sea and the rocks below. The most secure room.

The window was open, allowing the mildly warm sea breeze to come in, bringing with it all the scents of his childhood that he'd never forgotten: earth, sea, wild flowers. And the more exotic scents of spices and herbs that always managed to infiltrate the air were coming from the main town's market.

It had been a tumultuous few weeks, to say the least, but he was still here and that was something.

Leila. She was a constant ghost in his mind. Haunting him. Tormenting him. As soon as he'd returned to Isle Saint Croix on a wave of triumph the perfume of the island had reminded him indelibly of her. Of the perfume she'd made for him.

Was she sitting in a luxurious hotel suite right now, with her potions arrayed before her? Smiling at some hapless man? Enthralling him? *Witch.*

He still couldn't believe she'd turned her back on the opportunity to become his Queen. Or that her rejection had smarted so badly. He told himself it was a purely ego-based blow. He'd chosen Leila because he'd genuinely believed she had the necessary attributes. Plus he'd had the evidence that they got on well, and he'd felt she had integrity and that he could trust her.

Not to mention the insane chemistry between them.

And all along she'd had her own agenda.

An abrupt knock at the door interrupted his brooding and made him scowl. 'Come in.'

It was Andres, looking worried. Holding a tablet in his hand. When he got to Alix's desk he was grim. 'There's something you need to see.'

He turned the device around and Alix looked down to see rolling news footage. It took a second to compute what he was looking at, but when he did his entire body tensed and a wave of heat hit him in the solar plexus.

It was a picture of him and Leila, arguing in the street that day seven weeks ago. He had his hand on her arm and she looked angry. And beautiful. Even now it took his breath away.

The headline read: *'Want to meet the very fragrant mystery lover of the new King of Isle Saint Croix? Turn to page six...'*

Alix looked at Andres. 'Do it.'

Andres scrolled through and stopped. Alix read, but couldn't really take it in. Words jumped out at him:

Illegitimate secret daughter of Alain Bastineau...
next President of France?
Pregnancy test...positive...royal heir?
Does King Alix know if he's the father?
Scandal and controversy don't seem to want to leave
this new King in peace...

Leila was still in shock. It hadn't left her system yet even though she'd had since yesterday to come to terms with the news. She'd had it confirmed, after weeks of trying to deny the possibility when one period hadn't materialised and then the next one. She was pregnant—approximately eight weeks, according to the doctor she'd gone to see after doing three home tests: positive, positive, *positive*.

Pregnant and without the father. Just like her mother.

A sense of shame and futility washed over her. It was genetic. She'd proved no less susceptible to a gorgeous man intent on seduction. The only difference being that this time around the father would have been quite content to marry the mother of his child.

Leila smiled, but it was mirthless. Perhaps that was progress? Maybe by the next generation her child would manage *not* to get pregnant and would avoid dealing with the prospect of rejection and/or a convenient marriage?

Oh, God. Leila clutched her belly. Her child. A son or daughter. With this legacy in its past. How pathetic. Bitter tears made her eyes prickle.

A furious pounding on the door of the shop downstairs made her jerk suddenly upright. She heard a clamour of voices. She was late opening up, but her clientele hardly arrived in droves, so desperate to get into the shop that they'd pound on the door like that.

Momentarily distracted out of her circling thoughts, Leila hurried down to the shop, thinking that perhaps an accident had happened.

More banging on the door…urgent voices. Leila fumbled with the lock and swung the door wide—only to be met with a barrage of flashing lights, shouting voices and people pushing towards her.

It was so shocking and unexpected it took a moment for what they were saying to sink in, and then she heard it.

'Is it true you're pregnant with Alix Saint Croix's baby?'

'Are you getting back together?'

'How long have you been seeing him?'

'Why did you fight?'

'Are you in touch?'
'Does he know about the baby?'

The voices morphed into one and Leila finally had the presence of mind to slam the door shut again before someone got their foot in the door. Just before she closed it, though, someone threw in a newspaper and it landed at her feet.

She bent down to pick it up. Emblazoned across the front page was a picture of her and Alix arguing in the street that day all those weeks ago, his hand on her arm, her face tilted up to his: angry. *Hurt, humiliated.* She cringed now to see her emotions laid so bare. So much for believing she'd been in control.

And the headline: *'Leila Verughese, secret lover of Alix Saint Croix and the even more secret daughter that Alain Bastineau never wanted you to discover.'*

They knew about her father.

Leila's back hit the door and she slid down it as her legs turned to jelly. She barely noticed the pounding on the door, the shouting outside. She just knew that however bad she'd believed things to be just minutes before... when she'd known she was pregnant and it had still been her secret...they were about to get exponentially worse.

From somewhere came a persistent and non-stop buzzing noise. Leila dimly recognised that it was the phone. On hands and knees she crawled over to where the device sat under the counter. She picked it up.

Somehow she wasn't surprised to hear the familiar authoritative male voice. It caused her no emotion, though. She was numb with shock.

It told her that in one hour Ricardo would be at the back lane entrance of her property with a decoy. She was to let him in. In the meantime she was to pack a bag, and then leave with him when instructed.

The shock kept Leila cocooned from thinking too much

about these instructions, or the baying mob outside. And in just over an hour she let Ricardo in, with a girl who looked disconcertingly like her... Leila didn't think twice about letting them borrow one of her coats for the girl, nor about the fact that he sent the girl out through the front. The baying mob reached fever pitch and then suddenly died down again as she heard vague shouts of, *'She's getting away!'*

Ricardo was saying urgently, 'It won't be long, Miss Verughese, before they realise she's not you. Where is your bag? We need to lock up and go—now.'

And then Leila was being escorted into the back of a car with blackened windows and they were racing through the streets of Paris. At one point Ricardo must have been concerned by her shocked compliance and pallor as he asked if she was okay. She caught his eye in the mirror and said numbly, 'Yes, thank you, Ricardo.'

The shock finally started dissipating when they pulled up outside one of Paris's most iconic and exclusive hotels. It seemed as if a veritable swarm of black-suited men appeared around the car, and one of them was opening her door.

Leila looked at Ricardo, who'd turned around to face her.

'It's okay, Miss Verughese, they're the King's security staff. They have instructions to bring you straight to him.'

The King. He was a king now. Leila blanched. 'He's here?'

Ricardo nodded. 'He flew in straight away. He's waiting for you.'

The man almost looked sympathetic now, and that galvanised Leila. No way was she going to be made to feel that she was in the wrong here. Her life had just been torn to pieces and it was all *his* fault.

The wave of righteous indignation lasted until she was standing outside imposing doors on one of the top floors of the luxurious hotel and the bodyguard escorting her was knocking on the polished wood.

Indignation was fast being replaced with nerves and trepidation and nausea. *She was going to see him again.*

She wanted to turn and run. She wasn't ready—

A voice came from inside the suite, deep and cold and imperious. 'Come.'

The bodyguard opened the door with a card and ushered her in. Leila all but fell over the threshold to find herself in a marbled lobby that would have put a town house to shame.

It was circular, and doors led off in various directions. For a second she wanted to giggle. She felt like Alice in Wonderland.

And then a tall, broad shape darkened one of the doorways. *Alix.* He looked even bigger than before, dressed in a three-piece suit. His hair was severely short and he was clean shaven. Leila immediately felt weak and hated herself for it.

She fought it back and lifted her chin. 'You summoned me, Your Majesty?'

Alix's face darkened. A muscle pulsed in his jaw. He didn't rise to her bait, though, just stood aside and said, 'We need to talk—please come in.'

Leila moved forward and swept past him with all the confidence she could muster, quickly moving into the enormous room with its huge windows looking out over the Place de la Concorde, with the Eiffel Tower just visible in the distance.

She'd tried not to breathe his scent as she passed, but it was futile. She found herself drinking it in…it seemed to cling to her…but she couldn't find any of the notes she'd made for him. It was the scent he'd had *before*. She felt a pang of hurt. He wasn't wearing her scent any more…

She looked out of the window and folded her arms over

her chest, wishing she felt more presentable. Wishing she wasn't wearing the same old dark trousers, white shirt, flat shoes. Hair up in a neat ponytail for work. No make-up.

'Is it true? Are you pregnant?'

Leila fought the urge to bring a hand down to cover her belly protectively, as if she could protect the foetus from hearing this conversation.

'Yes, it's true,' she said tightly.

'And it's mine?'

She sucked in a breath and turned around. 'Of course it's yours—how dare you imply—?'

Alix held up a hand. He looked cold and remote. She'd never seen him like this apart from at that last meeting.

'I *imply* because *I* come with quite a considerable dowry.'

Leila bit out, 'Well, if you remember, you have come to me—not the other way around.'

Alix dug his hands into his pockets. 'And would you have come to me?'

Leila opened her mouth and shut it again, a little blind-sided. But she knew that her fear of how Alix would have reacted would have inhibited her from telling him—at least straight away.

She avoided answering directly. 'I've only just found out for sure. I haven't had much time to take it in myself.'

That was the truth.

Alix looked so obdurate right then that it sent a prickle of fear down Leila's spine. 'I'm not getting rid of it just because I'm not suitable wife material any more.'

He frowned. 'Who said anything about getting rid of it?' His frown deepened and then an expression came over his face—something like disgust. 'You suspected you might be pregnant that day, didn't you?'

Leila's face got hot. She glanced down at the floor, feeling guilty. 'I *hadn't* got my period.' She looked up again. 'But I didn't want to say anything. I had no reason to believe it wasn't just late, and I was hoping that...' She stopped.

'That there would be no consequences?' Alix filled in, with a twist to his mouth.

Leila nodded.

'Well, there are. And rather far-reaching ones.'

More than fear trickled down her spine now. But before she could ask him to clarify what he meant he moved towards her. He stopped—too close. She could smell him, imagined she could feel his heat. She wanted to step back, but wouldn't.

'You lied to me.'

Leila frowned. 'But I only just found—'

'About your father. You said he was dead.'

Leila felt weak again. She'd conveniently let that little time bomb slide to the back of her head while dealing with this.

She glared at Alix. 'You lied too. You lied about the fact that you were poised to take control of your throne again and just using me as a smokescreen.'

Alix appeared to choose to ignore that. He folded his arms. Eyes narrowed on her. 'Why did you lie about your father?'

Leila turned away from him again, feeling like a pinned insect under his judgemental gaze. He came alongside her. She bit her lip. He was silent, waiting.

Reluctantly she said, 'It was my mother. It was what she always said. *"He's dead to us, Leila. He didn't want me or you. And he only wanted me to prostitute myself for him. If anyone asks, he's dead."*'

Alix stayed silent.

'I was aware of who he was—his perfect life and family. His rise to political fame. Why would I ever admit that he was my father? I was ashamed for him. And for myself. It's one thing to be rejected by a parent who has known you all your life, but another to be rejected before they've even met you.'

She and her mother had seen both sides of that coin.

Alix's tone was arctic, he oozed disapproval of her messy past. 'We found out that the press sat on the story of your identity in order to dig into your past and see if they could find anything juicy. And they did. Your father is already doing his best to limit the damage, claiming these reports are spurious—an attempt to thwart his chances in the election.'

Leila hated it, but she felt hurt. Another rejection—and public this time. 'I'm not surprised,' she said dully. And in front of Alix. Could this day get any worse?

Apparently it could. From beside her he said briskly, 'The press conference will be taking place in an hour's time. I've arranged for a stylist and her team to come and get you ready.'

Leila turned to look at Alix. 'Press conference? Stylist? What for?'

Alix turned to face her. His expression brooked no argument. 'A press conference to announce our engagement, Leila. After which you'll be leaving with me to come back to Isle Saint Croix.'

For some reason Leila seized on the most innocuous word. 'Back? But I've never been...' Her brain felt sluggish, words too unwieldy to say.

A sharp pinging noise came out of nowhere and Alix extracted a sleek phone from his pocket, holding it up to his ear. He took it away momentarily to say to Leila, 'Wait here for the stylist. I'll be back shortly.'

And he was walking out of the room before she could react.

When she did react, Leila felt red-hot lava flow through her veins. The sheer arrogance of the man! To assume she'd meekly roll over and agree to his bidding just because he had a King Kong complex!

Leila stormed off after Alix, going down seemingly endless corridors that ended in various plush bedrooms and sitting rooms, and a dining room that looked as if it could seat a hundred.

She eventually heard low voices from behind a closed door and without knocking threw the door open. 'Now, look here—what part of *I don't want to marry you* didn't you understand the first time I said it?'

Leila came to an abrupt halt when about a dozen faces turned to look at her. There were two women in the group, scarily coiffed and besuited. Alix was in the middle, looking stern, and they were all watching something on the television.

A man around Alix's age detached himself from the group and came over to Leila, holding out a hand. 'Miss Verughese—a pleasure to meet you. I'm Andres Balsak, King Alix's chief of staff.'

Leila let him take her hand, feeling completely exposed.

Andres let her hand go and urged her in with a hand on her elbow. 'We're watching a news report.'

The crowd parted and Leila was aware of their intense scrutiny. She avoided looking at Alix's no doubt furious expression.

The news report was featuring a very pretty town full of brightly coloured houses near a busy harbour. An imposing castle stood on a lushly wooded hill behind the town.

A reporter was saying, 'Will King Alix be able to weather this scandalous storm so early into his reign? We will just have to wait and see. Back to you—'

The TV was shut off. Alix said, 'Everyone out. *Now.*'

The room cleared quickly.

The reality of seeing that report, as short as it had been,

brought home to Leila the stark magnitude of what she was facing.

She turned to Alix. 'What exactly is it that you're proposing with this press conference and by bringing me to Isle Saint Croix?'

Alix looked at Leila. She could have passed for eighteen. She was pale and even more beautiful than he remembered. Had her eyes always been that big? The moment he'd seen her standing in the foyer, his blood had leapt as if injected by currents of pure electricity.

And when she'd passed him, her scent had reminded him of too much. How easily he'd let her in. How much he still wanted her. How much he'd trusted her. Would she even have come to him to let him know about the baby? He had a feeling that she wouldn't, and his blood boiled.

Damn her. And damn that sense of protectiveness he'd felt when she'd revealed the truth about her father. He couldn't think of that now.

'You'll come because you're carrying my heir and the whole world knows it now.'

Leila looked hunted, her arms crossed tightly over her chest again, pushing the swells of those luscious breasts up. They looked bigger. Because of the pregnancy? The thought of Leila's body ripening with his seed, his child, gave him another shockingly sudden jolt of lust. A memory blasted—of taking a nipple into his mouth, rolling it with his tongue, tasting her sharp sweetness—he brutally clamped down on the image.

Leila was pacing now. 'What is the solution here? There *has* to be a solution…' She stopped and faced him again. 'I mean, it's not as if you're *really* intending to marry me. The engagement is just for show, until things die down again…'

She looked so hopeful Alix almost felt sorry for her.

Almost. Her reluctance to marry him caught at him somewhere very primal and possessive.

'No, Leila. We *will* be getting married. In two weeks. It's traditional in Isle Saint Croix to have short engagements.'

Leila squeaked, 'Two weeks?' She found a chair and sat down heavily. She looked bewildered. 'But that's ridiculous!'

Alix shook his head. 'It's fate, Leila. Our fate and our baby's. The child you're carrying is destined to be the future King or Queen of Isle Saint Croix. It will have a huge legacy behind it and ahead of it. Would you deny it that?'

Leila's arms uncrossed and her hands went to her lap, twisting. Alix had to stop himself from going over and lacing his fingers through hers.

'Well, of course not—but surely there's a way—?'

'And would you deny it the chance to grow up knowing its father? Surrounded by the security of a stable marriage? You of all people?'

Leila paled and stood up again. 'That's a low blow.'

Alix pressed on, ignoring the pang of his conscience *again*. 'We have a child to think of now. Our concerns are secondary. If you choose to go against me on this I will not hesitate to use my full influence to make you comply.'

'You bast—'

Alix spoke over her. 'There's not only our child to consider, but the people of Isle Saint Croix. Things have been precarious, to say the least, since I won back the throne. We are at a very delicate stage, and we desperately need to achieve stability and start getting the country back on its feet. Everything could descend into chaos again at a moment's notice. This scandal is all my enemies need to tip the balance. Would you allow that to be on your conscience?'

Leila thought of the pictures she'd just seen on the TV of the pretty town, the idyllic-looking island.

She swallowed. 'That's not fair, Alix. I'm not responsible for what happens to your people.'

'No,' he agreed. 'But I am, and I'm taking full responsibility for *this* situation.'

In the end it was the weight of inevitability and responsibility that got to Leila. And the realisation that she'd suspected all along that this might happen. Either this or Alix would have asked her to get rid of the baby. And the fact that he hadn't...

She put her hand over her belly now, that newly familiar sense of protectiveness rising up. She'd felt it as soon as the doctor had confirmed her pregnancy beyond all question. Along with a welling of helpless love. So this was what her mother had gone through... It put a whole new perspective on her mother, and how brave she'd been to go it alone.

And Leila wasn't even facing that. She was facing the opposite—a forced marriage to someone who pretty much despised her after she'd told him she'd used him. In a pathetic attempt to save face, to hide how hurt she'd been.

And now she'd have to live with that. But as long as she remembered Alix's phone conversation she wouldn't lose her way. He'd never intended this to be anything but a means to an end. And at least he hadn't fooled her into thinking he'd fallen for her.

Her child would not suffer from the lack of a father as she had done. Feeling rejected. Abandoned. Unwanted. Alix might want this baby purely for what it represented: continuity. But it would be up to Leila to make sure it never, ever knew how ruthless its father was.

'There, Miss Verughese, see what you think.'

Leila smiled absently at the stylist who'd been waiting with a rail of clothes when Alix had escorted her back through the suite like a recalcitrant child. Someone had also been there to do her hair and make-up.

She looked in the mirror now and sucked in a breath. She looked totally different. Elegant. She wore a fitted long-sleeved dress in soft, silky material. It was a deep green colour, almost dark enough to be blue. It was modest, in that it covered her chest to her throat, but it clung in such a way that made it not boring. It fell from her hips into an A-line shape, down to her knees.

Her hair was up in a chignon, showing off her neck. Her eyes and cheekbones seemed to stand out even more. She put it down to the artful make-up, and not the fact that her appetite had waned in the last month.

She was given a pair of matching high heels. And then Alix appeared. He'd changed suits and was now wearing one with a tie that had colours reflecting those in Leila's dress. She reeled at the speed with which he'd reacted to the news and been prepared.

'Please leave us.'

Once again the room emptied as if by magic. Alix's cool grey gaze skated over Leila and she felt self-conscious. This man was a stranger to her. But a stranger who made her body thrum with awareness.

He held out a velvet box and opened it. Inside was a beautiful pair of dangling emerald and gold earrings. Ornate—almost Indian in their design.

She looked from them to him. 'They're beautiful.'

Alix said, 'They're part of the Crown Jewels. They were protected by loyalists to the crown while I was in exile. Put them on.'

Leila glared at him.

'Please,' he said.

She lifted them out, one by one, and put them on, feeling their heavy weight dangling near her jaw.

'I have something else...'

Alix was holding out a smaller velvet box. Her heart thumped hard. She'd dreamed of this moment, even though she'd never have admitted it to herself—but not like this. Not with waves of resentment being directed at her.

Alix opened it and she almost felt dizzy for a moment. Inside was the most beautiful ring she'd ever seen.

Five emeralds—clearly very old. Set in a dark gold ring. It was slightly uneven, imperfect.

Leila reached out a finger and touched it reverently. 'How old is this?'

Carelessly Alix said, 'Around mid-seventeenth century.'

She looked at him, horrified. 'I can't accept this.'

Alix sounded curt. 'It matches your eyes.'

Something traitorous moved inside her to think of him choosing jewellery because it matched her eyes. That he'd thought about it rather than just picking the first ring he saw.

Alix took the ring out of the box and took up Leila's left hand.

Immediately her body reacted and she tensed. Alix shot her a look before sliding the ring onto her ring finger and Leila held her breath. It was as if the fates and the entire universe were conspiring against her, because it fitted her perfectly.

Alix's hand was very dark next to her paler one, his fingers long and masculine. Hers looked tiny in comparison.

He didn't let her go and she looked up, confused.

Alix's expression was unreadable. 'There's one more thing.'

'More jewellery? I really don't need—'

But her words were cut off when Alix's head lowered and his mouth slanted over hers. She was so shocked she didn't react for a second, and that gave Alix the opportunity to coax open her mouth and deepen the kiss.

When Leila recovered her wits she tried to pull away,

but Alix had a hand at the back of her head and stopped her from retreating. Everything sane in Leila was screaming at her to push him away, but her body was exulting in the kiss, drinking him in as if she'd been starved in a desert for weeks and had just found life-restoring water.

His scent intoxicated her, and before Leila could stop herself she was clutching at Alix's jacket and pressing her body closer to his.

A sharp rap at the door broke through the fog and Alix broke contact. Leila didn't have time to curse him or herself, because Andres was popping his head around the door and saying, 'They're ready for you.'

Alix said abruptly, 'We'll be right there.'

Andres disappeared and Leila realised she was still clinging onto Alix's jacket. He was barely touching her. She took a step back. He was looking at her almost warily, as if she might explode. And she *had* almost exploded—in his arms. It was galling.

'What was that in aid of?' Her tongue felt too large for her mouth.

'The world's press are waiting for us downstairs. We need to convince them that this was a lovers' tiff and we are now happily reunited. That the pregnancy is the happy catalyst that has brought us back together.'

The speed and equanimity with which Alix seemed to be reacting to this whole situation, not to mention his attention to detail—*that kiss*—just confirmed for Leila how ruthless he was. And how she'd never really known him.

She wanted to kick off her heels and run as fast as she could for as long as she could. But she couldn't. Together they had created a baby, and that baby had to come first. Exactly as Alix had said.

She smoothed clammy hands down her dress and drew her shoulders straight. 'Very well—we shouldn't keep them waiting, then, should we?'

Alix watched Leila walk to the door and open it. Her spine was as straight as a dancer's and her bearing was more innately regal than any blue-blooded princess he'd ever met. Something like admiration mounted inside him, cutting through the eddying swirl of lust that still held his body in a state of heightened awareness and uncomfortable arousal.

He'd tried to block out the effect she had on him, telling himself it couldn't possibly have been as intense as he'd thought. But it had been *more*.

CHAPTER NINE

THE PLANE THAT was taking them to Isle Saint Croix was bigger than the plane Alix had used before. The fact that Leila had only ever travelled on private jets was something she should have found ironically amusing, but she couldn't drum up much of a sense of lightness now.

The press conference had passed in a blur of shouted questions and popping cameras. Leila had just about managed to lock her legs in place so they hadn't wobbled in front of everyone.

Andres had sent someone to retrieve her most important and portable possessions from her apartment and they were in a trunk in the hold.

Alix's staff, whom she'd seen in the suite in Paris, were all down at the back of the plane now, including Andres, and she and Alix were alone in the luxurious front. There was a sitting room, dining room and bedroom with en-suite bathroom. Stewards had offered dinner, but Leila had only been able to pick at it. Her stomach was too tied up in knots.

She thought of how Alix had responded to a question about her father at the press conference.

He'd said curtly, 'If Alain Bastineau is so certain he is not my fiancée's father, then let him prove it with a DNA test.'

Huskily Leila said now, 'When they asked about my father...you didn't need to respond like that.'

Alix looked at her. 'Yes, I did. Any man who rejects his own child is not a man. You're to be the Queen of Isle

Saint Croix and I will not allow you to be speculated about in that way.'

Immediately Leila felt deflated. He'd only stood up for her because of concerns for his own reputation. She'd been stupid to see anything else in it, however tenuous.

'You need to eat more—you've lost weight.'

Alix was looking at her intently and Leila cursed herself for having drawn his attention. She felt defensive and, worse, self-conscious.

'Apparently it's common to lose weight when you're first pregnant.'

Alix's voice was gruff. 'We'll arrange for you to see the royal doctor as soon as you're settled. We need to organise your prenatal care.'

Leila was surprised at the vehemence in Alix's voice and had to figure that all this meant so much more to him than the fact of a baby. She and the baby now represented stability for the island's future.

She frowned then, thinking of something else. 'How did they find out?'

Alix was grim. 'I told you—they had that picture of us in the street and they sat on it, wanting to know more about you. Also, as I had just been crowned King again, they knew there was potentially a much bigger story in the offing. They were keeping an eye on you, Leila. We think someone went through your bins and found the home pregnancy tests you did.'

Leila instantly felt nauseous and put a hand to her mouth. She shot up out of her chair and made it to the bathroom in time to be sick. She knew it wasn't necessarily what Alix had just said—her bouts of nausea hit her at different moments of the night and day.

To her embarrassment, when she straightened up in the small bathroom she saw Alix reflected in the mirror, looking concerned. No doubt concerned for her cargo.

Weakly she said, 'I'm fine—it's normal.'

'You look as pale as a ghost. Lie down and rest, Leila. You'll need it.'

Alix went out into the bedroom and pulled back the covers. Leila kicked off her shoes and avoided his eye as she sat down. Then she thought of something else and looked up at him, panicked. 'What about my shop?'

Alix was grim. 'We can arrange for someone to manage it in the short term. It'll probably be for the best if you sell it. You'll be busy with your duties as Queen and as a mother.'

Furious anger raced through Leila's blood, galvanising her to stand, all weariness gone. 'How dare you presume to take my livelihood away from me just like that?' She snapped her fingers.

'Leila, look—'

'No, *you* look.' Leila stabbed a finger towards Alix, the full tumult of the day catching up with her. 'That business is my own family legacy. It's a vocation, making perfumes, and I will *not* be giving it up. If you insist otherwise then I won't hesitate to leave Isle Saint Croix on the first return flight out.'

She folded her arms tight across her chest.

'Or are you telling me that you'll incarcerate me like some feudal overlord? I'm sure the tabloids would love to hear about *that*!'

Alix's mouth was a thin line, and a muscle jumped in his jaw. Finally he said, 'Fine. We'll discuss how you can incorporate it into your life.'

And just as suddenly as the anger had come, it faded away, leaving her bone-weary again. Leila sat down on the side of the bed. Alix stood in her vision, huge and immovable.

Leila lay down and curled away from where he stood, eyes shut tight. Maybe when she woke up this would all be a bad dream...?

* * *

Alix stood looking down at the woman on the bed, seeing how her breath evened out and her muscles grew slacker. Her back was to him and that only compounded the frustration still rushing through his system. He knew he'd been out of line to suggest that Leila sell her business, but he found it hard not to operate from some base place when she was in front of him.

He'd noticed the minutely perceptible thickening of her waist. Her hand had rested there just now, as if to protect the child within. And suddenly an almost dizzying sense of protectiveness rose up within him.

He thought of those paparazzi hounding Leila, and recalled that when Andres had shown him the news footage, his primary instinct had been to get to her and keep her safe more than to confront her about the pregnancy.

It made him feel exposed.

Alix finally backed away from the bed and out of the room. When he sat down again he asked for a shot of whisky from the hovering attendant.

He swirled the dark amber liquid in the heavy crystal glass for a long moment. He'd always thought that having a child would be something he'd feel quite clinical about. Not entirely unemotional, of course. He would be as loving as he could be. But how could he be something he knew nothing of? A loving parent?

Alix had only ever really loved one person: his brother. And the pain he'd felt when his brother had been murdered had nearly killed him too. He would never forget that raw chasm of rage and grief. And he never wanted to feel it again.

Except now his gut was churning with dark emotions that felt far too close to the bone.

When he'd first contemplated making Leila his Queen it had felt like a relatively uncomplicated decision. He liked her. Liked talking to her, spending time with her. Liked that he'd been her first lover. *Just* that memory alone was enough to have Alix's body hardening.

His mouth twisted. Their intense mutual chemistry had told him that there would be no issues in the bedroom.

For someone who had always known that his choice of bride would be strategic above all else, it had felt like a very logical choice. A beautiful bride...a queen he would have no hardship creating a family with.

Until she'd rejected his offer outright.

And now she was pregnant with his child and he had no choice but to make her his wife. He was being mocked by the gods for his initial complacency.

Alix willed down the heat in his body and the darkness in his gut. He'd believed that Leila was falling for him when evidently she hadn't been.

He ignored the intensifying of the tightness in his chest and told himself that this would only make things easier. No emotion on either side. No illusions. This was about the baby and the future of Isle Saint Croix, and while Leila was not the bride Alix would choose if he had a choice right now, he *would* make this work. For the sake of his people and for the sake of his legacy into the future.

When they arrived in Isle Saint Croix it was after midnight. Too late for any kind of formal reception, much to Leila's relief. She was still feeling a little hollowed out and overwhelmed. Her sleep on the plane had been populated with scary dreams of her running and a tall, menacing figure trying to catch her. She didn't have to be a genius to figure that one out.

Her first impressions of the island were of warm, damp heat. Warmer than she'd expected. Stars populated the clear night sky. There was the zesty sea-salt freshness of the ocean nearby. And something much more exotic and intriguing.

On the journey to the castle Leila caught glimpses of small pretty villages and a bigger town down near the sea, lights twinkling in the harbour. Then they rounded a bend, and there on a hilltop in the distance stood the floodlit castle.

She couldn't hold in a gasp of pure awe. On the TV it had looked like a toy...now she could see just how massive and imposing it was. As if it had been hewn directly out of the rock of the mountainside.

Its influence was clearly Moorish, with its flat roofs and long walls and what looked like lots of quadrangular buildings. Something about it called to Leila—something in its stark beauty.

'That's the castle. Our home.'

Our home. It was surreal. Leila felt overwhelmed again and said, 'I don't even know what language you speak...'

Alix turned his head. 'It's a colloquial mixture of Spanish and French and Arabic. But the official language is French, thanks to the fact that the French were our longest colonisers until the mid-eighteenth century.'

'There's so much I don't know.'

'I'll arrange for Andres to find a tutor for you.'

The car was descending now, down winding steep roads into a sort of valley. Leila could see the lights of a town nearby—presumably the capital. And then they were by-passing it and climbing again, up towards the castle, in through ornate gates and up a long driveway.

When they arrived in a huge stone courtyard with a bubbling fountain in the centre the car drew to a stop. Leila could see through the tinted windows to where a large handsome woman was waiting for them.

When they were out of the vehicle Alix led Leila over to her and said, with evident fondness in his voice, 'This is Marie-Louise, the castle manager. She and her husband risked their lives to protect some of my family's oldest artefacts, including the Crown Jewels.'

Leila's engagement ring winked at her in the moonlit night. 'That was very brave of you.'

The woman beamed and then ushered them inside to where the castle spread out into what seemed to be a warren of imposing stone corridors and inner courtyards.

Alix spoke to the woman in his own seductive tongue. He was obviously telling her goodnight, because she walked away from them.

He let Leila's hand go and indicated for her to precede him down a long corridor. It was lit by small flaming lanterns and for a moment Leila had the sensation that they might have slipped back in time and nothing would have changed.

They were approaching a wall that held a huge wooden door, ornately carved. The guard there stood aside and bowed as Alix opened the door and led them through.

'These are the royal family's private apartments.' He stopped outside another door and opened it. 'And these are your rooms.'

Leila felt a kind of giddy relief mixed with disappointment. She looked at Alix. 'We won't have to share a room?'

Alix saw that vaguely hopeful look on Leila's face and it made him feel rebellious. He desisted from telling her that his own parents had not shared rooms. That it would be considered perfectly normal if they had their own suites.

He shook his head. 'This is just until we're married—to observe propriety.'

Leila's hopeful look faded and became something else—something cynical, hunted. She gestured to her belly. 'It's not as if people don't *know* we've already consummated our relationship.'

Alix had to battle the urge to remind her of just what

that consummation had felt like. The magnitude of the fact that Leila was here under his roof, pregnant, was hitting him in a very deep and secret place.

He ruthlessly pushed it down and walked into the suite. 'I hope you'll find the apartment comfortable.'

Leila had followed him in and was looking around with big eyes. He saw it as if for the first time again: the understated luxury that the ruling regime had seen fit to keep for themselves. It was a little shabby now, but still with shades of its former opulent glory.

A glory that would be fully restored.

With his wife by his side.

With that in mind Alix forced out all emotion and said, 'The sleeping quarters are accessed back through the main hall. I have instructed that you are to have everything you might need.'

Leila looked at him and he could see the faint shadows under her eyes. Like delicate bruises.

The fact that she didn't want to be here sat like a dense heavy stone in his chest. He ignored it. She wouldn't have that power over him.

'I've made an arrangement for a scan at the hospital tomorrow—apparently you're due one about now.'

Leila's mouth twisted. 'To check on the cargo? Make sure that it's all looking good before you commit?'

Alix gritted his jaw at the sudden urge he had to go over and slam his mouth down on hers, making those mutinous lines soften.

'Something like that.' He moved towards the door. 'You should rest, Leila. The next few days will be busy.'

And then he left, almost afraid that she'd see something of the lack of control he felt.

Leila watched Alix leave. She was barely aware of the beauty of her surroundings, only vaguely aware that they'd walked through an open-air courtyard to come into the living room.

She felt numb with tiredness, delayed shock and the lingering effects of adrenaline.

Exploring back through the main hall, she found a bathroom off the bedroom. It was massive, with a grand central sunken tub. The dressing room was a more modern room, luxuriously carpeted and filled from floor to ceiling with clothes. A central island held hundreds of accessories in various shelves and drawers—and underwear. Underwear that made her cheeks grow hot.

She hurriedly shut those drawers, knowing how wasted the lovely underwear would be—because clearly Alix felt no desire for her any more, despite that kiss earlier, which had just been for appearances. He'd looked at her since as if he could hardly bear to be in the same room as her.

She ignored the pain near her heart and found the least skimpy nightwear she could find. Silk pyjamas. After conducting a rudimentary toilette and carefully putting the jewellery away in a drawer, she climbed into a bed that might have slept a football team and tried not to be too intimidated by the grandeur.

For a long time she looked up at the ceiling. Leila couldn't stop thinking about the fact that if Alix didn't desire her any more, then what glue could possibly hold their union together beyond duty and a shared responsibility for their child?

The following early afternoon Leila was pacing in the sitting room of her lavish suite. Marie-Louise had appeared that morning with a meek-looking girl who apparently was to be Leila's personal maid. When Leila had protested she'd been ignored and all but marched into a small dining room, where a delicious breakfast had been laid out. Her stomach had still been in knots, so she hadn't eaten much.

She'd explored thoroughly now, and had discovered the beautiful open-air atrium had a small pool, with glittering mosaics on the bottom and brightly coloured fish darting back and forth.

There was also a terrace outside her bedroom doors, and a balcony that overlooked the town far below with its brightly painted houses and the harbour.

Smells had tickled her nostrils, making her tip her head back to breathe deep. Earth, flowers, the sea, a distant wood... And then she'd realised why Alix had reacted so strongly to the scent she'd made. She'd somehow managed intuitively to recreate the scents of this island without having ever been there before.

Hating it that she felt so hurt because he obviously didn't wear the scent any more, Leila focused on checking herself in a nearby mirror. She'd had to pick a dress from the vast array of clothes in the dressing room as her own clothes hadn't appeared yet. She'd chosen a simple wrap dress in a very deep blue, and matching shoes.

She plucked at the material now, feeling that it was gaping over her breasts, which were sensitive and felt inordinately swollen.

She put a hand on her belly, knowing that it hadn't grown perceptibly in size, but feeling a telltale bloatedness.

'How are you today?'

Leila jumped and whirled around to see Alix behind her, hands in his pockets, dressed in a simple dark suit and white shirt. Every inch of him exuded pure masculine power and sensuality. And that new reserve tinged with disapproval.

The carpet must have muffled his steps. She hated it that he'd caught her in a private moment like that. And that her body had immediately zapped to life in his presence, nerve endings tingling.

She lifted her chin. 'Time to confirm all is well with your precious heir?'

His eyes glittered, as if he was angry at her insolence. 'The doctor is waiting for us at the hospital.'

Alix stood back to let Leila precede him from the room and she prayed he wouldn't see how brittle her sense of control was.

They walked down another seemingly unending labyrinth of imposing stone corridors and Leila had much more of a sense of the grandeur of the castle. She had to admit it: she was *impressed*. It was a little overwhelming, to say the least.

As was the display when they got to the entrance of the castle and about a dozen bodyguards jumped to attention. Alix opened the passenger door of a Jeep for Leila and after she was in got in the driver's side.

She watched him take the wheel with easy confidence, the guards preceding them and following them.

Slightly nervously, Leila asked, 'You said things were precarious here—is there any danger?'

Alix flashed her a look and she saw his jaw tighten before he said, 'I would never put you or the baby in danger. We are being protected by the best security firm in the world.'

Leila was slightly taken aback at his vehemence and said, 'I didn't mean to imply that you'd put me—*us*— in danger.' She'd realised, of course, that Alix probably couldn't care less if she was in danger. It was the baby he cared about.

She saw his hands tighten on the wheel and then relax. 'Forgive me. But you don't have to worry. The opponents to the throne are small in number, and weakened after years of not living up to their promises to build an egalitarian society. They have no real power. I've made sure of that. Still, I would never take anything for granted—hence the protection until Isle Saint Croix is on a much more solid footing economically.'

They were driving through the town now, and Leila could see its charm up close. She could also see that it was badly in need of sprucing up, with a general sense of neglect pervading the air.

A few people waved at their Jeep and Alix waved back. He said now, 'It's going to take time for the people to adjust to having their King back. They're not sure how to deal with me yet.'

Leila asked, with a feeling of something like disappointment, 'And do you really want them bowing and scraping to you?'

Alix looked at her again, slightly incredulous. 'God, *no*. I couldn't imagine anything worse.'

He looked back to the road, one hand on the wheel, the other on his thigh. Which Leila found very distracting, as she remembered how those thighs had pushed hers apart so that he could sink deep—

'I want to live side by side with my people. To move among them as an equal. I don't want pomp and ceremony. But equally I want to be their leader and protector. To provide for them.'

Leila jerked her gaze up. Alix's voice was quiet but his words had a profound effect on her. He sounded so... *protective*.

Before she could truly analyse how that made her feel she saw that they were driving into a car park outside a beleaguered-looking building.

Alix grimaced slightly as he pulled to a stop. 'The hospital doesn't look like much, but it houses some of the best consultants in the world. I've personally put many of our medical students through college for this very purpose— to bring them home to work and teach others. We're in the process of building a new hospital on a site nearby, and this one will be pulled down once it's built.'

Once again Leila was surprised to discover the depth of Alix's commitment to his island. And to discover how little she really knew him.

He got out of the Jeep along with a flurry of movement from the cars before and behind them, and as Alix solicitously helped her out she saw staff lining up to greet them.

Alix kept hold of her hand and Leila figured that of course he'd want to project a united front. Promote the fairy tale that they were in love.

She was introduced to the staff and the doctor who would be taking care of her prenatally—a genial older man. And then she was whisked away to be prepped for the scan, leaving Alix behind talking to the staff. The nurse was shy and sweet, and Leila did her best to put her at ease even though her own nerves were jumping.

What if they found something wrong?

When she was dressed in a gown and lying on a bed the doctor came in with Alix. He was chatty and warm, but Leila couldn't help her nerves mounting as cold gel was spread on her belly.

She glanced at Alix, but he was looking intently at the monitor where the doctor was focusing his attention as he moved the ultrasound device over Leila's belly.

She winced a little as he pressed in hard and almost reached for Alix's hand—some reflexive part of her was craving his solid strength and support. Instead she curled her hands into fists and looked at the monitor too. Her mother had done this alone. And even though Leila's baby's father was beside her she might as well have been alone too, for all the emotional support he was offering.

Suddenly a rapid beat filled the room, and it took Leila a second to figure out that it was the baby's heartbeat.

The doctor smiled. 'He—or she—is strong, that's for sure.'

A shape was appearing on the screen now, like a curled-over nut. The head was visible. And the spine. So delicate and fragile, yet there. Growing. Becoming someone. A son or a daughter.

Emotion suddenly erupted in Leila's chest and she had to put a hand to her mouth to stop a sob escaping. The love she felt, along with a fierce protectiveness, made her dizzy. Up to now it had been largely an intellectual thing. But this was visceral and all-consuming. *Primal.*

The doctor was saying reassuringly, 'Everything looks fine to me. We'll have you back in another few weeks, to see how things are progressing, but for now just eat well, take some gentle exercise and get lots of sleep.'

Leila just nodded at the doctor, too emotional to speak. He patted her hand, as if he saw this every day—which he probably did.

When Leila felt a little more composed she looked at Alix. But even steeling herself didn't prepare her for seeing the closed-off expression on his face. His eyes were unreadable. He certainly wasn't feeling the same depth of emotion Leila was experiencing, and it was like a physical blow.

His gaze was still fixed on the screen, and then he seemed to come out of the trance he was in and he said curtly, 'So everything is fine, then?'

'Yes, yes…nothing to worry about.'

'Good.'

He didn't look at her. His jaw was hard, resolute. They'd established that the baby was well. That was all he cared about. Leila was far too emotional to deal with Alix's smug satisfaction now, and she welcomed the distraction of the nurse coming to help her change back into her clothes.

The doctor and Alix left, and Leila did her best to ignore the ache in her throat and the hollow hole in her chest. She'd never really imagined what this experience would be like, but even if she had she would have expected the father of her child to be slightly more interested.

This had obviously just been a clinical experience, as far as Alix was concerned. And she was a fool to have had even the minutest impulse to seek anything from him.

That protectiveness that had assailed her moments ago surged back at the thought of Alix being so distant once the baby was born.

Once she emerged into the corridor her ire increased when she saw Alix pacing up and down, on his phone. As if they'd *not* just established that their baby was well. He saw her and gestured to say that they were leaving. She had to almost trot to keep up with his long-legged stride, and with each step she felt angrier and angrier and more *hurt*.

Alix terminated his phone call once they were in the Jeep and silence reigned. Leila was determined not to break it, feeling far too volatile and emotional. She knew Alix was sending her glances, but she resolutely ignored him, looking at the pretty scenery but not taking it in.

When they pulled up outside the castle she opened her door and got out before he could do it—or anyone else. She all but ran back into the huge stone fortress and blindly made her way down corridors, hoping she was headed in the right direction.

Everything was bubbling up—her hurt, her unwelcome desire for Alix and the need to get far away from the man who had turned her world upside down.

She heard steps behind her. 'Leila, what the—? *Stop!*'

She did stop then, breathless and hopelessly lost. She turned to face Alix, who was glowering. Fresh anger bubbled up, and again that fierce protectiveness. She felt the walls of the massive building crowd in on her, squeezing her chest tight. But biggest of all was the *hurt*.

She put a hand on her belly. 'You didn't feel a thing in

that scan room, did you? Except maybe a sense of satisfaction that your precious heir is fine.'

Alix looked at Leila. She'd never been more beautiful. Her cheeks were flushed with colour, eyes sparkling with anger. And with something else that he didn't want to identify.

He saw movement in his peripheral vision and, aware of staff nearby, strode forward, taking Leila's arm in his hand. 'Not here.'

He looked around and saw a doorway, recognised what it was. He opened it and brought a resisting Leila in, shutting the door behind him.

She ripped her arm free of his hand and moved away, looking around, her cheeks flushing even more and her eyes going wide as she took in the lavish surroundings.

'What is this place?'

Leila's voice was shaky and Alix hated the fact that it twisted his guts. He strode forward into the room. It was an opulent stone chamber with a raised marble platform. Alcoves around the edges of the room held sinks and drains. The ceiling was domed, and inlaid with thousands of mosaic mother-of-pearl stars that glittered.

'It was the women's *hammam*. And the harem is in this section of the palace too.'

Leila sent him an incredulous look. 'A harem? I thought we were still in the civilised west—not some medieval desert kingdom.'

Alix pushed down his irritation. 'The harem hasn't been in regular use for some time.'

Leila let out a laugh. 'Wow, *that's* reassuring. But maybe you're contemplating starting it up again? Taking additional wives just to fulfil your royal quota of children?'

Alix's jaw was so tight it ached, and yet he couldn't stop a series of images forming of Leila being stripped, massaged, washed and dressed by an army of women. And of him coming here to these secret and sensual rooms to find her waiting for him. Supplicant.

He wanted her so badly right then that he shook with it. He curled his hands into fists and said, 'Want to discuss what that was all about?' He couldn't even articulate himself properly. This woman tied him into knots.

She folded her arms over her breasts and it only served to remind Alix that he kept noticing how much fuller they were. The wrap dress she wore accentuated every womanly curve. He'd found it near impossible not to look at her bared belly in that room in the hospital, his control feeling far too flimsy.

'I'm talking about the fact that you might as well have been looking at a weather report in the hospital... Did seeing our baby on that screen affect you at *all*?'

CHAPTER TEN

ALIX LOOKED AT HER. *Did seeing our baby on that screen affect you at all?* His mind reeled. It had affected him so much he'd almost doubled over from the rush of pride, mixed with love and an awful bone-numbing sense of terror. Terror that something would happen to that fragile life that wasn't even born yet. Terror that something would happen to Leila. Terror at the surge of an emotion he'd never expected to feel again.

Leila didn't wait for him to speak. 'You were so cold… impervious. I will *not* bring a baby into a marriage where there is nothing between us except a sense of responsibility and duty. It's obvious you feel nothing for this baby beyond valuing it for the fact that it will inherit—'

Alix put up a hand, stopping her. Her words scored at his insides and yet he couldn't let it out—it was too much. And all he could see was *her*. So beautiful, so vital, and *here*. In front of him. Pushing his buttons.

Suddenly Alix wanted all the turmoil he felt to be consumed by fire. He moved closer to her and was gratified to see the pulse grow hectic at the base of her neck. Her breasts swelled with her breath.

'You say there's nothing between us?'

She nodded her head jerkily. Not so sure of herself now. 'There isn't. You only pursued me to distract people from your plans. You used me. You don't want me—you just want a vessel for your heirs. And it's not enough—for me or the baby.'

Alix was so close to Leila now he could smell her scent. Her unique brand of musk and sweetness.

'You're wrong, you know.'

Something flared in her eyes—something that once again he didn't want to identify.

'How?' she asked defiantly.

Alix reached out and took a lock of long, dark, glossy hair, winding it around his finger, tugging her gently towards him. She resisted.

'There *is* something between us and it's enough to bind us together for ever.'

He saw Leila swallow. He tugged her hair again and she jerked forward slightly, almost against her will.

'You see, I *do* want you. I wanted you the moment I saw you. I have ached with wanting you for the past seven weeks. And I am afraid that I will never stop wanting you, no matter how much I have of you—*damn you.*'

And with that Alix's control snapped and he hauled Leila into his arms, driving his mouth down onto hers, crushing her soft abundant curves to his body that was aching with need to be embedded in her tight, hot warmth.

Leila's brain fused with white-hot heat and lust. For long seconds she felt only intense relief as Alix's mouth crushed hers and he finally relaxed enough to allow the kiss to deepen and become a real kiss.

Then Leila's brain finally cleared enough to recall his words: *I have ached with wanting you.* Just like her. And now that ache was finally being assuaged.

Alix's big hands were roving over her back and waist, finding her hips, squeezing. Cupping her bottom, lifting her against him so that the hard ridge of his erection slid against her...just *there*.

She moaned into his mouth, rubbing herself against him, wanting more. She was incoherent with lust. Warning bells telling her to stop and think about what they'd just been saying to each other were being drowned out, and Leila knew that she was complicit in this.

She also knew that she was proving some point for Alix—and it wasn't necessarily a point she wanted to prove. But it was too late. She needed him too badly. She needed *this*. Physicality. No words or confusing emotions or hurt. Just the satisfaction of needs being met. Transcending everything.

Alix broke the kiss and drew back. He yanked aside the material of her dress to expose her breast, encased in lace.

Leila bit her lip to stop herself from begging. She was only still upright because one of Alix's arms was around her. Her legs were like jelly. And now he was pulling down the lace cup of her bra, freeing her breast and thumbing her nipple, then squeezing it gently.

She was so sensitive there that she almost screamed, circling her hips against Alix, utterly wanton.

He looked at her, his eyes flaming dark silver with need. A need that resonated within her too.

In a swift move he lifted her into his arms before she knew what was happening. Her shoes fell off as Alix strode out of the main *hammam* room and deeper into the harem. It was dark and shadowy. Mysterious. Rooms led off the corridor all in different colours.

He shouldered open one door and Leila's eyes went huge when she took in an enormous circular bed, dressed in blood-red silks and satins. The walls were covered with murals and it took a second for it to sink in that the murals depicted *Kama Sutra*–like explicit drawings.

A courtyard filled with wild blooming flowers was visible through French doors and a brightly coloured bird flew away from a water fountain. It was as if this was some kind of fairy tale and these rooms had been suspended in time all these years.

And then Alix laid Leila down on the bed and she knew

this was no fairy tale. He was too intent...serious. Focused. And she knew she should care...should be getting up, walking away...but she couldn't move. And, worse, she didn't want to.

If this was all they had then she wanted it as fiercely as he did. Somehow, here, with Alix stripping off his outer urban layer, Leila could pretend that nothing else existed. For a moment.

When Alix was naked he lowered himself over Leila on his arms and dropped his head, his mouth feathering hot kisses along her jaw and neck down to where her pulse beat like a drum, sucking her there and biting gently. As if he wanted to leave his mark on her.

She reached for him, groaning with deep feminine satisfaction when she found his hard muscles, the defined ridges of his abdomen. And she reached down further, to where his erection jutted proudly from his body. Hot and hard. Silk over steel.

She wrapped a hand around him, suddenly more confident than she'd ever been before. She stroked him, loving how the muscles in his belly tightened at her touch.

Then he put a hand over hers and drew it away. 'I'll explode if you keep touching me like that. I need you—*now*.'

Suddenly Leila was frantic with the same urgency, and aware that she was still fully dressed—albeit with her dress gaping open and her bra pulled down.

Alix undid the tie of her dress and Leila wriggled out of it. Her bra was dispensed with and Alix pulled her panties and tights down and off.

He stood back for a moment and just looked at her. Waves of heat made her blood throb and her skin feel tight. And then he came over her again, nudging her legs apart. He lavished attention on her breasts, sucking her nipples into his mouth and making them wet and tight with need.

Then he trailed his mouth and tongue down over her belly, where their baby was nestled in her womb.

He seemed to linger there for a second, and Leila felt a rush of emotion, but she bit her lip to stop it coming out, afraid of what she'd say. And then she couldn't think, because Alix's mouth was moving lower, and so was he, hitching her legs over his shoulders and gripping her buttocks as he put his mouth on her *there*.

At the hot, wet seam of her body where she couldn't hide how much she wanted him.

She felt utterly exposed, but couldn't stop him as he stroked her with his tongue, opening her up to his ministrations, and then he found that cluster of cells and licked and sucked until she was gripping his hair and bucking towards his mouth, and his tongue was thrusting deep inside her.

And even though she'd climaxed, right into his mouth, it wasn't enough. She was panting, almost sobbing as he rose up like some kind of god. Her legs flopped wide and Alix moved his erection against her. After an enigmatic second of silent communication he thrust deep into her core. And her world shattered into pieces for a second time.

She became pure sensuality—engulfed in a never-ending moment of bliss. Alix moved within her, deeper and harder with each thrust. She was boneless, and yet she couldn't help the rising tide of another climax. Even after the last two.

She caught a glimpse of something above them and looked up. The ceiling was mirrored glass. Old and dark. But she could see Alix's sculpted and muscular buttocks moving in and out of her body, her legs wrapped around him, ankles crossed over the small of his back.

And it was as she saw his huge, powerful body flexing into hers with such beauty and strength that she fell apart for the third time, her orgasm so intense that she barely felt the rush of Alix's hot release, deep in her body, as he jerked spasmodically with the after-effects of his own climax.

When Leila woke she was completely disorientated. She was alone on the huge circular bed and the covers were pulled up over her chest. She could see herself reflected in the ceiling and her hair was spread around her head. Images came back... The sheer carnality of their union. The humiliating speed with which she'd capitulated.

'You're awake.'

Leila tensed and lifted her head. Alix stood by the open French doors of the room. It was dusk outside and birds called. The scent of the flowers was heady. Leila had to block out the immediate instinct she had to assimilate the smells.

She pushed herself up on her elbows, noting that Alix was in his trousers, but still bare-chested. 'Yes, I'm awake.'

She felt as if she'd been turned inside out. She tried to claw back her sense of anger from earlier, but it was hard when she felt as if someone had drained every bone from her body and injected her with some kind of pleasure serum.

She saw her dress at the end of the bed and sat up, holding the sheet to her as she reached for it. She put it on awkwardly, aware of Alix's intense regard, and tied it around her, sitting on the edge of the bed.

'You asked me earlier if it affected me, seeing the baby today?'

Leila went still and nodded.

'Of course it affected me. What kind of man would I be if I couldn't see my own child and feel something?'

Leila stood up, hoping her legs wouldn't fail her. She needed to move away from the bed—the scene of where she'd lost control so spectacularly. She saw a chair nearby and sank onto the edge.

'Why didn't you say something?'

Alix was terse, tense. 'Because I couldn't. It was too much all at once.'

Leila felt a very fragile flame of hope light within her. 'That's how I felt too. But when I looked at you, you were so closed off—as if you were just checking something off a list. I'm afraid that you won't love this baby. That it'll just be a means to an end for you.'

Like this marriage.

Alix looked as if he'd prefer to eat nails than pursue this conversation, but eventually he said, 'I should tell you about my brother.'

Leila frowned. 'You told me he was killed—with your parents.'

Alix nodded. 'Max was handicapped. A lack of oxygen to the brain when he was born prematurely. He wasn't severely disabled, just enough not to be able to keep up with kids his age. I was five when he was born. He spent a lot of time in hospital at first, in an incubator. My parents weren't interested, so I spent most of my time with him.'

Leila's heart lurched. She could imagine Alix as a serious, dark-haired five-year-old, with both his parents God knew where, keeping an eye on his brother.

'It was obvious to our father that he'd never become King, so he had nothing to do with him after that.'

Leila hid her shock. 'And your mother?'

His mouth twisted. 'She barely knew *I* existed, never mind Max.'

'He must have loved you very much.'

If anything Alix looked grimmer. 'He did, the little fool, following me everywhere... But I couldn't give him what he needed most: our parents' care and love.'

Leila sensed his reluctance to talk, even though he'd brought it up. But she needed to know this—because if they were to have a life together she couldn't bear for him to shut their children out.

'What happened the day he died?'

'They murdered him...' Alix moved a hand jerkily. 'Not just the actual murderers, but my parents. *They* were the ones who made sure I was protected so the precious line would go on, and *they* kept Max with them, knowing that he would die, hoping that seeing him would distract the soldiers enough to let me get away. The last thing I remember hearing was Max, screaming for me. He couldn't understand why I wasn't coming to get him, to take him with me—and I couldn't go back...they wouldn't let me. One of the men taking me away had to knock me out. I came to on a boat, leaving the island behind.'

He looked at Leila.

'It nearly killed me, knowing that I'd left him behind. I had nightmares for years. Sometimes they still come...'

Leila stood up. 'Oh, Alix...I'm so sorry.'

She could understand in an instant how something must have broken inside him that day when he'd lost his home and his beloved brother. She was going to walk over to him, but something in his expression stopped her.

Alix was harsh. 'Don't give me your pity, Leila, that's the last thing I want or deserve. I've told you this because you need to know that I wasn't unaffected today. But I won't lie to you. I have always envisaged myself keeping an emotional distance from my Queen and any children. My role as King is a *job*, and as such I need to avoid distraction. Focus on what's best for the country and the future. But when I saw the scan today it all came back—the love I felt for Max and the awful grief when he died.'

Alix shook his head.

'It terrifies me that I'll be unable to control how I feel about my own child in case anything happens. I couldn't survive that grief again.'

A gaping hollow seemed to open up in Leila's chest. What could she say? Wasn't every parent terrified of their child being hurt or worse? Terrified that they wouldn't be able to protect it from every little thing? What Alix didn't understand yet, and what she only had an inkling of herself, was that he wouldn't be able to control it.

He walked over to her then, and Leila tried desperately to call up some sense of defence. She felt raw with this knowledge, not sure what it meant now.

'I want you, Leila, and I want our baby. I will do my best to serve you both well—and any other children we may have.'

Leila went still. Nothing had changed. Not really. Even though he'd opened up to her his main concern was the baby. Not her. And she should be feeling relieved that he'd admitted he wanted this baby as much for itself as for its role as heir. That he would not shut it out.

Alix reached a hand out then, but Leila stepped back jerkily. If he touched her now she'd break into a million pieces.

She forced herself to sound far more calm than she felt. 'I'm quite tired now. I'd like to go back to my rooms, please.'

Alix still felt raw from the mind-blowing sex and what he'd just revealed about his brother. But he hadn't been able to bear the thought that Leila really believed he'd felt nothing for their baby. And she deserved to know the truth. That he wasn't prepared to go through that emotional wasteland again. Having lost everything.

His hand was out to touch her, but she'd stepped back out of his reach. His first instinct was to move closer…but something stopped him. If he touched her again who knew what else he might feel compelled to reveal?

His hand dropped. He'd never wanted a woman so badly that he wanted her again as soon as he'd had her, but right now he really could see no end in sight to this constant craving.

The lush surroundings of the old harem didn't help. And the fact that *she'd* been the one to step away made something prickle inside him. She had control when he was in danger of losing it.

He was terse. 'Okay, let's go.'

Alix put on the rest of his clothes and watched Leila step into her panties, sliding them up her slim thighs. Thighs that had been wrapped around him only a short time before, her inner muscles clasping his shaft with spasms so strong he'd almost climaxed twice in quick succession.

Damn.

She picked up her shoes on the way out and Alix was forced to feel a measure of shame. They were like teenagers, sneaking off to the nearest private space to have sex. He was a *king*, for God's sake. Not a randy schoolboy.

'What are you going to do with this place?' Leila asked as she walked out through the main door.

He watched as she went past him, his eyes tracking down her body and up to her tangled hair. Lust was sinking its teeth into him all over again.

'I had thought of getting rid of it, but now I'm not so sure.'

She looked at him, and before she could say anything he stepped up to her, so that there were just centimetres between their bodies. 'It won't be for more wives, Leila, it'll be for us alone,' he said.

Her cheeks coloured at that. 'But that's...outrageous. A whole *hammam* and harem, just for two people?'

Alix quirked a smile at the mix of expressions on her face: slightly scandalised, and yet interested at the same time.

'It'll be purely for your pleasure and mine, Leila. You're

to be my Queen, and I will want to make sure that you are satisfied.'

The colour faded from her cheeks and she said, 'I'll be satisfied when you don't shut our child out, Alix. Sex is just sex.'

Alix felt her words like a physical blow to his chest. He watched as she stepped out from where he had her all but caged against the wall and started to walk down the corridor. *Sex is just sex.*

'Leila,' he called out curtly.

She stopped and turned around with clear reluctance.

'It's this way.' He pointed in the opposite direction and watched as she came back down the corridor and past him, head held high. He had to stop himself from hauling her back into the harem to show her that he knew *exactly* that sex was just sex.

The irritating thing was he didn't *need* Leila to tell him sex was just sex. So why did he suddenly feel a need to prove that to her—and himself?

Leila wasn't sure how she made it back to her rooms with Alix behind her, boring holes in her back with the intensity of his gaze. She thought of that harem, existing just for carnal pleasure... She'd almost melted on the spot when he'd said that it would be solely for their use.

Sex is just sex—ha! Who was she kidding when she felt upside down and wrung out?

It had brought up all the emotions she'd been feeling the morning after they'd returned from Venice, when she'd felt so perilously close to believing she'd fallen for him.

There was no 'falling'.

The truth hit her like a slap in the face. She was in love with Alix and had been for some time, if she was honest with herself. And that last bout of *just sex* had left her nowhere to hide.

She almost sobbed with relief when she saw their door appear and the guard standing outside.

When they reached her room she was about to escape inside when Alix said, 'Wait.'

Leila turned around, schooling her features. No way would Alix know that what had just happened had been cataclysmic for her.

'Yes?' Reluctantly she looked at him, and saw his eyes were like grey clouds.

'We're having an engagement party at the end of this week. It's a chance to introduce you to society here, and there will be some international guests.'

Immediately nerves assailed Leila. She was a perfumer, a shop manager—not someone who walked confidently among the moneyed classes. Royalty!

But she needed space from Alix to process everything that had happened so she just nodded nonchalantly and said, 'Okay—fine.'

And then she slipped into her room and leant back against the door, letting out a long, shuddering breath.

She was in love with a man who had admitted to her that he was averse to love—based on the fact that he'd suffered so much pain due to losing his beloved brother. She could understand his trauma—and he would have felt it that much more keenly, being young and impressionable. But who was she to say to him that he wouldn't be able to control who or how he loved?

And yet he was willing to do his best for the sake of their child. Clearly that would have to be enough—and it should be. Everything Leila did now was for the sake of this baby. Her own personal needs and desires were not important.

Yes, they are, you'll wither and die in this environment with no love, whispered a rogue voice.

Leila pushed herself fiercely off the door and ignored

the voice. As much as she longed for a different life from the one she'd had with her mother, she'd be an absolute fool to hope, even briefly, that some kind of fairy tale might be out there.

She stripped off her clothes and stepped into a hot shower and tried not to think of how it had felt to have Alix surging between her legs, touching her so deeply that it had made a mockery of the words she'd spouted at him.

Sex is never just sex, crowed the same rogue voice.

She shut it out and blinked back the prickle of weak tears.

On the evening of the engagement party Leila was a bag of nerves. It didn't help that she'd barely seen Alix since their last conversation. But she'd welcomed the space—especially in light of what had happened. She'd been having lurid erotic dreams of the harem all week.

Alix had sent her messages and notes, explaining that he was caught up with political meetings and getting everything prepared for the wedding.

And Leila had been kept busy with lessons about the history of the island, along with etiquette classes, instruction on how she would be expected to behave as Queen. And with wedding dress fittings.

The magnitude of how radically her life was changing was overwhelming.

The last thing she needed was to see Alix and have him guess just how brittle she was feeling.

Her personal maid, Amalie, was just finishing dressing her now, and Leila winced a little at the increased sensitivity of her breasts—which only made her think of how it had felt to have Alix's mouth on her there.

Amalie obviously misread Leila's discomfort. 'Are you too hot, *mademoiselle*? Shall I open the doors?'

Leila shook her head quickly. 'No, I'm fine—honestly.'

She forced a smile and looked at herself in the mirror, not really recognising the sleekly coiffed woman in front of her and feeling a moment of insecurity that Alix would take one look at her and feel nothing but disappointment with his inconvenient bride.

Alix stood in the doorway, unnoticed for the past few minutes, and watched as Leila was transformed from beautiful to stunning. His breath caught in his throat. She wore a cream strapless dress with a ruched bodice that clung to her full breasts before falling in delicate chiffon layers to the floor. Her dark hair was coiled into a complicated-looking chignon at the back of her head. Make-up subtly enhanced her eyes and that lush mouth.

Alix's body reacted with predictable force. A force he'd spent the week avoiding by keeping busy at all costs. Like some kind of yellow-bellied coward. He'd stood face to face this week with one of the men who had shot his parents and his brother, and he hadn't felt half the maelstrom he was feeling now.

As if sensing his regard, Leila turned her head and saw him. Her cheeks flushed and Alix gritted his jaw to stop his body reacting even more rampantly. He felt like a Neanderthal. He wanted to throw her over his shoulder and carry her back to the heart of that harem, to sink himself so deep he'd never have to feel or think again. He wanted to lock them in there for a month.

He stepped into the room with a velvet box in his hand, vaguely aware of the young maid curtseying and disappearing.

Leila looked from the box to him. 'More jewellery?'

She said it as if it was a poisoned chalice, and bleakly he had to realise that perhaps that was what this marriage was for her.

Alix curbed his irritation. 'Yes, more jewellery.'

He came closer to Leila and opened the box, watching her eyes widen at the sight of the exquisite gold necklace and matching earrings. He put it down and lifted the necklace, already knowing it would look stunning on her flawless olive skin. It was faintly geometric in design, and circular. He opened it and placed it around her neck, burningly aware of her body so close to his. Of his straining erection.

Leila put a hand to it as he took his own away and stepped back. 'It's beautiful. I don't mean to sound ungrateful. I'm just not used to...*this*. I feel like I'm not qualified.'

Alix saw her insecurity and was amazed at how little she was aware of her own beauty and power. *Over him.*

Gruffly he said, 'You're just as qualified as anyone else ever was. Most of the Queens in this family were slave girls, transported from northern Europe on ships, taken by pirates.'

Leila looked at him, a rare spark of humour in her eyes. 'That's one part of your history I *didn't* particularly relish learning about.'

Alix handed her the earrings and watched as she slid them into her ears. *Dieu.* He even found that erotic.

Feeling compelled, he said, 'I'm sorry I left you alone all week. I had things to attend to.'

It sounded so lame now. Pathetic. No woman had ever made him feel as if he wasn't in complete control. Except for this one.

He forced his mind back from the brink and stepped back. 'Ready?'

She nodded and he saw how she swallowed nervously. Instinctively he reached for her hand and led her out of the suite and into the corridor, aware of her tension and wanting to soothe it. Reassure her. Alien concepts for Alix.

They were coming close to where the sound of over two hundred guests could be heard and she stopped in her tracks. He looked at her and his chest squeezed at the fear on her face. *He'd* done this to her. He'd never contemplated having a wife who wouldn't just take this in her stride.

Her eyes were huge. 'What if I can't do this? I'm not a princess...'

Alix couldn't stop himself from reaching out and putting a hand to her neck, massaging her muscles with his fingers, feeling them resist and then relax. Her eyes were all he could see: huge pools of green. Her skin was so soft under his hand, and then he couldn't resist tugging her into him and lowering his mouth to hers.

They sank into each other, mouths open and tongues tangling, their kiss growing hotter and deeper before he had a chance to claw back some control. They were in the corridor. About to face guests. And he was ready to lift her against the nearest wall and thrust into her tight sheath.

Alix pulled back, feeling dizzy. Leila looked equally disorientated. Mouth pink and swollen.

Somehow he managed to grit out, 'You'll be fine. Just follow my lead.'

Leila wasn't sure how she was able to make her feet move at all after that kiss, but somehow Alix's words and his hand anchored her—although she had to figure that the kiss had been a somewhat calculated move to make her look suitably starry-eyed before they faced his public.

And then suddenly they were standing at the top of the stairs at the entrance to the majestic ballroom and Leila's nerves were back. It was filled with portraits of his rather fearsome-looking ancestors. The crowd started to hush as people noticed them. Alix took her hand and placed it on his arm.

A man in an elaborate Isle Saint Croix uniform struck a tall staff on the ground. It made an impressive booming noise and then he shouted out, 'May I present to you the King of Isle Saint Croix, Alixander Saul Almaric Saint

Croix, and future Queen and mother of Isle Saint Croix, Leila Amal Lakshmi Verughese.'

Leila felt absurdly emotional at being called the mother of Isle Saint Croix as Alix led her down the stairs. She took a deep breath as they reached the bottom, and suddenly it was organised chaos as Andres appeared and led them around the room, introducing them to everyone.

CHAPTER ELEVEN

WHAT FELT LIKE aeons later, Leila wondered if her mouth would stay in a rictus smile for ever. Her cheeks ached and her feet were burning in the too-high heels. Thankfully the crowd had dissipated somewhat now, and she felt as if she could breathe again.

Alix's conversation with a man whose name Leila couldn't recall ended. He turned to her, looking genuinely concerned. 'Are you okay? You probably shouldn't be on your feet for so long.'

Leila had to stop her silly heart from lurching and forced a smile. 'Don't be silly—I'm pregnant, not crippled.' But in fact she *was* feeling a little hot and weary.

Alix was gesturing to a member of staff, giving him some kind of signal, and then he was leading Leila out to a secluded open courtyard off the main ballroom.

Leila sat down on a wrought-iron chair with relief, slipping off her shoes for a moment to stretch her feet. She caught Alix's look and said ruefully, 'Okay, my feet *were* beginning to kill me.'

The staff member appeared again, with a tray of hors d'oeuvres and some sparkling water. Alix sat down too and tugged at his bow tie, loosening it a bit.

More touched than she liked to admit, and surprised at this show of concern, Leila said, 'You don't have to wait out here with me. I just need a moment.'

Alix popped an olive into his mouth and shook his head. 'I could do with a break myself. The French ambassador was beginning to bore me to death.'

Leila smiled and felt a moment of extreme poignancy, imagining that it could be like this—this sense of communion, sneaking out to take a break during functions. She quickly slammed the door on those thoughts. It was heading for dangerous fairy-tale territory again.

She helped herself to a vegetarian vol-au-vent and savoured the flaky pastry and delicate mushroom filling, more hungry than she'd like to admit.

'You need to eat more.'

She looked at Alix and grimaced. 'I'm still nauseous sometimes, but the doctor said it should ease off soon.'

Alix stood up then and looked out at the view. Something about his profile seemed so lonely to Leila in that moment— it was as if she might never truly reach him or know him. She found herself wondering if anyone ever had, and didn't like the sharp spiking of something hot and dark. *Jealousy.*

She forced her voice to sound light. 'Have you ever been in love, Alix? I mean with a lover.'

He tensed, and Leila found herself holding her breath.

'I've thought I was in love once before, but it wasn't love. It was only a very wounded youthful ego.'

Swallowing past the constriction in her throat, Leila asked, 'Who was she?'

Alix turned around to face her, leaning back against the wall. His expression was hard. 'I met her in America when I was a student. I thought she only knew me as Alix Cross. I was trying to stay under the radar and I believed that she was attracted to me for myself—not who I was...'

He leaned his hands on the stone wall.

'She was English. She'd come to America to escape the public scandal of her father gambling all their money away. They were related to royalty. She was looking for a way to get back into Europe and restore her reputation via someone else. Namely me. I was young and naive. Arrogant enough to believe her when she said she loved me. But the truth was that she just used me to get what she wanted. And clearly I wasn't enough for her, because I walked into her room one day and found one of my undercover bodyguards giving it to her a lot rougher than I ever could or wanted to.'

Leila looked at Alix's hard expression. *She just used me.* Her own words that she'd thrown at him came back to her like a slap on the face. *I used you.* She felt sick.

Then Alix said, 'I've already told you Max was the only person I've loved. I was brought up knowing any marriage would be a strategic alliance, all about heirs. I saw no love between my parents. Love was never part of the equation for me.'

That was what he'd said on the phone to Andres that day in Paris.

'I *can* promise to honour you and respect you, Leila. You did well this evening, and I have no doubt you'll make a great queen. And mother of our children. But that will have to be enough, because I can't offer any more.'

There it was—the brutal truth, sitting between them like a squat ugly troll. Dashing any hopes and dreams Leila might have had.

'Well,' she managed to say, as if her heart wasn't being lacerated in a million different places, 'at least we know where we stand.'

In a desperate bid to avoid Alix looking at her too closely, seeing the devastation inside her, she stood up too. She thought of what he'd said about being used and her conscience smarted. She really didn't want to do this, but his honesty compelled her to be honest too.

She went to the wall and mirrored his stance. 'I owe you an apology.'

'You do?'

Leila nodded and avoided his eye. 'That day in Paris… when I told you I'd used you just because I wanted to get rid of my virginity…I lied.'

She turned and looked at him, steeling herself not to crumble.

'The truth is that I *was* humiliated and hurt. I lashed out, not wanting you to see that.'

Something like a flash of horror crossed Alix's face.

Before he could say anything she cut in hurriedly, 'Don't worry. I wasn't falling for you... It was wounded pride. That's all.'

His expression cleared and Leila felt a monumental ache near her heart to see his visible relief.

'Look,' she said, putting a hand over her belly, 'all I want is to go forward from this moment with honesty and trust between us. At least if we have that we know where we stand, and it might be something we can build on. I won't deny that this marriage won't give me all that I need and want emotionally, but I'm doing this for our baby, and I'll try to make you a good queen.'

Alix looked at Leila and felt flattened by her words when only a moment ago he'd been feeling relief that she hadn't fallen for him.

This marriage won't give me all that I need.

And her admission rocked him. The fact that she hadn't meant those words, *I used you.* It ripped apart something he'd been clinging on to since he'd seen her again. As if as long as he had that he'd be protected.

She humbled him, this woman who had walked out of a shop and into a world far removed from anything she'd known, and she'd captivated the entire crowd this evening, behaving with an innate graciousness that he hadn't even known she possessed. She was putting everyone around her to shame.

Including him.

He felt like a fraud. He felt for the first time as if he was taking something beautiful and tarnishing it. He should let her go—but he couldn't. They were bound by their baby.

He owed her full honesty now.

'There's something you need to understand. When I met you I was consumed with nothing more than you. I never set out to use you as a smokescreen. There was no agenda. When we took that trip to Isle de la Paix it *was* spontaneous in that I planned it once you'd mentioned you didn't want any press intrusion. But I *did* see an opportunity, and I *did* arrange for someone to take that photo, seizing the chance to keep attention diverted.'

Alix sighed heavily.

'I had no right to exploit you for my own ends. And I'm sorry for that. Ultimately it led them straight to you. But when I pursued you it was because I wanted you— pure and simple.'

His admission made Leila feel vulnerable. If anything it just made things harder to know that he *hadn't* ruthlessly used her from the start.

She said, as breezily as she could, 'Well, it's in the past, and we're here now, so I think we just have to keep moving forward.'

Terrified he'd read something in her eyes, or on her face, she stepped around him and walked back into the ballroom.

She spent the rest of the evening avoiding him, in case he saw how close to the surface her emotions were. Emotions that she'd denied she felt right to his face.

She knew they'd agreed to be honest, but there was such a thing as taking honesty too far. And Leila hated how this new accord made her feel as if they'd taken about ten steps forward and twenty back.

She realised that if she was to negotiate a life living with a man who could never—*would* never—love her, she was going to have to develop some hefty self-protection mechanisms.

'She's a natural, Alix. If you'd seen her... The kids loved her. The nurses and doctors are in awe of her. She's possibly done more for Isle Saint Croix in one visit to the children's ward of the hospital than you could have done in six months. No offence.'

Alix grimaced as he recalled his recent meeting with Andres. Of course he hadn't taken offence at the fact that apparently his fiancée was indeed bound to be as perfect a queen as he'd expected her to be. When he'd believed she was falling for him. The fact that she'd assured him she *hadn't* been was like a burr under his skin now.

In the past few days, since the engagement party, Leila had thrown herself into doing as much as she could to learn about her new role. Alix had gone to her rooms at night to find her sleeping, and as much as he'd wanted to slide between the sheets and slide between her legs, something had held him back.

The same thing that had held him back the night of the party, when he'd left Leila at her door. He'd wanted her so badly, but after everything they'd said he had been almost afraid that if he touched her something would spill out of him—something much deeper than a mere climax. Some truth he wasn't ready to acknowledge yet.

'Your Majesty? Your fiancée is here to see you.'

Conjured up out of his imagination to taunt him?

He turned around. 'Show her in, please.'

Leila walked in and Alix felt that all-too-familiar jolt of lust mixed with something else. Something much more complex.

She looked pale.

Alix frowned, immediately concerned. 'What is it?' He cursed softly as he came around and held a chair out for her. 'You've been doing too much. I told Andres that you're busy enough with wedding preparations—'

She put up a hand and didn't sit down. 'No, I'm fine. Honestly. I enjoyed the visit to the hospital.'

Alix smiled. 'You were a big hit.'

She blushed and ducked her head, and Alix felt a pang near his heart. Her ability to blush and show her emotions was one of the things that had made him fall for her...

Alix went utterly still as the words he'd just thought sank in—and dropped like heavy boulders into his gut.

Alix was so quiet that Leila looked at him. The smile was gone from his face and he was deathly pale. She put out a hand. 'Alix...are you all right? You look like you've seen a ghost.'

He recoiled from her hand and a look of utter horror came over his face. Leila flinched inwardly. But, if anything, this only confirmed for her the reason why she needed to talk to him. She had to do this to protect herself.

At least over the past few days she'd discovered a real sense that perhaps she *could* be a queen, that she could relatively happily devote her life to the people of Isle Saint Croix and her children.

But in order to survive she needed to create a very firm boundary where Alix was concerned.

The fact that he hadn't made any attempt to sleep with her in the past few nights had left her feeling frustrated and relieved in equal measure. She knew physical intimacy without love would eventually crack her in two—or that she'd end up blurting out how much she loved him, and she couldn't bear to see that horror-struck look on his face again.

Alix retreated around the desk—as if he needed to physically put something between them. Leila tried not to feel hurt.

She steeled herself. 'I wanted to talk to you about something. About us. And our marriage.'

Alix sat down, still looking a little shell-shocked. Leila sat down too, twisting her hands in her lap.

'Go ahead.' Alix sounded hoarse.

'I am committed to doing my best to be a queen that you can be proud of, and I will love our child—and children, if we have more. I do believe that we can have a harmonious union, and that's important to me for the sake of those children—I expect you will want more than one.'

Alix frowned. 'Leila—'

She spoke over him. 'But apart from with our children, and promoting a united front for social occasions or events, I would prefer if we could live as separately as possible. I don't want to share rooms with you. And I would prefer if any intimacies were to be only for the sake of procreating. I will understand if that's not enough for you, but I would just ask that you be discreet in your liaisons, should you feel the need.'

Alix's face was getting darker and darker. He stood up now and put his hands on the desk. Leila tried not to move back, or be intimidated.

'Let me get this straight. You want to maintain a separate existence in private and we'll only share the marital bed for the purposes of getting you pregnant? And if I'm feeling the urge in the meantime I'm to seek out a willing and discreet lover?'

Leila nodded, telling herself that it hadn't hurt so much or sounded so ridiculous when she'd thought it all through in her head. But this was the only way she felt she could survive this marriage, knowing he didn't love her.

At least if she could create a family then she would have some purpose in her life—love and affection.

But all at once she realised that that was the most selfish reason in the world for creating a family.

Alix's mouth was a thin line. 'My father paraded his many mistresses around the castle and did untold damage to this country. I vowed never to repeat his corrupt ways—so, no, I don't think I'll be taking you up on your helpful suggestion to maintain a discreet mistress.'

He came around the desk and towered over Leila. She stood up.

'And, no,' Alix continued, 'I don't believe I *do* agree that we should maintain separate existences. I believe that you will share my bed every night, and I expect intimacies to be many and varied. Are you *really* suggesting that I am going to be forcing myself on a reluctant wife?'

Leila had to stop a slightly hysterical laugh from emerging. Of course he wouldn't have to force himself on a reluctant wife. Even now she felt every cell in her body straining to get closer to him. But, standing so close to Alix now, she realised that she'd actually completely underestimated her ability to survive even if she could maintain some distance from Alix. And of course he wouldn't agree to her admittedly ridiculous terms. What had she been thinking?

A sense of panic made her gut roil. 'Then I don't think I can do this, Alix. I thought I could, for the sake of the baby...but I can't.'

She felt weak, pathetic, selfish.

'What are you saying, Leila?'

She forced out the words. 'I'm saying that I want more than you can offer me, Alix. I'm sorry...I thought I could do this, but I can't.'

Terrified she'd start crying, Leila turned and hurried out of the room.

Alix looked at the door that had just closed and reeled. He had to recognise the bitter irony of the fact that Leila had more or less just outlined the kind of marriage that he'd always believed he wanted.

Space between him and his wife. She would be his consort in public and mother to his children. She wouldn't infringe upon his life in any other more meaningful way.

He might have laughed if he hadn't still been consumed by the terrifying revelation that made his limbs feel as weak as jelly. The rush of love he'd felt while watching that scan had been for Leila as much as for the baby. He'd just been blocking that cataclysmic knowledge out.

She had just said she wanted more. And the even more ironic thing was that *he* wanted more too. He suddenly wanted the whole damn thing—and it was too late.

The gods weren't just mocking him…they were rolling around the floor, laughing hysterically.

Leila was aware of the bodyguards, standing at a discreet distance, and was doing her best to ignore them. Her chest ached with unexpressed emotion. She had taken a Jeep and driven away from the castle, needing some space and time to breathe. She should have expected that she wouldn't be able to move without triggering a national security alert.

And even the stunning view from this lookout point high on the island was incapable of soothing her.

The sound of another vehicle came from the narrow road and Leila heaved a sigh of frustration. She turned around. Really, this was getting ridiculous.

But her breath stopped in her throat when she saw Alix getting out of the driver's seat. He looked grim and went over to the bodyguards. After a couple of seconds they all got back into their vehicles and left.

When they were gone he looked at her for a long moment, and then came over. He stood beside her and gestured with his head to the view.

'On a clear day, with good binoculars, you can see both the Spanish and African coasts from here.'

Leila looked away from him. 'It's beautiful.'

'There are hundreds of shipwrecks around the island. It's my plan to use them as an incentive to get people to come wreck-diving. Part of the tourism package we're putting together.'

Leila's heart ached. 'The island is magical, Alix. You won't have a problem getting people to come.'

He turned to face her and said quietly, 'And what about

getting people to stay? I wonder what incentive I could offer for that...'

Your love, Leila thought bleakly.

But she had to come to terms with the futility of her position and she said, 'I'm sorry. I overreacted just now. Of course I won't be leaving. I can't. Our baby deserves two parents, and a stable foundation. It was just...hormones, or something.'

Alix didn't say anything for a moment, and then he held out a hand. 'Will you come with me? I want to show you something.'

Leila hesitated a moment, and then slipped her hand into his, hating how right it felt even as a gaping chasm opened up near her heart.

Alix brought her over to the Jeep and she got into the passenger side. She watched him walk around the front, her gaze drawn irresistibly to his tall, powerful form.

He drove in silence for about ten minutes, and then drove off the main road down a dirt track. They weren't too far from the main town, and Leila could just make out the castle in the distance.

After about a mile Alix stopped and got out. Leila got out too and looked around, but could see nothing of immediate interest. Alix led her over to where a vast area looked as if it was in the process of being cleared and levelled, even though there were no workmen at the site today.

'What's this?'

Leila looked at Alix when he didn't say anything immediately. He was so handsome against the sunlight it almost hurt. She could see that he truly belonged here, in this environment. And that somehow she was going to have to belong here too. And weather the emotional pain.

'It will be your new factory.'

Leila blinked, distracted. 'My new...*factory*?'

Alix nodded. 'The area is being cleared and I've lined

up architects to meet with you and discuss how you want it designed and built. There's also room for a walled garden, so you can cultivate and grow plants and flowers. We have a huge range on the island, including a rare form of sea lavender. There's room for a greenhouse too, if you need it. You'll know more than me what you need.'

Leila looked around, speechless. The area was massive. And in this environment she could grow almost anything. What Alix had just said was almost too much to take in. She turned around and saw the island falling away and the sea stretching out to infinity. She was simply stunned.

Alix said worriedly, 'You don't like the site? It's too small?'

Leila shook her head and blinked back tears, terrified that once the emotion started leaking out it wouldn't stop. 'No, no—it's lovely...amazing.'

When she felt more in control she looked at him.

Her voice was husky. 'I thought you said I'd have other priorities—the baby, my role as Queen?'

Alix looked serious. 'Leila, you inhale the world without even realising you're doing it—it's part of you. You're led by your nose. I want you to be happy here. And I hope that this will make you happy. I know you want more... you deserve so much more...'

A slightly rueful expression crossed his face.

'And I need you to make me more of that scent, because I destroyed the bottle you gave me in Paris. I destroyed it because I was angry and hurt.'

Leila's heart gave a little lurch. 'You weren't hurt. Your ego was wounded because I dared to say no to you.'

Alix nodded. 'That's what I believed. That it was my ego. Except it was a lie that I told myself and kept telling myself, even when I saw you again. The truth is that it wasn't just my ego—it was my heart. And I didn't have the guts to admit it to myself.'

He took her hands in his.

'It hit me today, Leila. Like a ton of bricks. I've been falling for you from the moment I saw you in your shop. When we were leaving Isle de la Paix I knew I had to let you go, but I didn't want to. I think I came up with the idea of proposing to you because it was the only way I could see to make you stay...'

Leila looked at Alix. She said a little dumbly, 'You're saying you *love* me?'

He nodded, looking wary now.

For a second Leila felt a dizzying sweep of pure joy—and then a voice resounded in her head: *Silly Leila...there's no fairy tale*. The joy dissolved. She had thought the chasm in her chest couldn't get any bigger, but it just had.

She pulled her hands free. 'Why are you doing this? I've told you I'm not leaving.'

Alix frowned. 'Doing what? Telling you I love you? Because I do.'

Leila shook her head, those damn tears threatening again. 'I can't believe you'd be this cruel, Alix. Please don't insult my intelligence. I tell you that I want to go, that I don't think I can marry you, and now suddenly you're claiming to love me? You're forgetting I heard your conversation on the phone that day: *"If I have to convince her I love her then I will."*'

Alix ran his hands through his hair, his frustration palpable. Leila folded her arms.

'Why would I do this now? Pretend?'

Leila felt ill. 'You've made a very convincing case for persuading me that you're incapable of love, and now I'm suddenly supposed to believe you've had some kind of epiphany? It's three days to the wedding, Alix, and I know how important it is for you and for Isle Saint Croix, but I never thought you'd be unnecessarily cruel.'

Alix looked as if she'd just punched him in the gut, but Leila steeled herself.

He opened his mouth, but she said with a rush, 'Please don't, Alix. Look, I appreciate what you're trying to do—and all this...' She put out a hand to indicate the site for the factory. 'It's enough—it really is.'

It'll have to be. At least he didn't know that she loved him. It was her last paltry defence.

She turned away and started to walk back to the Jeep, fiercely blinking back tears. She didn't see the way Alix's face leached of all colour as he watched her go. She also didn't see the look of grim determination that settled over his features.

Their journey back to the castle was made in tense silence. When they arrived Leila jumped out of the Jeep, but Alix moved faster than her and her hand was in his before she could react.

He led her into the castle, and when she tried to pull her hand free Alix only tightened his grip and looked at her, his face more stern and stark than she'd ever seen it.

'We have not finished this conversation, Leila.'

She had to trot to keep up with his punishing pace, and only recognised where they were when he opened a door.

Immediately Leila dug her heels in and pulled furiously on Alix's hand. 'I am not going in there.'

Alix looked at her and said tauntingly, 'Why, Leila? Sex is just sex, after all—isn't it?'

They were in the impressive *hammam* room before Leila could object and the door was closed. Alix stood in front of it, arms folded. She hadn't even registered him letting her hand go.

'You know, I never thought you were a coward, Leila.'

Leila's mouth opened, and she finally got out, '*Coward?* I am not a coward.'

Alix stepped away from the door and towards her. She eyed the door, wondering if she could make a run for it, and then his words sank in.

She couldn't run. So she rounded on him. 'What's that supposed to mean?'

He walked around her now, looking at her assessingly, and she had to keep turning, getting dizzy.

'You're a coward, Leila Verughese. An emotional coward. And I know because I was one too.'

Something like panic was fluttering in Leila's belly now. 'That's ridiculous. I'm not a coward and you're a liar.'

He arched a brow and made a low whistling sound. 'That's harsh. I told you I love you and you call me a liar?'

Leila changed tack. 'Why are you doing this? I've told you I'm happy to stay. You don't have to sweeten it up for me.'

Alix almost sneered now. 'You're "happy to stay"— like some kind of martyr? The days of pirates kidnapping European slaves and forcing them into marriage are over. When we marry it'll be because you want it as much as I do. Because you love me too—except you're too much of a coward to admit it. Why else would you want us to maintain a distance while we're married?'

Leila felt her blood draining south. Her last defence was crumbling in front of her eyes. 'I don't love you,' she lied.

'Liar.'

Alix stalked closer, tension crackling between them.

'If I'd been more honest with myself sooner I would have recognised it the day we left here—when you said sex is just sex. That was the key. Sex has *always* been just sex for me. Until you. That's why I haven't touched you since we were in here—because as soon as I touch you I'm not in control, and I was afraid you'd see it. And I think it's the same for you. *Dieu*, Leila,' he spat in disgust. 'You'd really want me to take a mistress?'

Leila could feel her insides tearing apart. 'But you don't love me—you can't. You said it.'

She sounded accusing now. The fairy tale was like a shimmering mirage, and she knew that the moment she committed herself to trusting, believing, it would disappear and she'd be left with less than she had even now.

Alix was ruthless. 'I can—and I do. You brought me to my knees and showed me that anything less than total surrender to love and all its risks is a life not worth living. It terrifies me, because I know how awful it is to lose someone you love, but I've realised that it's impossible to live in constant fear of that. I want more too—and I want it with you. No one else.'

Leila shook her head, tears making her vision blurry. It hit her then. Alix was right—she was a coward. Terrified to trust. Terrified that the dream didn't exist. Her mother's ghost whispered to her even now that it couldn't. She hadn't had it, so why should Leila?

Alix stepped right up to her. 'Say it, Leila.'

She shook her head. 'Please, don't make me…'

She had a terrifying vision of telling him she loved him only to see him go cold and shut down, satisfied that his convenient wife had surrendered to him completely.

Alix wrapped a hand around her neck. 'Then we do it this way… You're mine, body, heart and soul, and I will leave you nowhere to hide.'

Alix's head dipped and his mouth settled on hers like a scorching brand. Leila resisted. *This* was what she was afraid of, and suddenly speaking the words didn't seem so scary— what was far worse was the honesty he would wring from her now, because she literally would have nowhere to hide.

But it was too late for resistance. And Leila was weak. And again he was right. She *was* a coward.

She sobbed her anguish into his mouth as his tongue stroked hers and the flames licked higher and higher.

This time there was no way they could make it to the harem bedroom. Leila felt herself being lowered onto the raised platform of smooth marble. Their movements were not graceful or measured. There was a feral urgency to their coming together.

Clothes were ripped off. Alix's hands were rough, his mouth hard, teeth nipping and tongue thrusting deep into the slick folds of her sex. Leila's back arched. Her hands clenched in Alix's hair. His hands clasped her so tightly she knew she'd be bruised, but she revelled in it.

He was her man and she loved him.

And now he loomed over her, huge and awe-inspiring, face flushed and eyes glittering intensely. She saw the need on his face, making his features stark. She saw the uncertainty even now, in spite of his bravado, and her heart ached.

He sank into her body with slow and devastating deliberation, watching her. Demanding that she expose herself utterly.

Leila had nowhere to hide. He was true to his word. She wrapped her legs around him and finally broke free of the bonds of fear. He touched her so deeply she gasped and caught his face in her hands, the words spilling from her lips in a rush of emotion.

'Of course I love you, Alix. I love you with all my heart and soul. You're mine, and I'm yours, for ever.'

An expression of pure awe broke over his face. A look of fierce male satisfaction. And *love*.

Leila's heart soared free, and then the delicious dance of love started. And when Leila arched her back in the throes of orgasm and looked up, all she could see were thousands of glittering mosaic stars above their heads. And finally she believed in his love—deep down in the core of her body, where Alix had broken her apart and now put her back together.

EPILOGUE

LEILA HURRIED FROM the Jeep into the castle, greeting staff as she went in. Happiness and fulfilment were things that she felt every day now, but she didn't take them for granted for a second.

In the seventeen months since she'd married Alix, in a deeply emotional ceremony, they and the island had undergone seismic changes.

The island was thriving and growing stronger every day. Her factory had opened a few months ago and it, too, was beginning to flourish as she started to manufacture perfumes again. Her apartment in Paris was now an office over the shop, and she went back about once a month to keep an eye on proceedings.

She'd been stunned to get a call one day from her father's daughter—a half-sister. He'd been put under immense public pressure to do the DNA test which had proved his paternity of Leila and consequently ruined his political career. Leila's half-sister, Noelle, had confided that her and her brother's life had been blighted by his numerous affairs and their mother's unhappiness.

She'd already come to Isle Saint Croix to meet Leila, with a protective Alix by her side, and their relationship was tentatively flowering into something very meaningful.

But the real heart and centre of her life was right here in the castle. Everything else was a bonus.

When Leila walked into Alix's office she couldn't help a grin spreading across her face at the scene before her, featuring her two favourite people in the world. Alix and their dark-haired eleven-month-old son, Max.

Max was bouncing energetically on Alix's knee, simultaneously slapping his pudgy fists on the table while trying to cram what looked like a very mushed up banana into his mouth.

Alix had a big hand firmly around his son and was typing with one hand on his open laptop, safely out of destruction's way.

Then they both caught sight of her at the same time—two pairs of grey eyes, one wide and guileless, the other far more adult and full of a very male appreciation and love.

'Mama!'

Small arms lifted towards her and Leila plucked Max off Alix's knee. But before she could move away Alix's arm snaked around her waist and pulled her onto his lap. Max was delighted—clapping his hands, bits of banana flying everywhere.

Leila chuckled. 'I was trying to help you.'

Alix slid Leila's hair over her shoulder and pressed a kiss to her exposed neck.

She shivered deliciously and asked a little breathlessly, 'Where's Mimi?'

'I gave her the afternoon off. We were lonely without you—weren't we, little man?'

Max gurgled his agreement. Leila stood up and found a wet wipe to clean her son as much as possible, before putting him into his playpen and watching him pounce on his favourite cuddly toy.

She turned to face Alix, eyes sparkling, voice dry, 'I was in the factory for three hours and you got *lonely*?'

Alix stood up and took Leila's hand and drew her over to a nearby couch, pulling her down with him so she ended up sprawled on his lap again—this time in much closer proximity to a strategic part of his anatomy.

'I get lonely the minute you leave my sight,' he growled softly.

Leila's heart swelled. 'Me too.'

The playpen was suspiciously quiet, and Leila checked quickly to see their son sprawled on his back, thumb in his mouth, cuddly toy clamped to his side, fast asleep. Worn out.

She leaned back against her husband. 'I have something for you.'

He arched a brow and moved subtly, showing her that he had something for her too. 'Do you, now?'

She nodded and took a bottle from the pocket at the front of her shirt dress. The label read *Alix's Dream*. It was the perfume she'd first made for him. And one that was so personal she never sold it to anyone else.

He kissed her, long and slow and deep. 'Thank you.'

'Mmm,' she said appreciatively. 'I'll have to make it more often if that's the sort of response I'll get.'

Alix shifted so that she slid into the cradle of his lap. Leila groaned—half in frustration, half in helpless response. 'Alix…'

'I'm going to make a secret passage from here to the harem,' he grumbled.

Leila blushed to think of their very private space, which had been completely refurbished. The *hammam* was in use again too, and was open to local women and the women of the castle.

Leila loved going there amongst them and hearing their stories. It was one of the things that had earned them both the love and respect of their people—their unaffected ways and their wish to be considered as equal as possible.

Alix teased a strand of Leila's hair around his finger. 'Andres said you went to the hospital today? Another visit to the new children's wing?'

Leila nodded—and then the excitement bubbling inside

her couldn't be contained any more. 'Yes, but I also had an appointment to see Dr Fontainebleau.'

Alix immediately tensed at the mention of the royal doctor. 'Is there something wrong?'

Leila shook her head and took his hand, placing it over her belly. 'No, everything is very okay...but we'll be a little bit busier in about eight months.'

The colour receded from Alix's face and then rushed back. His arms tightened around her and then he lowered her down onto the sofa. His formidable body came over her, his happiness and joy palpable.

When he spoke his voice sounded a little choked. 'You do know that you've made me the happiest man in the world, and that I love you to infinity and beyond?'

Leila blinked back emotional tears and wound her arms around her husband's neck, drawing him down to her.

'I know, because I feel exactly the same way. Now, about that secret passage to the harem...do you think we could get it done before the baby arrives?'

* * * * *

THE PREGNANT PRINCESS

ANNE MARIE WINSTON

For Sandy,
sister of my heart

RITA® Award finalist and bestselling author **Anne Marie Winston** loves babies she can give back when they cry, animals in all shapes and sizes and just about anything that blooms. When she's not writing, she's managing a house full of animals and teenagers, reading anything she can find and trying not to eat chocolate. She will dance at the slightest provocation and weeds her gardens when she can't see the sun for the weeds anymore. You can learn more about Anne Marie's novels by visiting her Web site at www.annemariewinston.com.

One

God, it was hot. Rafe Thorton ran a hand through his thick black hair and pulled his sunglasses down over his eyes. Arizona might be a great place for a guy employed year-round in construction, but he could do without the heat. It was only late January and the temperature today had reached the mid-eighties.

Rafe took a long pull of the water he'd just bought, then swung away from the cool interior of the convenience store into the heat of the afternoon. Juggling the bottle, he stripped off his T-shirt and swiped it across his chest, absently smiling at two women whose eyes widened in appreciation as they passed him. He glanced at the newspaper box on the sidewalk outside the store—and stopped mid-stride.

Wynborough Princess Dedicates Hospice.

Rafe stared at the headlines of the daily paper. Slinging the T-shirt over one shoulder, he set his drink atop the machine for a moment while he fished coins from the pocket of his faded jeans. He dropped a quarter and a dime through the slot, then opened the door and pulled out a paper.

Wynborough was a tiny kingdom; its royalty rarely received the kind of press that Britain's royals were subjected to regularly. There was a brief press release accompanied by one small candid photo, a blurry shot of a small, slender woman stepping out of a car.

Holding the paper close to his face as if that might bring it into better focus, he stared at the grainy picture. The woman's hair obscured much of her face and he couldn't discern its color from the black-and-white shot. Still...it could be her.

The features that had consumed his dreams for the past five months floated before his mind's eye as he scanned the article. Memories bombarded him, and his pulse sped up. Princess Elizabeth would be arriving in Phoenix, Arizona, this afternoon. She'd be staying for several days, making an appearance tomorrow to raise funds for a local children's hospice.

Elizabeth! Was that *her* name?

He tossed the paper across the seat as he climbed into his truck and started the engine. Wynborough. Five months before, he'd attended one of the royal charity events, a masquerade ball. It had been the first time he'd been home in ten years, the first time since the day he'd informed his father, the Grand Duke of Thortonburg, that he had no intention of assuming the title or of living under his father's thumb. And hearing himself addressed as the Prince of Thortonburg by his family's servants, the title that had descended onto his shoulders along with all the other responsibilities he'd been trained to handle all his life, had reminded him forcibly of all the reasons why he'd made the decision to live in the States.

He didn't want those responsibilities.

Wryly, he wondered what his father, who'd harped on

responsibility all his life, would think if he knew Rafe had
seduced one of the Wynborough princesses in a garden
house five months ago. Not a very *responsible* act, even if
the lady had been as hot and ready as he had been.

He'd thought about her a great deal since then. She'd
been gentle and sweet, with a hint of innocence that had
turned out to be more than a hint. But she'd been so warm
and willing that he'd found himself unable to resist her,
even though he had better sense. At least he'd told her right
up front that he would be leaving the next morning, he
thought. She couldn't accuse him of not being honest about
his intentions.

But that was a moot point. He hadn't told her who he
was, and he had never expected to see his pretty lover
again. He just hadn't anticipated that she'd be so deeply
embedded in his memory that he caught himself thinking
of her at all hours of the day and night.

Yes, he'd thought about her far too much.

Irritably, Rafe drummed his fingers on the steering
wheel, waiting for the light to change. Although he couldn't
imagine that she'd known who he was, years of thwarting
his father's machinations had honed his suspicious nature.
His mouth tightened. Did he discern his father's match-
making hand in the princess's sudden appearance in Phoenix? Had the old man found out somehow about that night?

He felt his shoulders tensing and he took a deep breath,
forcing himself to relax. Maybe it was simple coincidence.
Maybe it wasn't even the right princess, if indeed his mystery lover had been one of the Wynborough princesses.

Then again, maybe years of living away had dulled his
instinct for self-preservation. His father had an incredible
capacity for trying to force the issue of a royal marriage on
his firstborn son. If he'd even heard any of Rafe's firm
denials, there certainly was no evidence of it.

But he didn't intend to marry anybody with royal blood.
Ever. Being heir to the damned title his family so revered

had caused him more grief in his childhood than any kid should have had to bear. He had no intention of foisting it onto any offspring of his own. No, the Duchy of Thortonburg would pass to his younger brother Roland.

As for marriage…when and if he ever felt the time was right, he planned to find a nice American girl of common ancestry and settle down in anonymous wedded bliss.

No way was he marrying a princess!

He picked up the discarded paper and read the article again. She was staying at the newly opened Shalimar Resort. Now that was handy. His company had gotten the bid to complete work in a courtyard at the Shalimar, and he still had a crew there. Maybe he'd run by there right now and see how the work was progressing.

It was a lovely hotel, Elizabeth thought, admiring the muted dusty rose and pale marble colors of Phoenix's newest five-star resort. But then, she was used to lovely things. What she wasn't used to was freedom.

She supposed to most of the people milling around in the lobby as she moved toward the restaurant, walking alone through a five-star hotel was so ordinary as to be forgettable. But to her, accustomed as she was to bodyguards and security systems, schedules and surveillance cameras, it was incredibly exciting. Daring.

A little scary.

"Ma'am, do you have a reservation?" the maitre d' asked as she approached.

She smiled. "Yes. Elizabeth Wyndham. One for dinner."

Instantly, the man's inquiring expression changed to one of delight. "Ah, Princess Elizabeth! Your Royal Highness, may I welcome you to La Belle Maison. Your table has been prepared." He bowed low and gestured for her to precede him, pointing to a candlelit alcove where a server stood with napkins at the ready.

Elizabeth took the seat they had prepared, allowing the men to fuss over her every comfort, refusing wine and asking for a menu. But as she perused the selections, her mind was still out in the lobby, where for a few minutes she'd walked alone, free, with no one to worship her, no one to worry about every step she took or every person she passed.

She sighed. "I'll have the special, a salad with your house dressing, and the carrots. No potato, thank you."

As the waiter rushed off, she felt a slight but very real movement pushing at the wall of her womb. Discreetly covering her abdomen with one hand, she patted the small bulge beneath her fashionably loose-fitting pants and tunic top. *Hello, my sweet one. Perhaps we'll meet your daddy today.*

She rested her chin on one hand. Oh, how she hoped she'd be able to find the mysterious man with whom she'd shared such a wonderful night of loving five months ago. He'd said he was American, though he'd sounded as if he'd been a native of her father's kingdom. And though he'd had to return to the States, he'd left behind his card—a clue—letting her know where she could find him.

Thorton Design and Construction, Phoenix, Arizona. U.S.A. Apparently her baby's father worked for the firm.

She'd hoped he would come back for her and, of course, that was still possible. In fact, she was sure he would, since she was absolutely positive he had felt the extraordinary bond between them as strongly as she had.

But she couldn't wait much longer. He didn't know she was on a rather urgent schedule now. Her spirits took a mild plunge. Soon she was going to have to tell her parents about her pregnancy. It was becoming difficult to hide it with clothing. When she'd had the opportunity to come to the States with her three sisters to search for their long-lost brother, she'd seized the chance, hoping for the opportunity to slip away and seek out her mystery lover.

It had been the sheerest good fortune that their search

had led them to Hope, Arizona, to a foster home where their kidnapped brother might have been brought nearly thirty years ago. And even better fortune that Catalina, where she was going to interview a man who might be that brother, was but a few hours' drive from her current location, providing her with a perfectly good reason to stay in Phoenix.

Arranging a charity event for the hospice project had been easy. Now she could only hope that the excuse the event had given her to visit Phoenix brought back into her life her Prince Charming from the charity ball.

Oh, he'd been so handsome, so wonderful. From the moment their eyes had met across the crowded ballroom at her sister Alexandra's annual Children's Fund Ball, she'd known he was destined to be someone very special in her life. They'd danced and drunk champagne, and within hours she'd fallen head over heels in love with a man whose name she didn't even know! No, that wasn't true. She'd fallen in love the moment their eyes had made a connection across the ballroom. And she was fairly sure her lover had felt the same way.

The memory of that perfect evening still made her smile. She'd talked Serena into telling the guards she already had retired to her rooms for the night. And then Elizabeth had led him to the little octagonal pavilion at the far end of the formal gardens.

The glass-walled house was furnished with simple chaise lounges for whiling away long, lazy summer afternoons. One of those lounges would forever linger in her memory. He'd kissed her until she thought she might die of pleasure, and then he'd gently drawn her down onto the chaise and—

"Take me to the princess's table." The brusque, masculine voice penetrated her daydreaming.

"The princess is dining alone, sir. I don't think—"

Her heart began to beat frantically as it recognized her lover's voice. She'd planned on visiting him tomorrow, hadn't expected to see him so soon! She half stood, and her napkin slid to the floor.

But she didn't notice. All her attention was riveted on the man standing in the archway of the dining room.

The man whose steady gaze compelled her not to look away, as memories of their hours together sizzled through the air between them as surely as a silky finger over sensitive skin.

His eyes were a dark, dangerous blue, screened by thick black eyelashes that any woman would have killed for. The last time they'd met, those blue eyes had been warm with desire. Right now, they were flashing with a combination of puzzlement, wariness and what she was pretty sure was a touch of anger.

"Never mind. I see her." His voice was deep and tough as he started forward, completely ignoring the fluttering waiters hovering around him.

"But...sir! You are hardly dressed for—sir! A tie and jacket are required in the dining room...."

As her broad-shouldered lover advanced toward her alcove, she took a deep breath, ignoring the sudden doubts that fluttered through her brain.

He'd be happy to see her. Of course he would. And he'd be as thrilled about the baby as she was.

The baby! Some protective maternal mechanism prompted her to resume her seat. Quickly, she reached for her napkin and draped it over her lap, pulling loose the folds of her tunic so that the barely noticeable swell of her abdomen was hidden. She didn't question the instinct that told her this was not the time to tell him of his impending fatherhood. That could come later. After they'd gotten to know each other better.

The thought made her feel hot all over. Raising her chin, she let the warmth of her feelings show in her eyes as she smiled at the man approaching her table. The man whose set, unsmiling face didn't offer anything remotely resembling the welcome she'd prayed he would extend.

He was huge. That was the first thing that registered now that she'd gotten over the surprise of seeing him so unexpectedly. Oh, she'd remembered he was big, but the man striding toward her, wearing a white T-shirt, faded jeans cinched by a snug leather belt with a heavy silver buckle and dust-covered work boots was simply enormous. But as she focused on his face, she knew he was indeed the man to whom she'd given her heart—and so much more—five months ago.

His hair was raven-black, gleaming in the discreet lighting of the dining room. It had been ruthlessly groomed the night they'd met, but by the time the evening had ended, it had been every bit as rumpled and disheveled as it was right now. Shadows emphasized the hollows beneath high, slanted cheekbones, and his firm lips, lips she remembered curved in a sensual smile, were as full and sensual as ever, though they were pressed into a grim line at the moment.

"How did you find me?"

Whatever she'd expected, that wasn't part of any greeting she could imagine. "Your card," she said, raising her hands helplessly. "The one you left for me."

"I didn't leave you any card."

"Oh, yes, don't you remember? It was on the chaise when I—" She halted in sudden acute embarrassment.

Then the meaning of his denial struck her. *He hadn't meant to leave his card behind. Hadn't intended that she ever know who he was.* The idea was crushing, and for a long moment she couldn't even force herself to form words. Finally, lifting her chin, she put on the most regal expression she possessed, the expression her entire family used to cover emotion from prying eyes and paparazzi. "Apparently I was wrong to assume you intended me to look you up if I was in the States," she said in a cool, smooth voice. "I apologize."

"I told my father years ago I wouldn't marry any of you."

Her face reflected her bewilderment. This conversation was making no sense. "What?" She shook her head. "What are you talking about?"

"About an arranged marriage. To one of the princesses." He crossed his arms and scowled at her. "To *you*." He stabbed a finger in her direction. The move made his muscular arms bulge and the shirt strained at its seams across his chest. He still stood over her, and if he wanted to intimidate her, he was doing a darn good job.

But she wasn't going to let him cow her. Never mind that her hopeful heart was breaking into a thousand little pieces. Thank heavens she hadn't had a chance to share any of her foolish dreams with him. "I didn't come here to marry you," she said in a slow, measured tone that barely squeezed past the lump in her throat.

His expression darkened even more, if that was possible. Slowly, he uncrossed his arms and leaned forward across the table, planting his big palms flat on the surface. He was invading her space and she forced herself not to scoot backwards, away from him.

"I am not amused by your little act," he said through his teeth. "If you came here hoping to take me back to Wynborough like some kind of damned trophy, you can think again, Princess."

It was so far from the passionate greeting that she'd imagined all these months, like a stupid fool, that she had to fight the tears that welled up. What was wrong with him? She hadn't done anything to make him so angry.

"I didn't come here to take you anywhere," she said, swallowing hard to keep the sobs at bay. "I am here on another matter entirely—although I did wish to talk to you."

There was a tense silence. The man who'd been her lover didn't move a muscle for a long second. She felt a tear escape and trickle down her cheek, but she didn't even raise a hand to brush it away. "Who are you, anyway?" she asked in a shaky voice.

He smiled. A wide baring of perfect white teeth that somehow was more of a threat than a pleasantry. Reaching across the table, he picked up her small, fisted hand and bowed low over it. "Raphael Michelangelo Edward Andrew Thorton, Prince of Thortonburg and heir to the Grand Duke of Thortonburg at your service, Your Royal Highness," he said. "As if you didn't know. Expect me for dinner in your suite tomorrow evening at seven."

Before she could pull away, he pressed an overly courteous kiss to the back of her hand, his gaze holding hers. Despite the animosity and antagonism that radiated from his big body, a vivid, detailed image of the intimacy with which those finely chiseled lips had traveled over her body leaped into her head. Her cheeks grew hot and she mentally cursed her fair complexion, because in his eyes flared awareness—he knew exactly what she was thinking.

Then his lips compressed into a thin line as he straightened abruptly. "And be ready to answer my questions this time, *Princess*."

Elizabeth paced the suite nervously as the clock struck seven the following evening. The Prince of Thortonburg! She still couldn't believe it.

As children, she and her sisters had made fun of the stern Grand Duke. She could still remember Serena swaggering across the playroom, doing a deadly accurate imitation of the man, boasting about his eldest son's educational achievements in England and America, that had had Katherine and her in stitches. Even Alexandra, whose overdeveloped sense of responsibility and position as the eldest had often made her seem stuffy to the younger girls, had laughed until the tears ran.

When the girls grew old enough to be presented at court

and began to attend the balls and royal functions of the kingdom, they'd speculated about the invisible Thortonburg heir. Though he wasn't that much older than Alexandra, none of her sisters had ever seen him. He'd been away at Eton and Oxford for years, then to the States to Harvard, she'd heard, and not long after that there had been rumors of a quarrel between the Grand Duke and his elder son. If it weren't for Roland, the personable younger son of the Grand Duke, who vouched for his brother's existence, she would have thought Raphael was a hoax. When he hadn't even shown up for Roland's twenty-first birthday party, it had only fueled the fires of her sisters' curiosity.

Well, he existed, all right. She rested a hand on the slight swell of her belly, hidden beneath the loose, floating gauze of the dress she'd chosen to wear this evening. She could guarantee that he existed.

The worries of the present receded beneath a wave of memories that could still make her blush. She remembered the first time she'd seen him. He'd been wearing severe black evening dress, which had made him look impossibly tall and broad-shouldered compared to every other man in the room, as indeed he was. His only concession to the masquerade ball had been a small black silk mask that concealed the upper half of his face.

She'd been standing across the ballroom, dressed in the costume of a medieval princess, when their eyes had met. Within minutes, he'd cut a decisive path through the crowd to reach her side.

"Good evening, fair lady. Might I have the pleasure of your company in this dance?"

Up close, he was so much larger than she that he could have been intimidating. But as she allowed him to take her gloved hand, his eyes glowed a warm blue through the slits in the mask, and she had felt the oddest sense of security surround her. He drew her into a very correct ballroom position for the waltz that followed, and silently they danced. He didn't even ask her name. Enjoying the game, she preserved the pretense of two strangers, but as the evening progressed, he gently urged her closer to him until she could feel his big hand splayed across her back, his long fingers nearly caressing the upper swell of her bottom, the strength of his muscled thighs pressing against her through the light gown she wore.

They'd danced like that for hours, until every nerve in her body quivered with desire. Her fingers had explored the heavy muscles of his arms and shoulders, slid up into his hair, and she felt his big body shudder against hers.

He brushed a kiss over her ear. "Let's get out of here."

A jolt of need surged through her. Had she ever felt like this before? The answer was so clear—none of the polished suitors who came sniffing around the royal residence had ever made her feel so much as a fraction of what she felt for this man.

She lifted her face to his, studying his thick-lashed eyes through the mask, the clean line of his jaw and the slight curve of chiseled lips. His gaze held hers, demanding her answer, and, as suddenly as that, she knew this was the man with whom she wanted to spend the rest of her life. She'd lifted herself on tiptoe and brazenly brushed her lips over his, then reached back and unlinked his hands from behind her back.

"Just let me visit the powder room," she said. "I'll meet you on the terrace."

But as she turned away, he caught her by the wrist and lifted a big hand to her face, caressing the soft flesh along her cheek with one long finger. "Don't be long," he said in a deep voice that sent shivers of excitement racing through her, and her body contracted in an uncontrollable sexual response.

Turning her head, she kissed his finger as she slipped away. "I won't be," she promised.

And she wasn't. It took her mere moments to locate Serena, flirting cheerfully and shamelessly with a crowd of young men, and she unapologetically drew her aside. ''Cover for me tonight. I met someone.''

''Who?'' Serena's green eyes went wide with anticipation.

But Elizabeth shook her head. ''I'll tell you tomorrow. Just cover for me, okay?''

''Okay.''

Since they'd been children, the two of them had shared a longing for freedom from the ever-present bodyguards who shadowed their every move. Alexandra, immersed in correctness, and dear, quiet Katherine never seemed to mind the oppressive atmosphere, but she had longed for freedom, as had Serena. It had been a great game to elude the guards, and often, one of them would murmur, ''Cover for me,'' just before committing some daring vanishing act, invariably sending the guards into frantic scurrying which the hidden sister watched with glee.

It wasn't particularly difficult to shake her observers. The royal bodyguards took their work seriously, but they were no match for a young woman who'd had years of practice in evading them.

Slipping out a side door into the garden, she approached the terrace from the lawn, her heart thumping heavily as she recognized her handsome dance partner standing on the other side of the low stone wall of the terrace.

''Hello, there,'' she murmured.

He turned, immediately picking her out of the darkness and strolling to the edge of the wall. ''Hello, beautiful,'' he said. And in one powerful, lightning-swift move, he vaulted over the wall and dropped to the ground beside her.

She pressed a startled hand to her mouth, then released a nervous laugh. ''Some people use the steps,'' she pointed out, gesturing to the marble stairs at the center of the terrace.

"But you weren't near the stairs," he replied in a perfectly reasonable voice.

She smiled. "No, I wasn't, was I?"

He cupped her elbow, drawing her away from the lights of the terrace and into the dim evening coolness of the gardens. "I thought perhaps you weren't coming."

She caught her breath in dismay, turning to face him and clutching his arm. It suddenly seemed vitally important to reassure him. "I'm sorry. It took longer than I expected. You see, I had to—"

But her words were stilled when he gently placed one large finger against her lips. "Hush. It doesn't matter."

His gaze held hers as he slowly, without any hurry or fumbling, placed his hands at her waist and drew her closer. She found she was holding her breath as his mouth drew nearer and nearer. "I've been wanting to do this all evening," he murmured. His lips were a heartbeat away now, and she found she was holding her breath as she leaned forward the scant distance that separated them and allowed his lips to meet hers.

It was heaven, was all she could think. His mouth was warm and tender, competently molding hers as he gathered her closer. Suddenly, within the space of a second, a flash-fire raced through her system as desire spread. She sank against him, and instantly his arms tightened, his mouth grew firmer, less tentative and more demanding. He kissed her as though she were the only thing in his entire world, his tongue invading her mouth in a basic, primitive rhythm that grew stronger, more insistent and demanding until she locked her arms around his shoulders, straining against him as he plundered her lips.

He groaned, deep in his throat, and one hand slid down her back to her bottom, sliding around and over the tender flesh, tracing the crease of her buttocks with one long finger, then clasping her firmly in his hand and lifting her strongly against him. She gasped against his mouth as she felt his hard body pressing into her, the blatant surging against her soft belly and the driving need his shifting hips communicated. She realized her hips were moving, too, slipping back and forth against him as her body sought relief from the need racing through her.

His mouth blazed a trail down her throat, pressing a string of stinging kisses to her collarbone and firmly sliding down over her heated flesh until his face was pressed into the full swell of her breasts. He turned his head, and she jumped as a hot breath seared her tender flesh, and then his mouth began to move again. Her head fell back as he brushed over one straining nipple, suckling her through the thin fabric of her gown, and she moaned, twisting against him, her hands coming up to clutch at his hair, combing restlessly through the black silk strands.

He lifted his head, and he was breathing heavily, harsh gasps for air. "Where can we go?"

His voice was so deep and guttural, it was nearly a growl, and her feminine nature recognized the primitive possession in the sound, her body drawing into a nearly painful knot of need. "The—the garden house," she said breathlessly. "Down this path—oh!"

Before she could complete the sentence, he had lifted her into his arms, his head coming down again, his lips slanting over hers in a complete claim that it never occurred to her to resist. She might not know his name, but her body recognized his. And as he began to stride down the path, she relaxed in his arms and gave herself to the embrace that should have felt strange but only felt...right, as if finally, after twenty-seven years of waiting, she'd found what she hadn't even known she'd been waiting for.

Two

On the dot of seven, Rafe knocked on the door of the Royal Princess of Wynborough's suite. Almost immediately, the double doors swung inward, as if Elizabeth had been waiting on the other side.

Elizabeth. She'd been nameless for five months now. Her real name was going to take some getting used to.

Her eyes widened, and he knew she must be contrasting the image he'd presented yesterday in his work clothes with the charcoal suit he donned now. She shouldn't be that surprised—she'd seen him in a tux.

For that matter, he thought with a surge of grim humor, she'd seen him wearing a whole lot less.

"Good evening," she said, stepping back and waving a hand in invitation for him to enter. "Please come in."

"Thank you, Your Highness." He gave the title the faintest emphasis and was gratified to see a blush climb her neck as he stepped into the room.

She was dressed simply, in a pretty, lightweight dress in

a silky fabric that swirled loosely around her body and draped over the full swells of her breasts, drawing his eye as he passed her. His body sat up and took notice as he remembered the soft mounds that had filled his hands a few months ago.... He mentally shook himself, annoyed that he was letting his sex drive get the better of his good judgment again. Just like the first time he'd seen her.

The Children's Fund Ball was an annual masquerade event, and he still didn't know what had possessed him to attend. Once he'd seen this woman, though, he'd ceased to wonder. He and his mysterious lady had complied with the ball's unspoken rule, not identifying themselves. Still, he was almost positive his paramour had been one of the princesses. Her demeanor had been refined, almost archaically elegant compared to the brash American women whom he'd seen throw themselves at a man. Even compared to other women at the ball, British royals as well as those of his native isle, she'd seemed exceptionally genteel.

If she were one of the princesses, that would make sense. He'd never even met one of them, despite his own royal status. Granted, they were all several years younger than he, and he'd been away at school most of his life before he'd escaped Thortonburg, but rumor had it that King Phillip employed the tightest security to keep his remaining family safe.

Rafe supposed that if *his* infant son had been kidnapped and presumably killed, he'd be overprotective with his other children, too. Yes, given all those factors, he'd been nearly positive that his lady fair had been one of King Phillip's four beautiful daughters.

"Could I offer you a drink?" She had moved across the room behind him and now stood behind the small breakfast bar.

"Please." He walked to the bar and hooked one foot around a stool, drawing it to him and propping himself on the edge of the seat with his feet splayed. "Nice place."

"Yes. It's very comfortable."

"I guess you wouldn't know what it's like to live somewhere that wasn't."

Her eyes flickered to his for an instant. "I've never had the opportunity to find out," she said in a neutral tone. Busying herself for a moment, she laid a napkin on the bar and set a highball glass in front of him.

He stared at the drink for a minute. "How do you know what I drink?"

The color that had begun to subside began to climb her neck again. "If you'd prefer another drink, that's fine. This is what you were drinking...the last time."

"This is fine." Abruptly, he picked up the drink and took a quick gulp. When she'd first seen him yesterday in the restaurant, there had been warm, intimate welcome in the depths of her green eyes until he'd scared it away. Today, the same wide eyes held only wariness. Her hair was a beautiful copper, shiny as a new American penny. Tonight she wore it down, curling softly around her shoulders and framing her heart-shaped face.

He recognized that face. Now that he knew who she was, he felt like an idiot for doubting his instincts before. It could almost have been her mother's face at a younger age, except for a slight dimple in her chin, courtesy of her father, the king.

The king.

Anger began to rise again and he ruthlessly pushed it back and shut the door on it. He intended to have his questions answered this evening.

Elizabeth continued to hover behind the bar. She had made herself a drink as well, though he'd seen her put nothing in it but cranberry juice. She gestured to the center of the room, where a coffee table surrounded by several chairs and love seats held a silver tray full of canapés. "Shall we sit down?"

He rose from the stool and gestured for her to precede him. "Certainly."

Her gaze flew to his, then whisked away again, and he saw her swallow. Then she stepped from behind the bar and quickly walked to one of the chairs, sinking down and demurely crossing her legs at the ankle while she fussed with the loose folds of her oversize dress.

Rafe followed her, taking a seat at an angle to hers and accepting the plate she offered him. He'd worked all day and had only gotten home in time to shower and change before heading over to the hotel, and he was starving. As he filled his plate with a selection of the hors d'ouevres, he glanced at her. "Aren't you going to eat?"

She gave a single nervous shake of her head. "I'm not particularly hungry. You go ahead."

"If you're sure." This rigid courtesy was getting to him already. One more of the reasons he didn't intend to return to Thortonburg.

She only nodded.

There was an uncomfortable silence for a few moments. Judging from the way she fidgeted, it bothered her a lot more than it did him. He applied himself to his food until his plate was empty, but he held up a hand in refusal when she offered him a second helping.

"No thanks, this will hold me for the moment."

A faint smile crossed her face. "As you wish." She studied him curiously. "You're very American, aren't you?"

He supposed she meant the slang expression, because he knew his voice still carried the clipped accents of his homeland. "This is my home now," was all he said.

"This country appeals to you so much more than Thortonburg?" she asked softly.

"When I was younger, anyplace that didn't have my father in it was appealing," he said with grim self-mockery. "Now...yes, I like it here. It's warm, it's sunny almost all the time—you certainly can't say that for the North Atlan-

tic.'' Only a short distance off the coast of the United Kingdom, the country of his birth was frequently rainy, cloudy
and chilly. On its good days.

"No.'' Again, a small smile played around her lips.
''You certainly can't.''

He watched her lips curve, aware of the flare of sexual
attraction deep in his gut. She was every bit as beautiful as
he remembered, and every bit as seductive. His good humor
faded.

"Why did you seduce me?'' he asked bluntly.

Her green eyes widened and her head snapped up as if
he'd struck her. Her face went white, then vivid color filled
every centimeter of her fair complexion. ''I didn't seduce
you!''

He considered that. ''Okay. I'll give you that. It was
definitely a two-sided deal, as I recall.''

For a moment, she simply stared at him silently and he
watched, fascinated, as a deep rosy hue flushed her cheeks.
Finally, in the same neutral voice she'd used a minute ago,
she said, ''Why ever would I want to seduce you?''

"Does the word *betrothal* ring any bells?''

She had a bewildered look on her face as she shook her
head. ''But I'm not betrothed to anyone.''

He snorted. ''Do we have to continue this little game of
make-believe? Okay, so it didn't have to be *you*. My father
isn't particular as long as the union occurs. You know full
well one of you will marry the future Grand Duke one day.
You were trying to get a jump on your sisters, weren't you?
After all, if you can't have a king, a grand duke is the next
best thing.''

"You think I'd marry for a *title?*'' She gaped at him for
a moment, ignoring the rest of his heavy-handed sarcasm.
''My father never arranged a marriage in his life. I don't
know why you believe he would do something like that.''

"Maybe because my father's been telling me since I was

four years old that I would marry one of the princesses one day?''

''We'll marry whomever we want, your father's wishes aside.''

''Umm-hmm.'' It was a skeptical sound.

''There was no arrangement of any kind!'' she insisted. ''Anyway, my eldest sister is already married. She married a rancher from right here in Arizona. They're expecting their first child—''

''I don't give a bloody damn if they're expecting ten children,'' he said through his teeth.

Her eyes widened again and though she didn't actually move, he had the impression she'd reared back out of his reach.

''You're...what? Second eldest?'' he asked.

She nodded. ''Third, actually. My brother was—*is*—the eldest. Katherine and Serena are younger than I am.''

Why had Elizabeth been steered his way instead of one of her sisters? It was a puzzle that he couldn't find the right pieces for, and he didn't like unfinished puzzles. But for now, he set it aside. ''My father and your father must have gotten their heads together since I left the country,'' he said. ''And you were the sacrificial lamb. I wonder how the King decided which daughter to send. A roll of dice? A flipped coin?''

''I told you my father would never arrange a marriage for me,'' she insisted, and her voice was agitated. ''There is no scheme.''

''Not anymore there isn't,'' he said, not caring how cold and implacable he sounded. ''You might have been a virgin, and you might even have been the hottest sex I've ever had, but I'm still not falling for it. Go home and tell your daddy I'm not marrying you.''

The color that had infused her cheeks drained away. For a minute, he thought she was going to cry. Then she drew a deep breath. ''I'll tell my father nothing of the sort.'' She leaped to her feet and stomped across the room, yanking open the door of the suite. "He didn't plot for us to meet *or* marry, and if you think I'm trying to trap you into matrimony you couldn't be more wrong. You may leave, sir, and don't come back. I plan to forget we ever met." Grandly, she flung her arm wide to encourage him to leave.

About to take her up on the invitation, Rafe rose from the chair—and stopped in his tracks, all thoughts of leaving forgotten. His eyes narrowed in disbelief.

She was pregnant.

Shock ripped through him as the silhouette of the princess was outlined through her thin dress against the light flowing in from the hall...the light that clearly showed the bulge of pregnancy beneath the flowing style he'd assumed was merely fashionable. Her outflung arm pulled the garment tight across her midsection, making it impossible to miss her condition.

Temporarily struck dumb, Rafe stalked across the room toward her.

Elizabeth must have recognized the bone-deep rage tearing through him, because she backed up until the wall beside the door stopped her retreat.

He didn't hesitate until he was practically standing on her toes, the protrusion of her belly only inches from his body and her wide, fear-filled eyes gazing up at him defensively.

"You...little...*bitch*," he ground out. "So *that's* what this surprise reunion is all about. You've got a bun in the oven and let me guess..." He paused and allowed a mocking grin to slide across his face. "I'm supposed to believe it's mine."

She gasped. When her hands came up and shoved hard at his stomach, he was surprised enough that he let her push him back a step or two. Again, she was flushing that bright red that only a redhead could manage, her whole body shaking. Her face looked shattered, and he thought she was going to cry, but when she spoke, her voice trembled with rage. "It *is* your child," she said. "My sister Serena thought it was only fair that you know."

Her words rocked him to the core, but he managed to cover his reaction with a sneer. "And you expect me to believe that? Do I really look like that big a sucker?" He crossed his arms and his own rising anger made his voice rough. "That could be anybody's baby."

Her eyes darkened, dulled, and she swayed. Alarmed, he reached out to steady her, but she backed away from him so quickly that she nearly fell over a chair. She slapped his hand away.

"As you so kindly reminded me, I was a virgin." Her voice was low and unsteady, and her body shook from head to toe. He had a moment's instinctive concern for her condition, but before he could think of anything to say that might calm her a little, she whipped around and ran across the suite to a far door, entering it and slamming the door so hard the frame shook.

Considering she'd caught him by surprise, he reacted quickly, sprinting after her. But she'd had just enough of a start that by the time he reached for the doorknob, he heard the distinct metallic click of a lock and then the final hammering sound of a deadbolt being thrown into place.

"Elizabeth!" he roared, rattling the knob. "Come out here!"

There was no answer, but through the door he could hear the sound of water running in the bathroom. And then another sound. Weeping. He rested his fists against the door, fighting the urge to batter it down. Frustration and fury mounted as the feeling of being trapped rose within him. Any sympathy that her crying had aroused died as echoes of his childhood swamped him. He'd sworn he would never have a child, would never do to a child what had been done to him. *Never.*

He gave the door a hefty kick with the flat of his foot.

"Nobody makes my life plans for me!" he shouted through the door before he spun on his heel. "Not my father, and not you!"

His mood was only marginally better at nine the next morning. He had tossed and turned half the bloody night. This morning, his eyes felt gritty and he was drinking industrial-strength coffee in an effort to revive the brain cells that were comatose from lack of sleep.

But there were a few brain cells that were alive and well. With no effort at all, he could recall the look on Elizabeth's face when he'd told her that the baby she carried could belong to anyone.

She'd been shattered.

He felt like pond scum. He might not have any intention of marrying the girl, but he wasn't a total jerk. He knew, as sure as he knew his own name, that she'd never had another lover. Before him, impossible. After him... If she'd been a bedhopper, she wouldn't still have been a virgin when he had met her. He wasn't sure how old she was, but he knew she had to be in her mid-twenties. Definitely not promiscuous.

And her baby was his.

My sister Serena thought it was only fair that you know. What in bloody hell did that mean? That Elizabeth wouldn't have told him otherwise?

He might not want it, might be furious about this whole bloody mess, but he wasn't a man who walked away from his responsibilities. He'd fathered a child, and he'd support it. She'd waited, damn her, far too long for abortion to be an option. He'd counted in his head during the endless nighttime hours, and he figured she was about five months along now.

Abortion. In his heart, he knew he couldn't let her do that, anyway. It certainly would have been the easy way out, but the solution gave him a sick feeling. Together, he and Elizabeth Wyndham had created a life, and he didn't believe either of them had the right to end it.

No. Biologically, he was going to be a father, though he had no intention of getting involved in this child's life. He wondered if Elizabeth had considered adoption. As far as he was concerned, that would be the best thing all around, but somehow, he doubted his redheaded lover would see it that way. Nor would the royal family, come to think of it.

Oh, well. If she wanted to raise the kid, he couldn't stop her. And he certainly wouldn't have any trouble supporting it financially. Even though he'd refused to use any of his family's money, except that from his grandmother's trust, he'd managed to build quite a respectable business for himself here in the States. Regardless of the hidebound, ambitious schemer he had the misfortune to call his father.

Hell. He wasn't going to get any more sleep, and he knew he couldn't work until he'd straightened things out with Elizabeth. Dumping the coffee in the sink, he grabbed his car keys and headed for the garage.

Twenty-five minutes later, he stood in the suite where he'd been only last night, clinging to his temper by a thin thread while the personal assistant provided to Elizabeth during her hotel stay spread her hands helplessly. "I'm sorry, Mr. Thorton, but the princess insisted. I didn't think it was wise for her to rent a car for herself, but there was simply no stopping her."

"How many were in her party?"

"Her party? Oh, no one else, sir. She was alone."

She hadn't even taken a driver or a bodyguard? The vague tingle of apprehension that had hovered since he'd learned the princess had left the hotel that morning became a full-fledged itch. "What about her bodyguard?"

"She didn't bring one, sir."

Rafe swore, a string of curses that clearly shocked the young woman before him. "Where did she go?"

"I don't know, sir. She was meeting a man, I believe.

All she told me was that she planned to be back by the dinner hour.''

Dinner hour. In Wynborough, that could easily mean eight or nine in the evening. No way was he waiting that long to be sure she was all right. With the hotel employee to vouch for him, it was an easy task to get the concierge to supply him with Elizabeth's intended destination and to get a description of the vehicle she was driving.

Driving! As sheltered as her life had been, he would bet she'd rarely, if ever, driven herself anywhere in her whole life.

Not to mention the little fact that Americans drove on the other side of the road from what she was accustomed at home.

As he waited impatiently for the facts he'd requested, the assistant's other words sank in. Meeting a man. A man! Who the hell would Elizabeth know in Phoenix other than him? She was pregnant with *his* baby, damn it!

Five minutes later, he was climbing back into his truck and heading for the highway.

He drove south out of Phoenix on Interstate 10, heading toward Casa Grande. The concierge had told him that Elizabeth had asked for directions to Catalina, a little town nestled between the Tortolita mountain range and the Coronado National Forest just north of Tucson. She had maybe an hour's start on him—how the hell was he going to find her?

Especially if she was meeting some other man.

It was only with the greatest restraint that he could keep himself from snarling at the woman's naïveté. She didn't know the first thing about men. Elizabeth had no business haring off to meet another man, and when he found her he was going to let her know in no uncertain terms that as the father of her baby, he wouldn't tolerate another man hanging around his...

His what?

Nothing, he told himself. *Nothing.* She doesn't belong to you. You need this princess in your life like you need heat rash.

It was hot.

She didn't think she'd ever experienced this kind of heat before. She'd vacationed on islands in warm climates, but nothing she could recall resembled this dry, draining heat that leached every ounce of energy from her. Of course, she'd never been on a tropical island when she was pregnant, either, and she'd nearly always had a pool or a beautiful ocean in which to cool off.

Elizabeth bent over the motor of the rental car again. This was dreadful. She had no idea what she might be looking for among all the black, greasy parts and metal pipes. All she knew was that a white, billowing cloud of smoke had begun to leak from beneath the bonnet of the automobile about thirty minutes ago, and that when she'd pulled off the road to investigate the sedan wouldn't start again.

Fear coiled and her fingers shook as she tentatively reached forward and lightly tapped a piece of metal. It was easy to call herself a dunce. An hour ago, a jaunt down an American highway to find the man who might be her brother had sounded like a grand lark. Now it sounded like the height of folly.

No chauffeur. No bodyguard. No car phone. Off the main road on a little side highway with not a building in sight. Her parents would be terribly distressed if they knew. It hadn't seemed so foolish to her when she'd had the idea. She was so awfully weary of being followed, escorted, fussed over everywhere she went. This had seemed like the perfect time to see how it felt to be *normal.*

Now all she could think was that if someone would rescue her, she'd offer him a title in his own right. Peering into the engine one more time, she picked up the black

umbrella she'd brought along and held it open above her
head, providing a bit of shade from the sun if not from the
heat.

The thought of what Rafe would say if he were here only
served to lower her spirits even more. He thought she was
a silly, helpless girl who'd been sheltered from the real
world her entire life. She could see his disdain in his eyes
when he looked at her.

Was he right? She thought of the organ donor campaign
with which she'd consented to work, of the hospital visits
she'd made in the name of her other charity, a hospice in
Wynborough's capital city. She'd seen suffering. She'd
seen death. She wasn't a hothouse flower who had fluff for
brains.

*Oh? Then why are you standing here in the heat beside
a crippled auto?*

She was going to pray to God Rafe never found out
about this. Then again, why should he? When he'd
slammed out of her suite last night, she'd known she would
never see him again.

Far down the road, something distracted her from her
morose thoughts. A car! A car on the highway coming toward her. It was moving quite fast over the straight, flat
terrain, and as it drew closer she could see it was a truck.
Not that it mattered as long as the driver would be willing
to take her to Catalina. In Catalina she could accomplish
her goal, which was to locate Samuel Flynn, the man who
once was an orphan in The Sunshine Home for Children,
the home she and her sisters were sure their kidnapped
brother had been brought thirty years ago.

Her stomach quivered, and she hoped it was at the
thought of locating her brother, presumed dead for so long.
What a coronation anniversary gift that would make for her
father!

Her stomach quivered again, and she wiped a drop of
sweat from her temple before it could trickle down her

cheek. The truck was drawing to a halt behind her car now, and she squinted as the driver stepped out, forcing her dry lips into a welcoming smile. Until she recognized the big broad-shouldered figure of the Prince of Thortonburg walking toward her.

Curses. The day was rapidly assuming the proportions of a major disaster. She closed her eyes, hoping he was a mirage, but she was forced to open them quickly by a wave of vertigo. He was still there.

His expression was forbidding as he strode toward her. "What do you think you're doing?" he demanded.

"It's lovely to see you again, too, Mr. Thorton. How coincidental that you should be traveling the same road as I." She tilted her chin, determined not to give him the satisfaction of seeing her squirm.

"You know perfectly well it's not coincidence. I was coming after you. You have no business traipsing around an American desert without an escort."

"Thank you for your opinion. Where I traipse and with whom is not your concern, sir." She would have stuck her nose even higher in the air, but she was forced to close her eyes as another round of dizziness seized her.

"Elizabeth!" She felt his big hands catch her elbows.

"You may address me as 'Your Royal Highness'—oh!" She squeaked in alarm as Rafe scooped her up in his arms and swung her around, and she clutched at his shoulders as the world spun crazily around her. "Put me down!"

"Gladly." His booted feet crunched on gravel as he set her on her feet, and she opened a cautious eye to see that he had brought her around to the passenger side of his truck. Keeping one arm about her, he leaned around her and opened the door, then set his hands at her waist and easily lifted her into the enclosed cab.

He'd left the engine and the air conditioner running. Beneath her legs in her thin dress the leather seat was cool, and she was blessedly shaded from the vicious sun. She almost whimpered with delight, but she wasn't going to give him the satisfaction. Instead, she lay her head against the back of her seat and blotted her forehead with a tissue from her purse.

"What's wrong with the car?" he asked.

"I don't know," she said. "I was trying to figure that out when you came along."

"Right." He gave a snort of amusement. "Why did you stop along the road in the middle of nowhere?"

"There was smoke coming from beneath the bonnet."

"Smoke?" He looked alarmed. "Are you sure it wasn't steam?"

She shrugged. "I haven't a clue. Smoke, steam, something like that."

"There's a pretty big difference," he informed her. Then he straightened. "Put your seat belt on." He slammed the passenger door with more force than necessary, making her wince.

She watched through the windshield as he walked back to the blue Lincoln and retrieved the keys before locking its door and coming back to the big truck. Today he was wearing jeans again, jeans that caressed the solidly muscled contours of his legs like a lover's hands. She remembered the feel of those strong limbs against hers, the heat of his skin and the rough texture of the hair liberally sprinkled over it. The feminine core of her tightened with pleasure, but she sternly reminded herself that theirs had been a single encounter, that the Prince of Thortonburg had made it abundantly clear that she was going to be no part of his life.

A lump in her throat warned her to change the direction of her thoughts, and as Rafe approached the truck, she catalogued the rest of his clothing. With the jeans, he had donned a white shirt, the sleeves of which he'd turned back several times. On his head was a broad-brimmed white straw hat like American cowboys wore. And, as he had since she'd first seen him again, he was wearing a pair of boots. She'd noticed last night that even with his suit he'd worn a polished pair of black leather boots with intricate stitching.

He slid easily into the driver's seat and fastened his own seat belt before backing the truck up and turning a wide circle in the highway.

"Wait! I want to go to Catalina," she said.

"Tough." He didn't even look at her. "You're coming back to Phoenix and going to the doctor, then you're going to lie down and rest."

"To the doctor?" She gaped at him. "I don't need a doctor."

"I want you to be looked over anyway," he said. "You were mighty close to heatstroke back there." He reached behind the seat and pulled a thermos forward. "Drink. You didn't even have extra water with you," he said in a scathing tone.

"I'm not used to the climate here," she said with quiet dignity. "I'm aware that you think I'm a brainless fool, so you can stop rubbing my nose in it."

"Princess," he said, "I haven't even started. What in hell are you thinking, running around here without a bodyguard?"

"I don't need a bodyguard," she said through clenched teeth. "I'm perfectly capable of taking care of myself. And anyway the hotel assistant and the concierge knew my destination."

"They wouldn't have been much help if you'd spent hours out here in the sun."

The only answer to that was silence, and she turned her head to gaze out the window, closing her eyes to shut him out.

She must have napped, because she woke, groggy and disoriented, as they were entering the outskirts of Phoenix.

Hastily, she straightened in her seat, hoping he hadn't noticed.

"Have a good nap?"

So much for wishes. She didn't answer him.

"Why were you going to Catalina?"

She was growing mightily sick of his constant interrogations. "I wanted to visit the next of my many lovers to see if he could be the father of my child," she snapped.

There was a moment of silence in the truck, a silence that nearly vibrated with electricity.

"I apologize," he said in a low growl. "I know it's my child."

He did? Momentarily stunned, she turned her head to stare at him. He glanced over at her and his blue eyes were dark and sober. He looked nearly as shocked as she felt.

There didn't seem to be much to say after that. She went back to staring out the window, though she was no longer seeing the landscape that was so foreign to her, no longer enjoying the contrast between what she'd grown up with and the stark, dry, blindingly bright Arizona desert.

He believed her. That one thought kept running through her mind, and she wondered what had convinced him. Yesterday he'd appeared to doubt her claim. The memory of her naïveté made her wince inwardly, and she took a deep breath to stave off the tears that wanted to rise again.

She'd promised herself last night that Rafe Thorton, under whatever name he chose to use, was never going to make her cry again. She'd been stupid and she'd learned a lesson from her stupidity. Several, in fact.

"How do you feel?" Rafe's voice broke into her thoughts, gruff and deep and distinctly noncommittal.

As if you care, she thought.

"Fine, thank you." She made her voice as chilly as possible while still being scrupulously polite.

"You're not used to this climate," he stated. "You'll

have to be doubly careful of the heat, especially in your condition.''

''Thank you for the advice. I'm sure it will prove invaluable.''

His mouth tightened and she was pleased to see that she was annoying him. He didn't speak to her again, but picked up the phone that was installed in the truck and punched in a number, then tapped his fingers impatiently against the wheel while he waited.

She wondered who he was calling, then decided she didn't really care. But she couldn't prevent herself from glancing over at him.

''Hey, gorgeous!'' Rafe suddenly became animated. Apparently someone had answered on the other end. Someone female, she suspected, from the way his face relaxed and his teeth flashed in a grin that sent an arrow through her heart. He'd smiled at *her* like that once, she remembered.

And you fell for it, dummy.

''In the desert,'' he said and she reasoned that the woman had asked him where he was. ''Listen,'' he said, ''I have a weird question. I need to know the name and number of a reputable obstetrician in Phoenix.''

There was silence on his end and one black eyebrow quirked up, then he laughed, a low and intimate chuckle that set Elizabeth's teeth on edge. ''A friend,'' he said. ''That's all you need to know.''

He scrabbled in the side pocket on his door and came up with a piece of paper and a pencil, tossing them at Elizabeth. ''Write this down,'' he mouthed.

She glared at him, but as he repeated the name and number she did take them down, then slid the paper back across the seat to him.

''Okay, babe. You're one in a million. I'll call you later today.'' Removing the phone from his ear, he punched the button to cut off the connection and let it dangle from his fingers for a moment while he drove. Then he studied the information on the paper and dialed again.

While he was talking, Elizabeth sat in miserable silence. Could things get any worse? Obviously, Rafe had a girlfriend, or someone special in his life. The silly fantasies she'd woven about him—about them together—seemed pathetic and ridiculous now. How could she have been so stupid? She might have led a somewhat sheltered life, but she knew what the world was like. Men got women pregnant every day of the week because they acted on sexual attraction without thinking. The resulting condition had nothing to do with affection or love or respect or long-term plans.

Now she was another one of those sad statistics, and her child would be fatherless because of her carelessness.

The words *appointment this morning,* penetrated her absorption, and she was startled into looking over at Rafe again.

"No! I don't need a doctor."

He ignored her.

"I won't go." She tugged at his forearm to get his attention. A mistake. Beneath her fingers, his bare flesh was hot, and the thick hair that grew along his arm was silky in texture.

"Cancel it," she said fiercely.

"Thorton," he said to the person on the phone. "Elizabeth Thorton."

Her fingers clenched on his arm. Then she realized she was still holding on to him and she snatched back her hand. Again his eyebrow slid up into a bold dark arch as he threw her a questioning look. But before she could find her voice, he'd concluded the call and hung up again.

"What are you doing?" she demanded.

"Making you a doctor's appointment," he said easily. "I want to make sure you and the baby are none the worse for wear after spending the morning standing in the sun."

"I don't need a doctor. Go on back to your girlfriend and leave me alone." She tried to infuse the words with command, but even to her she sounded weak and cranky.

"My girlfriend…" He shot her a smug grin. "That was my secretary on the phone. She has twin grandsons, so she's not exactly competition."

"I'm not competing." So there. "Why didn't you use my real name?"

"Would you rather I'd given your real name?" he asked.

She drew in a sharp breath as his words penetrated, then slumped back against the seat. "No," she admitted in a muted tone. "My parents don't know yet."

"Mind if I ask how long you were going to wait?" He sounded more than slightly shocked.

"I wanted to tell you first," she said quietly. "When I get home, there won't be any reason to delay."

"You're going home soon?"

Did she imagine the slight sharpness in his tone? She shrugged. "As soon as my business here is concluded."

"Your business in Catalina? You never did tell me why you were going there."

"No," she said with more calm than she felt. "I didn't."

Three

She wasn't one bit happy with him, Rafe reflected as he unlocked the door of his Phoenix home shortly after lunch. He eyed the rigid line of Elizabeth's back and the regal tilt of her small, dimpled chin. They didn't call her Princess for nothing.

When she'd realized that despite her protests he was adamant about taking her to a doctor, she'd become quietly furious. Through the appointment, and the quick lunch they'd had afterward, she hadn't spoken one word to him beyond the absolute minimum civility required. If she appreciated his concern for protecting her anonymity, it sure didn't show.

Now he ushered her into his spacious foyer, wondering what she thought of the skylights that let in the bright, cheerful sunlight, the flagstone floors and the soft pastel colors of the desert that he'd wanted for his private spaces. He'd designed it himself, initially intending to use it as a display for potential clients. But he'd liked it so much, he hadn't been able to part with it in the end.

Elizabeth halted about three feet into the foyer and turned to face him. "May I use your telephone, please? I'll put any charges on my calling card."

He glared at her, oddly disappointed that she didn't even seem to notice his home, and irritated that she would bring up a silly thing like telephone charges. "The phone is right through here."

He showed her into his casually appointed den, then left her to go into the kitchen and get each of them a cold drink. The doctor had felt that Elizabeth was in good condition although he had advised her to drink plenty of fluids while she was in Arizona, a dictate Rafe fully intended to see she followed.

From his vantage point around the corner he could clearly hear Elizabeth's conversation. His upbringing and conscience protested the eavesdropping, but since she wouldn't talk to him, he told himself he'd have to find out all he could through any method available.

"Yes, this is Elizabeth. Is my mother there?"

A ten-pound load dropped from Rafe's shoulders. So she wasn't calling another man! She was calling her parents. Not that it mattered terribly to him, he assured himself.

"Mummy? Hello, it's Eliz—yes, yes, I'm fine. Yes, I was afraid you'd worry since I didn't call on time. Oh, please don't cry. Mummy? Maybe you'd better put Daddy on the line."

There was a pause, and Rafe remembered to clink a few ice cubes around in the glasses so she wouldn't think he was spying.

"Hello, Daddy. Of course I'm fine. I'm sorry I didn't call first thing this morning as I promised. I rented a car but it broke down on a highway while I was on a little day trip. But I'm fine. I've met someone you know. Well, I suppose he's an American now, but he was from Thortonburg once. He calls himself Rafe Thorton now, but you know him as the Prince of Thortonburg. What's that? Oh, no, I doubt I'll see much of him. It was really more of a courtesy call on his part—Rafe!'' She glared at him as he removed the receiver from her hand and held it to his own ear.

"Hello, Your Majesty. This is Thorton.'' He knew he sounded clipped and discourteous, but talking to King Phillip was the last thing he'd planned on doing today. Or any day, for that matter.

"Hello, Raphael.'' The King's voice sounded warm and cordial. "It's been far too long. The States must agree with you.'' He didn't sound annoyed, particularly.

"Give me that!'' Elizabeth reached for the phone he'd taken out of her hand, but he held it above her head until she hissed at him and backed off.

He couldn't resist grinning at her as he returned the receiver to his ear. She might pretend to be a lady, but there was fire beneath her calm surface. "Excuse me, Your Majesty. I rescued your daughter this morning from a spot of folly. Did she tell you she had no bodyguard or driver with her?''

"No one at all?'' King Phillip sounded alarmed, but not particularly surprised. "I'm afraid Elizabeth doesn't fully understand how careful she must be. She and her youngest sister spent hours trying to outwit their bodyguards as children. She'd become quite adept at sneaking about, and it's made her a bit overconfident.''

"I agree, Your Majesty. I was a bit concerned myself.''

"Thank you for your assistance.'' The monarch's tones were as friendly as Rafe remembered from his childhood. He never had been able to understand how a man who appeared as nice as the King could conspire with a man as class-conscious as his own father. "Elizabeth will soon be leaving. I believe the dedication ceremony occurred yesterday.''

''It did.'' Rafe hesitated. He should be leaping at the chance to get the princess out of his hair, but the thought of her flying back to Wynborough, thousands of miles away, bothered him. He needed more time to think, to decide how to handle this sticky situation with her and the baby before he let her get away.

''Sir, I don't believe the princess should fly right now,'' he said, turning his broad back on Elizabeth's accusatory face. ''She was through a bit of an ordeal this morning. Nothing serious, of course, but I'd be happy to offer her my hospitality until she feels herself again.''

''Thank you, Raphael.'' The King sounded relieved. ''That's quite kind of you to look after her for us.''

''It will be my pleasure to look after her,'' he said, turning to pin Elizabeth with a meaningful glance.

Her fair skin colored. She avoided his gaze as she reached for the phone, which he let her have this time. ''Daddy, I'm twenty-seven years old,'' she said into the receiver. ''I hardly think I need looking after. In fact, I'd planned on leaving Phoenix today. I want to do a little sightseeing and then I'll be returning to Mitch and Alexandra's for a few days before I come home.'' She laughed a little, but to Rafe's ears it was a forced sound. ''Yes, I know I'm the only one left. No, I promise I won't run off with a cowboy.''

Damn right she wouldn't, he thought.

After a few more exchanges, she punched the button that ended the call and replaced the phone in its cradle. For a moment she simply stood, one hand on the receiver, and Rafe could practically feel the weariness radiating from her.

''Have you a telephone book?'' she asked without looking at him.

''What for?''

She sighed. "Not that it's any of your business, but I'd like to call a taxi and return to the hotel."

"No."

Clearly startled, she turned and stared at him. "Excuse me?"

"I don't think you should return to the hotel right now." His brain was racing a mile a minute. "You look exhausted. Why don't I show you to a guest room and you can rest for a little while, then I'll take you back when you're refreshed."

She hesitated. "No, I really—"

"I insist," he broke in smoothly. Without giving her a chance to argue further, he took her elbow and led her down the wide wood-floored hall to the second room on the left. "Consider this yours for the time being," he said.

Elizabeth looked around, then turned to survey him suspiciously. "Why do I get the feeling you're plotting something?"

"You have an overactive imagination," he said, shrugging.

She stared at him for a second longer, then let out her breath in a long sigh. "Thank you for your offer. I'll just rest for a little while, and then I can get myself back to the hotel."

He shut her in the bedroom before she could change her mind, hoping she didn't notice that he hadn't agreed. Then he strolled back to the kitchen and picked up the telephone. She wasn't going anywhere.

When she woke, it was twilight. Twilight! Momentarily panicked, not recognizing the quietly attractive room around her, she sprang out of the bed—

And had to sit back down quickly when the room spun around her.

As she sat waiting for the alarming vertigo to abate,

memory sneaked back. A second glance around the room confirmed her recall. This wasn't a hotel room. She was in a guest bedroom at Rafe Thorton's home.

She glanced at her watch and was appalled to see it was after six. She'd slept the entire afternoon away!

There was a telephone on the table beside the bed and she decided she'd better use it while she had the chance. Fishing the paper with Sam Flynn's number on it out of her bag, she quickly punched the buttons.

It was an office number, she realized when an answering machine picked up. And as she listened to the message, her heart sank. Mr. Flynn would be out of town on business for several days. Emergency calls were referred to another number.

Somehow, she didn't think another person could help her. She'd just have to wait until Sam was back again.

A spacious bath off the bedroom afforded her the opportunity to freshen up before she twisted the doorknob and stepped into the hall. She had to resist the urge to tiptoe as she walked into the comfortably decorated family room.

Rafe was nowhere in sight. A pass-through counter at one side of the room connected it with the kitchen so she walked through the nearby doorway. She had to admit, his taste was impeccable. Done in a blond wood that complemented the muted tones echoed in the family room, Rafe's kitchen was sleek and modern yet still warm and inviting.

Wide French doors at one end led to a covered terrace, beyond which lay a glistening blue pool. And in the pool, she could see a dark head and powerful arms that were rhythmically slicing through the water. Rafe.

The muscles in her stomach contracted involuntarily, and her breasts felt as if they tightened as well, drawing her flesh taut and smooth as if waiting to welcome him.

No! How dumb could one woman be? How pathetic? He'd made it more than plain that he didn't want her. Stupid as it had been, she'd come here hoping, maybe even expecting him to greet her with…affection. Warmth. She'd dreamed of his delight at learning she carried his child and of how he'd cuddle and coddle her through the rest of the pregnancy.

Well, she wasn't dreaming anymore. And the ache that seemed to have settled permanently around her heart was only because her child was going to grow up without the traditional family she'd believed was possible.

Opening one of the doors, she stepped through onto the terrace.

Immediately Rafe altered his pattern, cutting through the pool to the side nearest her. "Welcome back," he said, a grin lighting his chiseled features and giving him the handsome, roguish look she remembered so well. "I thought maybe you'd sleep straight through 'til tomorrow."

"Hardly." She kept her voice low and expressionless. "I wanted to thank you for your hospitality. I'll be leaving as soon as I can get a cab out here."

"Elizabeth…" He said her name in a hesitant manner at odds with his usual imperiousness.

"Yes?"

"You're going to have a hard time getting a cab out here."

"Not if I make the deal sweet enough." She spoke with the confidence born of growing up with money and seeing its tiresomely predictable effect on people.

"The thing is…" He let his voice trail off as he put both hands on the side of the pool and smoothly lifted himself from the water, the powerful muscles in his back and shoulders flexing and bulging and sliding over each other in a way that made her mouth go dry and her heart thump in her breast.

He straightened, taking the single step that brought him to her side. His wet bathing trunks molded steely thighs, defining well-remembered muscle. Little drops of water caught in his eyelashes, his beard stubble, clung to his wide shoulders. The water caught in the curls springing from his chest succumbed to gravity's pull and began a steady trickle downward to his navel and below.

She had to force herself not to let her gaze follow the droplets' path. Instead, she repeated, "The thing is...?"

"The thing is," he said again, "you don't have a room to return to anymore."

"I don't—*what?* What do you mean?"

Rafe crossed his arms. Part of her instinctively recognized the defensive posture and her own body tensed in response.

"I checked you out of the hotel," he said.

Surely he couldn't have said what she thought he'd said. She stared at him. "I beg your pardon?"

"Your bags are in the front hallway."

"Are you crazy?" She spun around and stalked back into the house, needing visual confirmation of his claim. Sure enough, the two big bags and smaller grip she'd brought from Alexandra's were sitting in his foyer.

Furious, she stalked back to where he dripped water on the kitchen floor. "What do you think you're doing?" By the slimmest of margins she caught hold of her temper and reined it in.

"Keeping you here for a while," he said bluntly.

"Keeping me...for what purpose?"

"Because," he said, and though his tone sounded reasonable and courteous, she got the impression he was gritting his teeth. "You can't waltz into my life again, announce that you're carrying my child and just leave."

"I made no such announcement," she muttered.

"What did you say?" He took her by the arms and turned her to face him, and she was overwhelmed by the power of his physical presence.

"You can't keep me here against my will." She tried to ignore the tanned flesh of the naked chest only inches in front of her. Turning to the side, she twisted in an attempt to slide from his grip. But Rafe didn't let go. Instead, he pulled her the few inches remaining between their bodies until she was held firmly against him.

Elizabeth gasped as the water droplets clinging to his body and the soaking fabric of his swim trunks quickly penetrated her thin clothing. She closed her eyes, hoping he hadn't seen in her eyes the way this sham of an embrace affected her senses.

Leaning away from him, she attempted to step back, but Rafe didn't release her. Well, she wasn't going to dignify his behavior by struggling. She'd just stand here until he let her go.

But her grand plan backfired. With her eyes closed, her world was defined by her other senses. He smelled of the fresh, clean scent of the water in which he'd been swimming, and his naked flesh was cool where their arms touched. Against her body, his much larger frame felt solid and hard, and, unlike the cool skin of his arms, an intense heat radiated from him. She felt dwarfed by him, strands of her hair clinging to his tanned bare shoulders.

His breath stirred the hair near her ear, and as they stood there locked in silent confrontation, she felt his breathing change, become faster as his chest rose and fell.

"Elizabeth." He put one hand to her face and cupped her cheek, and she opened her eyes again. His face was only inches from hers, his blue eyes so compelling that she couldn't look away. His thumb caressed the line of her jaw and then he slipped it beneath her chin and exerted a light pressure, tilting her face up to his.

His features became a blur as his face moved closer, and then his lips closed over hers.

She'd kissed him before, so she really shouldn't be so

overwhelmed. His mouth was gentle but firm and insistent, warm and mobile as he explored her. His tongue traced the shape of her upper lip, then flicked along the closed line of her mouth before firmly delving between her lips, forcing them to part for him.

When her head fell back, he cradled it against his shoulder, keeping his mouth angled over hers while he plumbed the depths of her mouth. His free hand smoothed up her body from her hip to her shoulder, then firmly back down again to press her against him. She could feel him growing aroused through the thin, wet fabric between them and her body, recognizing him as surely as it had from the first, relaxed into his embrace.

Her hands had been clutching his muscled arms, prepared to push him away, but as warm pulses of fevered arousal swept through her, she slowly stroked her palms up over his shoulders, feathering delicate fingers up the back of his neck.

He shuddered. Then he tore his mouth from hers and pressed her face against his shoulder. He was panting and she hoped he wouldn't notice that she was, too.

"So you'll stay." It wasn't a question.

The self-satisfied tone in his voice had the effect of a thousand gallons of water being sprayed on a bonfire. She stiffened in his arms and, with one of the hands still around his neck, she plunged her fingers into his thick, black hair and tugged. Hard.

"Hey!" He released her immediately. "What was that for?"

"For assuming you can use sex to get me to do whatever you want."

"It worked once, didn't it?" His eyes were dark and furious.

"Now wasn't *that* the height of chivalry speaking." She knew her fair complexion was slowly becoming the vivid orange of an Arizona sunset and the knowledge only made her angrier.

"I never claimed to be a white knight," Rafe said. He thrust his own fingers through his hair and clenched his hand into a fist, his frustration evident. Then he heaved a great sigh. "I'm sorry. I don't want to get into a shouting match with you."

"Then I'll leave and you won't."

He ignored the deliberately provocative statement. "Can we start this conversation from the beginning again?"

She shrugged. Part of her wanted to get as far away from him as fast as she could. But another part, a treacherous, yearning hopefulness that she seriously despised, kept raising its own little chorus in her head, reminding her of the ecstasy she'd known in his arms and the dreams she'd woven during the long weeks since she'd seen him last. "I suppose we might."

"You're planning on keeping the baby, correct?"

She nodded. "That's correct. But I don't expect anything from you. I merely felt an obligation to inform you that you had fathered a child."

"You mean your *sister* felt that obligation," he reminded her. She bristled immediately and he held up a placatory hand. "I'm sorry. The point is, I would like you to stay in Arizona for a while as a guest in my home."

She couldn't keep the suspicion from her voice. "Why?"

He took a deep breath. "We—you and I—are going to be parents. We barely know each other. For the baby's sake, we need to learn more about each other and discuss the rearing of the child."

"This baby is mine!" Elizabeth put a protective hand over her stomach. "You wouldn't even know about it if you hadn't noticed for yourself, and you certainly weren't thrilled when you did. I told you, I don't want or need anything from you." On the verge of tears, she halted, unwilling to relive the hurt and shock she'd felt after their meeting in the restaurant, when she'd realized how little the moments in the garden house had meant to him.

"You're being unreasonable," he said. "You just walked into my life again two days ago and I learned you're carrying my child. It was a shock, and I'm sorry if I reacted badly. Elizabeth…" His voice softened, and those devastatingly direct blue eyes caught and held her gaze. "I'd like to get to know you better."

She hesitated. Staying here was a very bad idea, when all the man had to do was walk into the room, and her body began to yearn for his touch. But he was probably right. They did have some things to talk about. If she could just remember that his caresses meant nothing, that he had only kissed her in an effort to get her to weaken and agree to stay, she could handle a few days of this.

The problem was that she couldn't even remember her own name when he touched her, much less any principles.

Still, she owed this to her child. If her baby's father wanted to be involved in its life, then she was just going to have to learn to deal with Rafe Thorton. Only for the baby's sake, she reminded herself as she felt her insides automatically loosen and warm beneath the smoldering intensity of his gaze. He was only interested in her because she carried his child.

Slowly, she nodded her head. "All right. I'll stay for a few days. But you have to promise me one thing."

"Anything," he said, clearly pleased with his persuasive technique.

"No more kissing," she said.

His big body had relaxed when she'd agreed to stay. But now his muscles tensed, and his dark brows snapped together in clear displeasure. "Why?"

"Promise me." She ignored his question.

"We're attracted to each other. Don't you think it's natural for us to want to…kiss?"

The devil. She knew exactly what he was doing. His
purposeful hesitation had brought all manner of memories
rushing to the surface of her mind, distracting her from the
conversation as she remembered the hot, wild ecstasy she'd
known in his arms. Firmly, she said, "I'm not interested in
casual sex. Promise me you won't start that kissing again
or I'm getting the first plane out of here."

"All right," he said, and there was a grim set to his
mouth. But as she watched, his lips curled into a lazy grin
that curled her toes inside her shoes. "There was nothing
'casual' about the night we were together and you know it.
Pretending you don't want me and I don't want you isn't
going to work."

"It will have to," she insisted, though her stomach did
a wild flip-flop at the look in his eyes, "or I won't stay."

It was probably just as well that he hadn't told her she'd
be staying longer than a few days, Rafe reflected the next
afternoon as he pulled into his driveway. He had no intention of letting her go back to Wynborough. His child was
going to be a citizen of the United States of America.

He strode into the house, wondering what she'd done
with herself all day. They'd agreed that she would rest and
he would work as usual. He'd spent his time at the office
getting things in order so that he could take a few days off.

"Hello." Elizabeth stood framed in the doorway to the
kitchen.

He told himself the relief and satisfaction that rushed
through him were merely a response to his concern that she
might have packed and left while he was out, though she'd
promised him she wouldn't. "Hello," he said. "How are
you feeling?"

To his surprise, she laughed. The sound of her husky,

feminine chuckle touched chords of sexual awareness inside him, but he firmly shoved those impulses away.

"I feel fine," she said. "I'm pregnant, not ill, you
know."

He smiled in return. "I know. It's just instinct, I suppose,
to feel protective toward a woman carrying a child. Especially to a mere man who can't even imagine what it must
be like."

*Especially when that woman looks like a green-eyed an-
gel, and she's carrying your child.*

He started forward. "What did you do today? I felt
badly, leaving you to your own devices, but I wanted to
get my staff in order so that I could take a few days off."

"You're not working?" She sounded startled and a little
dismayed.

"Not for the next few days," he said easily, though he
hadn't missed her reaction. "We can't get to know each
other if we don't spend time together, right?"

"I suppose you're right." She sounded less than gracious.

"Did you lounge around all day? Looks like you spent
a little time in the sun."

Instinctively, she touched the tip of her nose with a fin-
gertip, obviously making an effort to smile and match his
friendly tone. "Is my complexion giving me away? I swam
this morning, and I swear I sat by the pool for less than
thirty minutes slathered in sunscreen, but these freckles
can't be banished."

"I didn't notice the freckles. You simply have a little
extra glow."

"Oh." She appeared to be at a loss for words. "I
watched a chef on your telly this afternoon," she offered
in what he recognized as a bid for a safer subject. "He
made the most scrumptious-looking chicken dish. My
mouth was watering by the time he finished. I wrote down

the recipe, but I'm not really sure why—I've never cooked in my life. It looked like fun.''

Rafe chuckled. ''Most women don't consider cooking fun. They're so busy rushing around with careers and family commitments that cooking is just one more thing on the list to get finished. Where's your recipe?''

She turned and gestured behind her. ''On your kitchen counter.''

''Would you like me to teach you how to make it?''

She stared at him. ''You can cook?''

''I have become a thoroughly modern American male,'' he announced in an overly grand tone. ''I can cook, I can clean, I can provide. And all this with one hand tied behind my back, of course.''

''I'd like to learn to cook,'' she said in a somewhat hesitant tone. Then she smiled, and her eyes grew soft. ''My family will be so surprised when I get home.''

And in that moment, he promised himself that by the time she got home, she was going to think of him and smile like that, with that faraway look of familiar intimacy that made onlookers feel they'd been left outside the magic circle. But he didn't tell her any of that. ''Then I'll teach you,'' was all he said.

Over the next few days, he worked hard to make Elizabeth feel at ease. He gave her the big guest suite at the far end of the hallway from his room, and he let her have private time by the pool. He helped her learn her way around his kitchen and took her shopping for a few clothes and things to extend her stay.

She wouldn't let him hang around while she browsed the women's clothing section, which he thought was amusing. And she guarded her packages fiercely when he tried to find out what she'd bought.

"Just odds and ends," she said. They were seated in a little ice-cream café with her bags beneath the table.

"What kind of odds and ends?"

"*Ladies'* odds and ends," she said repressively.

He had to laugh. "I've seen ladies in their odds and ends before, you know. Out of them, too, come to think of it—" He stopped at the look on her face. "Magazines," he said hastily. "Men's magazines."

"Right." She made a little pout. "Here I am, buying stretchy knickers and getting fatter by the day, and you're talking about seeing women in the altogether. Thin women, no doubt."

So that was why she'd been so coy about her purchases. She was shy about buying maternity clothes. And it suddenly struck him that he was being less than a gentleman when she was probably feeling insecure enough about her body. "Elizabeth," he said. "There hasn't been a serious woman in my life in…well, ever." He leaned across the table. "And you don't have to buy *any* knickers for my benefit. I like you just fine without them."

Her face was a study in consternation. "Sh-h-h! This is hardly the place to talk about my lingerie!"

He couldn't agree more. The thought of Elizabeth as he'd seen her the night they made love, clothed only in moonlight and shadow, had its usual effect on his body. Why, he wondered, could one special woman make every one of your senses sit up and take notice while the rest… Since he'd met Elizabeth, he couldn't even remember another woman's face.

Still, he was glad he'd brought up the topic. Or pursued it. Whatever. She might insist on no kissing, but he planned to make sure she didn't forget what it had been like between them that night.

Because he fully intended to repeat it. Soon.

Her eyes were alive with wary sexual recognition and he

smiled at her, a predator's smile, lazy and content because he knew that eventually he'd get what he wanted. "Okay, we'll change the subject. What would you like to do tomorrow?"

"Cook breakfast," she said eagerly.

He stared at her for a second, then threw back his head and laughed. "Okay, we'll cook breakfast. Shall I teach you how to make French toast?"

As she nodded, it occurred to him that she was changing, absorbing American ways and independence and enjoying herself in the process.

She was never going to fit comfortably into her sheltered royal life-style again. He'd have her thoroughly Americanized soon.

The thought was more satisfying than it should have been.

A few days later, in yet another restaurant, where they'd gone at Elizabeth's request for a taste of authentic Mexican cuisine, she had the nerve to laugh at him when he suggested some of the spicier fare might not be good for the baby.

"The baby won't suffer, but I might." She smiled as she liberally splashed a hot sauce over her dish.

"Tell me about your childhood," he said, taking the bottle and setting it beyond her reach. "Not the official bio—I know that. What were you and your sisters like as children?"

A soft smile touched her lips and he wondered if she knew what her smile did to his nervous system.

"As children...well, I suppose it depends on which of us you're discussing," she said. "Alexandra is the eldest and she was a very responsible little person who took her duties much too seriously. I think she felt she had to be especially good at doing 'the royal thing' since Mummy and Daddy had lost their only son.'' The laughter in her eyes dimmed and he could see shadows of sadness. ''My parents were very loving, but there was always an awareness, if you can call it that, that our family wasn't complete. It's rather silly sounding, but true. James, my brother, was kidnapped before any of us was even born, so it wasn't as if we'd known him and missed him. It's hard to explain.''

''He was a part of your family,'' Rafe said quietly. ''I remember the kidnapping. I was about five then, I think. The whole world mourned. I remember my mother sitting in front of the television crying.''

There was a moment of silence between them. Elizabeth looked as if she was about to say something more on the topic, but then her lips firmed into a line as if she was pressing back the words.

To get her mind off the sober twist in the conversation, he said, ''Tell me about your other two sisters.''

Elizabeth's introspection vanished in the blink of an eye and she smiled that fond, intimate smile that reminded him that back in Wynborough she had a life waiting for her that didn't include him. ''Katherine is two years younger than I am. She's the quiet one most of the time.'' She grinned. ''Unless you make her mad. She was the one who put the brakes on some of our crazier stunts.''

''So you were the wild one?''

''Not quite. Serena's the baby. We all treated her like a little princess—literally—when she was small and we spoiled her terribly. If she wasn't such a sweet person, she'd be a terrible brat. Serena could twist anyone around her finger. She came up with some of the most outrageous ideas.'' She paused. ''Or shall I say that Serena came up with the ideas that got us in the most hot water?''

''I can't imagine it was too bad. All the press I ever saw portrayed you as well-behaved young ladies.''

''Oh, we were,'' she assured him. ''For the most part.''

"And the other part?"

Her eyes twinkled with mirth, and her lips parted in laughter. When she began to speak again, the little dimple in her chin deepened, and he had to resist a sudden, insane urge to reach over the table and lay his finger right in the center of that small depression.

"When I was about twelve, Serena had this great idea involving buckets of syrup and bags of feathers suspended over a doorway. Katherine tried to talk us out of it, but then she decided it might be fun and she quit whining. We did it in the stable where we could hide in the hayloft and watch. We figured we might get one of the stable lads, maybe the trainer if we were lucky."

"And did you?"

She shook her head, miming sorrow. "Unfortunately for us, my father had gone riding that day."

"You poured syrup over the *king?*" He was still steeped in his royal roots enough to be truly horrified. And he could only imagine his own father's wrath over such a stunt.

"And feathers," she added. "For what it's worth, it works magnificently."

"I just bet." He could feel the laughter bubbling up, and he let it go. When she joined in, he howled even more, mentally envisioning the reigning monarch of Wynborough covered in sticky feathers. Finally, his amusement died away to an occasional chuckle. "Remind me never to get on your sister Serena's bad side," he said.

And just that quickly the atmosphere changed. Her face sobered instantly, and she picked up her taco again. "I doubt there will ever be any occasion for you to meet," she said.

Her attitude got under his skin and before he could restrain himself, he leaned across the tiny table until he was right in her face. "As the father of your child, I'm going to be meeting *all* of your family eventually."

"Why should you?" He could tell he'd shaken her, but still she didn't back down. "It's not as if we were getting married. We barely know each other."

Her tone irritated him thoroughly, and her words annoyed him even more. "In case you haven't figured it out yet, we're going to get to know each other a whole lot better."

Four

"**F**ine. You want us to get to know each other, now it's your turn." Elizabeth gestured at him with her taco. He could tell he'd unsettled her when he'd spoken in that tone of voice that told her he meant every word he said, but she clearly didn't intend to let him think she was just going to *listen*. God forbid she should make it easy.

"My turn to what?" he asked.

"Tell me about your childhood."

"I only lived at home for five years before I got shipped off to boarding school," he said dismissively. "There's not much to tell."

Elizabeth set down her food and her green eyes began to flash. "I know evasion when I hear it. This getting-to-know-you bit was your idea to start with, so don't try to wriggle out of your half of the deal."

He shrugged. "There really isn't anything exciting to tell. I was sent to boarding school, went to Eton over in the U.K. from there and eventually to Oxford. That was when I decided to come to the States for further study at Harvard University.''

''You have a brother. I know him.'' Elizabeth was prompting him as if he were slightly slow and he sighed, having learned enough about her by now to know she wouldn't give up—or shut up—until he had satisfied her curiosity.

''Roland. I was nine when he was born. You probably know him better than I ever will. Each of us was raised virtually as an only child.''

Elizabeth raised her eyebrows. ''I can't imagine not being close to my family. You must have missed them terribly when you went away to school.''

''No.'' When she turned startled green eyes on him, he realized his answer had been too immediate, too final. ''My father and I are like oil and water,'' he said, shrugging to indicate how little it mattered. ''It was a relief to everyone, I'm sure, when I was at school. When I came home on holiday, we only seemed to get on each other's nerves.'' An understatement of the greatest proportion. But there was no reason for her to know the rest. He'd forgotten half of it himself.

She was looking at him speculatively, and he could see that she wasn't done with the topic. So it was a surprise when she spoke again.

''So what shall we do this afternoon?''

''That depends on you,'' he said. ''Are you tired? If you'd like to nap, we can go home.'' The sound of the phrase struck him forcefully. What would it be like if Elizabeth lived with him? If they really could go home together?

She wouldn't be napping alone.

The basic truth annoyed him. He wondered how many

men thought a pregnant woman was the sexiest thing they'd ever seen.

It was only that his body remembered Elizabeth's, he assured himself. It was normal to wonder if that first time had become better in retrospect than it had really been. Just because he couldn't ever remember better sex in his life was no big deal.

Then the significance of the earlier thought drowned out all others. *If Elizabeth lived with him...!* Where had that come from? True, he fully intended to marry one day, which would certainly entail sharing his home with a wife. But why was it that he could so easily picture his pregnant princess in the role?

Could there be a woman anywhere on the globe less suited to his life-style than a blueblood who'd known luxury every waking moment of her life?

The incongruity of it would be laughable if it wasn't so damned irritating. He'd spent the better part of his adult life running from his aristocratic status and here he was, about to become a father to a child who would have even more ties to royalty.

He and Elizabeth might not agree on many things, but they'd always be stuck with each other now, all because of his irresponsible behavior. For the rest of his life, he'd have royal ties that could never be broken. That much he was sure of. No child of his would be raised in the rigid, duty-demanding manner that he had been. He intended to be a warm, loving father in every way.

"I'm not tired," she said, interrupting his racing thoughts. "For the first three months all I wanted to do was sleep, but now I feel great most of the time."

The first three months.

Before he could squash the curiosity that welled, he asked, "How long was it before you realized our night together had lasting consequences?"

She slanted him an enigmatic look even though he could see the pretty pink blush deepening in her cheeks again. "You mean other than losing my virginity? *That* I realized right away."

"That wasn't what I meant and you know it." He pushed his plate aside, no longer hungry. He'd been a cad and he knew it; she didn't have to keep reminding him of how careless and thoughtless his actions had been. "When did you first suspect you were pregnant?"

She finished the last bite of her taco and set her plate aside as well, then took her sweet time dabbing at her mouth with her napkin and studiously wiping her fingers before laying it aside. She didn't look at him. Instead, her eyes were unfocused as she looked into the past. "I was worried about it right away. So I took a pregnancy test as soon as it was recommended. It confirmed my fears."

"What did you do then?" His conscience jabbed even more sharply.

Unexpectedly, she smiled. "After the first day or so of panic, I realized I was happy about it. I'm looking forward to being a mother."

"Even without a husband?"

Her smiled dimmed slightly. "Even without a husband. Though that's going to make it difficult when I tell my parents."

"Don't you think you've waited a bit long?"

Her smile grew brittle around the edges. "It's *my* baby. When and how I choose to share the news with my parents isn't your concern."

Want to bet? His jaw ached from grinding his teeth to keep from informing her that it damned well was his concern. But he knew that would be the worst thing he could say to her. A glimmer of an idea teased at the edges of his mind. If her parents didn't know yet, he might be able to use that as leverage to get her to stay. Satisfied with his own cleverness, he let it pass. "So you aren't tired. Is there anything special you'd like to do?"

She tilted her head to one side. "What I'd really enjoy is a hot air balloon ride. I read somewhere that you can take a one-hour ride over the Sonoran Desert that includes a champagne brunch—"

"No way."

"I beg your pardon?" It was her snootiest royal tone. He decided not to tell her how much it turned him on. If he did, she'd probably never use it again, just to be perverse.

"You're not going up in a hot air balloon," he said instead.

"And you would be the one making that decision?" she asked in a too-gentle tone.

"I would," he confirmed. "You're five months pregnant. They probably wouldn't take you anyway. Besides, you can't drink champagne until after the baby's born."

When she suddenly shoved her chair back from the table and stood, he was caught off-guard. "I *don't* take orders from you," she said through her teeth, both hands flat on the table. "What I do with my body and my baby is my affair and no one else's." And she spun on her heel and began to stomp out of the restaurant.

Rafe jumped to his feet. He fished money from his clip and tossed more than enough on the table to cover their meal, then surged through the tables after her.

"Go get her, buddy!" shouted some delighted onlooker from behind him.

She hadn't reached the door when he caught up to her. He didn't give her a chance to register his presence when he took her elbow and half-turned her, then swung her into his arms and began to stalk out of the eatery. Scattered clapping and scandalized laughter followed them as he carried her into the blinding midday sun. His damn sunglasses were in his shirt pocket and he couldn't get to them without setting her down, which steamed him even more.

Elizabeth was squirming and struggling. "You Neanderthal! I hated this the last time you did it! Put me down immediately."

"Not until you promise me you won't do anything stupid," he said, grimly quelling her struggles.

"Stupider than sleeping with you, you mean? That would be hard to top. That was definitely the stupidest move I ever made," she said in a bitter tone.

He set her down beside the car then, crowding her with his body to keep her from getting away as he fished his keys from his pocket. "You weren't complaining at the time," he reminded her. He yanked open her door. "Get in."

"No. I don't wish to ride with you." She folded her arms.

Rafe leaned very, very close. "Either you get in the car or you're going to be the first pregnant woman ever to get turned over a man's knee in this parking lot."

She glared at him.

He stared at her with stony implacability.

Then she turned her back on him, sliding gracefully into the passenger seat. As he slammed the door and came around to the driver's side, she said, "You don't know that."

"What?" he barked, still furious and wondering what in the hell she was talking about.

"You don't know if I would have been the first pregnant woman to get her bum smacked in this lot."

She *wasn't* going to make him smile. But he could feel the anger draining away. "No, but I'd be willing to bet on it," he said grudgingly.

There was a silence that lasted until he had pulled out

of the lot and wound his way through the streets back to the freeway.

"Look," he said, wondering why in hell he felt compelled to explain himself. "I wasn't trying to give you orders. I was concerned for your safety."

"You mean you were concerned for the baby's safety," she said quietly.

"No, that is *not* what I meant," he said. "Could you possibly quit taking exception to every word I utter? The baby is still an unknown, an abstract to me, although I know that to you it's a very real presence by now. Yes, it's important, but not as important as your safety."

"Because of your promise to my father."

He wanted to strangle her. "Fine. If that's what you want to believe, then yes. I promised your father you'd be safe with me." Another reason, far more accurate, tried to rear its head, but he ignored it. He was *not* going to let her get under his skin.

Another silence. She was looking out her window, and she had to have realized he wasn't headed for home by now, but she wouldn't look at him or speak to him.

Finally he said, "Would you like to drive out to Saguaro Lake? We could rent a canoe and paddle around the lake. It's not hot air ballooning, but it's pretty and peaceful."

She turned to face him then, and he could read surprise in her face. "That sounds lovely."

"But I'm not bringing champagne," he warned.

She gave him a small, smug smile. "I can't stand the stuff. Never drink it."

He shook his head. "You were just trying to rattle my cage back there, weren't you?"

"Maybe a little," she conceded. "May I apologize?"

"Only if you'll accept one from a Neanderthal."

She chuckled. "Done."

"Tomorrow, in Scottsdale," he said, "they celebrate the Parada del Sol. I'll take you to it if you like."

"Sol...sun? A festival for the sun?"

"Yes. The sun and wonderful climate have been good to Phoenix. The locals figure a little appreciation is in order. Did you know it's the ninth largest city in the nation?"

Her eyes widened. "But it seems so...I don't know. When I think of big cities, I think of London, New York. Everything here is golden and open, not gray and overpowering."

He nodded, relieved that she'd accepted his olive branch. "There's plenty of space here to spread out. And the climate can't be beat."

She laughed. "Growing up where we did, I suppose this is very appealing to you."

He nodded, smiling. "No rain. None of any consequence anyhow. When I wake up in the morning and walk outside, I can be assured that the sun will be there to greet me."

"You really like it here."

He took his attention from the road to glance at her. "Yes, I really do. When I first came out here, my plan was to get as far away from my father as possible. Another state farther and I'd have been in the Pacific Ocean, so I figured this was far enough."

"And has it been?" Her voice was quiet.

He sobered, reflecting. "No, not really. It's amazing that the man can still try to manipulate me from across a damned ocean."

"But you don't allow it."

"No." He shook his head firmly, positively. "There's nothing he can do or say that will affect me anymore."

"You don't say much about your mother," she observed. "The Grand Duchess has been a guest at my mother's ladies' bridge game on many occasions. She's a wicked player as I recall, having been suckered into playing against her more than once."

Rafe nodded. "She always enjoyed those afternoons. Having no daughters of her own, I imagine she missed female companionship."

He spent the rest of the drive to the lake pointing out native plants and animals to her. She was amazed to see the numbers of creatures that existed in the barren, dry world of the desert where there was no water for months on end. Phoenix itself, he explained, had grown from a village into a truly disreputable outlaw town by the end of the 1800s and it wasn't until a couple of public hangings were conducted that the frontier town began to assume a semblance of civilization. After the Roosevelt Dam was created, significant power for industrial enterprise was generated, and the city began to grow and spread.

"How do you know so much about American history?" she asked him at one point.

Rafe shrugged. "Architecture is a field of study that often demands some knowledge of what came before in order to create a structure that reflects an area's heritage. I've always enjoyed learning about new places, and once I'd decided to settle here I was doubly interested in learning about its past." He chuckled. "If you were to ask me other questions about American history, you'd find me woefully lacking in knowledge."

She snorted. "Somehow I doubt that."

When they arrived at the lake, Rafe wasted no time in renting a canoe and taking her out on the water. But first he made her cover herself in sunscreen while he went into the little store and bought her a wide-brimmed hat. That creamy complexion wouldn't stand up to the strong Arizona sun, and he would never forgive himself if he let her get sunburned.

She was skittish at first when the little craft rocked slightly from side to side as he paddled.

"This is certainly different from a rowboat," she said.

"I enjoy canoeing," he said. "A canoe is easy to maneuver in the water."

She trailed her fingers over the side, letting gentle wavelets lap at her hand as she relaxed into the rocking rhythm of the little craft. "It's so peaceful out here."

He watched her from his seat at the back of the canoe as she swept a hand beneath her shoulder-length tumble of sun- touched curls, pulling them into a heavy twist atop her head, which she then anchored with a firm tug of the hat's brim. The nape of her neck was white and vulnerable and he wondered if the skin there would feel as silky under his lips as the rest of her had the night they'd made love.

Mentally, he shook his head. How could she imagine that he was never going to kiss her again?

She dipped her hand into the water again. Such a small, dainty hand. She was a small, dainty woman, more than a foot shorter than he was. She wasn't too tiny, though. As he remembered how perfectly she'd fit around him, his breath grew short and he had to look away from the languid motion of that pretty, pale hand with its long, slender fingers. Those fingers had touched him intimately, shyly at first, then more boldly when he'd shown her how much he liked it—

Damn! If he'd set out specifically to drive himself insane, he couldn't have done a much better job.

"Put sunscreen on the back of your neck," he said.

She half turned and looked over her shoulder at him, a wry smile curving her lips. "You're keen on giving orders, aren't you?"

He shrugged. "I guess it's a habit. Sorry."

She nodded her acceptance of his apology. "My father's much the same, you know. The dear man doesn't realize

how autocratic he sounds at times." Her light laugh floated
out over the lake. "Unfortunately for him, we know there's
no bite behind his bark."

"I bet you and your sisters have him wrapped around
your little fingers."

She laughed again. "I won't deny that he finds it hard
to say no to us."

A new thought struck him. "Do you know yet…?" He
motioned in the general direction of her abdomen. "Is this
baby a boy or a girl?"

"I don't know. And I don't plan to ask, either." She
lifted a hand and tucked a trailing wisp of auburn curl back
beneath the hat. "Personally, I'm hoping for a little girl I
can dress in ruffles and lace."

He grimaced. "As long as it's healthy, I'll take whatever
we get and be delighted with it."

"I'll agree with that," she said.

"Although it might be nice to have some warning if it's
a daughter. What I know about little girls would leave
plenty of room on the head of a pin."

She didn't answer him, but he saw her cheek dimple in
a smile before she turned her head to face out over the
water again.

An hour later, he tied up the canoe, and they headed back
into Phoenix.

"I have to stop at the grocery store," he told her as they
neared the suburb where his home was located.

"May I come along?" She seemed instantly intrigued.

Her enthusiasm reminded him of his first years in the
States when he'd done so many things for the first time.
Things that most people took for granted, a part of everyday
life that had to be done. They had no idea how exhilarating
true freedom was. He knew she must be experiencing the
same feelings. She had known restrictions that most people

never even dreamed of. Restrictions he understood better than she might imagine.

A cage with velvet bars was still a cage.

"Of course you can come along," he said. "Have you ever been in one before?"

She shook her head. "No. There was no reason to at home. What kinds of things do we need to buy?"

We. Such a simple little word. How could it change so many things? He wondered if she even realized she'd used it as he answered.

"Breakfast foods. Lunch meats. The ingredients for the chicken dish you wrote down. Fruits and vegetables. Cleaning supplies—"

"Stop!" She was smiling. "I get the picture."

She wanted to push the cart at first, simply for the novelty of it all. Then she wanted him to explain the price comparisons and the meaning of the dietary listings on the back. What would normally have taken him less than thirty minutes became a two-hour tour of the grocery market.

When they finally had finished and he'd loaded the last of the groceries into the back of the truck, he swung into the driver's seat and snagged his seat belt. Automatically he glanced over at her. Then he frowned.

"You shouldn't be wearing your seat belt like that."

"Like what?" She glanced down at herself, then back at him, clearly mystified.

He leaned across the seat, snagging his fingers in the lap belt she'd pulled over her belly and tugging it down beneath the bulge of his child to rest across her hips. "I've seen warnings about this. Pregnant women should be careful not to position the belt too high. If there was an accident, the belt could harm the baby."

"Oh." Her voice was slightly breathless.

With sudden, shocking clarity Rafe became aware of how close they were. His breath stirred the copper curls about her ears, and the arm he'd draped over the back of the seat was very nearly an embrace around her shoulders. His fingers, where he'd hooked them beneath the seat belt, rested against soft feminine flesh. He'd pulled the belt down as he'd spoken so that now his hand was practically nested in the warm pocket where her thighs met her body. His fingers were held firmly against her by the constriction of the seat belt.

She froze.

So did he, largely because his entire being was caught up in the battle raging inside him: the gentlemanly part of him that knew he should move away versus the purely male impulse to extend his fingers down and brush over the sensitive flesh he knew lay just beyond his loosely curled hand. It was a toss-up as to which one would win.

And then she took the choice from him.

Slowly, her hand came up and snared his wrist, her small fingers braceleting his hard male sinew, not even meeting around the thickness of his arm. It was clearly a signal to halt. She didn't tug his hand away, though, only turned her head and tilted up her chin to look at him with wide, questioning eyes.

The desire to lower his head and take her lips was nearly too much for him to resist. But he'd promised her. No kissing.

Damn that promise!

Holding her gaze, he slowly, slowly slid his hand from beneath the seat belt fabric, caressing her flesh with the back of his hand as he withdrew, moving higher to let his knuckles lightly skim over a nipple, which elicited a swiftly indrawn breath from her. Not a moan, but not far from it, either.

Without a word, he slid his arm from behind her and turned his attention to starting the truck and pulling out of the lot. She didn't speak the whole way home and neither

did he, though he was hard-put to contain the elation dancing around inside him.

She'd said no more kissing, but she hadn't said a word
about touching—and she hadn't objected just now to what
had been a whole lot more intimate than some kisses he'd
experienced.

What in the world had she been thinking? Or not thinking?

Washing up before joining Rafe to work on the recipe
she'd copied from the television, Elizabeth held a cool face-
cloth to cheeks that burned at the very memory of his hard,
hot fingers pressed firmly against her body. If she'd been
naked, those fingers would have been nestled in the curling
hair that protected her most private flesh.

*If you'd been naked he would have been doing a whole
lot more with those fingers.*

She groaned and flopped the sopping cloth over her entire face. She was an imbecile. An imbecile ruled by her
hormones. And she didn't mean pregnancy hormones, either. She couldn't even be in the same room with the man
without her heart beating faster and her mind conjuring up
vivid pictures of him embracing her, his body hard and
demanding against her soft, yielding one.

Staying here in his home was the dumbest thing she'd
done since...well, since she'd slept with a perfect stranger
and gotten herself pregnant.

But in her heart she didn't consider Rafe a stranger. Not
then and not now. They might not know each other well,
but her body and her heart knew all they needed to know
to assure her that he was the only man she'd ever want.

She snatched the cloth off her face and stared at herself
in the bathroom mirror.

Oh, no. No, no, no, no, *no!* She was *not* in love with
Rafe Thorton.

He didn't want her, at least not in any way other than the purely physical, and she'd *promised* herself she wasn't going to weave any more foolish romantic fantasies around him.

But oh, it was hard to make her heart listen to her common sense. All her life she'd dreamed of a man who would breach the fortress of security around her and carry her off to a world where she could be just another ordinary person. These easy-flowing hours the past few days had given her more contentment than she'd known in her entire life.

She loved living in a single-story home with only a few bedrooms as opposed to an entire wing of bedroom suites with drafty hallways half a kilometer long. She loved the casual atmosphere in which one simply drove one's car out of the garage and went to the market instead of calling a chauffeur. She loved everything about the life Rafe had created for himself, and that was part of the problem.

She couldn't let his life-style confuse her. She couldn't fall for him simply because he embodied the kind of life she'd always longed for in her most secret heart.

But this experience had been good for her in some ways. She was determined that her child wasn't going to be raised in a hothouse environment. She wasn't blind to the fact that she might always need discreet security, but she was determined to make as normal a life for her baby as she could.

And that didn't include being escorted everywhere she went every minute of the day. So far, Rafe had treated her exactly in the hothouse-flower way that her own parents always had. He might be content with his lifestyle, but he clearly didn't think it was right for her.

Before she'd known who he was, she'd woven the most ridiculous romantic fantasies about her mysterious lover. Now, she could only thank heaven that she'd gotten wise.

Of course she didn't love him.

She repeated that to herself the whole way out to the kitchen where he was waiting for her.

"Ready for another lesson in preparing American cuisine?" Rafe stood at the counter, where he'd assembled what looked like half his kitchen's worth of cooking equipment.

"Ready for another lesson in preparing any kind of cuisine," she said lightly, walking across the room to join him. It was hard to meet his eyes after the thoughts that had just been running around in her brain, so she concentrated on the items before her.

Without thinking about what she was doing, she opened the cabinet doors beneath his sink and withdrew a dishpan, drainer, dish soap and a cleaning cloth. Automatically she began to fill the dishpan with hot water.

"What are you doing?"

She glanced at him. "Getting out the cleaning things so we can get rid of the mess as we make it."

"Since when does a princess think about cleaning up? Don't you have servants for the menial tasks?"

His tone had been merely curious, but it still made her bristle. "You were raised much as I was. You already know the answer to that."

"But I wasn't," he said. "Remember? I lived at school most of my childhood. And, believe me, one learned to clean up at those venerable institutions."

"Kitchen duty for breaking the rules?" She smiled, determined to keep a civil distance between them. After all, he was her host.

"Occasionally." He grimaced. "Bathroom duty was worse."

"Infinitely." Genuine amusement lit her eyes. "Although there's a tremendous satisfaction to be gained from seeing porcelain and steel gleam through your efforts."

"And how would you know that?" He raised his eyebrows skeptically. "I can't imagine you scrubbing toilets in the family castles."

She chuckled. "I can't quite see that myself. But for the past three years, I've volunteered at a children's hospital."

"And they asked you to clean their bathrooms?" He was grinning.

"I did anything that was necessary," she said, her face growing serious. "It would be a terribly bad example for others to see me pick and choose tasks as if I were too important for some."

He didn't want to let her see how impressed he was by her attitude. By all rights, she should be a spoiled, demanding brat, but she wasn't. In fact, she was one of the most conscientious, sensible women he'd met in a long time, he thought, recalling her concern when she thought her parents might be worrying about her.

But all he said was, "Good point. Now, are you ready to make your first jen-yoo-wine American entrée?"

She laughed. "Ready."

It wasn't until later that the fragile truce ended.

They'd put together the casserole she'd chosen, which thankfully had been pretty straightforward. While he'd become a credible cook since he'd been forced to feed himself, Rafe was under no illusions about the limitations of his culinary skills.

As she'd insisted, they cleaned up the dishes as they went so there wouldn't be a huge mess at the end. He liked the idea since he usually had a mini-disaster area in his kitchen after any cooking effort.

As she passed him the final mixing bowl to dry and put away, she folded the dishtowel over its bar. They worked well together, he realized. That would be helpful after they were married, one area in which they could be relatively compatible.

After they were married. A few weeks ago—hell, a few *days* ago—he'd have thought someone who mentioned marriage and Rafe Thorton in the same sentence was insane.

But everything was different now. When had he realized that? So, okay, maybe she wasn't what he'd envisioned when he'd entertained hazy, half-formed thoughts of a wife and family. But she was carrying his child and that made all the difference. *That and the way she goes up in flames every time you touch her.*

It would be best to get things settled between them quickly, he decided. He clattered the bowl into the cabinet and closed the door, then turned and walked to her. She merely looked at him with puzzled, wary eyes when he took her hands.

"Elizabeth. Marry me." It might not have been the most romantic proposal in the world, but it wasn't as if they were in love or anything. This was strictly a necessity in his eyes, to give his child a name.

"No, thank you." She spoke as calmly as if she were declining a second helping at a meal. She slipped her hands free of his and linked them together at her waist.

There was a long, taut silence while his brain processed the fact that she'd refused his offer. *She'd refused him!* Summoning a calm tone that he was proud matched her cool little voice, he said, "No, thank you? Any possibility you'd expand on that?"

She hesitated. "You do me a great honor with your offer," she said formally, politely, not meeting his eyes. "But I have no wish to marry solely to provide a family unit for this child. You and I lead very different lives."

"That we do," he said grimly, annoyed at the way she'd reduced his proposal to a mere matter of convenience, conveniently ignoring the fact that he'd done exactly the same thing a few minutes ago. "And there's no way I'm ever going back overseas, not for you, not for anyone."

"I didn't ask you to!" Her tone wasn't so calm anymore. Pivoting, she flounced to the other side of the counter and stood staring out the window with her back to him.

The unspoken dismissal broke the thin threads by which he'd been holding together his temper. "You'd like that, wouldn't you, if I'd fall into line like a good little subject and—"

She whirled. "If you were a good little subject, you'd be even more objectionable than you are now!"

"Well, you aren't exactly my first choice, either." Her belligerent words had stung. "My plan was to marry a home-grown American girl who doesn't have a drop of blue blood or aspirations to a title when I was good and ready. A *princess* doesn't exactly fill the bill."

"Good!" Her face was flushed, and unless he was mistaken, her eyes held the sheen of tears. "Then you have no problem accepting that you did the honorable thing and proposed and I chose to decline."

"Fine!" He was as mad as she was now. Then he thought about what he'd just said. "Hold it. *Not* fine. My child isn't going to be born a bastard."

Her brows snapped together. "That's a nasty word and I don't appreciate you applying it to our child."

"Why not? Other people will."

One of the tears that had been swimming around in her eyes broke the dam and spilled down her cheek. "They wouldn't dare."

"Of course they would. You know how people love good gossip. Just imagine the fodder an illicit liaison between royals of Wynborough and Thortonburg would provide them—" The look on her face stopped him midsentence.

A moment of silence as pregnant as the woman before him hung in the air between them.

"You weren't going to tell them, were you?" A part of him wondered why it bothered him so much. After all, it would get him out of an inconvenient marriage and ensure that he didn't get sucked back into his father's title-seeking sphere again. But a bigger part of him rejected the idea that his child wouldn't bear his name.

"You weren't even going to tell them," he accused again. "You planned to go home to Wynborough with this baby in your belly and never tell your parents who the father was, didn't you?"

"Why not? It makes sense." Her face was still flushed with anger. "Neither of us wants to marry the other. You weren't planning on becoming a father now. There's no reason to involve yourself in my life."

"No reason?" He was so mad, he had to clench his fists to keep from reaching for her. "You're going to bear my child in a matter of months. *My child.* Not that of some anonymous man who you can dismiss for his rather negligible role in the conception." He stalked around the counter until he was only inches from her, leaning forward to speak right into her startled, defiant face. "This baby is going to be legitimate if I have to tie you up and fly to Las Vegas for a quickie wedding."

Her eyes rounded. "You wouldn't dare."

"Try me," he invited. "And while I'm at it, I'll get on the telephone and call your parents. I'm sure your father would be pleased to know I'd done the right thing by you."

Her face drained of color. "You *can't* tell my parents," she said. She half turned away from him. "This baby can't be—" She stopped abruptly and put a hand out toward the counter, and he saw her sway. "I feel…" He didn't wait for any more. He'd never seen anyone faint, and he wasn't going to start now. Taking a half step that brought him to her side, he drew her into his arms.

She gave a startled squeak that trailed off into a moan, but she didn't fight him, merely laid her head against his chest. After a moment, he led her into the living room and laid her on the couch, then placed a pillow under her feet.

She moaned again, but this time there was an element of relief in the sound. The band of tension squeezing his throat relaxed marginally and he nudged her over gently to make space to perch beside her.

"Can I get you anything?" His voice was deep with concern, and he didn't care if she noticed.

"No, I'll be all right." She groped for his hand. "Just— don't go."

Her small fingers found his and clung, and he was astonished by the force of the emotion that roared through him. His throat grew tight again and he had to clear it roughly before he squeezed her fingers and said, "I'm right here."

Long moments passed. He watched her closely. Her eyes were closed, dark silky lashes lying soft against her cheeks, and gradually a hint of pink crept back to replace her pallor. Her clutch on his hand lessened. Even so, he made no move to release her.

Finally, her eyelashes fluttered and slowly her eyelids rose to reveal deep, mysterious emerald pools that swam with emotions he couldn't name. "I'm sorry," she said quietly.

"Don't be. I'm the one who should be sorry." Disgusted with himself, he looked away from her. "I should be treating you more carefully—"

"I'm not sorry about almost fainting," she said, smiling. "I meant I was sorry to have gotten into a shouting match with you. I'm not usually such a shrew."

"You have nothing to apologize for," he told her firmly.

"You weren't the only one shouting, in case you hadn't noticed."

"I'd noticed," she said in a dry tone. Then her face sobered. "I'm also sorry for treating your feelings and wishes as if they count for nothing. I don't want to deny you your child."

"We can talk about that later," he said, anxious not to let more discord mar the day. She still might not understand that marriage wasn't negotiable; it was a *fact,* but there was nothing to be gained by antagonizing her again right now.

An odd odor assailed his nostrils, almost as if something was burning—

"The casserole!" they shouted in unison as Rafe bolted for the kitchen.

Five

Marrying him was out of the question.

As she applied mascara to her lashes several days later, Elizabeth felt a definite kick just beneath the right side of her rib cage. Laying her hand gently over the swell of her belly, she thought again of the father of the baby growing within her.

Again? That was a bit of a lie, she thought ruefully. Rafe Thorton had been in her thoughts since the night he'd taken her into the garden house and he hadn't left yet.

What was she going to do? He hadn't sounded as if he was kidding when he'd told her she would marry him. Not kidding at all. Even though she knew he didn't love her, knew she was one of the last women on earth he'd ever take as wife of his own free will, he planned to marry her to provide his child with a legitimate heritage.

An admirable intent, certainly. It would be even more admirable if she wasn't the one he was intent on marrying.

Rafe's intense blue eyes materialized in her mental meanderings and she groaned. If only the darned man wasn't so appealing. Irresistible. Adorable... He'd die if he heard *that* description, she thought with a soft chuckle. But the chuckle dried in her throat when she recalled the sharp words they'd exchanged.

Since their last confrontation they'd been as polite as casual acquaintances, avoiding anything the least bit controversial. He'd taken her to the Parada del Sol, they'd watched the beginning of a hot air balloon race and, at dawn the day before he'd driven her into the desert to watch the sun rise. He'd been gracious, friendly...and as remote as a distant moon.

There was no way they could marry. Aside from the attraction that seemed to charge the air between them, they had nothing in common. He'd been independent for more than a decade, had lived in the States long enough to be truly an American now. She was enjoying her experience in the country immeasurably, but she'd never known the kind of freedom these people took for granted.

She loved and respected her family. Though Rafe had said little about his own, she had gotten the distinct impression he wasn't particularly fond of his nearest kin.

She'd been raised with an exceptionally fine liberal arts education that had prepared her for no practical work. Rafe had used his education to carve out an amazingly successful career for himself.

No, marriage was definitely out of the question, regardless of what Rafe had said about Las Vegas.

Las Vegas! Oh, how she'd love to see it. Serena had been married there a short time ago in one of those "have to see it to believe it" chapels, as her sister had put it, laughing gaily. Elizabeth had gotten on the Internet this afternoon and looked up some information on the town that had risen in the middle of the Nevada desert. It certainly looked like a fascinating place and she was determined to visit it one day.

The baby stirred beneath her palm and she rubbed her hand over her belly again, sighing. The next few months couldn't go fast enough. Not only was she aching with the need to hold her child in her arms, she was nearly as excited at the thought of having a waistline again.

It was bad enough that Rafe had to provoke her into acting like a fishwife, but even worse that she felt so fat and unattractive around him. She longed for her former slim figure, the figure she'd had when they'd first met and he hadn't known who she was.

A knock on the door of her suite startled her and she nearly dropped the mascara wand she was still holding.

"Are you ready?"

"Almost. Just give me a moment."

Hastily she finished adding the little makeup she normally wore and picked up her jacket and bag from where she'd laid them on the bed. Opening the door, she stepped into the hallway to face Rafe and her breath caught in her throat.

He was so handsome. In a simple cream shirt and khaki pants, he managed to look better to her than other men did in a tux. He smiled when he saw her, and the deep creases his dimples made flashed in his lean cheeks.

"Ready to go?" he asked her.

"Ready." As he took her elbow and escorted her through the house she added, "Though it might be nice to know where we're headed."

"I told you it's a surprise," he said, grinning smugly. He led her into the garage and held the door of the sleek Mercedes she'd discovered he kept in addition to his serviceable truck. "You'll just have to wait and see."

He drove her northeast through the city to Scottsdale Municipal Airport where he apparently already had arranged a flight. But when they walked onto the airfield, Elizabeth stopped and resisted his hand on her arm urging her forward.

"That's a *small* plane," she said in dismay. And it was. Though she'd often taken puddle-jumpers back and forth between Wynborough and the U.K., this plane looked like a life-sized toy. Two men standing outside the single door waved when they caught sight of Rafe and again he urged her forward.

"It's a twin-engine and it's bigger than some private planes," Rafe said. "If I had a pilot's license, we could have taken a two-seater."

"And how many seats are there in this?" she asked apprehensively.

"Four. That's the pilot and co-pilot waiting for us."

"It takes two men to fly something this small?"

"Not normally, no. This usually is only used for pleasure tours around the city."

"Ah-hah! So we're going somewhere outside Phoenix."

By then they had reached the waiting pilots, and after quick introductions Elizabeth was led up a very small, very steep flight of steps into the tiny cabin.

It was beautifully appointed, far nicer than she'd expected. Served her right for forgetting that while Rafe might act like nothing more than an American businessman, he had a small fortune at his disposal.

As she settled into the comfortable leather seat she asked, "Now do I get to know where we're going?"

"Actually, we have two destinations," Rafe told her. "We'll only be doing a flyover of the first one, though. Just settle back and enjoy."

"Settle back and enjoy," she grumbled. But the anticipation dancing in his eyes seduced her into an equally good humor, and as the little plane rose and circled to the north, she relaxed and enjoyed the receding view of the city and the interesting combination of desert and mountain around it.

"That's Flagstaff," Rafe told her a few minutes later. "And in just a minute, if you look out your window, you'll see the highest point in the state of Arizona, Humphrey's Peak."

"Who was Humphrey?"

He laughed. "I don't have a clue. See, I told you I didn't know everything about this country."

She continued to gaze out her window at the peaks and valleys they passed, and then they flew over a densely wooded forest. "Where are we now?" she asked.

"Just keep watching." Rafe unbuckled his seat belt and came to kneel at her side. "In another minute or two, you should be able to see it."

"See *what?*" She was intensely aware of his big warm body so close, the clean smell of newly showered man and cologne. To distract herself she angled an elbow at his ribs, but he dodged away, chuckling. He was impossible to resist in this mood. And she was so tired of forcing herself to ignore the pull of sensual promise that his intense eyes promised.

"Now look," he said in her ear and she turned her head and peered out her window, resolutely ignoring the shiver that rushed down her spine at the sensation of hot breath bathing her sensitive earlobe.

"Oh! It's—it's incredible. Beautiful. *Huge.*" Below their little plane the Grand Canyon yawned wider and deeper than she'd ever thought possible. She turned to him, overwhelmed. "Oh, Rafe, thank you! I hadn't expected to get to see this during my trip."

His face was only inches away, his broad shoulders and arms bracketing her seat and creating a small haven of intimacy. Before she allowed herself to think too much about it, she leaned forward and brushed a soft kiss over his lips.

Then she quickly turned her head and looked out the window again.

"What happened to the 'no kissing' edict?" he asked in her ear. His voice was deep and seductive, and she took deep breaths until the urge to turn back into his arms subsided enough to control.

She cleared her throat. "I made the rule. I can break it if I like," she said.

He laughed yet again and warm breath played over her ear. Slowly his arms came around her from behind, drawing her back against his chest, surrounding her with heat and scent and the feel of his hard forearms clasped over her belly. Her breasts rested against his arms and her breath began to come faster as desire rushed through her.

To distract herself from her body's messages, she concentrated on the glowing colors of the canyon and the distinct striations in the rock that she knew marked different periods of Earth's geological history dating back millions of years.

The plane banked to the left, turning away from the morning sun and heading west as they followed the shining ribbon that was the mighty Colorado River winding through the canyon. The canyon narrowed, then widened again and finally a huge, gleaming lake appeared beneath them.

"That's Lake Mead," Rafe explained. "It's man-made, a result of the Hoover Dam, which you'll see in a minute."

And then the dam was past, and they were turning due west once again. The flat plain of a desert spread below them and in the distance some sort of city rose out of the desert like a mirage—

"Where are we?" Suspicion tinged her tone.

"Don't recognize Tinseltown? I wish I'd been able to bring you in at night, but we'd have had to miss the canyon then." Casually, Rafe withdrew his arms and straightened, returning to his seat to buckle himself in as if he was completely unaffected by the embrace in which he'd been holding her.

"Las Vegas! We're going to Las Vegas?" She didn't know whether to be apprehensive or excited. It couldn't be a coincidence that he'd brought her here when they'd been dancing around the topic of marriage for days. Could it?

"It's a unique place."

"My sister was married here recently," she informed him. "I'm not sure this is such a good idea."

Rafe shrugged his shoulders. "I thought you'd enjoy spending the day here. But if not, we can just refuel and head back home."

"No, it's not that. I'm sure I would enjoy it. But…" There was no way to say it without sounding paranoid and silly. *I'm afraid you'll make me marry you?* Too ridiculous for words. She was entirely too suspicious for her own good.

As if he'd read her mind, Rafe laid a hand gently over hers. "You'll like it, I promise," he said. "I would never make you do something that you didn't want to do."

And so she found herself in a taxi less than half an hour later, heading through the glaring sunshine to a city that never slept.

He took her to Caesar's first, leading her through the casinos to the huge shopping plaza beyond. They lunched at the Italian restaurant in the center and she marveled at the sky that changed from dawn to dusk, through night and back to day again in less than an hour.

At the Mirage, Rafe had gotten tickets to a special showing of Siegfried and Roy's magic show that included unbelievable special effects as well as their trademark white tigers and other animals. When the show ended, Rafe escorted her to the front desk, where the mention of his name produced quick and efficient service in a private office.

Pocketing the key he had received, Rafe smiled at her

startled expression as he led her to the elevator. "Well, you can't expect to go all day without rest, can you? I got a suite so that you could take a nap if you like."

The concierge attendant led them to their room and didn't blink an eye when Rafe told him they had no luggage. "Very good, sir," was the man's only reaction before he shut the door, leaving the two of them standing in the foyer of the spacious suite.

"I'm impressed," she said lightly, trying to conceal the sudden attack of nerves that assailed her. "Don't they usually reserve these for the folks who drop a significant bundle with their establishment every year?"

"There are ways around that." Rafe prowled the room like the great tigers they'd just seen, opening doors and cabinets. He gestured. "The bedroom's through here. Why don't you lie down for a while?"

She *was* tired, even if she hated to admit it to him. The day had been full of fun and excitement and a lot of walking—more than she was accustomed to, if she was honest. While she hadn't gained a great deal of weight yet, the eight pounds she'd added to her slender frame made a difference and her feet were aching.

"What are you going to do?" she asked. The thought of sleeping in the single bedroom of the suite while Rafe prowled the living area made her feel vulnerable in a not entirely reasonable way. Which was stupid, she reflected, when she slept in his home every night.

Still, their bedroom suites were at opposite ends of the hallway in his house and she didn't even see him after dinner unless she so chose.

"I'll find something to occupy an hour or two," he assured her. "I'll go downstairs and gamble away enough money to make our hosts happy. I'll be back near six, though, because I want to show you the volcano outside the hotel and then watch the pirate ship battle the British down at Treasure Island. You have to see it to believe it. Somewhere in there, we'll get some dinner.''

''That sounds lovely.'' She smiled at him across the room and his gaze seemed to snare her so that she couldn't look away. His eyes were deeply blue and compelling, as if he were willing her toward him. The moment stretched and shimmered between them.

In a deep, rough voice, he said, ''Lovely enough for another kiss?''

Every nerve in her body sprang to life. She wanted to kiss him and she didn't. Stalling, she said, ''Is that the price for today?''

He was already starting across the room. ''No price tag on the day,'' he said. ''This would be purely a bonus for extraordinary service.''

He was directly in front of her now, and she had to tilt her head back to see his face. ''Well,'' she said, ''I guess you should get a bonus. It's been a pretty spectacular day.'' She lowered her gaze to the open neck of the shirt he wore, waiting for him to take the lead.

''But I'm not allowed to kiss you, remember?'' He was breathing faster and his eyes were even more intense than usual, narrowed and brilliant with desire, but there was indulgent humor in his voice.

''I'd forgotten,'' she said. ''In that case...'' Taking a deep breath for courage, she stepped closer and lifted her hands to his shoulders to balance herself, then stood on tiptoe. ''Thank you,'' she whispered and pressed a soft kiss to his smiling lips, momentarily molding her mouth to his firm, warm one.

His hands came up to her wrists, holding her in place, and he made a sound of approval deep in his throat. Then before she could back away, his mouth shifted against hers, hardening in demand. The kiss became his instead of hers and she whimpered at the surge of sensation that tightened her body with a desire she'd been suppressing for days.

Her hands gripped his shoulders and he slid his own down from her wrists, traveling over the curves of her body as he held her mouth with his, demanding a response that she gave without thinking, without hesitation. His thumbs briefly caressed her hipbones, still evident despite the mound of his child in her womb, and then he gripped her soft curves, pulling her against him and shocking her system with the hard warm promise of his big body.

This, she thought hazily, was what she'd remembered from their first meeting, this magnetic pull that erased conscious decision and attracted her to him. Opposite charges creating a bond. The hard probe of his tongue sought out every response from her own; his muscled arms and shoulders blocked out the light as he loomed over her, making her feel small and fragile. Against her belly, taut masculine flesh swelled, and when he lifted her off her feet and his arousal found the hidden pocket of warmth at her thighs, her startled intake of breath matched the groan wrenched from his throat.

This was the man about whom she'd woven her foolish fantasies, the man whose skillful hands and hard body had claimed her, making it impossible for her to forget him. She had to remember...what? Her distracted thoughts whirled in her head under the sensual onslaught, and as desire mounted it became less and less crucial that she recall what her brain was struggling to bring into focus.

His hands stroked restlessly up and down her back; he no longer needed to bind her to him. One big palm slipped around her rib cage to cover a breast. Even through her clothing, his thumb sought out the tender peak, circling her nipple until it stood out in bold relief, the contact sending arrows of arousal straight to the aching flesh between her legs. Restlessly she pressed herself closer. As if he recognized her need, he slipped one hard thigh between hers, pressing upward so that she was firmly lodged against his leg, the small press and release of his muscled thigh spiraling her closer and closer to the reckless edge of passion.

Finally he released her mouth, sliding his lips along her jaw and down to the vulnerable flesh beneath her chin, sucking and licking, flicking a relentless rhythm over the tender skin as he worked his way down to the upper swells of her breasts. He nuzzled aside the button-front shirt she wore, but eventually the fabric frustrated him and he abandoned his efforts, simply closing his lips over the taut nipple shielded from his view and suckling strongly.

She gave a high, smothered cry as the shock reverberated through her system, and though she wouldn't remember it later, her back arched and her hands came up to plunge into his thick hair and hold him closer. Her fingers flexed and kneaded his scalp and he dragged one hand away from her back to begin working at the buttons of her blouse until he'd freed enough that he could pull the fabric aside and lift her breast free of her bra.

His mouth on her bare flesh was yet another shocking wonder. How could she have forgotten this? Logical thought receded and she gave herself to the hot magic flowing between them, her knees giving way so that she sank to the thick carpet, pulling him down as she went. Within minutes, they were sprawled in a needy tangle of limbs struggling to remove clothing even as they explored newly bared skin.

When he had removed the bikini panties that still fit beneath the bulge of her belly, Rafe sat back on his heels for a long moment, studying the changes in her form since the last time they'd been together. Under his intense scrutiny she blushed, raising a knee and covering her breasts with her arms.

He gave a quiet chuckle, then stretched his length beside

her, propping himself on an elbow and laying a hot, hairy leg over hers, gently but inexorably tugging until she relaxed her arms from their defensive posture. Bending his head, he touched a light kiss to the crest of the nearest breast.

"You are so beautiful," he said almost reverently. "Before, in the dark, I wished I could see you better." He placed his open palm at her throat and slowly smoothed it in a long, slow glide down the midline of her body, dragging it through the valley between her breasts, down past her navel and finally stopping when his big palm covered the place where their child was sheltered.

She raised her own hands to his broad, bare shoulders, exploring the muscular flesh with gentle fingers, running her hands up to cradle his stubbled jaw, marveling at the differences in a man's body. Oh, she was no naive schoolgirl. She knew a lot about what happened between men and women, courtesy of many gossipy, giggly late-night sessions with the girlfriends her parents made sure were a part of their daughters' lives.

And she'd had that one wondrous, magical night with Rafe...when everything had seemed dusted with magic and moonlight, and her inhibitions had slipped away into the shadows under his expert handling.

He leaned over her then, kissing her deeply, caressing her silky skin until she was arching against him, small whimpers escaping each time his hand ventured into sensitive territory. She didn't want to talk, didn't want to think. She only wanted to feel, to savor every brush of his fingers, every inch of his body against hers.

His hand slipped lower and lower over her belly and into the warm thatch of curls below, and she gave a strangled cry of shock as he deliberately pushed on. One long finger slid between her soft folds, spreading the moisture he found there in ever-widening circles until her nails were digging into his shoulders and she tugged at his lean hips, trying to drag him closer.

He answered her wordless plea with his body, moving atop her and settling himself in the space she willingly made between her thighs. She could feel him, throbbing and silky against her belly and she slipped a hand between them, needing to feel the proof of his desire for her. He groaned as she cupped him and his hips thrust involuntarily at her, then he captured her hand and kissed her fingers before anchoring both hands above her head with his own.

Slowing, he drew back, allowing his heavy flesh to find its home between her thighs, nudging at her gently but insistently until the slick channel he'd prepared for himself opened. He thrust forward in one strong stroke then, pushing into her in the ultimate joining while he kissed her again and again, hard, stinging kisses that spoke more clearly than words of the control he was exerting. She wriggled beneath him to lodge him even more firmly in place, then rocked her hips lightly, savoring the slippery movement of flesh in flesh.

Looking up at his chiseled features, she felt her heart swell with love. It was ridiculous to deny it. Oh, she might never tell Rafe, but it was silly to pretend she didn't love him, had begun to lose her heart when their eyes had met across a ballroom. She'd loved him since that night, the one night he'd been all hers without any of this baggage between them muddying feelings and relationships.

He kissed her again as if he would never stop, and she closed her eyes, wanting to impress every memory into her mind, to save these precious moments for the long, lonely days that she feared were ahead. She didn't know what the rest of her life might hold; she only knew that Rafe wouldn't be there, and she doubted she'd ever feel about another man the way she felt about him. It had happened for her parents—mutual, instantaneous love that defied social class and expectations, and she'd been raised to respect the sacred joining of two souls. Marriage shouldn't happen unless there was love between the parties involved.

Rafe drew back, then pushed forward again, and the sensations his body produced where he moved within and over her were so exquisite that she couldn't prevent the soft sound of need that escaped.

"I thought of you." His voice was a rough confession in her ear. "So many times, I nearly hopped on a plane and came to find you."

It was the first time she'd had any indication that he might have been as affected by their night of lovemaking as she had been, and it was the most powerful aphrodisiac she'd ever known.

"I wish you had," she whispered. Then she shifted her legs higher, clasping his lean waist, and gave herself to the moment. As he began to move heavily against her, she turned her face into his chest and moved in counterpoint, meeting his thrusts. He unclasped her wrists and drew his hand down to brace himself, and she laid her palms over the smooth muscles of his shoulders, feeling the heat and sweat, feeling a throbbing tension drawing taut at the point where his body slammed into her over and over. She'd noticed an increased sensitivity in her breasts and other places as her pregnancy progressed, and the rhythmic thrusting was quickly more than she could take.

With an incoherent cry, she convulsed in his arms, writhing as climax ripped through her. Rafe followed almost immediately, as if he'd been waiting for her and she wrapped her arms around him, dimly feeling the pulses of his own release flooding warmly within her, awareness slowly returning as ecstasy receded into a lethargic satisfaction.

She yawned against his chest and felt a chuckle rumble

through him. He started to shift away, but she wrapped her arms around his shoulders. "Stay."

"I'm planning to." He lifted a hand and smoothed her hair back from her face, lingered over the curve of her cheek. "But I have to move. I don't want to hurt you or the baby."

Reluctantly, she relaxed her grip, hating the moment when he pulled away from her, but nearly as quickly he slid to her side and shifted her so that he lay on his back with her cuddled against him. His arm was hard around her and the hair on his chest was tickling her nose. She'd never been so content in her entire life. Heaving a sigh that made him chuckle again, she closed her eyes and slipped into sleep, safe in his embrace.

Two hours later, Rafe stepped out of the shower and wrapped a towel around his waist. Quietly he walked through the bedroom, and, as the knock he'd been expecting sounded at the door, he quickly pulled it open before the man standing on the other side could knock again.

"The things you requested, sir," the valet said. The man pushed a garment cart with several bagged items hanging from it into the room, then efficiently dealt with the bags piled on its bottom rack. As Rafe watched, all kinds of toiletries and accessories appeared: a shaving kit, a selection of makeup, the ladies' maternity underclothes he'd specified, perfume and men's cologne and more, right down to a handbag and pretty, low-heeled sandals for his sleeping beauty.

Rafe signed the bill the man discreetly presented, adding a generous tip before he ushered him out, closing the heavy door quietly. Elizabeth was still sleeping on the bed where he'd carried her after their lovemaking, and he suspected she needed a little more rest before their evening began. She was going to be hard enough to handle when she found out what he had planned; no point in having her tired and cranky as well.

He'd sworn he would never wind up like his parents, and now he was doing nearly the exact same thing.

The bitter thought tore through his mind and he felt compelled to defend his decision. He was not doing the same thing his parents had done. Well, not exactly. His parents' marriage had been a power deal and his mother hadn't been pregnant at the time of the ceremony. Although it certainly hadn't been long before she was.

The thought boggled the mind. He couldn't imagine two people less likely to indulge in hot, sweaty, draining but delightful bouts of sex than his parents. Victor and Sara were the least passionate people he'd ever met.

Unless you were talking prestige or finances, he thought with a bitterness that hadn't subsided over the years. His father lived to ingratiate himself with the royalty of every European nation that hadn't gotten rid of the archaic idea of a ruling class. Anyone who dared to thwart Victor in one of his never-ending attempts to link himself with yet another royal name found out just how passionate he could get.

As a child, Rafe had learned quickly that protocol and etiquette were the keys to success in his home. One didn't run to one's mother for a kiss upon her return from a trip, or cry over a skinned knee. His father's favorite phrase, without doubt, was ''stiff upper lip.''

And Rafe was damned if his child was ever going to hear it.

He pulled on the black evening trousers and slipped into the shirt, fastening the studs and adding the formal bow tie before working on the cuff links he'd had sent up with the other accessories. Then he crossed to the little writing desk in the living area and quickly penned a note for Elizabeth before slipping into new Italian leather shoes and the rest of his tux and letting himself out of the suite.

He had a lot of things to do if he was going to get married tonight.

She knew he was gone when she woke.

Rafe was an overwhelming presence; if he were still in the suite, she would know. She stretched and immediately a thousand small sensations reminded her of his lovemaking. Though there was no one there to see, she smiled a slow, happy smile of contentment. At least physically she was sure that he wanted her.

Slowly she sat up, then rose from the bed and padded into the bathroom. Donning one of the luxurious robes that were compliments of the casino, she used the facilities and washed her face, then went to the mini-bar and got a large bottle of spring water.

On the bar lay a note. The first time she had seen Rafe's handwriting, she'd been privately amused. She could have predicted the bold, aggressive strokes like these in which he explained that he'd had clothing and accessories sent up, that she should go ahead and dress and he'd be back by…oh, heavens!

The clock on the wall told her she had little more than twenty minutes before his return. If she wanted to be beautiful, she'd better get moving. She snatched up the toiletries and cosmetics and headed for the bathroom.

She took the quickest shower on record. As she was slipping into the strappy little sandals that were in one of the boxes, she heard the door of the suite open. Hastily she crossed to the vanity area and picked up her bag, applying a quick dash of lipstick. Then with a nervousness she didn't entirely understand, she started for the door leading to the living room.

Before she could get there, the door opened.

Rafe seemed to fill the doorway, and she was struck by his size, as she always was when she saw him after an absence. His shoulders were so broad, they blocked the light behind him.

"Sleep well?" His voice was warm as he started across the room.

"Yes, I—Rafe!"

He'd seized her by the waist and pulled her up against him. Her protest was purely a formality because already she was winding her arms about his neck and relaxing into his embrace. He put a finger beneath her chin and lifted her face up to his, then cupped her jaw as he set his mouth on hers and parted her lips with his, invading the tender depths with his tongue until she curled against him in restless surrender.

When he lifted his head, he was smiling complacently, a purely male expression of satisfaction. "I'd like to keep you naked in bed for the rest of the evening, but I'd better feed you, for the baby's sake."

She stepped back, smoothing her dress as a warm feeling of hope spread through her. He sounded so tender and concerned...maybe there was a chance he could come to care for her the way she wanted—no, *needed*—him to.

He linked his fingers through hers and held her hands wide. "You look beautiful." Then he grinned. "I've seen pictures of your mother at your age and you're a dead ringer."

She shrugged, smiling. "Strong genes, I guess."

"No wonder your father says he never had a chance." Then his face sobered and his gaze slid down to the gentle curve of her abdomen barely noticeable in the unbelted pale pink dress. "If this baby's a girl, I'm going to have to lock her up to keep the boys away."

Her smile faded as he escorted her out the door and they turned down the hallway to the elevators. "I don't want my child to be as shielded from the world as I was. Until I was ten or so, I thought everyone's parents employed bodyguards around the clock.''

Rafe nodded. ''I can see why your father is so overprotective, though.''

''Yes.'' It was on the tip of her tongue to tell him about Sam Flynn, the man she was going to look up when she got back to Phoenix—the man who might be her brother. She'd been neglecting her duty—it was time to call and see if he had returned to work. She made a private vow to do exactly that first thing in the morning. But instead she said, ''Mother and Father were devastated when James was kidnapped.'' She shuddered and put a hand protectively over her stomach. ''I can't even imagine what it must have been like.''

''No.'' Rafe's face was grim. ''I'm sure losing his only male heir was devastating to your father, especially since he never had another son.''

She glanced up at him, frowning. ''Losing his *child* was devastating to my father.''

''It was a terrible thing,'' he agreed. The elevator bell rang and the doors slid open. ''Shall we go, my pretty princess?''

First they walked out to the front of the hotel, where he secured her a place at the rail in front of the volcano. Despite the warmth, it still got dark relatively early and already the sun was gone. After a short wait, the volcano erupted.

Elizabeth was delighted by the display. Then he hustled her down to Treasure Island just in time to watch the British man-o'-war engage the pirate ship in battle. She clapped when the cannons flashed, and when the British ship finally sank with its captain bravely going down with his command, she gasped at the sight of the lone tricorne floating on the waves. When the ship rose again after a long, tense wait, and the actor portraying the captain spouted a stream of water high into the air, she laughed herself silly.

Next, he took her to a chic French restaurant which boasted burgundy leather seats, quaint low-lit lamps and wildflowers on tables covered in lace-edged linens. After seating her and allowing the maitre d' to unfurl napkins edged in matching lace across their laps, he smiled across the table at her. "It seems a crime to come to a place like this and not drink wine, but you aren't permitted to have alcohol."

"One small glass would be acceptable," she said. "Nutritional value, you know."

He arched an eyebrow. "Umm-hmm. If you say so."

They chatted over dinner, the small, getting-to-know-you rituals that couples on a normal date would enjoy. Because he seemed so fascinated, she let him draw her out, telling him story after story of the scrapes she and her sisters had gotten into as children.

They both declined dessert and while Rafe drank strong coffee and she had a cup of decaffeinated tea, she seized an opening in the conversation to ask him a few questions. It was like pulling teeth with a pair of tweezers, but finally he told her about completing Oxford and deciding to study architecture at Harvard, a move which had appalled his father. Though Rafe didn't elaborate, she sensed there was a great deal more to the story.

"So how did you get from Harvard to owning a Phoenix construction company?"

He shrugged. "I decided I wanted to design unique structures. But I also wanted to see them built to the standards I envisioned, so creating my own company seemed a logical next step."

"This can't have made your father happy." She thought about the Grand Duke she knew. "He's big on tradition.

Doesn't he want you nearby, taking over the reins from him one day?''

A heavy silence fell over the table. "My father's plans for my life are irrelevant," he finally said in a tone that indicated discussion was at an end. "He threatened to disown me when I wouldn't fall in line, though he hasn't resorted to that yet. Periodically he stops in Phoenix or calls just to browbeat me, thinking I'm going to get less bullheaded as I age. So if your father hoped to cement his relationship with Thortonburg through me, he made a major miscalculation. He'd have done better to throw you at my younger brother.''

The words were such an unexpected attack that she felt as if he'd leaned across the table and struck her. Very slowly, she set down her teacup with trembling hands. "I've told you before, my father isn't the least interested in arranging marriages for any of his daughters. My parents fell in love and married, and they have given us the same opportunity.''

Rafe snorted. "My father and your father made an agreement decades ago to marry one of you off to me. I expected it would be the eldest—''

"Alexandra.''

"But for some reason they must have decided you would be more suitable.'' He chuckled, but there was no mirth in the sound. "Obviously, they had no idea just how well we suit each other or they'd never have left us alone.''

The perfect filet she'd eaten rolled in her stomach at the callous reference to what she had been hoping was lovemaking. A wave of nausea, so strong that she had to grit her teeth, made her set her napkin aside and reach for her purse. "I'm going to visit the ladies' and then I'll be ready to leave. I'll meet you in the entry.''

Rafe rose, a frown of concern creasing his broad brow. "You don't look well.''

"I'm not."

"I knew you shouldn't have had that wine. Is there anything I can do?"

"You've done quite enough, thank you." Her words were clipped and she saw his eyes narrow at the tone, but she was past caring. The beat of her heart in her chest was nearly painful as she pushed away the hopes she'd had of love. Rafe had been hurt in the past, but he wouldn't share that part of himself with her. And she couldn't live with a man who couldn't love her, no matter the reason.

Six

Elizabeth was so quiet on the drive back to the hotel that Rafe could feel his gut twist with worry. She'd started getting weird again when he'd mentioned their fathers and the marriage deal. Mentally he kicked himself. That had upset her before, as well. He should have remembered. What did it matter if she didn't want to believe she was part of an arranged marriage? Women liked a little romance. Well, he thought, she'd forget about their conversation soon enough when she saw what he had done for her.

He led her back to their room and passed his keycard through the lock, then opened the door and motioned for her to precede him. As she did so, he pressed the button on the entry wall for the lamps in the living area.

Halfway into the room, stopped dead.

Behind her he was grinning. The florist had done a good job. On the glass table in front of the couch stood a huge crystal vase with an arrangement of red roses, three dozen if they'd done as he ordered, beautifully displayed against a background of greenery and some fine-textured, airy white stuff.

"What's this?" Her voice sounded strange.

"They're for you." He stepped forward and took her hand, drawing it to his lips. "For the mother of my child."

She half turned and her eyes were wide as she stared up at him. Then she burst into tears and bolted into the bedroom, sobbing.

What the hell—? He was so stunned, he didn't react at all for a moment.

Then he sprinted to the bedroom door as a feeling of déjà vu assailed him. She wasn't locking him out again!

But the doorknob turned easily beneath his hand. The bedroom was empty and he could hear water running in the adjoining bathroom. Tentatively he knocked on the door. "Elizabeth?"

"Just a moment." Her voice sounded strained and muffled.

She didn't sound as if she planned on camping in there for the night, so he lounged against the closest bureau and waited. It took a while, but finally the doorknob turned and she opened the door. The skin around her eyes was red and puffy, but she wasn't crying, at least.

He straightened. "What's wrong?"

She sighed. "Nothing. Thank you for the roses. They're beautiful." But her tone was lackluster and she looked at the floor rather than at him. "I'm very tired," she said. "I'd like to go to bed."

"All right." He knew perfectly well she meant *alone,* but there wasn't a chance of that. He walked back into the other room and locked the door for the night, then turned off the lights in the living area. By the time he returned, she'd slipped out of the pink dress and wore nothing but the silky undergarments he'd bought her.

She turned, startled, as he came back into the bedroom, but he ignored her reaction, crossing to the bath to turn out the lights. Then he rounded his side of the bed and casually began to undress, removing the tux jacket and unfastening his cuff links and studs.

"What are you doing?" Her voice had the same odd tone it had carried when she'd seen the roses.

Calmly he continued undressing, stepping out of his clothes until he wore nothing but his briefs. "Getting ready for bed. I thought you said you were tired."

"I am." She paused and made a helpless gesture with one hand. "I didn't intend to sleep with you."

"There's only one bed," he pointed out.

"No!" Her voice rose an octave. "I am not sharing a bed with you. Not for sleeping, not for...for any other activity, either."

He'd had it with guessing what was going through her head. Slowly, deliberately, he began to walk around the bed to where she stood.

She took a step backward for every one of his until finally she was literally backed against a wall and he was directly in front of her. If she wanted to get away from him now, she'd have to crawl across the bed.

"I thought you'd like the roses," he said. "I'm sorry if they upset you. Will you please tell me why?"

She hesitated, opened her mouth, closed it again. Finally she said, "Red roses are for lovers, for—for special relationships."

Now he was the one to hesitate. Slowly, feeling as if he was walking down a tunnel without a single glimmer of light, he said, "You...are special to me. Not just because you're going to have my child."

Her eyes were shadowed in the light of the single bedside lamp she'd lit. She shook her head. "Don't sugarcoat it,

Rafe. If I weren't pregnant, if I hadn't come and sought you out, we'd never have seen each other again.''

He opened his mouth automatically to protest. Then he shut it abruptly. She might be right. Five months ago—hell, *one* month ago—he couldn't have imagined himself feeling like this, couldn't have imagined his life without her. She'd been there in the back of his mind for months, and now that she was in his life he wasn't letting her go. Baldly, he said, ''You're probably right. If you'd stayed in Wynborough, we never would have seen each other again. But—'' he reached out and slowly cupped the warm, soft flesh of her cheek in his hand, framing her jawline with his thumb ''—you did come after me. You were smarter than I was. And I'm glad. I don't want to be without you. Not because of the baby. Because of *you*.''

She swallowed. He felt the movement beneath his hand. ''Rafe, I can't—''

''Shhh.'' He stepped closer, gathering her into his embrace, rubbing his chin over the top of her head and tucking her against his heart. ''Don't analyze it to death. Just accept it.''

Bending his head, he kissed her temple then her cheek, then tilted up her face with his thumb beneath her chin and brushed soft kisses over her eyelids, the bridge of her nose, finally nuzzling his way down to her mouth. She was warm and soft and pliant in his arms and he could feel her begin to tremble as she became aware of the arousal he couldn't hide as his body reacted to the scents and feel of woman, *his* woman.

''I want you,'' he said against her mouth. He bent his knees and kissed her throat, then trailed tiny kisses down the smooth flesh swelling at her breasts until the silky fabric of her slip stopped him. ''May I?'' he whispered.

She was leaning back against the wall now, her hands in his hair, eyes closed. Without opening them she nodded her permission, and his blood heated as he realized he'd convinced her to stay with him.

Slowly he reached down and found the hem of the slip, drawing it over her head. Her bra clasped in the front and he set his fingers at the little hook, gently snapping it apart and pushing it back off her shoulders, letting her pretty, pink-tipped breasts bob free. She was so beautiful. His throat grew tight at the realization that she was his now. He wondered if she knew he never planned to let her get away...but this wasn't the time to discuss it. Slowly he raised his hands, cupping the soft, full globes in his palms and gently brushing his thumbs back and forth across the nipples.

She began to breathe faster, her head lolling back against the wall, and the lamplight slanted across her face, making her look mysterious and sensual and desirable. He bent again and placed his mouth right at the place where her breasts met in the center, licking his way down the sweet crevice and then continuing on around the base of one pretty mound. He moved his hand and flicked his tongue over her flesh in an ever-decreasing spiral until finally, he was nearly at the peaked nipple. But he didn't close his mouth over the enticing tip until she moaned and her hands came up to his head, threading through his hair to cradle his skull and guide him to her.

Victorious, he suckled the tight bud, lashing it again and again with his tongue, moving finally to treat the other nipple to the same attentions. Her fingers clenched and loosened and clenched again in his hair, and the unconscious actions fired his own arousal, pushing him heavily against the restraining fabric of his briefs and making him ache with the need to bury himself within her.

But he wanted this time to last. He wanted her to want him, to need the sweet invasion of his body as badly as he needed to immerse himself in her hot depths. And so he

lingered over her breasts, suckling strongly then gently lav-
ing the puckered flesh until she was quivering before him,
her hips shifting in small circles, tiny moans escaping her
throat each time he increased the sweet torture.

Finally he allowed her hands to push him down, away
from her breasts and he trailed his lips over the satiny flesh
of her abdomen to the swell that contained his child. Turning his head, he slid to his knees and lay his cheek against
her, savoring the sweetness of the moment. But she was
too needy to be satisfied with such gentle actions and soon
he explored the tender flesh below with his mouth until the
edge of her panties, riding low beneath the fullness of her
womb, made him pause.

He grasped the lacy fabric with his teeth and tugged
gently, pulling the garment down, burying his nose in the
spicy curls that lay exposed before him. Hooking his fingers
into the fabric, he slid her panties down and off, and sat
back to view the results of his labor.

If he could stand the thought of another man seeing her
nude, he'd have her painted just like this, head thrown back,
red hair a wild tangle down her back, hands braced on the
wall behind her and one leg cocked slightly open, inviting
him to search the sweetness hidden in her shadows. But
there was no way any other man was getting within a mile
of her naked glory. He didn't care how primitive and possessive it sounded. She was his and his alone. Forever.

The thought shook him slightly. And because it was an
uncomfortable one to contemplate, he let her siren's call
distract him, freeing himself from his confining briefs, letting his straining flesh spring free in anticipation. Leaning
forward again, he placed his mouth directly over the shadowed crease in her feminine mound, gently blowing a warm
stream of breath over her. She made a low sound of surprise, and he drew back, putting his hands on the insides

of her thighs and shifting her stance wide, baring her pink, pouting flesh to his gaze.

His own body was urging him to move faster, but he resisted its pleas. Leaning forward yet again, he used his tongue to open her slick softness and when she cried out, he plunged deeply into her, tasting the hot wet warmth of woman that greeted him. He lifted a hand and rubbed his fingers along the plump folds until he could enter her easily with one finger. As she arched against his hand, he set his mouth over the tiny nubbin that he knew awaited his touch, stroking over it with a rhythmic licking that he mimicked with the movement of his finger.

She was crying with each breath, her hips plunging, her hands in fists beating against the wall. She tolerated only a few of his intimate caresses before she climaxed, her body squeezing his finger in tight, hard contractions as her knees gave way and she began to slide down the wall to the floor.

He would have liked to wait, wanted to spin out the pleasure even more, but he was so hard even the brush of his flesh against his own belly pushed him dangerously close to release. Frantically, he took her by the hips and guided her down onto his jutting staff, arching up and plunging deeply into her just as a series of harsh, hard pulses left him gasping for breath, his head bowed as weakly on her shoulder as hers was on his.

When he could breathe enough to speak again, he chuckled softly. "How in the hell am I going to manage to go six weeks without this after the baby comes?"

She lifted her head from his shoulder and though she still sat astride him, though their bodies were still sweaty and joined together, there was a distant quality to her smile. "You managed for five months last time."

He wanted to shake her. Instead, he leaned forward and nipped lightly at the smooth flesh of her shoulder. "Yes, but that was when I'd convinced myself you were a figment of my imagination.''

She yelped and shrank back. ''Your imagination?'' She sounded slightly indignant.

''My imagination,'' he repeated. ''Too good to be true. A hallucination caused by years of disappointing experiences. I wanted the real thing so badly that I created it. Or so I thought.''

''And this is the real thing?''

''I'm going to pretend I didn't hear that,'' he said, frowning to disguise his smile. Little smart aleck. He took her by the shoulders and pulled her forward, kissed her hard and deep one final time and then lifted her off him.

She promptly collapsed in a heap on the floor.

Groaning as his cramping leg muscles protested, he stood and pulled back the covers on the bed, then lifted her and laid her on the mattress. She immediately snuggled into the pillow, and he patted the smooth, bare buttock she presented before turning out the light and climbing in behind her. He gathered her into his arms and as he closed his eyes and sank into the sweet oblivion of sleep, he felt more content than he could ever remember feeling before in his life.

The morning's bright white light streamed into the room through the sheer curtains over the window, slowly calling him awake. He'd forgotten to close the heavier drapes the night before. It didn't really matter, though. They needed to get up and get going today anyway.

Elizabeth stirred in his arms. Or rather, beneath his arm. During the night she'd stretched out flat on her stomach. He lay on his side with one arm and one leg possessively chaining her to him. He smiled at the thought.

''Good morning, Sleeping Beauty.''

''Mmm. G'morning.'' She turned onto her side, then

rolled onto her back. "What am I going to do when I can't sleep on my stomach anymore?" she asked the ceiling.

"I guess you'll just have to let me hold you all night," he offered.

She turned into his arms, snuggling in and pressing small kisses across his chest. "That sounds nice."

"Elizabeth." He spoke slowly and quietly, not wanting to disturb her unduly. This was going to be the tricky part. Turning his head, he kissed her temple, his thumb caressing the ball of her shoulder where his arm lay around her. "We should get married."

As he'd expected, her body stiffened. She didn't pull away, though, and he was cautiously optimistic. Maybe she'd realized that what they had between them on the physical plane was extraordinary, that some people lived entire lives without experiencing the connection they had.

Finally, she spoke. "I believe we already had this discussion. No, thank you."

"Why not?" His instinct was to lift himself over her and demand that she acquiesce, but he knew her well enough by now to know that that approach would get him nowhere.

"Physical infatuation isn't a good enough foundation for a lifetime together."

"But it's a solid part of that foundation," he argued. "How many married couples do you suppose *aren't* sexually attracted?"

"It's only a part, though, as you just said." There was a hint of sad weariness in her voice. "And it's about the only part we do have."

"We have more than that," he insisted.

"Rafe, I'm not going to marry you and that's final." Her body was stiff and unresponsive, and suddenly he couldn't stand to be in the bed where she'd been so warm and sweet the night before.

Heaving himself upright, he stalked into the bathroom to

shower and shave, then donned the second set of clothes he'd ordered for himself yesterday. While he dressed, he steeled himself to do what he was going to have to do if she continued to be stubborn.

Damn woman! He couldn't understand the wall of resistance she erected each time he mentioned marriage.

Walking back into the bedroom, he said, "I'll ask you one more time. Elizabeth, will you *please* marry me?"

She was looking out the window, clad only in a sheer dressing gown; all he could see was her profile as her lips formed the word, "No."

He sighed. "Then you leave me no choice." He walked across the room and picked up the telephone. Fishing his wallet out of the pants he'd flung across a chair the night before, he extracted a piece of paper and started punching in the numbers.

"What are you doing?"

"Calling your father."

"My father!" She turned her head and glared at him. "Put that telephone down."

He ignored her.

"Why are you calling my father?"

"To tell him that you're pregnant with my child, and you won't marry me even though I've begged you to." He knew it was harsh, but he sensed that there was no other way to force her to agree, and he was determined. His child was going to have his name, and Elizabeth was never leaving him again.

"No!" Her response sounded so agonized that Rafe had to steel himself not to take her in his arms again and comfort her.

Slowly he replaced the receiver and turned to face her. "Why not?"

Elizabeth swallowed. Her gaze was still defiant, but he sensed the decisiveness draining away from her and gradually her defiance changed to a sad acceptance. "I'll marry you," she said quietly. "Just don't tell my parents."

"You're going to have to tell them sometime."

"I know." She shook her head and looked away. "You don't understand. I should be the one to tell them."

"All right." He eyed her. "We'll go get married."

"What? You mean *today?*" She rounded on him and her face went slack with shock for a moment. Then almost as quickly, the fire that he was beginning to recognize lay just beneath the surface of her ladylike demeanor flashed in her eyes. "You had this planned all along," she accused. "Even before I got on that plane yesterday morning, you intended to force me to marry you today. Didn't you? *Didn't you?*" she demanded when he remained silent.

Rafe regarded her for a moment, lightning bolts zinging his way from those emerald eyes. Finally he raised both hands in surrender. "I hadn't decided for sure, but after last night there isn't any reason why we shouldn't get married. I told you I mean my child to be legitimate. I'm prepared to do whatever I have to do to ensure that this baby never has to question his rightful heritage."

She all but sneered. "Noble words for a man who's turned his back on his own heritage."

The barb was a direct hit. "Bull."

"Hah." She crossed her arms and regarded him scornfully. "You're afraid to face your own family. The one time you were near your home in more than a decade, you came incognito and didn't even speak to your parents before sneaking off."

"I'm not afraid of my family," he said, feeling rage welling up from a hidden cache deep in his mind. His lip curled. "They've already done everything they can to make me buckle under and it hasn't worked."

Her face lit with the curiosity he was beginning to realize

was an integral—if damned annoying—part of her personality. "What did they do?"

"Never mind." He knew he sounded like a surly schoolboy, but the memories bombarding him made him feel like a child again as he relived some of the scenes he'd endured with his father.

I never said he wasn't a nice boy. But he's the butcher's son. Hardly a suitable companion for you, Raphael. I've already explained to his family that the friendship simply cannot continue.

With an effort, he shook off the voices from his past, focusing on the woman who would be his future. "Just be dressed and ready to go in thirty minutes."

"I'm having breakfast and taking a shower first," she said. "I'm not going to rush around just so you can be on whatever little schedule you have planned."

"Fine. Will sixty minutes be enough?"

"Plenty. Shall I meet you at the bar?"

He was still trying to forget the things her question had called to mind. "All right. I'll have another dress sent up. Be in the bar in an hour."

"Yes, sir."

He ignored the pert salute she aimed his way as he left the suite and stalked toward the elevator.

Hours later, she remained so angry, she couldn't stand still as she waited impatiently for the royal limo to be called to the VIP queue. As she paced back and forth, she checked her watch. By now, Rafe knew she'd gone and unless he was a lot less resourceful than she suspected, he knew she'd boarded an international flight. And he knew she was going home.

It hadn't been easy. She'd placed one quick call to Laura Bishop at the Colton ranch. Laura had agreed to make her travel arrangements and called back a short time later with all the necessary information.

Laura also agreed to explain to Alexandra that so far Sam Flynn had been unavailable. Elizabeth had hoped so much that she and her sisters would be able to locate the man they were all convinced was their brother, kidnapped as an infant and presumed dead. Only he hadn't been killed, after all. And though the records at The Sunshine Home for Children had left something to be desired, she and her sisters had narrowed down the field of possibilities. Now only two remained: Sam Flynn, the man she had been supposed to make contact with in Phoenix, and John Colton, the younger brother of Alexandra's new husband, Mitch, who, according to Mitch, was unable to be contacted until he decided to show up.

Elizabeth felt bad about letting her sisters down just when they were getting close to finding their brother, but... They would understand, she was sure. She had to talk to her parents before Rafe did. After that, Laura could make sure Sam Flynn was available before Elizabeth returned to speak with him.

With her conscience resting easier, she'd packed rapidly. Then she'd sneaked out of the hotel and caught a flight with minutes left in the hour he'd granted her. At JFK, she'd left her connecting flight to board the private plane her father had sent at Laura's request.

The limo arrived and before she was ready, before she really wanted to be there, she was being driven through the familiar gates of the palace to the main entry stairs where her mother and father, wearing smiles wide enough to crack their faces, waited to greet her. They hurried down the steps as the chauffeur opened the door, and as she slid out, she was enveloped in her mother's arms.

She knew the moment her mother realized what the bulge between them was. Gabriella's body stiffened. She pulled away and stood back, holding Elizabeth at arm's length to look at her. *All* of her. Shock, surprise, bewilderment all flashed across the Queen's face. Then compassion filled her eyes.

"Oh, my darling," she said. "Is this an occasion for celebration? Are you happy about this?"

"Happy about what?" Her father's voice boomed over her mother's softer tones.

"Brace yourself, Phillip," said Queen Gabriella. "Our little girl is pregnant." She shepherded Elizabeth up the steps as she spoke, issuing orders to the staff for refreshments in the family drawing room.

"Pregnant! But where...who...how...?" The King's voice trailed off into astonished silence as he strode along at his wife's heels.

"I imagine we'll learn *where* the father is and *who* the father is very shortly, dear," her mother said over her shoulder. "And if you don't know *how* by now, I truly despair of you."

Despite the tears that threatened to fall, Elizabeth had to giggle. She'd been so afraid to tell them. Well, afraid wasn't exactly the right word. More like sorry. She knew being an unwed mother must be the last thing her parents wanted for one of their daughters. She'd put off this moment for so long because she hadn't been able to face the thought of their disappointment in her.

And there was another reason, as well.

They *had* to locate James! If they didn't, and if this baby she carried was a son...she couldn't bear to think about what it would mean for her child. Please, God, let this be a girl.

"So." Her mother pressed her into a wingbacked chair and lifted her feet onto the matching hassock, making Elizabeth smile. "Would you like something to drink?"

"Some kind of juice would be wonderful. Cranberry, please?"

Her mother nodded, and the hovering maid took off at light speed. Anyone in the palace employ who hadn't already heard that Princess Elizabeth had come home with a baby on the way would know in a matter of minutes, she was sure.

One more reason she dreaded the idea of raising her child in the palace environment in which she'd been raised.

"How are you feeling?" her mother asked.

Simultaneously the king asked, "Do you know if it's a boy?"

Her father was pacing back and forth in front of the wide windows, looking rather...agitated. She supposed he had the right to be.

"I feel fine," she answered her mother. "A little bit of morning sickness early on, but now I couldn't feel better." Unbidden, an image of the heated lovemaking she had experienced only hours ago flashed through her head and she felt herself blush.

Her mother raised her eyebrows with a knowing smile, but didn't comment.

"I'm about five months along," Elizabeth went on. "The baby's due in mid-June. And, no, I don't know its gender. We'll have to wait and be surprised."

"Is the father in the picture?" Her own father had stopped his pacing and turned to toss the question at her.

Elizabeth hesitated. "Yes. But not in the way you might hope."

"In other words, he's not prepared to marry you." Her father was glowering.

"No, Daddy," she said, smiling gently. "It's the other way around. *I'm* the one who won't marry *him.*"

"Does this man have a name you'd like to share with

us?'' her mother asked. ''If you'd rather not, I suppose we can accept that.''

Elizabeth couldn't think of anything she wanted to do less, but she knew there was no point in hiding it. The truth would come out sooner or later. Sooner probably, if she knew Rafe. She wasn't stupid enough to think that this was anything but a successful skirmish in what looked to be a long siege.

''He has a name,'' she said reluctantly. ''You know him.''

''The Prince of Thortonburg,'' her father said.

''Yes. Although he goes by Rafe Thorton these days.'' She looked at him in surprise. ''Has he already spoken to you?''

''No, but it makes sense,'' her father said. ''That young man couldn't shake his royal title fast enough to suit him. When he told me you'd be staying with him, it seemed out of character.''

''Raphael.'' Her mother smiled. ''I always did like his spirit. Victor never succeeded in training that one to his ridiculously outdated notions of aristocratic conduct.''

''He didn't know who I was when we…when we… met.'' Her face felt hot again, and the disappointment in her mother's eye didn't help.

''I see,'' the Queen said.

''He was upset at first,'' Elizabeth confessed. ''As you said, he doesn't have a very high opinion of royalty. But once he'd gotten over the shock, he decided we would get married.''

''And that's a problem for you?'' her mother asked in a soft voice. She stood and came around behind the chair, setting her hands on Elizabeth's shoulders and rubbing gently.

''I don't want to be married out of duty.''

''Is that the only reason he wants to marry you?''

Elizabeth shrugged and avoided the question. "This is all Serena's fault. She's the one who talked me into tracking him down and telling him."

Her father turned from the window. "Coming from Serena, that was amazingly sensible." But his voice was indulgent and he was smiling. Serena had been a handful since the day she was born. Every silver hair in his head could be attributed to her, he'd said more than once.

"Daddy..." She hesitated, feeling ridiculous for even asking the question when she knew the answer. Still... "Rafe has some notion that you and his father arranged, or at least promised, that he'd marry one of us. I told him it's not true." But she knew her eyes were asking her father for the truth.

Phillip shook his head. "Victor hounded me about that for years. I always told him that I'd never oppose a match if one of my daughters chose either of his sons. As you said, it's not true." The King hesitated. "Does Thortonburg understand the manner in which the Wynborough crown is passed on?"

Elizabeth shook her head. "I—I'm not sure."

Her mother clucked her tongue. "You'd better be sure, dear. If this child is the first-born grandson to the King—"

"I know." Elizabeth linked her fingers. "I know."

The King moved to the side of Elizabeth's chair and bent to press a kiss to her cheek. "I have an appointment with the Minister of Public Works, but when I return I want to be filled in completely."

As he rose, a commotion in the hallway had them all turning. Trained to react instantly to threatening situations, the guard on duty slammed the door shut. As he did so, Elizabeth could see him drawing the gun from his holster.

Then she recognized the voice echoing down the hall, though it had an imperious quality that she'd never associated with it before. "...Thortonburg and I'm going to be marrying the Princess Elizabeth, so *do not* tell me they're unavailable. I'll search every damned room of this palace if I have to.''

She half rose from her chair, but the King moved faster. Throwing open the door to the room, he spoke at the top of his considerable voice. ''The Prince of Thortonburg is welcome. Put away your arms, everyone. Thank you for your vigilance, though in this instance it isn't necessary.''

Elizabeth closed her eyes. If Rafe had wanted a demonstration of the ridiculous lengths her father went to with security, she couldn't have provided a better one if he'd specifically asked.

When she opened her eyes again, he was there, striding into the room. Bigger, as always, than she remembered and looking as totally furious as she'd ever seen him. His expression today made his face the day he'd found her by her broken-down rental car look almost friendly.

His blue eyes speared her in the chair where she sat, and he took three steps forward before realizing he was in the presence of the King. Abruptly, he spun and bowed formally from the waist. ''Your Majesty.''

He crossed to the Queen and took the hand she extended, bowing low over it and kissing it in a formal salutation. ''Your Majesty.''

''Welcome, Raphael.''

Before the Queen could add anything else, Rafe stalked around to stand before Elizabeth. He held out his hand in regal demand, and when she placed hers in it, he bowed again. But he didn't give her hand the perfunctory peck she expected. Instead, he turned it over and slowly, leisurely pressed a kiss into the center of her palm. When she felt his tongue tracing secret patterns on her flesh, she tried to jerk her hand away, but Rafe held it firmly for another moment before raising his head. ''Your Royal Highness.''

''Subservience doesn't suit you,'' Elizabeth said, snatching her hand back and linking it tightly with the other in her lap, ignoring both her mother's snort of amusement and the leap of her own pulse at his touch. "So just stop it. How on earth did you get here so fast?"

"Ever heard of private planes?" His voice was surly. Grouchy. Thoroughly out of sorts. She guessed she couldn't blame him.

"Raphael, Elizabeth has just finished telling us of your intentions." King Phillip stepped forward. Gone was the indulgent father, and in his place was the commanding monarch few ever saw in action.

"Good." Rafe didn't even appear to notice the monarch's attitude. "Then you know that I have chased your stubborn, spoiled, opinionated daughter across the Atlantic Ocean because I intend to marry her. I shouldn't think that would be a problem for you."

"Of course not." The King's stern face softened slightly. "You are more than welcome in this family... *if* you can convince my 'stubborn, spoiled, opinionated daughter' to marry you." He looked over Elizabeth's head to his wife, then, offering her his arm, said, "Come, my dear. These young people have things to discuss."

"Really, that's not necessary," Elizabeth began, turning around, trying to send her mother a silent message with her eyes. "Mother, you don't have to leave."

"I'm afraid duty calls me, as well," the Queen said, shrugging as if she were helpless to alter the matter. She winked at Elizabeth—winked!—and took her husband's arm as the two of them exited the room.

Seven

A heavy silence fell. She kept her eyes on her clasped hands, refusing to look at Rafe. Finally, when he didn't speak, she could stand the suspense no longer. "You can't make me marry you."

"All right."

She raised her head abruptly and stared at him. "All right?"

He shrugged, and the motion of his wide shoulders shifted the fabric of the fine leather jacket he wore. "I can't force you to marry me. We'll let a judge decide what kind of custody arrangements would work best."

"You—you wouldn't do that." She put a hand to her throat.

"By now you should know me well enough to realize I mean exactly what I say."

"But that's half the problem," she said heatedly. In her agitation she rose from the chair and gestured wildly with her hands. "I *don't* know you. We've spent a total of only a few weeks in each other's company in our entire lives. How can you think we could make a marriage work?"

Standing had been a mistake. Rafe stepped toward her, slipping his arms around her and gently rubbing his big hands up and down her spine. "Why couldn't we? Lots of people make successful marriages from much less." His embrace felt so wonderful, his arms so strong and secure, that she could feel her willpower draining away like an overused battery.

"Name some." Her voice was muffled against his chest.

"That's easy. My parents."

She looked up at him. Another mistake. His hard lips and the enticing dimples grooving his cheeks were much, much too close. Hastily she put a hand against his chest, holding him away when he would have pulled her closer. "No kissing!" She could see the amusement gleaming in his eyes. Averting her gaze, she stared at the metal zipper tab where he'd left it halfway up its track on his jacket. "Was their marriage arranged?"

"Their families wanted to cement a business relationship," Rafe said. "My grandfather ran through enough of the Thortonburg money that a marriage to a wealthy noblewoman was a necessity for my father."

"How sad." She couldn't imagine having her husband picked out for her. "My father did the exact opposite. He defied his own father to marry a penniless American. Quite a scandal at the time." She smiled. "But they never have regretted it."

"They seem very happy." Rafe sounded almost as if he doubted it. "But we aren't discussing your parents. We're talking about us. When I realized you'd slipped out of Vegas without me—"

A knock at the door interrupted whatever he had been going to say. Hastily, Elizabeth pulled herself away from his embrace and smoothed her wrinkled travel clothes. "Come in."

"Welcome home, Your Highness." The tall, handsome man in the uniform of royal security stopped before her and bowed over Elizabeth's hand.

"Lance!" Ignoring protocol, Elizabeth reached up to hug the dark-haired man. "Lose any princesses lately?"

The guard bared his teeth at her, but his eyes were a warm, smoky gray. "Serena was sly, I'll grant you that. But I will never lose anyone on my watch again. Cost me a promotion, you know."

She laughed. "I hardly think so. I've heard of your recent success." Belatedly she realized Rafe was glaring at the stranger who still had a muscled arm familiarly about her shoulders. "Rafe, this is Lance Grayson—newly appointed head of the Investigative Division of the Royal Security Detail of Wynborough. Recently he had the misfortune to be assigned as my sister Serena's bodyguard." She slipped from beneath Lance's arm and stepped a pace away, aware of the aura of leashed aggression flowing from Rafe. "Lance, may I present the prince of Thortonburg."

There was a silence that lasted a beat too long as the two men, so alike in height and build, assessed each other.

"My Lord Thortonburg." Lance bowed formally.

"When will you be leaving us?" Elizabeth asked.

"This is my final week in the King's employ," Lance informed her.

"Was there a reason for your interruption?" Rafe's tone was courteous, but he left no doubt that he wasn't pleased.

"The King asked me to extend his invitation to stay here at the palace during your visit. If you wish to do so, I'll attend to your personal security."

"Please thank the King for me, but I'll decline his invitation. I've already made arrangements at the Royal Drake Hotel."

"Very good, sir." Lance bowed, turned to Elizabeth and smiled. "I beg your pardon for the intrusion."

As the door closed behind him, Elizabeth rounded on Rafe. "Why were you so rude to Lance?"

"I didn't like how familiar he was with you."

"Don't be ridiculous."

"I'm not." It was nearly a snarl.

Taken aback, she decided it was time for a little soothing of the savage beast. Warily she said, "You're more than welcome to stay here if you like. I'm sure my parents would be pleased."

Rafe gave a bark of laughter that wasn't amused. "Right. Until they caught me sneaking out of your bedroom, you mean." He reached for her so swiftly that she didn't have a chance to evade his arms. "I don't intend to sleep under the same roof with you unless you're in my bed. And I don't intend to sleep under another roof from you for very damn long. You're marrying me. Soon. Before I actually have to kill the next man who puts his hands on you."

His words sent a thrill of purely primitive reaction down her spine, though she refused to admit that his attitude made her feel cherished and protected and…safe. "I didn't say I'd marry you. As I recall, before we were interrupted, we were discussing the possibility of a marriage."

"The eventuality of our marriage."

"The *possibility*," she reiterated.

"There's no good reason we shouldn't marry," Rafe said, pulling her to him again. "Kiss me, Princess. I've been away from you for more than half a day, and now I'm condemned to spend the night elsewhere, too."

"I don't *want* to kiss you," she said irritably. "All that does is confuse the issue." But as his hands roamed down her back and over her bottom, pulling her up against him, she moaned.

"Just think what we could be doing right now if we were

still in Las Vegas.'' His voice was a rough growl in her ear, his breath hot against her cheek. He pushed his hips firmly against her and when she shifted her legs incrementally to give his growing erection a snug home in the warm cove of her thighs, he caught his breath in a harsh gasp. ''You love to tease me, don't you?'' He bent his head and seized her earlobe in his teeth, worrying the sensitive shell with a not-entirely-gentle series of nips.

The stinging sensations, soothed as they were by his agile tongue, were a stimulating caress, and she could feel her breath growing short, her body softening as it set up an insistent throbbing in the one place that so desperately needed his touch. She squirmed against him, rubbing her aching mound against the rigid flesh pushing at her.

''We can't do this here,'' she whispered into his shoulder.

''I know, but isn't it fun pretending for a few minutes?'' His mouth slid down the side of her neck.

She shuddered, feeling her willpower draining away. How could this one man make her brain cells go on holiday every time he touched her? ''Would you really try to take the baby away from me?'' It was an effort to focus.

He stilled against her. Finally his broad chest rose and fell in a heavy sigh. Setting her on her feet away from him, he said, ''I will do anything I have to to get you to marry me, Princess. You're never going to be on the other side of the Atlantic from me again.''

And as she stood there, bereft of his big, warm presence, dazed and trying to comprehend his words, Rafe made an impatient gesture. ''Elizabeth, I want you. Not just today but for a long, long time.'' He didn't sound that thrilled by the admission. ''Can you tell me you don't want me, too?''

She hesitated, but honesty won out. ''No,'' she whispered.

''Then marry me.'' That quickly, she was in his arms

again and he was kissing her with wild, unrestrained passion, his hands roving familiarly over her body, pulling up her sweater to slide his palms around the pliant mounds of her breasts, murmuring in quiet satisfaction. When she dropped her hands to his waist and slid them around him, pulling his lower body against her so that she could feel the proof of his need for her hard and ready against her belly, he growled. Lifting his mouth so that it hovered just above hers, he dropped small, harsh kisses on her lips. *"Marry me."*

"I—" She sighed. "All right."

His big body stilled completely for a moment. Then he kissed her again, only this time there was a tenderness in it that made her heart expand with hope. "You won't be sorry," he promised.

The next day, they made the short flight to Thortonburg and Rafe took her to the vault at Thortonburg Castle where his family's heirloom rings were kept. His family fortune was easily as extensive as Elizabeth's own, and the array of rings he brought out to show her was dazzling even to a woman used to the finest of gems. When she threw up her hands helplessly and told him there were too many beautiful rings to choose from, he leaned forward and picked up a square-cut emerald surrounded by diamonds.

It was a beautiful ring and when he slipped it on her ring finger, it fit as if it had been made for her. "It's a sign," he said in satisfaction. "This ring belonged to my great-great-grandmother on my mother's side. She had green eyes just like you and her husband gave her an entire set of emerald jewelry to match this." He leaned forward and kissed her, lingering over her mouth until they were both panting. "If you're good, I'll give you the rest for a wedding present."

"And just what does 'being good' entail?" She could

hardly believe that throaty purr had come from her own throat.

He chuckled as he rose and rang the bell for the waiting servants to enter and replace the rest of the gems in the vault. "Not nearly enough while we're each sleeping under a different roof," he said "Not *nearly* enough."

He was looking forward to seeing his parents again as much as he looked forward to his biannual dental checkups. And the woman sitting in the passenger seat on his left wasn't going to help the situation any, he thought darkly as he drove the imported luxury car from the royal airstrip through the countryside toward the hills of Thortonburg proper, where his entire family awaited his visit.

They were having dinner with the Grand Duke and Duchess. Elizabeth had been hesitant to accept when his mother Sara had called yesterday with the invitation, and he appreciated her concern for his feelings. Still, he'd told her, it was an excellent way for her to get to know him better, a lure he knew she'd swallow like a trout.

"Tell me more about your childhood." Elizabeth shifted in her seat, and he took his eyes off the road long enough to appreciate the way her skirt climbed up one long, slender thigh. They'd brought evening dress for tonight's dinner, but the simple houndstooth suit with gray suede trim at the collar and cuffs was almost elegant enough to suffice.

Last night, he'd been amazingly miserable without her, considering that they'd only spent one whole night together in the same bed in this whole crazy relationship. And as much as he longed to have her moving under him in ecstasy and sleeping in his arms, he knew there was more to it than that. The days they'd spent together in Phoenix had gotten him accustomed to her presence, to her quiet humming as she flitted around the house, to the gentle scents of perfume—and Elizabeth—that occasionally wafted down the halls. He hadn't particularly wanted to analyze the feeling that had swept over him when he'd presented himself at the palace for luncheon earlier today and seen her come sedately down the hall to greet him.

No, he'd much rather relive the passionate moment they'd shared when he pulled her into the deserted library for a few kisses to tide him over.

"Rafe? Where are you?"

He came back to the present with a jolt. She was eyeing him with what looked to be compassion and he realized she thought he'd been thinking of his childhood.

"My childhood? Not much to say, as I already told you. I was away at school."

"What did you do on holiday?"

A ball of ice formed in his stomach. "I spent most of my holidays at school."

There was a moment of silence as she digested that. But he knew she wouldn't let it go. "Why didn't you go home?"

Raphael! Come down from there at once. Climbing trees is for peasants. Time for your riding lesson and I'll be most unhappy if you're late again.

He shrugged. "I don't know. My father and I didn't get along very well. It seemed...simpler."

Second place in the national geography competition. Second place? *Really, Raphael, we expected more from you than this. The Thorton name is one of the oldest and finest in all Europe...*

"How about your mother?"

"What about her?"

She sighed as if she were dealing with an intransigent child. "Did you get along with your mother?"

"Sure. But when there were any decisions to make, she deferred to Father's judgment."

"How long has it been since you've seen them?"

He counted. "Almost two years. They stopped to harass me briefly on a trip to California."

"Two years! And you haven't been to see them since?" She was truly shocked. He could feel it flowing across the car toward him like a tangible presence. "But..." she was clearly at a loss "...they're your *family*."

"Look," he said, wishing he were anywhere else but having this conversation. "Your parents adore you. Not everyone in the world has the same good fortune. Don't expect them to fall all over themselves with joy at the sight of me." He couldn't suppress the bitter laugh that escaped. "On the other hand, you and I both will probably be honored guests now that my father's gotten what he wants. That baby is his fondest dream."

"Don't tell me we're back to this arranged marriage nonsense. My father says it's not true." Her tone was aggressive, and for the first time a kernel of doubt worked its way into his mind. Was it possible the old goat had lied to him all these years?

But all he said was, "You'll see what I mean."

He turned into the high, gated entrance to the castle a few minutes later. The guard on duty greeted him by his title—his *former* title, he thought grimly as he made the drive through the forested grounds and out through the expanse of lawn to the circular drive that fronted the enormous old keep.

He hoped his father didn't think this visit was made for the purpose of effecting a reconciliation, because nothing could be farther from the truth. The castle might be an outstanding example of Norman architecture, but Roland could have the moldy old ruin—and all the others—as well as the yoke of responsibility that went with them.

As they walked up the wide marble steps of the castle, memories battered at his brain. He'd come up these steps many times as a child. His father would be standing at the top, waiting, and the little boy he'd been dreaded those first words.

Fell from your horse in the polo match. Fell from your horse! If you want the King of Wynborough to consider you a suitable match for one of his daughters, you'll have to do better than that.

The little boy in his memories nodded docilely, but behind the blank face resentment brewed.

"You look positively ferocious." Elizabeth laid a small hand on his arm. "What on earth are you thinking?"

With an effort, he shook off the past. "Just reliving the happy scenes of my youth. Come on, let's get this over with."

But she didn't move forward with him and he stopped and looked at her. "Uh-oh. You don't think we know each other that well, but I already know exactly what you're going to say next."

"You do not." But her voice was indulgent.

"What scenes from your childhood were you reliving?" He did his best imitation of a cracked feminine voice, and she laughed.

"All right. I confess. Maybe it's just that women in general are invariably nosy? And I'm just like every other woman."

"Not a chance." Rafe took her hand and pulled her nearer. "Believe me, there's no other woman on earth like you." He raised her hand to his lips. "And I mean that in the best possible way."

She swallowed, and the rosy blush he so loved warmed her cheeks. He hadn't thought a simple compliment, if it even qualified as such, could unsettle her like that.

"Thank you," she said. But as the heavy door began to swing open, she smiled at him, flashing the little dimple in her cheek he found so fetching. "Don't think you've sidetracked me. We'll get back to this conversation later."

A butler in formal dress opened the door and Rafe noted it was the same stodgy old coot his father had employed for eons.

"Good afternoon, Trumble. How have you been?"

"Very good, my lord. Welcome home." The old man's face was a study in blank disapproval, a look he'd worn since the days when Rafe was a young boy trying to sneak in the kitchen door with the garden snake he'd captured. "May I take your wraps?"

Rafe stepped behind Elizabeth and removed the car coat draped over her shoulders, then handed over his leather jacket. "We have bags in the car. Could you have them taken to a guest suite, please?"

"Certainly, my lord. If you'll follow me...?" As the man turned and started down the hallway, Rafe spoke again.

"Don't bother showing us in, Trumble. I know the way. Family in the drawing room?"

"As you wish, sir." The aged servant nodded stiffly, and Rafe could see his insistence on informality was a source of irritation. Some things never changed. As they moved down the hall, Rafe leaned close to Elizabeth's ear. "Trumble's been here since the place was built. He was born that age and he wins yearly awards for his personality and charm."

She laughed, a soft, musical sound. "He certainly seems a bit on the...sour side."

"Lemons are sugar in comparison, believe me."

They continued down the hall and turned left, heading for the room where he knew the family would be gathered, having their pre-dinner drink. Routine rarely, if ever, varied in his father's house. As they passed a large linen closet, Rafe paused and opened the door. Ha! Empty. Grabbing Elizabeth's wrist, he dragged her behind him into the small, dark room, reaching out to flip on the single light.

She turned her face up to his and her green eyes were wide and alarmed. "What are we doing in here?"

He looked down at her and smiled. Then his gaze dropped to her lips, the luscious field of soft pink slightly parted as she waited for his response. He could see the instant the intimacy of their position dawned on her. Slipping one arm around her, he drew her close while with his other hand he covered her hard little tummy, his fingers nearly brushing the top of the warm feminine mound below as he cupped the small bulge. He slipped one hand up to the back of her neck, drawing her up on tiptoe against him while he still held his other hand over her unborn baby. "Stop thinking so much," he growled as he bent to her lips. "Turn off your brain and go with your instincts."

Then he kissed her, and just as it had every other time he touched her, the world fell away and all he could feel, all he could smell and taste and touch was her, surrounding his senses so that he could think of nothing else. But this time there was a new element of intimacy in the meeting of their mouths, a recognition that this was meant to be. It was as if each of them had realized in their one day apart just how much they needed each other.

"You have to marry me soon," he said, and his voice was so rough and deep and hoarse that it didn't sound like his at all.

There was a moment when her gaze flew up to meet his and he couldn't read her thoughts. A cold arrow of fear shot through him at the idea that he'd been mistaken, that she hadn't really agreed—

"All right."

He might not have heard it if he hadn't been watching her face. Jubilation expanded within him until he thought he might have to shout aloud. But instead he forced himself to release her, then gently turned her around while he brushed the wrinkles out of her skirt and she fished a tissue out of her purse for him to wipe her lipstick from his lips.

"Let's get this over with," he said. "The sooner we can get home to Phoenix, the better."

It was a little like facing a firing squad, she thought, as Rafe opened the double doors. She'd met every one of the three people in the room many times before. *But you weren't pregnant and unmarried,* said the little voice inside her head that still shamed her from time to time.

The Thorton family stood as she preceded Rafe into the room. Though not a one remarked on her pregnant state, she knew it was obvious in the simple wool maternity suit she'd worn, and she felt her cheeks heat in embarrassment at the slight widening of their eyes before they all hastily dragged their gazes to her face.

Training kicked in and she went from one to another, exchanging a small word with each person as Rafe followed behind her. As they approached his father, she caught a flash of deep emotion in the older man's gaze as he looked at his eldest son. But in an instant it was gone, and, after greeting her, the Grand Duke turned to Rafe with a stern cordiality so remote he could have been addressing a peer whom he barely knew.

"Welcome home, Raphael."

"Thank you, Father."

Rafe didn't bother to add any small talk to ease them past the moment, and when she glanced at him, the muscle working in his jaw warned her just how difficult this was for him. Quickly she stepped into the breach.

"My father says you've got an exceptional colt out of the mare you bred to his stallion," she said. Then she blushed as she realized breeding practices probably weren't the wisest topic of conversation under the circumstances.

But Victor Thorton only nodded and smiled at her. "Yes,

indeed. The last time we bred them, we got that pretty little filly who has gone on to win every two-year-old race out there. Your father kept that one, and I'm hoping this colt will be as superb a piece of horseflesh.''

They moved past him then to where the Grand Duchess of Thortonburg stood beside the wingback chair in which she'd been sitting doing needlework before they arrived.

''Your Grace.'' Elizabeth touched her cheek to the older woman's, noting the still-beautiful skin and, more importantly, the open warmth in her green eyes as she gazed at her son. ''Thank you for receiving me.''

''It's my pleasure, dear.'' The Grand Duchess spoke to Elizabeth, but her hungry eyes barely left her son. As Elizabeth moved aside, the slender woman stretched up to enfold her eldest child in her arms. ''Oh, Raphael, it's good to have you home. You've been missed.''

''It's only a visit, Mother.'' Again, Rafe was stiff and abrupt, though Elizabeth noticed his arms tightened for a long moment about his mother's slender frame.

''One we hope you'll repeat often.'' The Grand Duchess smiled serenely, but Elizabeth saw the hurt she couldn't hide.

''And Roland.'' Elizabeth held out both hands to the waiting man. A year younger than she, they'd attended balls and house parties and all manner of things with the same crowd of young aristocrats.

''Princess Elizabeth. It's been too long.'' Roland drew her close and kissed both cheeks.

''Hmm.'' Elizabeth drew back and considered. ''Nearly four months. The last time I saw you, you'd been unseated during a hunt and landed in a mudhole as I recall.''

Roland gave her a mock-scowl, then grinned and her heart stuttered at the resemblance to his brother. ''You have a good memory. Too good.'' He turned to his older brother with his hand extended. ''Welcome home, Raphael.''

"Thank you." Rafe took the outstretched hand and the brothers shook.

An awkward silence fell. It was as if these people didn't know how to make small talk with each other, she thought. Then she realized that was probably the literal truth. Rafe had lived at schools most of his life. Any attempt at "catch-up" conversations would be severely limited because they simply didn't know each other well. Comparing them to her own boisterous, warm, loving family, she felt her heart constrict. No wonder Rafe had trouble allowing himself to feel.

As the silence grew oppressive, she opened her mouth to say something, anything, but Rafe forestalled her by taking her hand in his and holding up the engagement ring he'd given her.

In a curiously formal tone, he said, "Father, Mother, Roland, we have an announcement to make." He paused for a moment and looked down at her, holding her gaze with his as he said, "Elizabeth has agreed to do me the honor of becoming my wife. We'll be married in Wynborough in two weeks."

Two weeks? Suddenly time seemed to be rushing past.

He must have read the shock in her eyes because he smiled then, a small, private smile just for her before turning back to his family. "In case you hadn't noticed, there's a bit of a need for haste," he added wryly.

She was blushing, she knew she was and she made a face at him. Darn the man for pointing out something that didn't need any additional notice.

"Well!" The Grand Duke's tone was too loud, too enthusiastic. "That's wonderful news, Raphael. Congratulations to you both."

The Grand Duchess looked happy but hesitant. "I wasn't aware that you two had ever met," she said.

"We became acquainted at the Children's Fund Ball last

fall,'' Rafe informed her. "Elizabeth has been a guest in my home in Phoenix recently. We'll be living there after the wedding.''

She had to admire the way he left out all sorts of pesky details which would have required a rather more in-depth explanation.

''But you weren't home at that time—'' Sara Thorton stopped abruptly as she realized that her eldest son had indisputably been in Europe at that time. He simply hadn't chosen to visit his family.

The Grand Duchess bit her lip and turned away, and Elizabeth saw the sheen of tears in the older woman's eyes. ''It was a very quick trip,'' she offered impulsively.

A muffled choking sound from across the room drew her attention. Roland's eyes were dancing with laughter and she realized she was only making things worse. Rafe obviously had had time for *some* things. She could feel her cheeks heating again.

''We'll be married in Wynborough, but we will continue to make our home in Phoenix,'' Rafe said.

''In Phoenix! But you can't take the potential heir to the throne out of the country,'' the Grand Duke protested.

''Elizabeth cannot take the throne,'' Rafe said sharply. ''Alexandra's the eldest, so her firstborn son will ascend the throne. I *do* remember a few things from my classes in governmental policy, Father.''

''There's been a change—''

Rafe's mother cut off her husband's blustering tone. ''Where will the wedding take place?''

''At Wynton Chapel,'' Elizabeth volunteered gratefully. She could practically see Rafe's temper rising perilously close to the boiling point, and apparently his mother did, too. She put a gentle hand on his arm. This topic was *not* one she wanted to discuss at the moment.

The Duchess was determined to get the conversation

back onto safer topics. "Then we'd better get on with the arrangements. I shall call the Queen tomorrow and offer my assistance."

"Thank you, Mother." Rafe stepped forward and kissed her cheek and again Elizabeth saw the woman blink back tears. "Now if you'll excuse us, I'm sure Elizabeth would like to rest before dinner. Is there a room prepared?"

Roland strolled to the door. "Can you imagine that there isn't?"

That succeeded in drawing a chuckle from Rafe and Roland beckoned for them to precede him. "I'll show you to her room."

They followed the younger man to the second level of the old castle and down several long hallways until he halted and turned the knob of a door. Along the way, she surreptitiously watched Rafe's face as he absorbed the ambience of his childhood, but his expression was completely blank and she had no clue as to what was going through his mind. The only suggestion of tension came from the rigid set of his shoulders and the muscle ticking in his jaw.

At the door of the room they all paused. "It really is good to see you again, Roland," she said, breaking the silence that hung between the brothers.

"And you," he responded, reaching for her hand and holding it for just a moment. "Good luck with this baby. It'll be easier if it's a girl, I'm sure. No decisions to be made."

She nodded, and she knew her voice sounded troubled when she answered him. "Thank you."

"Rafe…" The younger man hesitated. "I know it hasn't been easy to come back."

"I wouldn't have come at all if a certain skittish woman hadn't made me chase her through three time zones." Rafe reached out and gave a lock of Elizabeth's hair a gentle tug.

"I know." Roland smiled. "But maybe it's a good thing. You and Father needed this." Then he hesitated. "He's sorry, you know, even if he can't say it. He's been different lately—mellower—largely because it broke his heart to realize he had driven you away."

"You're trying to tell me he learned from his mistakes?" There was sarcasm in Rafe's voice.

The affable mask over Roland's handsome face dropped away, and suddenly Elizabeth felt the aggression that charged the air. The two men faced each other, and if the atmosphere hadn't been so tense, she would have laughed at the sight of the brothers who looked enough alike to be twins but for their age disparity glaring at each other.

"I'm not *trying* to tell you, I *am* telling you," Roland said levelly. "I remember very little of what happened when you two got together. If you can't forgive him, I'll try to understand. But I hope you'll think about it."

Rafe sighed. "You ask a lot."

Roland shrugged, smiling, then he extended his hand. "Thank you for coming, whatever the reason. I'm glad you're here."

Rafe hesitated. Then, grabbing his brother's hand, he pulled the younger man into an awkward embrace. "It surprises me to admit that I'm glad I'm here, too. Thanks."

In the next moment, the door closed behind Roland, and Rafe and Elizabeth were alone in the room. For an instant, he wondered about his brother's odd words when he'd spoken to Elizabeth. But when he looked across the room at his woman, everything else faded from his mind except the need to reassert his claim.

He closed the space between them in three quick steps, taking her by the shoulders and dragging her into his arms.

Eight

"**R**afe!" She squeaked and struggled, but he caught both
wrists in one big hand behind her back, arching her against
him and rubbing his body back and forth against hers, feeling the heady rush of arousal course through him. Her body
was soft and warm and when he bent his head and covered
her mouth, she didn't fight him but opened to his probing
tongue as if she'd been waiting for him.

Maybe she had. He hoped he wasn't the only one who'd
been driven crazy by the hours and the night they'd spent
apart.

Lifting his head a fraction, he said, "Do you know how
I felt when I realized you were gone?"

Her body stilled. "Furious?" she ventured.

"Well, that, too." He framed her jaw with one big hand.
"I was worried sick. Not that you had decided to travel
independently—" He forestalled her when she would have
spoken again. "You're pregnant. You shouldn't be running

around the globe.'' He paused for a moment, and his next words were more of a thought spoken aloud. ''I don't want you away from me overnight ever again.''

Her eyes widened. They stared at each other for a moment and again he recognized that something had changed between them. But her body was calling to him, soft and enticing against him, and he couldn't think of anything but making her his again in the most basic way there was, telling her without words how much she meant to him.

Putting a hand on her hip, he explored the inside of her mouth as he urged her toward the high, antique bedstead with its tapestry canopy. When the backs of her knees bumped against the mattress, he slid his free hand around to palm one smooth, rounded buttock, but the fabric of her skirt got in the way.

Releasing her wrists, he muttered against her mouth, ''Get these clothes off,'' as he plunged his hands beneath her skirt and tugged both her knickers and her tights down and off. She was unbuttoning the line of tiny buttons running down the front of her blouse when he stood again. Impatiently he pulled the blouse and her slip over her head in one smooth move, then tossed them aside and reached for her bra. As he unclasped the garment and drew it aside, her breasts fell free. He cupped them in his palms, feeling their cool weight warming beneath his touch as he slipped his hands around and around in small circles, brushing repeatedly over the sensitive nipples that rose to meet his stroking.

He leaned down and kissed her again, then dropped his head to her shoulder and pressed a kiss to the fine-grained flesh he found there, marveling at the bounty of feminine beauty he'd exposed. She was making small noises in the back of her throat and she brought her hands up between them to deal with the buttons of his shirt, shoving it aside and dragging up his T-shirt beneath to expose his broad, rough-haired chest. He felt her breath hot against him and then he jumped at the startling sensation of tiny teeth closing gently but firmly over one of his flat male nipples, using her tongue and her teeth to draw it into the same nubbin of aroused flesh that he had called from her.

Arrows of desire sizzled a path through his nerve endings from her teasing tongue straight to his groin, and he groaned, abandoning her breasts to slide his hands around her bottom and pull her higher against him. He pushed a muscled knee between her slim legs, parting them and moving steadily forward until she rode one hard thigh. She brought a hand down then, exploring him through his pants, and the feel of her small palm rubbing over his cloth-covered erection drove him wild. Holding her in place, he fumbled with his belt, roughly unzipping his pants and then stepping away from her momentarily to discard the rest of his clothing.

Elizabeth stood with her back against the bed, her chest rising and falling with her quickened breathing, her arms braced behind her on the mattress. He stepped forward again, pulling her against him, and they both made anguished sounds of frustration and delight at the feel of naked flesh against naked flesh. His hot, pulsing column pushed at the mound of her belly and when she slowly rocked back and forth, caressing him with the small motion, he closed his eyes and threw his head back, giving himself to her ministrations.

With his eyes closed, every touch of her fingers to his skin made him tremble. She smoothed her hands over his chest, flicking lightly over his nipples again, then made small circles that moved steadily lower and lower. Over his rib cage, down into the tiny well of his navel, then even lower until she was brushing the thicket of black curls that surrounded his aching hardness. She toyed with him, straying down to the creases where his thighs met his torso, stealthily sliding her fingers along those folds to the heavy sac that hung between his legs, gently cupping him in her hand with her fingers slowly slipping back and forth. But she didn't touch him as he longed for her to, and he felt himself getting harder and larger, and more and more frantic for her touch.

Finally he couldn't take another second of her sly teasing. ''Touch me,'' he growled, dropping his head to seize her earlobe between his teeth and deliver a not-so-gentle nip of warning. He slid his own hands down her body to her hips and held her firmly with one, while with the other he dipped boldly into the shadowed cleft between her legs, finding her hot and wet and unbelievably slick and ready.

She wrapped her fingers around his straining shaft, feeling the silky heat, running her thumb up over the tip and discovering the slipperiness already forming there. She rubbed her fingers around the broad head, then down again, clasping him in a firm hand and beginning to stroke him rhythmically.

''Like this?'' she whispered.

His breath whistled in and out between his teeth in agonized pleasure. His hand between her legs pushed her thighs apart until she widened her stance, then found the humid entrance to her and pushed one long finger steadily, slowly but firmly up into the tight feminine channel. ''Like that,'' he managed. He matched his finger's motion to the strokes of her hand, feeling the pace quicken far too fast, knowing this was going to be over in a matter of moments, but he couldn't bring himself to drag her hand away. Instead, he found himself covering her hand with his free one and showing her an even more intense rhythm, tutoring her in the hot, fierce pleasures of sensual fulfillment.

But all too soon, he began to shake uncontrollably with the effort to retain control, and he had to force himself to draw her hand away, twining her fingers with his when she made a sound of protest and reached for him again. The tip of his erect staff brushed against her belly and he groaned. He knew he didn't have much time. Withdrawing his hand from her steamy center, he grabbed her by the hips and boosted her up to perch on the edge of the high bed, placing her in a perfect position to receive him. His body was so ready for release that he groaned aloud as he clasped himself in one big hand and positioned himself for the final claiming. Then he pulled her off the edge of the bed.

She slid onto him in a deep, smooth stroke so perfect she might have been made for the moment, wrapping her legs around his hips and drawing him even more closely to her. He thrust deeply into her and she cried out as her most sensitive knot of tiny nerves banged against his pelvis.

She threw her head back and looked up at him, her eyes wide, pupils dilated with passion. "I can't...I can't—"

"Yes, you can." Scarcely able to restrain himself, but still in control enough to know that he didn't want to go without her, he pushed his hand between them and found the little bump of pouting flesh with his thumb. Her body was quivering around him and he'd barely started a steady circling when her back arched and she screamed.

Inside her, strong muscular contractions squeezed his bursting flesh, and as she shuddered and heaved in his arms, Rafe felt himself gathering into one giant sensation all centered on the hot flesh snugly ensconced within her body. His hips thrust, withdrew and thrust again, slamming against her, and she screamed with each contact of flesh against flesh. His body drew taut, sensation dancing down his back, starting deep within him and pushing his seed up and out, arching him against her again and again, bucking wildly as he emptied himself into her receptive woman's well.

Finally there was nothing left to give, nothing left to feel but satiated pleasure and drowsy exhaustion. His legs trembled; her ankles slipped from their clasp behind his back and her legs slid to the floor.

He reached behind her to the gold coverlet, pulling it back before lifting her and placing her gently on the crisp sheets. Drawing the cover up around her, he walked around the foot of the big bed to the other side and climbed in. She turned to him as she had the night before on another continent and he slipped one arm beneath her, drawing her close, conscious of how small and fragile she seemed. Her hand came up to rest on his chest and she nestled against him with one leg over his thigh; the mound of their child pushed into his side, cradled between them and he felt her give a deep sigh.

Rubbing his thumb over the silky skin of her upper arm, he turned his head and kissed the top of her head. "Tired?"

"Mmm-hmm." She snuggled closer.

It was amazing what a warm, sweet woman cuddling up to you could do...when it was the right woman. He lifted a hand and put a finger under her chin, tilting her face up to his so that he could kiss her, long and tender. "Then sleep. I'll hold you."

He woke before she did. Easing his arm out from under her head, he grinned when she grumbled and curled into a little ball next to him. Shifting himself onto one elbow, he took a moment to study her features.

She was so pretty. Her complexion was roses and cream with a light sprinkling of freckles over the bridge of her nose. Her dark lashes concealed those incredible eyes— those penetrating eyes that made him feel she could see every thought in his head.

The first night they'd met, she speared him with one look from those eyes and he'd been lost. His body had leaped with interest, but it was more than that—it was as if he'd known from the very start that she was going to be his.

And she was. Satisfaction filled him. She'd finally agreed that marriage was their best choice given the situation. Idly, he wondered what would happen if he'd met her today, in Phoenix, with no pregnancy to make marriage a necessity.

Would he still have been drawn to her so strongly? Would he have called her again? Would he even consider asking her to be his wife?

Of course. That was how it was supposed to work. Arranged marriages were ridiculous, and seemed even more so now that he understood what it was like to be anticipating marriage to the woman he loved—

The woman he loved.

My God, it had been between them the whole time. How had he not known? How had he not recognized it?

On the other hand, why would he? He hadn't grown up knowing what it felt like to be loved. He'd never allowed himself to need another person, either, like he needed her. He *needed* her. It was a frightening thought to know that his happiness depended on this one small woman lying beside him.

Shifting onto an elbow, he watched the slow rhythm of her breathing. The milky globes of her breasts were hidden beneath the arms she had folded under her chin and one leg was drawn up, hiding the soft female treasure that had welcomed him earlier. Her belly, stretched and swollen, was tilted down to rest against the bed and he wondered how much bigger she would get.

She was going to need him, too, in a very physical sense that had nothing to do with sex, he realized. For assistance as her body grew even more bulky and cumbersome, but more than that, for reassurance. He wouldn't let her doubt for a single moment that he found her desirable despite her pregnancy. The fact that she carried a child made from the two of them, from their very first, memorable meeting, only made her more precious in his eyes.

Gently, he laid his hand over her stomach, over the womb where his baby rested.

His baby. *Their* baby. For a few moments he allowed himself to dream about the child growing within her womb. What would he be like as a father? he wondered. He'd promised himself over the years that any children of his never would have to know the sting of critical words, never would cry themselves to sleep because they hadn't measured up, never would choose to spend lonely holidays at boarding school rather than go home. Hell, his kids wouldn't even go to boarding school.

He's sorry, you know, even if he can't say it. Roland's words echoed in his head.

Oh, his father couldn't have been an easy man to live with even if he had mellowed, as Roland claimed. And his mother...she'd followed her husband's lead her entire life. Rafe had sensed more than once that she'd have liked to be warmer, more demonstrative and loving with him, but she'd never disobey the Grand Duke's edict that too much coddling would spoil the boy.

Rafe's children were going to know they were loved in every way there was. If that spoiled them, then too bad. It beat rejection.

He came out of his reverie then to see Elizabeth lying quietly, sleepy emerald eyes studying his face. She reached out a hand and laid it gently on his cheek and he turned his face into her palm, pressing a whisper-light kiss there before taking the hand and bringing it to the back of his neck. Slowly he leaned over her and set his mouth on hers, kissing her with all the tenderness his newly realized love gave him. When he lifted his head, there were tears in her eyes and he knew she'd caught something of his feelings in the gentle caress.

Dinner with his family was more of a success than he'd have believed was possible before this day. But now, Rafe caught himself thinking of the legions of ancestors who had lived in this very building. It would be exciting to share that with his child someday, on a visit to his father's homeland.

On a visit... For the first time he had a moment's dissatisfaction with his life-style. His child's heritage was here, where hundreds of years had passed under his family's rule. It was a remarkable legacy...was he wrong to reject it so completely?

Flying back to Wynborough that evening, to the palace where Elizabeth was staying with her parents, he remembered what she'd been pestering him about during their trip the previous afternoon. Though talking about his childhood wasn't high on his list of favorite activities, he said abruptly, "My parents—my father in particular—had very set ideas on how to raise a little duke-to-be. I had to ride, hunt, fish, speak French, read Latin, excel at mathematics and science, study the classics, recite every rule of etiquette, know proper forms of address—you name it, my father believed I should do it."

Elizabeth put a hand over his where it rested on the wheel of the car he drove. "Your childhood must have been busy."

"Busy." He laughed, but even he could hear the pain in the sound. "I wanted to please. I can remember lying awake as a very small boy, rehearsing over and over again how to greet the King of Wynborough at my first formal presentation the next day. But when the next day came, I was so nervous that I threw up while we were waiting in line to be presented. My father was livid."

Her fingers tightened briefly on his.

"They sent me to school when I was five because my father felt I lacked proper self-discipline. It was horrible. Cold showers every morning, standing in perfect lines at all times, no extra servings at meals. For a growing boy, that alone was torture. But do you know what the worst thing was?''

He sensed rather than saw her shake her head in the dark interior of the vehicle. ''The worst thing was that soon, too soon, I preferred that hellish school to my own home. At school, hard work had rewards. At home, hard work only meant more difficult tasks and more criticism.''

He stopped speaking. There was no point in going on. She got the picture.

''Rafe...'' Her voice was soft and hesitant and when he glanced at her he could see the tracks where tears had slipped down her cheeks. ''I promise our child will never be a...a product to be perfected. Our children will be works of art, great treasures to be protected and preserved for their own unique characteristics.''

Her words moved him, and the fact that she'd said ''children'' wasn't lost on him. Reaching across the car, he wiped away the telltale moisture with the pad of his thumb and caressed her cheek before returning his hand to the wheel.

''Mother, I'll be back in five days, I promise.'' Elizabeth hugged the Queen of Wynborough. ''Plenty of time to get your wedding gown altered to fit a pregnant bride.''

''But why go at all?'' her mother asked plaintively. ''It isn't as if there's anything in Phoenix for you to do in the next two weeks.''

But there is. According to Laura, Sam Flynn is back in town. It would be wonderful if I could bring my brother home for my wedding!

But aloud all she said was, ''I have to go. I don't want to be away from Rafe so long. You make the rest of the arrangements as you see fit.'' That wasn't a lie. She *didn't* want to be away from Rafe. At all.

"We'll keep it simple," Gabriella promised. She smiled wistfully. "Although it would have been nice to throw a huge wedding for at least one of my daughters!"

Elizabeth laughed ruefully, thinking of the men who had claimed each of her sisters, the whirlwind weddings and the after-the-fact announcements. "Oh, Mother, I'm sorry. We spoiled your dreams, every single one of us."

The Queen took her daughter's face in her hands and kissed her forehead. "No, dear, you didn't. In fact, you've all fulfilled the only dream your father and I have ever had for you. You've found love."

Elizabeth looked over her shoulder at Rafe, talking with the King. "Is it that obvious?"

"What, that you adore each other?" Her mother smiled. "Only to eyes that know how to spot it."

If only it were true, Elizabeth thought as they completed their good-byes and Rafe helped her into the car. He'd begun to treat her as if he truly did care for her. She'd started to hope that maybe her marriage would be more than a one-sided love affair for the rest of her life.

The trip back to Phoenix was tiring, if uneventful. She slept much of the way on both planes while Rafe read and watched movies. When they stepped out of the car into the brilliant winter sun outside his home, Elizabeth smiled and raised her face to its warmth. "I didn't even realize I'd missed this until now. Oh, Rafe, I do love this town!"

He laughed as he walked around to the trunk to get their bags. "It's a good thing. My business is firmly established here. I'd hate to have to move it now."

Halfway up the sidewalk, she stopped and turned to him. "You'd actually consider moving if I asked you to?"

There was a moment of stillness in the dry air. Slowly Rafe set down the bags he carried. "Well," he said, "I'd prefer not to move to Wynborough unless you can't be happy anywhere else, but yes, if you really wanted me to, I'd move my business.'' He reached down and took her hands, holding them in his much larger ones as he held her eyes with his intense blue gaze. ''Don't you know I'd do anything to make you happy?''

She felt her eyes filling with tears at his tender tone, and she swallowed. ''All it takes to make me happy is you.''

Something wild and bright flared in his eyes for a moment, then he dropped her hands and gathered her into his arms. ''I might have been too stubborn to admit it, but you've owned my heart since the first time I looked across a ballroom and saw those green cat-eyes watching me.'' Dropping his head, he found her mouth with his, kissing her until she hung limp in his arms, gasping for breath with her body melded to his from breast to knee. ''Let's go inside,'' he growled against her lips, ''so I can make us both very happy.''

In the middle of the night he was awakened by an odd sensation.

Rafe came fully alert in an instant with Elizabeth still in his arms. Confused, he glanced around the shadows of the bedroom he'd soon be sharing with his wife—*his wife!*—and then he felt it again.

A tiny thudding right at the spot where the mound of Elizabeth's full stomach was pressed against his side. Shifting himself fractionally, he placed his hand on the spot, then waited impatiently. There! Again, the same motion. And now that he was watching more closely, he could see by the full moonlight streaming in the window that there was a slight but definite movement beneath the surface of her skin. *Someone in there wanting to come out,* he thought whimsically.

''Hey, you in there,'' he whispered. ''It's the middle of

the night. This is when people sleep. You might as well get that concept down right now.''

A snuffling noise told him Elizabeth had awakened. Then she giggled more loudly. ''Are you talking to the baby?''

''Yes. He's keeping me awake.''

He could see her raised eyebrows in the dim light. ''He? I'm hoping 'he' is a 'she.'''

The words jogged a memory, and without really thinking about it, he said, ''You and Roland. Am I the only one who wants a boy?''

She went still beneath his hand. So still that he'd swear she wasn't breathing. Then, in an instant, she relaxed. ''Maybe,'' she said. But there was something in her voice that bothered him.

The memory came back more clearly now and he recalled the odd phrasing that he'd been too distracted to question that day. ''Roland said it would be simpler if it was a girl. Why?''

The moment the words hit the quiet night air, he wished he could get them back. Erase them and go on, blissfully unaware. A chill crawled up his back, though he didn't know why, and he felt a slow, inexorable change imbue the very air around them with dread. Moving deliberately, he sat up and looked down at her.

''Why?'' he demanded again.

She hesitated. Pushing herself to a sitting position also, she scooted back a little, moving away from him. She linked her fingers together in her lap, looked down at them, and sighed. The sound carried a distinct note of resignation. ''Your father started to tell you, but he was interrupted. There's been a great deal of discussion in recent years, in light of Wynborough's current lack of male heirs to the crown, as to how to proceed when the time comes.''

''That's great. But it doesn't affect us.''

''Well, actually, it might.'' She moved back even farther

as if she wanted to be out of his reach. "Two months ago a new proviso to the law was enacted."

"What kind of proviso?" He had a sick feeling jittering around in his stomach, and abruptly he recalled the vehement tone in his father's voice when they'd spoken of living in Phoenix. Unable to sit for another minute, he sprang from the bed, snatching a pair of sweatpants from the bedpost and stuffing his legs into them. "I'm waiting," he barked when she didn't respond.

"A proviso to ensure that the Wyndham line continues," she said in a low voice. "Since there is no eldest son to inherit, the eldest grandson will be the one to ascend the throne when my father...isn't the king anymore."

"The eldest grandson?" he repeated cautiously.

She nodded, apprehension clearly visible. "No matter which princess is his mother, the eldest grandson will be the next king."

He was incredulous. Fury rose as he realized fully what her words meant. There was a distinct possibility that his child, were it a son, would be the heir to the throne of Wynborough. "I can't believe this!" His voice was tight with the rage erupting inside him. "You know how I feel about this whole royalty thing and now you tell me if we have a son, he might be the next *king?*"

"Rafe, I didn't *plan* this," she said, a note of pleading entering her voice. "I certainly didn't intend to get pregnant the first time we met. And I didn't intend to marry you, remember?"

"You still expect me to believe that?" He was too angry to care about the words he hurled at her. "You knew who I was at the ball that night. Our fathers didn't have as much to do with this as I'd thought, did they?"

"That's not true! I had no idea who you were—"

"Sure. And pigs fly, Princess."

"I told you my father would never arrange a marriage for me. He doesn't believe in such an archaic custom."

"Maybe not, but he didn't mind sacrificing a virgin daughter for the good of the Crown, did he?"

She gasped. Tears were swimming in her eyes and as he watched, one fat drop slipped down her cheek. And still he went on, every suspicion he'd ever harbored erupting in a raging river of fury.

"I was right all along, wasn't I? You nearly had me fooled. But now your real agenda's been exposed. If you can't be the king—which you can't, being a female—then be the next best thing. Elizabeth, the Queen Mother. And I'm the perfect catch. Heir to the Grand Duchy of Thortonburg. *If* I were to inherit the title. I bet it was one hell of a shock when you found out I'm just plain old Rafe Thorton and intend to remain that way!"

The tears were pouring down her face now. "That's not what happened!" she screamed at him. She came off the bed in a rush, dragging the sheet around her to conceal her nakedness. As if he gave a damn. "I didn't know who you were when we met. I didn't even make the connection to Thortonburg when I found your card." She was shaking with rage, and he had a sudden moment of concern for the baby she carried.

"Eliz—"

"I *loved* you," she said, dashing the tears from her cheeks with one hand. "All I ever wanted was to marry you and have a family. Here in America or any other place you chose. That stupid title doesn't appeal to me any more than it does to you," she said fiercely.

"Right. And when were you planning to share this little 'proviso' with me?" He crossed his arms over his chest. "You knew about this months ago, no doubt. These kinds of laws aren't passed overnight. Were you afraid one of your sisters was going to beat you to the prize?" His heart was pounding so hard, he could feel it hammering against his wrist where it pressed against his skin and he felt as if his head was going to explode. How could she have done this to him? *Easily. You were just the means to the end, buddy.*

"I was waiting until the baby was born to tell you," she said in answer to his original question. Her voice was flat and dull. "I knew how you'd react. But if it's a girl, there would be no reason for concern. Alexandra's already expecting her first baby and my other two sisters recently married—I have every hope that one of them will produce the heir instead of me."

"Every hope," he repeated tightly.

"Every hope," she enunciated. "But you have such a phobia about your ties to the crown that it won't really matter even if it is a girl, will it, Rafe? Even if this baby is a daughter, you're still going to be stuck with a royal connection that's only one step away from the King. And you'll blame me for that for the rest of my life. I'll never be able to change my blood to something less blue. And you know what?" She stormed across the room until she was right in his face and he could see the deep, open wound he'd torn in her heart reflected in her eyes. "I wouldn't even if I could. I love my family. They're not my enemies, and I won't pretend to be somebody I'm not, even for you." She stopped and took a deep breath that hitched twice before she regained control. "You can forget this marriage. I'm going back to Wynborough to be with people who love me the way I am."

Her words stunned him. She stomped out the door and down the hall to the other end, where the room she'd slept in before still held most of her things. He heard the door slam violently and he knew there would be no talking to her the rest of the night.

You can forget this marriage.

She couldn't back out! She'd said she would marry him. *Forget this marriage.*

He felt himself begin to shake as he fully grasped what those words meant. She wasn't going to marry him. His child would not be born legitimate. His child would be raised on a separate continent from its own father with a mother who didn't want to have anything more to do with him. But worse, much worse, was the loss of the love he'd come to depend on. She'd said she was leaving, going back to Wynborough. She was leaving him.

He hadn't anticipated that when he'd accused her of wanting his title. What woman was going to stand and let a man shout at her, accuse her of all kinds of things, scoff at her honesty?

The sick feeling in his stomach returned full-force and he had to grope for the edge of the bed. He'd been wrong. He *had* to have been. No one had schemed to push her into his arms. Otherwise, she'd never be giving up the chance at marriage. He'd half assumed, stupidly, that she was only playing hard-to-get when she'd refused him before.

But she hadn't been. He could see that now. It was so clear. All she'd wanted from him was love. Not legitimacy for her child, not a "second-best" title for a woman who couldn't wear the crown. Just love. She'd refused to marry him repeatedly because she'd loved him and had no hope of the feeling being returned.

He dropped his head into his hands and squeezed his skull between his palms. How blind could a man be?

Oh, God, he'd been so stupid. He'd taken her love and trampled it beneath both feet, with less than no regard for her feelings. He'd been so steeped in his own bitter memories that even after his family had made a legitimate attempt at reconciliation he was still determined to punish someone.

And he'd taken it out on Elizabeth. He'd sensed her love

for him before she'd confessed it, and he'd been so confident that her heart would be his forever that he hadn't realized how easily hearts can be broken.

He'd just ground hers into dust.

Could he repair the damage? The sick feeling told him it wouldn't be easy. But he had to try.

Rising, he walked slowly down the hall to her suite and knocked on the door. But as he'd expected, she didn't answer. He listened carefully, but she wasn't sobbing—at least, not loudly enough for him to hear. With a weariness deeper than anything he'd ever felt before, he slid down the door into a sitting position and prepared to wait. When she opened that door, he intended to be there.

No matter how long it took.

Because she was the bottom line. Elizabeth was what mattered most to him. If she wouldn't forgive him, if she didn't love him anymore, he didn't know what he'd do.

Dawn came a few hours later and he still didn't hear her. Good. She must have fallen back asleep. God knew how—he hadn't been remotely tempted to close his eyes.

By eight he was tired of sitting. She rarely ever slept this late. He straightened from the cramped position in which he'd been sitting and stood, then knocked on the door. Not hard enough to make her think he was still angry, but firmly enough that she couldn't sleep through it.

Not a peep.

Fifteen minutes later he was getting worried. She still hadn't made any sound at all and his imagination was starting to rev into overdrive, quickening his pulse and shortening his breath.

"Elizabeth! Open this door. I only want to talk to you." He paused.

No answer. Oh, God, was she hurt? Lying on the bathroom floor unconscious? Those tiles were so slippery....

"Either you open it *now* or I break it down." That was an idle threat. He'd designed the house himself. There was no way anyone could kick in one of these doors.

Keeping an ear tuned for her, he hurried to his tool closet and got a few items, then returned and began taking the door off its hinges. One way or another, she was going to talk to him.

Finally, the door came free and he set it to one side, then rushed into the room. She wasn't there. Heart pounding, he checked the adjoining bath but she wasn't there, either.

Then he noticed the French doors leading to the pool terrace. The deadbolt was unlocked as was the lock on the doorknob. As he started across the room, something white and out of place on the bed's forest-green quilt caught his eye.

Snatching up the note, he scanned its contents.

Rafe
I will contact you when the baby is born. Please inform your family of the change in plans.
          HRH Elizabeth, Princess of Wynborough.

Nine

The sunlight hurt her eyes even through the dark glasses she wore.

As the driver of the rental car she'd hired sped along the highway toward Catalina, Elizabeth wished for the tenth time that she was allowed to take a painkiller for the headache that was pounding behind her eyes.

When she extracted the sheet of paper from her purse, her hands were shaking and abruptly she clasped them together in her lap, squeezing tightly enough that her knuckles turned white. She had to get herself under control before she reached Catalina, or Sam Flynn would think she was crazy.

Sam Flynn was likely to think she was crazy, anyway. After all, how many people knocked on your door and explained that you might be a long-lost prince?

She should be more excited about this venture. It was quite likely that she would be meeting her older brother for the first time in her life in less than an hour.

But nothing seemed exciting to her after the events of last night.

She swallowed and told herself to think of something— *anything*—else. But over and over again, like a scratched CD that kept skipping back to the same spot, she heard Rafe's voice in her head: *You knew who I was at the ball that night... Heir to the Grand Duchy of Thortonburg.*

The pain battered her skull. Dear God, how could he have believed that of her? She was right to break it off. He would never be able to get past his doubts, never be able to work through the anger he still felt at his father and his family for trying to make him into something he wasn't.

She recalled the look she'd seen on the Grand Duke's face the day they'd gone to visit. Victor Thorton was a man who loved his son...a man who would have to live the rest of his life knowing he had driven away his own child with his demands and his untruths. But Rafe would never fully understand that. Because he would never choose to allow himself to believe it.

Her eyes began to sting again, though she would swear there couldn't be any more tears left to fall. Last night she'd called a taxi and quietly left the house through her terrace door as soon as she could dress. Getting over the fence around the property hadn't been as easy as it might have been normally, but she'd managed it and then checked into a motel for what was left of the night. She'd cried endlessly into a pillow and risen at dawn to stare vacantly at the television until a decent hour arrived and she could place a call to Catalina.

Sam Flynn had been noncommittal on the telephone, but he'd agreed to meet with her. So after a hasty shower she'd rented this car, complete with driver this time. She would accomplish what she and her sisters had really come to the States to do—find their brother—and then she'd go home. To Wynborough.

Even if Wynborough didn't feel like "home" anymore, it was a better place than most to raise her child... Rafe's child. Her breath caught, and she turned the sob into a cough. She'd already alarmed the driver once when he'd looked in the mirror and seen the tears flowing down her cheeks. So now she wore the dark glasses and told herself to buck up, quit sniffling. After all, she was a princess. She had an obligation to present herself well in public.

Samuel N. Flynn was an attorney-at-law, according to the listing in the telephone book. Since it was a Tuesday morning, she'd called his office and been lucky enough to find him in.

Now, as the car pulled to a stop in front of the sign announcing Flynn's business, situated in a professional building, she stepped out and mentally closed the door on all thoughts other than the task at hand.

A receptionist sat busily working at a keyboard in the waiting room. Elizabeth announced herself simply as she had on the phone, as Elizabeth Wyndham, and the woman disappeared down a long hallway. A moment later, she reappeared and invited Elizabeth to follow her.

The attorney sat behind an enormous desk which held a small assortment of objets d'art and a larger collection of neat stacks of files in rows across the top of the desk. He rose when she entered and courteously came around the desk to shake her hand and offer her a seat as the receptionist retreated to her post.

"Miss Wyndham. A pleasure to meet you. Now tell me how I can help you with this 'urgent matter' you mentioned on the phone this morning." Sam Flynn had thick, wavy brown hair and a strong jaw with a dimple in his cheek. A good-looking man in a rough, tough way that went with the broad shoulders beneath his conventional white shirt. But it was his eyes that caught her attention. Piercing, blue and compelling, they reminded her of Rafe's eyes, and she felt her composure falter as Rafe's beloved features appeared in her mind once more.

"Ah, Mr. Flynn, thank you for seeing me on such short notice."

"Sam, please, Miss Wyndham." He leaned forward to look pointedly at her ring finger, grinning mischievously. "It *is* Miss, isn't it?"

"Um, actually, it's Princess." She was wearing an unrevealing pantsuit this morning and the handsome attorney must not have noticed her pregnancy. But she found herself completely unable to respond to his lighthearted flirtation; the comment only made her want to burst into tears again. "My father is King Phillip of Wynborough."

"Good God." Sam Flynn looked mildly thunderstruck. He assessed her expression. "You aren't kidding, are you?" Then his face sobered and he leaned back against the edge of his desk, crossing his ankles and folding muscular arms over his chest in a manner that made her fear for the seams at the shoulders of his shirt. "Now you've really got me curious. What's going on?"

"Are you the Samuel N. Flynn who was once at The Sunshine Home for Children in Hope?"

He nodded, his eyes alive with interest. "One and the same."

"What does the *N.* stand for?"

He grinned again. "No-middle-name. I was dumped at the home without a middle name and they listed it on my records the same way. Hence, my *N.*"

"Mr. Fl—Sam, you may remember that years ago I had a brother who was kidnapped as a child."

"Presumed dead." He shook his head. "I was just a baby then, but I've read about it. Must have been a horrible time for your parents."

"It was. The thing is, you are exactly the same age as my brother. Until recently we believed he was dead. But new evidence led us to The Sunshine Home, where my brother is believed to have been brought a few weeks after the kidnapping.''

''I see.'' Sam spoke slowly and she could see why he was a lawyer. His mind worked at top speed. ''And you think there's a chance I'm your brother.''

''There's a chance,'' she agreed.

''Nah.'' He unfolded his arms and boosted himself to sit on the desk, long legs dangling. ''You're too gorgeous to be related to me.''

''When my brother disappeared, he had dark hair and blue eyes. We know he was big for his age. He looked a great deal like pictures of my father at the same age and he probably still would today.'' She fumbled to open her bag and pulled out two sheets of paper, unfolding them and smoothing out the creases. She passed the first one to him. ''This is a picture of my father at age thirty, the age my brother would be today.''

''The age I am.'' Sam studied the copy. ''It's possible. Although I don't see any great resemblance.''

''It's hard to tell from a photograph.'' She studied him, thinking that he could indeed be James. So why wasn't she more excited? Wasn't this what she'd come to the States for?

You also came to the States to find the man who made love to you in a garden house.

She took a deep breath, banishing another pair of blue eyes from her mind. ''Would you be willing to have some bloodwork done?''

Flynn considered. ''Sure. Why not?'' He passed the photo back to her. Then he snapped his fingers. ''Wait a minute. Did your brother have any identifying marks? Birthmarks, scars—anything like that?''

She consulted the second sheet of paper she still held, though she knew its contents by heart. ''Yes. He had a small patch of freckles clustered closely together on his upper right arm. We have been warned, though, that such a mark may have faded over the years.''

''No scars?'' Sam was watching her closely.

She shook her head. ''None that would have been large enough to have lasted. James never had any kind of surgery or stitches. He was only a year old when he was kidnapped.''

''Well, then I'm afraid you've had a wasted trip, Your Highness.'' Sam heaved his bulky body off the desk and began to drag the front of his shirt free of his pants. ''I have a surgical scar that was already healed when I was brought to the Sunshine Home, so they figured it had to have occurred at least three months before. It must have been a doozy when it happened, because they could still count the stitch marks. Twenty-one in all.''

She was horrified at the thought of a tiny baby undergoing such trauma. ''At least three months before you got to the home?'' she said, thinking aloud. ''My brother hadn't been missing that long before you both turned up at the Sunshine Home.''

She stood and examined the scar in the muscle just below his ribs, seeing that despite the age of the wound, it obviously had been a ''doozy.''

''Good heavens. Surely a doctor would remember that kind of suture on a baby so young. Have you ever pursued it?''

Sam shrugged. ''They checked it out when I was dumped, but nothing turned up. That was in the days before computers, so I imagine the search was a local kind of thing. I've never bothered,'' he added. ''Whoever left me there didn't want me. I don't need them now.''

She nodded, though she felt a small ache in her heart for the little boy whose hurt still showed. The ache expanded as it reminded her of another grown man with his own childhood hurts—*No, don't go there, Elizabeth.*

Stepping back, she gathered up the papers and began to fold them before replacing them in her purse. "Sam, I'm sorry to have wasted your time. Thank you for seeing me today."

"My pleasure, Your Highness." He extended his hand and engulfed hers in a huge bear paw, holding it gently for a moment. "Good luck finding your brother."

When she got back to the car, the driver was waiting as she'd asked. He immediately headed for her next destination, a small public airstrip where she had booked a commuter flight to Tucson and then a flight to the east coast where she would leave for the transatlantic flight to Wynborough. It wasn't the most direct route she could have taken, but there was no power on earth that could induce her to go anywhere near Phoenix, not even to transfer from one airplane to another.

At the airport it suddenly dawned on her that she had the information that she and her sisters had been waiting to confirm for so long. Hurriedly, she sought a telephone and placed a call to Mitch Colton's ranch where Laura Bishop still was staying with Mitch and Alexandra, coordinating the remaining leads on finding the prince.

"Laura? It's Elizabeth."

"Princess Elizabeth! Congratulations on your engagement." Laura Bishop sounded as sweet and delightful as ever. "I'll be seeing you soon, back in Wynborough. I can't wait for the wedding and I can't wait to meet Raphael Thorton!'"

"Laura, listen to me." Elizabeth stopped and struggled to regain control of her voice, trying desperately to hold the tears at bay. She couldn't bear to talk about the wedding nor her dashed hopes of a lifetime of love. "I found Sam Flynn. He's not the one."

"He's not...then the only one left—" Laura's voice rose in excitement "—is John Colton! Alexandra's brother-in-law!"

"Yes. Is he there? I need you to talk to him right away."

"I can't." The secretary's voice was regretful. "He's still not here. Mitch and Alexandra have left messages in several locations for him, but he hasn't contacted them as far as I know."

"Tell them to send more urgent messages. We *have* to talk to him." If she concentrated hard enough on the task of finding her long-lost brother, perhaps some of the devastating pain that pierced her heart would go away. Or at least become more bearable. "I'm heading back to Wynborough soon. Call me there if you have any new information. But be careful. I don't want my parents to learn anything about this until we know for sure."

When Rafe disembarked from the flight onto which he'd bullied his way earlier in the day, Roland stood waiting in the airport lounge, his blue eyes dark with worry.

"Rafe, sorry to greet you with bad news, but I don't think she's come here. At least not yet."

Rafe nodded stoically. "Thanks for checking."

"Father has someone looking at all the flights. If she does come home, you'll know it."

"All right." He was so disappointed, he could barely force out the words.

They began walking through the airport.

"I was sure she was in love with you," Roland said. "Was I wrong?"

"You weren't wrong." Rafe shook his head. "But I—I didn't handle it very well, I'm afraid."

"Is there any way I can help? Or would you rather I just shut up?"

Despite his bone-deep misery, Rafe had to smile at his

younger brother. "Just being here is help enough." Regret for the years he could have had with Roland coursed through him and he tossed an arm around the other man's shoulders in a quick and affectionate hug.

When they reached the chauffeured limo waiting at the exit, Rafe was surprised to see his father seated inside the car.

Before he could utter a greeting, Victor held up a hand. "I know what you're thinking."

"You do?" Rafe smiled wryly. "Good, because I'm not sure I do anymore."

"Raphael, I'm sure you think I'm being so helpful out of a desire to link my house with the Wyndhams'." He grimaced. "And I admit, there's a part of me that would like that very much. But that's not why I'm here. In fact, I'll leave if you'd prefer I not involve myself in your life."

It was a shock to see that his father's intent blue eyes were the same ones that stared back at him every morning. Quietly, he said, "I believe you have my best interests at heart, Father. And that's good enough for me." And he realized it was true.

The moisture that gleamed in the older man's eyes embarrassed them both, and there was silence in the car for a moment.

The Grand Duke inclined his head. "I never should have tried to force you into a marriage based on—"

"Lies?" asked Rafe.

"Half truths, at the very least." The older man cleared his throat. "I know what it's like to love someone. And it was clear when we saw you together that you and Elizabeth were very much in love. Being my son, it's entirely possibly that you've done something unforgivably stupid—"

Both his sons laughed and the tension in the vehicle dissipated.

Then Rafe sobered. "I hope it's not unforgivable."

Slowly, hesitantly, his father reached over and laid a comforting hand on his son's knee. "We'll do whatever we can to help you make it right."

Several hours later, a servant knocked on the door of the smoking room where Rafe, his father and his brother were closeted.

The Grand Duke bellowed, "Enter," and Trumble came into the room, carrying a single sheet of paper on a silver tray.

"A telephone message for you, Your Grace."

Victor practically leaped on the man. "Well, give it here! What does it say?" The paper slipped from his grasp and fluttered toward the floor, but before it could land Roland had snatched it up again.

"The Princess has arrived at the palace," he announced. Then he cleared his throat. "She, ah, visited a man, an American attorney named Samuel Flynn in Catalina, Arizona, before leaving the States." He looked questioningly at Rafe. "Friend of yours?"

Rafe shook his head. "Apparently a friend of *hers,*" he said in a grim tone.

"Will she see you if you call on her?" asked his father.

"Not a chance." Once he would have endured torture rather than admit to his father that he'd made a mistake. Today, it no longer seemed to matter.

"Well, then, we'll have to get you in without being announced."

Two hours later, Victor's limousine was pulling up to the guardhouse at the palace gates.

"The Grand Duke of Thortonburg and my son Roland, Prince of Thortonburg," he announced imperiously to the guard as the man checked the two men seated in the rear interior of the vehicle.

The guard punched some buttons on the face of a cell

phone and received permission to admit them. As the gates slowly opened, and the limo rolled into the lush green gardens that led to the palace, Roland eyed the back of their chauffeur's head and chuckled. "Very good, Father. Very good."

The chauffeur glanced over his shoulder, blue eyes gleaming. "Thank you, Father."

In the end, it was even simpler than Rafe had anticipated.

Roland and the Grand Duke left him along a deeply wooded riding path close to the inner edge of the estate. Striding along the path, Rafe looked around to get his bearings. He'd chosen this location because he knew the woods grew up to the edge of the gardens near here. The guards around the palace grounds generally stayed within sight but not necessarily within hearing of the royal family. With that in mind, he hoped to get close enough to the house so that when Elizabeth came out for a stroll, he could speak to her even if he had to sit out here all night.

He couldn't believe how easy it had been, considering the King's well-known fetish for security. But the Grand Duke would never be expected to be a threat. And since the King's own security team had personally approved any chauffeurs entering any premises where the royal family was in residence, the man driving the Grand Duke's own limo had been cleared when his uniform insignia identified him as someone previously checked out.

To his right Rafe could see the beginning of a small clearing. As he got a better look, he muttered, "I'll be damned."

The palace grounds were enormous and he wasn't at all familiar with them. The sight of a glass-walled gazebo in the middle of the clearing made him shake his head wryly. Could it be the same one? It looked exactly like the one engraved in his memories—surely there couldn't be another so similar?

The drop of rain that hit his left cheek surprised him, so immersed in his surveillance was he. But as the drops quickly became a deluge, he sprinted for the only available cover, the little glass gazebo where he'd made love to Elizabeth the very first time.

Only moments after he rushed through the little entrance into the dry interior, a noise had him whirling to look for a pursuer. Elizabeth halted halfway through the door, her hand to her throat in a gesture of shock that matched the expression on her face.

"Rafe!"

He'd recovered his wits while she goggled at him, though her appearance was as much a surprise to him. "Why don't you come in before you get soaked?"

"I—" She glanced behind her at the downpour. "What are you doing here?"

"Coming after you."

She straightened, and he could see her regaining her composure. She wore jeans and an oversize sweater, but when she moved into the room, her manner was so regal that she might as well have had on a crown. "You've wasted a trip." The words dripped ice.

"Why did you come in here?"

Her eyelids flickered. "I was out for a walk and when it started to rain, I simply ran for the nearest cover. I *didn't* come here for any other reason."

He might have said something at that, but a man getting ready to beg for his life was smart not to antagonize the woman he wanted to share it with.

Again, she questioned him. "Why did you come here?"

"I can't forget it."

She blinked, looked at him through cool green eyes. "I beg your pardon?"

"Back in Phoenix you told me to forget about marriage. I can't."

"*That's* what you wormed your way in here to tell me? How did you get in here, anyway?" She held up a hand. "Never mind." Turning, she looked through the glass panes of the gazebo window. "Go away."

Her back was rigid, her arms hugged closely together over the swell of the baby. He could see her in profile, her lips pressed tightly together and her chin trembling.

"I've made peace with my father," he said softly.

"That's nice." She didn't look at him, but her tone wasn't quite so belligerent.

There was another awkward silence while he tried to think of something brilliant that would persuade her to give him another chance. Finally he just blurted out the words that were reverberating in his mind. "You said you loved me."

She flinched. Lifting a hand, she placed it against the condensation on the window. When she removed it, her small handprint was visible. But it was so humid in the garden house that even as they watched, the outline began to fade. "Some things aren't meant to be permanent," she said sadly.

"Elizabeth…" Was there no way to reach her? "If you don't want to get married, we don't have to. We can live together for the rest of our lives without making it legal. Just please—" His voice cracked. Stopping for a moment, he closed the space between them and stood directly behind her. "Elizabeth, I don't want to live without you. Please come back to me."

She didn't respond, but she didn't rebuff him, either. Raising his hands, he nearly placed them lightly on her shoulders but after a moment he let them drop. "Please," he repeated. "Give me another chance. I was wrong about everything. Your father, my father, you—"

"You would live with me even if I refused to marry you? Why? So you can hound me to death until I agree to make your child legal?" The words were lightly mocking, but he heard the pain underlying them, and his heart sank.

Quietly he said, "Some of us learn lessons more slowly than others. It took me far too long to learn mine."

He took a deep breath. "I love you."

Her emerald eyes widened and he could see the flare of an emotion she couldn't hide.

"I love you," he said again, pressing his advantage. "I should have told you before. I should have trusted you—"

She put a hand over his lips. "It's all right, Rafe. We'll make it all right now." She cradled his face in her hands and lifted herself on tiptoe against him.

Rafe gathered her closer and fit his mouth to hers, sweet relief flowing through him. Despite everything, she'd forgiven him. Could she ever understand how much he loved her? His mouth grew more demanding as he dragged her close, his body urging him to demonstrate his need for her.

Her hand smoothed over his shoulder and slipped around to the back of his neck as her tongue began to dance with his and her body softened and melted against him. In seconds the kiss heated into a flashfire that threatened to rage out of control.

The only thing that saved him from dragging her to the floor where they stood was the moisture on his face.

No, on *her* face.

The little annoyance crept into his consciousness, interrupting the intensity of the kiss, and he tore his mouth away from hers so he could wipe the rain from their faces. Only it wasn't rain.

Elizabeth was crying.

He gentled his hands on her, slipping his palms up to cradle her jaw. "What's wrong, Princess? Is it me?"

"N-no." She shook her head. Her eyes were as green as

spring grass, wet as the windowpanes around them, and tears continued to flow down her cheeks. She brought her hands up to cover his.

"I'll retain the title," he said desperately. Though it wasn't the path he'd intended his life to take, he'd do it in a minute if she'd agree to stay. To his shock, the words didn't bother him as once they would have.

But she shook her head again. "It's not the title. I'll love you no matter what you want to do with your life."

As the impact of what she was saying sank in, he felt the fist squeezing his heart begin to loosen its grip. He let his hands slide down from her face, turning them to take hers in a gentle clasp as he kissed her gently. "So if there's no problem, why are you crying?"

"I'm crying because I'm so happy." She leaned toward him for another kiss.

But at the last moment, he remembered something. "Just who in the hell," he said, holding his mouth a breath above hers, "is Samuel Flynn of Catalina, Arizona?"

"Who do you think he is?" Though she didn't withdraw, there was a sudden still quality about her that told him what she feared.

"I don't believe you're involved with him, because you love *me.*"

She laughed, her face lightening and her body relaxing again. "So modest."

"But he's someone very important. He's the 'other matter' you came to Phoenix about, isn't he?"

She nodded. "There's reason to believe my brother James survived the kidnapping."

"What?" He was thunderstruck. Feeling the mound of their child pressed against him, he could appreciate for the first time the hell the King and Queen must have gone through and the thought made him nearly ill.

"It's true," she confirmed. "He almost certainly survived. We traced him to an orphans' home in Arizona and narrowed our search to three men. Sam Flynn was the second.''

''And—?''

''He isn't my brother. He has a scar to prove it. Which means that the third man probably is the heir to the throne. My sisters are waiting for him to return home so we can speak with him.''

''My God! Your parents will be so—wait a minute. *That's* why you weren't quite as concerned about this new law, isn't it?'' Remorse struck him anew for the horrible words he'd thrown at her.

She hesitated. ''Until James is found, the first male heir *could* well be the Crown Prince. I am worried, but I also know my chances are as good of having a female child. If it's a son and we don't want him to be king, it could be done, but it would be a tedious process. As a last resort, we can petition the parliament to pass over him.''

Rafe gathered her into his arms. ''We'll deal with it together when the time comes, *if* the time comes. And if your brother is found, then we can just be an average pair of doting parents.''

She smiled. ''Well, perhaps not quite average.''

''The important thing,'' he said, drawing her even nearer, ''is that we spend the rest of our lives together.''

And as he found her lips and claimed his princess, he felt something inside him click into place, something he'd waited for his whole life. He was loved.

Epilogue

Elizabeth stood at the back of Wynton Chapel, her sisters gathered around her.

Alexandra, ever practical, had a list in her hand. "Now, Serena, don't forget to hand your flowers to Katherine right before they go up to the altar. She'll hand them to me. When Elizabeth hands you her bouquet, you two repeat the same thing so your hands are free to help with her train—" She broke off, fishing a tissue from her bodice to dab at her upper lip.

"Are you all right?" Katherine stopped adjusting Elizabeth's bridal veil and took her eldest sister by the elbow. "I thought this morning sickness stuff was only for the first three months."

"The doctor swears it will ease any day now," Alexandra replied, taking deep, shaky breaths. "If he's wrong, I'm going to have him beheaded."

"All you have to do is make it through the wedding," Serena said. "Then you can throw up all you want."

"Thanks," said Alexandra dryly.

"The *wedding*," Serena repeated. "I'm so glad at least one of us is getting married here. The rest of us will live vicariously through you, Elizabeth."

"And it will make Mummy and Daddy so happy." Katherine's face lost a bit of its happy glow. "I still feel badly that I deprived them of the chance to throw us a big 'do.'"

"Mummy and Daddy are happy for all of us," Elizabeth reassured them all, thinking back to her mother's words before she'd left for Phoenix the last time. "They wanted each of us to find love and hold it tight for the rest of our lives. And we have."

"I only wish we could have found James," Alexandra said. "What a wedding present that would have been!"

There was a moment of silence as they contemplated how very close they might be to giving their parents the gift of a lifetime.

"One last group hug," Serena said as she sniffed and dabbed at a tear. "The music's started and we have to start down the aisle any minute."

The four sisters huddled together, Katherine fussing at them not to wrinkle Elizabeth's gown.

She loved them so much, Elizabeth thought, swallowing tears of her own. It was almost inconceivable to think that they'd set out for the States mere months ago. So many events had occurred that it seemed much longer.

And now they would all be married. The wedding would barely be over before preparations for the coronation anniversary celebration would move into high gear. Mitch and Alexandra, along with Katherine and her new husband, Trey, as well as Serena and Gabe, would be staying in Wynborough until after the festivities.

Her smile faded a bit. The only person missing was Laura, whom they all cared for dearly. But she was needed at the Colton ranch in case John Colton showed up during Mitch's absence.

The wedding coordinator hissed at them then, and a maid handed Katherine her flowers. Katherine blew Elizabeth a kiss as she started up the aisle, and Alexandra gave her a sickly smile when her turn came. Serena accepted her bridesmaid's bouquet and flashed her one last wink before moving toward the front of the enormous old church.

Then it was her turn. King Phillip, who had been watching his other three daughters, came to her side and offered her his arm. One single tear slipped down his cheek and she reached up and wiped it away with her thumb.

"Don't *you* start," she said. "Serena was bad enough. I refuse to get married with smudged mascara."

Her father's chuckle was genuine. "Sorry. I was remembering you as a bare-bottomed baby and it suddenly hit me that very soon you'll have a baby of your own."

She grimaced. "I did things a bit out of order."

"It doesn't matter." Her father's tone was fierce, but his eyes softened as he looked toward the front of the chapel where the woman he'd loved for more than thirty years waited to see him give away their child. "What matters is that you and Rafe love each other, and for that, your mother and I are very, very thankful—for all four of our daughters' marriages. Not everyone is so lucky."

"We had a fine example to show us what it should be like." She gave him one last, misty smile. "I love you, Daddy."

He led her forward then. As she got near enough to the front of the church to see the tall, broad-shouldered man waiting there with his father and brother and a line of other attendants, she gave Rafe a radiant smile.

Her father was right. They *were* lucky.

And she intended to show Rafe every day for the rest of their lives just how much she valued his love.

THE PRINCE'S
SECRET BABY

CHRISTINE RIMMER

For my family.
For the joy, the laughter and the tears.
You've made my life rich
and full beyond my wildest dreams
and I love you all so very much!

Christine Rimmer came to her profession the long way around. She tried everything from acting to teaching to telephone sales. Now she's finally found work that suits her perfectly, she insists she never had a problem keeping a job – she was merely gaining "life experience" for her future as a novelist. Christine lives with her family in Oregon. Visit her at christinerimmer.com.

Chapter One

"Stop here," Rule Bravo-Calabretti said to the driver.

The limousine rolled to a silent stop at the head of the row of parking spaces in the shadowed parking garage. The Mercedes-Benz sedan Rule had been following turned into the single empty space at the other end of the row, not far from the elevators and the stairs that led into the mall. From where he sat behind tinted windows, Rule could also see the breezeway outside the parking structure. It led directly into Macy's department store.

The brake lights of the Mercedes went dark. A woman emerged from the sedan, her head and shoulders appearing above the tops of the row of cars. She had thick brown hair that fell in well-behaved waves. Settling the strap of her bag on her shoulder, she shut the car door and emerged into the open aisle, where she turned back and aimed her key at the car. The Benz gave an obedient beep.

She put the key away in her bag. She looked, Rule decided, just as she'd looked in the pictures his investigators had taken of her—only more attractive, somehow. She wasn't a pretty woman. But there was something about her that he found much more interesting than mere prettiness. She was tall and slim and wore a blue silk jacket, which was perfectly and conservatively tailored. Her matching blue skirt kissed the tops of her slender knees. Her shoes were darker than her suit, with medium heels and closed toes.

He watched as she settled her bag in place again, straightened her jacket and turned for the door to the breezeway. He thought she looked very determined and somehow he found that determination utterly charming.

She hadn't glanced in the limousine's direction. He was almost certain she had no idea that he'd been following her.

And his mind was made up, just like that, in the sixty seconds it took to watch her emerge from her car, put her key in her purse and turn to go. He had to meet her.

Yes, he'd always told himself he never would. That as long as she was running her life successfully, taking good care of the child, it would be wrong of him to interfere. He'd relinquished all rights by law. And he had to live with the choices he had made.

But this wasn't about rights. This wasn't about challenging her for what was hers.

He had no intention of interfering. He simply had to... speak with her, had to know if his first reaction to seeing her in the flesh was just a fluke, a moment of starry-eyed idiocy brought on by the fact that she had what mattered most to him.

All right, it was playing with fire. And he shouldn't even be here. He should be finishing his business in Dallas and rushing back to Montedoro. He should be spending time with Lili, learning to accept that they could be a good match, have a good life.

And he *would* return to Montedoro. Soon.

But right now, today, he was going to do the thing he'd wanted to do for far too long now. He was going meet Sydney O'Shea face-to-face.

Sydney could not believe it.

The totally hunky—and oddly familiar—guy down the aisle from her in Macy's housewares department was actually making eyes at her. Men like that did not make eyes at Sydney. Men like that made eyes at women as gorgeous as they were.

And no, it wasn't that Sydney was ugly. She wasn't. But she wasn't beautiful, either. And there was something much too...practical and self-sufficient about her. Something a little too focused, as well. She also happened to be very smart. Men tended to find her intimidating, even at first glance.

So. Really. It was probably only her imagination that the drop-dead gorgeous guy by the waffle irons and electric griddles was looking at her. She pretended to read the tag on a stainless-steel sauté pan—and slid another glance in Mr. Eye Candy's direction.

He was pretending to read a price tag, too. She knew he was pretending because, at the exact moment she glanced his way, he sent a sideways look in her direction and one corner of that sinfully sexy mouth of his quirked up in a teasing smile.

Maybe he was flirting with someone behind her.

She turned her head enough that she could see over her shoulder.

Nope. Nobody there. Just more cookware racks brimming with All-Clad stainless-steel pots and pans, Le

Creuset enameled cast-iron casseroles and complete sets of Calphalon nonstick cookware—which, she firmly reminded herself, were what she *should* be looking at. She put all her attention on the business at hand and banished the implausibly flirty, impossibly smooth-looking man from her mind.

Yet another coworker was getting married, a paralegal, Calista Dwyer. Calista hadn't bothered to set up a bridal registry anywhere. The wedding was something of an impromptu affair. Tomorrow, Calista was running off with her boyfriend to some tropical island for a quickie wedding and a two-week honeymoon in paradise.

Sydney had left the office before lunch to choose a wedding gift. It was a task she had come to dislike. It happened so often and always reminded her that other people were getting married all the time. She really should do what a man in her situation would do, just have her assistant buy the wedding gifts—especially in a case like this, where she had no clue what Calista might be wanting or needing.

But no. She was still her grandmother's granddaughter at heart. Ellen O'Shea had always taken pride in personally selecting any gift she gave. Sydney continued the family tradition, even if she sometimes found the job annoying and a little bit depressing.

"Cookware. Necessary. But not especially interesting," a voice as warm and tempting as melted caramel teased in her ear. "Unless you love to cook?"

Good gravy. Mr. Hot and Hunky was right behind her. And there could be no doubt about it now. He was talking to her—and he *had* been giving her the eye.

Slowly, as if in a dream, Sydney turned to him.

Breathtaking. Seriously. There was no other word for this guy. Jet-black eyes, sculpted cheekbones, a perfect, square jaw, a nose like a blade. Broad, broad shoulders. And the way he was dressed…casual, but expensive. In light-colored trousers and a beautifully made navy jacket over a checked shirt.

He arched an ebony brow. "Do you?"

She forced herself to suck in a breath and then asked warily, "Excuse me?"

"Do you love to cook?" He gazed at her as though he couldn't tear his eyes away.

This could not be happening.

But wait. A gigolo? Maybe she looked like gigolo bait. Well-dressed and driven. Maybe it was the new black, to go trolling for a sugar mama in housewares.

And then again, well, he did look somehow familiar. She probably knew him from somewhere. "Have we met before?"

He gave her a slow once-over, followed by another speaking glance from those black-velvet eyes. That glance seemed to say that he wouldn't mind gobbling her up on the spot. And then he laughed, a low, sexy laugh as smooth and exciting as that wonderful voice of his. "I prefer to think that if we'd met in the past, you wouldn't have forgotten me so easily."

Excellent point. "I, um…" Good Lord. Speechless. She was totally speechless. And that wasn't like her at all. Enough with the stumbling all over herself. She stuck out her hand. "Sydney O'Shea."

"Rule Bravo-Calabretti." He wrapped his elegant, warm fingers around hers. She stifled a gasp as heat flowed up her arm.

The heat didn't stop at her shoulder. Arrows of what she could only categorize as burning excitement zipped downward into her midsection. She eased her hand from his grip and fell back a step, coming up short against the steel display shelves behind her. "Rule, you said?"

"Yes."

"Let me guess, Rule. You're not from Dallas."

He put those long, graceful fingers to his heart. "How did you know?"

"Well, the designer clothes, the two last names. You speak English fluently, but with a certain formality and no regional accent that I can detect. I'm thinking that not only are you not from Dallas, you're not from Texas. You're not even from the good old U.S. of A."

He laughed again. "You're an expert on accents?"

"No. I'm smart, that's all. And observant."

"Smart and observant. I like that."

She wished she could stand there by the cast-iron casserole display, just looking at him, listening to him talk and hearing his melted-caramel laugh for the next, oh, say, half century or so.

But there was still Calista's wedding gift to buy. And a quick lunch to grab before rushing back to the office for that strategy meeting on the Binnelab case at one.

Before she could start making gotta-go noises, he spoke again. "You didn't answer my question."

"Ahem. Your question?"

"Sydney, do you love to cook?"

The way he said her name, with such impossible passionate intent, well, she liked it. She liked it way, way too much. She fell back a step. "Cook? Me? Only when I have no other choice."

"Then why have I found you here in the cookware department?"

"*Found* me?" Her suspicions rose again. Really, what was this guy up to? "Were you *looking* for me?"

He gave an elegant shrug of those fine wide shoulders.

"I confess. I saw you enter the store from the parking garage at the south breezeway entrance. You were so... determined."

"You followed me because I looked determined?"

"I followed you because you intrigued me."

"You're intrigued by determination?"

He chuckled again. "Yes. I suppose I am. My mother is a very determined woman."

"And you love your mother." She put a definite edge in her tone. Was she calling him a mama's boy? Maybe. A little. She tended toward sarcasm when she was nervous or unsure—and he did make her nervous. There was just something about him. Something much too good to be true.

Mr. Bravo-Calabretti either didn't get her sarcasm—or ignored it. "I do love my mother, yes. Very much. And I admire her, as well." He studied Sydney for a moment, a direct, assessing kind of glance. "You're a prickly one, aren't you?" He seemed amused.

So he *had* picked up on her sarcasm. She felt petty and a little bit mean. And that made her speak frankly. "Yes, I am a prickly one. Some men don't find that terribly attractive."

"Some men are fools." He said it softly. And then he asked again, "Why are you shopping for pots and pans, Sydney?"

She confessed, "I need a wedding gift for someone at the office."

His dark eyes twinkled at her, stars in a midnight sky. "A wedding gift."

"That's right."

"Allow me to suggest..." He reached around her with his left hand. She turned to follow the movement and watched as he tapped a red Le Creuset casserole shaped like a heart. "This." She couldn't help noticing that he wore no wedding ring. And the casserole? Not bad, really.

"Very romantic," she said dryly. "Every bride needs a heart-shaped casserole dish."

"Buy it," he commanded. "And we can get out of here."

"Excuse me. We?"

He still had his arm out, almost touching her, his hand resting lightly on the red casserole. She caught a faint, tempting hint of his aftershave. It smelled fabulous—so subtle, so very expensive. He held her eyes, his dark gaze intent. "Yes. We. The two of us."

"But I'm not going anywhere with you. I don't even know you."

"That's true. And I find that very sad." He put on a teasingly mournful expression. "Because I want to know you, Sydney. Come to lunch with me. We can begin to remedy this problem." She opened her mouth to tell him that as far as she was concerned there was no problem and lunch was out of the question. But before she got the words out, he scooped up the heart-shaped dish. "This way." He gestured with his free hand in the direction of the nearest cashier stand.

She went where he directed her. Why not? The casserole was a good choice. And he was so charming. As soon as the clerk had rung her up, she could tell him goodbye and make him see that she meant it.

The clerk was young and blonde and very pretty. "Oh! Here. Let me help you!" She took the casserole from Rule and then kept sliding him blushing glances as she rung up the sale. Sydney sympathized with the dazzled girl. He was like something straight out of a fabulous romantic novel—the impossible, wonderful, hot and handsome, smooth and sophisticated lover who appears out of nowhere to sweep the good-hearted but otherwise perfectly ordinary heroine off her feet.

And did she actually think the word *lover?*

Really, she needed to get a grip on her suddenly too-vivid imagination.

"This casserole is the cutest thing. Is it a gift?" the clerk asked.

"Yes, it is," Sydney replied. "A wedding gift."

The girl slid another glance at Rule. "I'm sorry. We don't offer gift wrapping in the store anymore." She spoke in a breathy little voice. Rule said nothing. He gave the girl a quick, neutral nod and a barely detectable smile.

"It's fine," Sydney said. Like her grandmother, she not only bought gifts personally, she wrapped them, too. But she didn't have time to wrap this one if she wanted to give it to Calista before her wedding trip. So she would need to grab a gift bag and tissue somewhere. She swiped her card and signed in the little box and tried not to be overly conscious of the too-attractive man standing beside her.

The clerk gave Sydney the receipt—but she gave Rule the Macy's bag with the casserole in it. "Here you go now. Come back and shop with us. Anytime." Her tone said she would love to help Rule with a lot more than his shopping.

Sydney thanked her and turned to him. "I'll take that."

"No need. I'll carry it for you."

"I said I'll take it."

Reluctantly, he handed it over. But he showed no inclination to say goodbye and move on.

She told him, "Nice chatting with you. And I really have to—"

"It's only lunch, you know." He said it gently and quietly, for her ears alone. "Not a lifetime commitment."

She gazed up into those melting dark eyes and all at once she was hearing her best friend Lani's chiding voice in her head. *Seriously, Syd. If you really want a special guy in your life, you have to give one a chance now and then....*

"All right," she heard herself say. "Lunch." It wasn't a big deal. She would enjoy his exciting, flattering attention over a quick sandwich and then say goodbye. No harm done.

"A smile," he said, his warm gaze on her mouth. "At last."

She smiled wider. Because she did like him. He was not only killer-handsome and very smooth, he seemed like a great guy. Certainly there could be no harm in giving herself permission to spend a little more time with him. "So. First I need a store that sells gift bags."

He held her eyes for a moment. And it felt glorious. Just standing there in Macy's, lost in an endless glance with a gorgeous man. Finally, he said, "There's a mall directory, I think. This way." And then he shepherded her ahead of him, as he had when he ushered her to the cashier stand.

They found a stationery store. She chose a pretty bag and some sparkly tissue and a gift card. The clerk rang up the sale and they were on their way.

"Where to?" she asked, as they emerged into the mall again.

"This is Texas," he said, his elegant face suddenly open and almost boyish. "We should have steak."

He had a limo waiting for him outside, which didn't surprise her. The man was very much the limo type. He urged her to ride with him to the restaurant, but she said she would follow him. They went to the Stockyards District in nearby Fort Worth, to a casual place with lots of Texas atmosphere and an excellent reputation.

An antler chandelier hung from the pressed-tin ceiling

above their corner table. The walls were of pine planks and exposed brick, hung with oil paintings of cowboy boots, hats and bandannas. The floor was painted red.

They got a table in a corner and he ordered a beautiful bottle of Cabernet. She refused the wine when their waiter tried to fill her glass. But then, after he left them, she gave in and poured herself a small amount. The taste was amazing, smooth and delicately spicy on her tongue.

"You like it?" Rule asked hopefully.

"It's wonderful."

He offered a toast. "To smart, observant, determined women."

"Don't forget prickly," she reminded him.

"How could I? It's such a charming trait."

"Nice recovery." She gave him an approving nod.

He raised his glass higher. "To smart, observant, determined and decidedly prickly women."

She laughed as she touched her glass to his.

"Tell me about your high-powered job," he said, after the waiter delivered their salads of butter lettuce and applewood smoked bacon.

She sipped more of the wine she shouldn't really be drinking, given she had that big meeting ahead of her. "And you know I have a high-powered job, how?"

"You said the wedding gift was for 'someone at the office.'"

"I could be in data entry. Or maybe a top executive's very capable assistant."

"No," he said, with confidence. "Your clothing is both conservative and expensive." He eyed her white silk shell, her lightweight, fitted jacket, the single strand of pearls she wore. "And your attitude…"

She leaned toward him, feeling deliciously giddy. Feeling free and bold and ready for anything. "What about my attitude?"

"You are no one's assistant."

She sat back in her chair and rested her hands in her lap. "I'm an attorney. With a firm that represents a number of corporate clients."

"An attorney. Of course. *That,* I believe."

She picked up her fork, ate some of her salad. For a moment or two they shared a surprisingly easy silence. And then she asked, "And what about you? What do you do for a living?"

"I like variety in my work. At the moment, I'm in trade. International trade."

"At the moment? What? You change jobs a lot, is that what you're telling me?"

"I take on projects that interest me. And when I'm satisfied that any given project is complete, I move on."

"What do you trade?"

"At the moment, oranges. Montedoron oranges."

"Montedoran. That sounds exotic."

"It is. The Montedoran is a blood orange, very sweet, hinting of raspberry, with the characteristic red flesh of all blood oranges. The skin is smooth, not pitted like many other varieties."

"So soon I'll be buying Montedorans at my local Wal-Mart Supercenter?"

"Hardly. The Montedoran is never going to be for sale in supermarkets. We won't be trading in that kind of volume. But for certain gourmet and specialty stores, I think it could do very well."

"Montedoran…" She tested the word on her tongue. "There's a small country in Europe, right, on the Côte d'Azur? Montedoro?"

"Yes. Montedoro is my country." He poured her more

wine. And she didn't stop him. "It's one of the eight small-est states in Europe, a principality on the Mediterranean. My mother was born there. My father was American but moved to Montedoro and accepted Montedoran citizen-ship when they married. His name is Evan Bravo. He was a Texan by birth."

She really did love listening to him talk. He made every word into a poem. "So...you have relatives in Texas?"

"I have an aunt and uncle and a number of first cousins who live in and around San Antonio. And I have other, more distant cousins in a small town near Abilene. And in your Hill Country, I have a second cousin who married a veterinarian. And there are more Bravos, many more, in California and Wyoming and Nevada. All over the States, as a matter of fact."

"I take it that Calabretti is your mother's surname?"

"Yes."

"Is that what they do in your country, combine the hus-band's and wife's last name when they marry?"

He nodded. "In...certain families, anyway. It's similar to the way it's done in Spain. We are much like the Span-ish. We want to keep all our last names, on both sides of our families. So we string them together proudly."

"Bravo-Calabretti sounds familiar, somehow. I keep wondering where I've heard it before..."

He waited for her to finish. When she didn't, he shrugged. "Perhaps it will come to you later."

"Maybe so." She lowered her voice to a more confiden-tial level. "And I have to tell you, I keep thinking that *you* are familiar, that I've met you before."

He shrugged in a way that seemed to her so sophisti-cated, so very European. "They say everyone has a double. Maybe that's it. You've met my double."

It wasn't what she'd meant. But it didn't really matter.

"Maybe." She let it go and asked, "Do you have brothers and sisters?"

"I do." He gave her a regal nod. "Three brothers, five sisters. I'm second-born. I have an older brother, Maximilian. And after me, there are the twins, Alexander and Damien. And then my sisters—Bella, Rhiannon, Alice, Genevra and Rory."

"Big family." Feeling suddenly wistful, she set down her fork. "I envy you. I was an only child." Her hand rested on the tabletop.

He covered it with his. The touch warmed her to her toes—and thrilled her, as well. Her whole body seemed, all at once, completely, vividly alive. He leaned into her and studied her face, his gaze as warm as his lean hand over hers. "And you are sad, then? To have no siblings?"

"I am, yes." She wished he might hold her hand indefinitely. And yet she had to remember that this wasn't going anywhere and it wouldn't be right to let him think that it might. She eased her hand free. He took her cue without comment, retreating to his side of the table. She asked, "How old are you, Rule?"

He laughed his slow, smooth laugh. "Somehow, I begin to feel as though I'm being interviewed."

She turned her wineglass by the stem. "I only wondered. Is your age a sensitive subject for you?"

"In a sense, I suppose it is." His tone was more serious. "I'm thirty-two. That's a dangerous age for an unmarried man in my family."

"How so? Thirty-two isn't all that old." Especially not for a man. For a woman, things were a little different—at least, they were if she wanted to have children.

"It's time that I married." He said it so somberly, his eyes darker than ever as he regarded her steadily.

"I don't get it. In your family, they put you on a schedule for marriage?"

Now a smile haunted his handsome mouth. "It sounds absurd when you say it that way."

"It *is* absurd."

"You are a woman of definite opinions." He said it in an admiring way. Still, defiance rose within her and she tipped her chin high. He added, "And yes, in my family both the men and the women are expected to marry before they reach the age of thirty-three."

"And if you don't?"

He lowered his head and looked at her from under his dark brows. "Consequences will be dire." He said it in a low tone, an intimate tone, a tone that did a number on every one of her nerve endings and sent a fine, heated shiver dancing along the surface of her skin.

"You're teasing me."

"Yes, I am. I like you, Sydney. I knew that I would, the moment I first saw you."

"And when was that?"

"You've already forgotten?" He looked gorgeously forlorn. "I see I'm not so memorable, after all. Macy's? I saw you going in?" The waiter scooped up their empty salad plates and served them rib eye steaks with Serrano lime butter. When he left them, Rule slid her a knowing glance as he picked up his steak knife. "Sydney, I think you're testing me."

Why deny it? "I think you're right."

"I hope I'm passing this test of yours—and do your parents live here in Dallas?"

She trotted out the old, sad story. "They lived in San Francisco, where I was born. My mother was thrown off a runaway cable car. I was just three months old, in her arms when she fell. She suffered a blow to the head and died instantly, but I was unharmed. They called it a miracle at the time. My father was fatally injured when he jumped off to try and save us. He died the next day in the hospital."

His dark eyes were so soft. They spoke of real sympathy. Of understanding. "How terrible for you."

"I don't even remember it. My grandmother—my father's mother—came for me and took me back to Austin, where she lived. She raised me on her own. My grandfather had died several years before my parents. She was amazing, my grandmother. She taught me that I can do anything. She taught me that power brings responsibility. That the truth is sacred. That being faithful and trustworthy are rewards in themselves."

Now his eyes had a teasing light in them. "And yet, you're an attorney."

Sydney laughed. "So they have lawyer jokes even in Montedoro?"

"I'm afraid so—and a *corporate* attorney at that."

"I'm not responding to that comment on the grounds that it might tend to incriminate me." She said it lightly.

But he saw right through her. "Have I hit a nerve?"

She totally shocked herself by answering frankly. "My job is high-powered. And high-paying. And it's been… important to me, to know that I'm on top of a very tough game, that I'll never have to worry about where the next paycheck is coming from, that I can definitely take care of my own and do it well."

"And yet?"

She revealed even more. "And yet lately, I often find myself thinking how much more fulfilling it might be to spend my workdays helping people who really need me, rather than protecting the overflowing coffers of multibillion-dollar companies."

He started to speak. But then her BlackBerry, which she'd set on the table to the right of her water goblet the way she always did at restaurants, vibrated. She checked the display: Magda, her assistant. Probably wondering why she wasn't back at the office yet.

She glanced at Rule again. He had picked up his knife and fork and was concentrating on his meal, giving her the chance to deal with the call if she needed to.

Well, she didn't need to.

Sydney scooped up the phone and dropped it in her bag where she wouldn't even notice if it vibrated again.

With the smooth ease of a born diplomat, Rule continued their conversation as though it had never been interrupted. "You speak of your grandmother in the past tense...."

"She died five years ago. I miss her very much."

"So much loss." He shook his head. "Life can be cruel."

"Yes." She ate a bite of her steak, taking her time about it, savoring the taste and tenderness of the meat, unaccountably happy that he hadn't remarked on her vibrating BlackBerry, that he hadn't said he was "sorry," the way people always did when she told them she'd grown up without her parents, when she confessed how much she missed her grandmother.

He watched her some more, his dark head tipped to the side in way that had her thinking again how he reminded her of someone. "Have you ever been married?"

"No. I'm Catholic—somewhat lapsed, yes, but nonetheless, I do believe that marriage is forever. I've never found the man I want forever with. But I've had a couple of serious relationships. They...didn't work out." Understatement of the year. But he didn't need to hear it and she didn't need to say it. She'd done enough over-sharing for now, thank you very much. She added, "And I'm thirty-three. Does that seem...dire to you?"

"Absolutely." He put on a stern expression. On him, sternness was sexy. But then, on him, everything was sexy. "You should be married immediately. And then have nine children. At the very least. You should marry a wealthy man, Sydney. One who adores you."

"Hmm. A rich man who adores me. I wouldn't mind that. But the nine children? More than I planned on. Significantly more."

"You don't want children?" He looked honestly surprised.

She almost told him about Trevor right then. But no. This was a fantasy lunch with a fantasy man. Trevor was her real life. The most beautiful, perfect, meaningful, joyful part of her real life. "I didn't say I didn't want children. I do. But I'm not sure I'm ready for nine of them. Nine seems like a lot."

"Well. Perhaps we would have to settle for fewer than nine. I can be reasonable."

"We?"

"A man and a woman have to work together. Decisions should be jointly made."

"Rule." She put a hand to her breast, widened her eyes and asked him dramatically, "Could this be...oh, I can't believe it. Is it possible that you're proposing to me?"

He answered matter-of-factly, "As it happens, I'm wealthy. And it would be very easy for me to adore you." His dark eyes shone.

What was this feeling? Magical, this feeling. Magical and foolish. And that was the beauty of it. It was one of those things that happen when you least expect it. Something to remind her that life could still be surprising.

That it wasn't all about winning and staying on top—and coming home too late to tuck her own sweet boy into bed.

Sometimes even the most driven woman might just take a long lunch. A long lunch with a stranger who made her feel not only brilliant and clever, but beautiful and desired, as well.

She put on a tragic face. "I'm sorry. It could never work."

He played it stricken. "But why not?"

"You live in Montedoro." Grave. Melancholy. "My career—my whole life—is here."

"You might change careers. You might even decide to try a different kind of life."

Hah. Exactly what men always said. She wasn't letting him get away with it. "Or *you* might move to Texas."

"For you, Sydney, I might do anything."

"Perfect answer."

A moment ensued. Golden. Fine. A moment with only the two of them in it. A moment of complete accord.

Sydney let herself enjoy that moment. She refused to be guarded or dubious. It was only lunch, after all. Lunch with an attractive man. She was giving herself full permission to enjoy every minute of it.

CHAPTER TWO

Chapter Two

The meeting on the Binnelab case was half over when Sydney slipped in at two-fifteen.

"Excuse me," she said as she eased through the conference room doors and they all turned to stare at her. "So sorry. I had...something of an emergency."

Her colleagues made sympathetic noises and went back to arguing strategy. No one was the least angry that she was late.

Because she was never late—which meant that of course there had to be a good reason for her tardiness. She was Sydney O'Shea, who graduated college at twenty, passed the bar at twenty-four and had been made partner at thirty—exactly one year before her son was born. Sydney O'Shea, who knew how to make demands and how to return a favor, who had a talent for forging strong professional relationships and who never slacked. She racked up the billable hours with the best of them.

If she'd told them all that she'd been sidetracked in Macy's housewares by a handsome orange salesman from Montedoro and allowed him to talk her into blowing off half of the Binnelab meeting, they'd have had zero doubt that she was joking.

She knew the case backward and forward. She only had to listen to the discussion for a few minutes to get up to speed on the direction her colleagues were taking.

By the end of the meeting, she'd nudged them in a slightly different direction and everyone seemed pleased with the result. She returned to her corner office to find her so-capable assistant, the usually unflappable Magda, standing in the middle of the room holding an orchid in a gorgeous purple pot. Magda stared in dismay at the credenza along the side wall where no less than twelve spectacular flower arrangements sprouted from a variety of crystal vases.

The credenza was not the only surface in the room overflowing with flowers. There were two vases on the coffee table and one each on the end tables in the sitting area.

Her desk had six of them. And the windowsill was likewise overrun with exotic blooms. Each arrangement had a small white card attached. The room smelled like a greenhouse.

Rule. She knew instantly. Who else could it be? And a quick glance at one of the cards confirmed it.

Please share dinner with me tonight. The Mansion at Turtle Creek. Eight o'clock. Yours, Rule

She'd never told him the name of her firm. But then again, it wouldn't have been that hard to find out. Just her name typed into a search engine would have done it.

"Smothered in flowers. Literally," she said to her nonplussed assistant. She felt that delicious glow again, that sense of wonder and limitless possibility. She was crushing on him, big-time. He made her feel innocent and free.

And beautiful. And desired…

Was there anything wrong with that? If there was, she was having trouble remembering what.

"They started arriving about half an hour ago," said Magda. "I think this orchid is the last of them. But I have nowhere left to put it."

"It would look great on your desk," Sydney suggested. "In fact, take the cards off and leave them with me. And then let's share the wealth."

Magda arched a brow. "Give them away, you mean?"

"Start with the data entry crew. Just leave me the two vases of yellow roses."

"You're sure?"

"Positive." She didn't think Rule would mind at all if she shared. And she wanted to share. This feeling of hope and wonder and beauty, well, it was too fabulous to keep to herself. "Tell everyone to enjoy them. And to take them home, if they want to—and hurry. We have Calista's party at four."

"I really like this orchid," said Magda, holding out the pot, admiring the deep purple lips suspended from the velvety pale pink petals. "It looks rare."

"Good. Enjoy. A nice start to the weekend, don't you think? Flowers for everyone. And then we send Calista happily off to her tropical honeymoon."

"Someone special must be wild for you," Magda said with a grin.

Sydney couldn't resist grinning right back at her. "Deliver the flowers and let's break out the champagne."

Calista loved the heart-shaped casserole. She laughed when she pulled it from the gift bag. "I guess now I'll just have to learn how to cook."

"Wait until after the honeymoon," Sydney suggested and then proposed a toast. "To you, Calista. And to a long and happy marriage."

After the two glasses of wine at lunch, Sydney allowed herself only a half glass of champagne during the shower. But the shortage of bubbly didn't matter in the least. It was still the most fun Sydney had ever had at a bridal shower. Funny how meeting a wonderful man can put a whole different light on the day.

After the party, she returned to her office just long enough to grab her briefcase, her bag and one of the vases full of yellow roses. Yes, as a rule she would have stayed to bill a couple more hours, at least.

But hey. It was Friday. She wanted to see her little boy before he went to bed. And she really needed to talk to Lani, who was not only her dearest friend, but also Trevor's live-in nanny. She needed Lani's excellent advice as to whether she should go for it and take Rule up on his invitation to dinner.

At home in Highland Park, she found Trevor in the kitchen, sitting up at the breakfast nook table in his booster chair, eating his dinner of spaghetti and meatballs. "Mama home! Hug, hug!" he crowed, and held out his chubby arms.

She dropped her briefcase and bag, set the flowers on the counter and went to him. He wrapped those strong little arms around her neck, smearing spaghetti sauce on her cheek when he gave her a big smacker of a kiss. "How's my boy?"

"I fine, thank you."

"Me, too." She hugged him harder. "Now that I'm home with you." He smelled of tomatoes and meatballs and baby shampoo—of everything that mattered.

At two, he was quite the talker. As he picked up his

spoon again, he launched into a description of his day. "We swim. We play trucks. I shout *loud* when we crash."

"Sounds like fun." She whipped a tissue from the box on the counter and wiped the red sauce off her cheek.

"Oh, yes! Fun, Mama. I happy." He shoved a meatball in his mouth with one hand and waved his spoon with the other.

"Use your spoon for eating," Lani said from over by the sink.

"Yes, Lani. I do!" He switched the spoon to the other hand and scooped up a mound of pasta. Most of it fell off before he got it to his mouth, but he only gamely scooped up some more.

"You're early," said Lani, turning to glance at her over the tops of her black-rimmed glasses. "And those roses are gorgeous."

"They are, aren't they? And as to being early, hey, it's almost the weekend."

"That never stopped you from working late before." Lani grabbed a towel and turned to lean against the sink as she dried her hands.

Her full name was Yolanda Ynez Vasquez and she was small and curvy with acres of thick almost-black hair. She'd been working for Sydney for five years, starting as Sydney's housekeeper. The plan was that Lani would cook and clean house and live in, thus saving money while she finished college. But then, even after she got her degree, she'd stayed on, and become Trevor's nanny, as well. Sydney had no idea how she would have managed without her. Not only for her grace and ease at keeping house and being a second mom to Trevor, but also for her friendship. After Ellen O'Shea, Yolanda Vasquez was the best friend Sydney had ever had.

Lani said, "You're glowing, Syd."

Sydney put her hands to her cheeks. "I do feel slightly warm. Maybe I have a fever...."

"Or maybe someone handsome sent you yellow roses."

Laughing, Sydney shook her head. "You are always one step ahead of me."

"What's his name?"

"Rule."

"Hmm. Very...commanding."

"And he is. But in such a smooth kind of way. I went to lunch with him. I really like him. He asked me to dinner."

"Tonight?" Lani asked.

She nodded. "He invited me to meet him at the Mansion at Turtle Creek. Eight o'clock."

"And you're going." It wasn't a question.

"If you'll hold down the fort?"

"No problem."

"What about Michael?" Michael Cort was a software architect. Lani had been seeing him on a steady basis for the past year.

Lani shrugged. "You know Michael. He likes to hang out. I'll invite him over. We'll get a pizza—tell me more about Rule."

"I just met him today. Am I crazy?"

"A date with a guy who makes you glow? Nothing crazy about that."

"Mama, sketti?" Trev held up a handful of crushed meatball and pasta.

"No, thank you, my darling." Sydney bent and kissed his plump, gooey cheek again. "You can have that big wad of sketti all for yourself."

"Yum!" He beamed up at her and her heart felt like it was overflowing. She had it all. A healthy, happy child, a terrific best friend, a very comfortable lifestyle, a job most high-powered types would kill for. And a date with the best-looking man on the planet.

Sydney spent the next hour being the mother she didn't get to be as often as she would have liked. She played trucks with Trev. And then she gave him his bath and tucked him into bed herself, smoothing his dark hair off his handsome forehead, thinking that he was the most beautiful child she had ever seen. He was already asleep when she tiptoed from the room.

Yolanda looked up when she entered the family room. "It's after seven. You better get a move on if you want to be on time for your dream man."

"I know—keep me company while I get ready?"

Lani followed her into the master suite, where Sydney grabbed a quick shower and redid her makeup. In the walk-in closet, she stared at the possible choices and didn't know which one to pick.

"This." Lani took a simple cap-sleeved red satin sheath from the row of mostly conservative party dresses. "You are killer in red."

"Red. Hmm," Sydney waffled. "You think?"

"I *know*. Put it on. You only need your diamond studs with it. And that garnet-and-diamond bracelet your grandmother left you. And those red Jimmy Choos."

Sydney took the dress. "You're right."

Lani dimpled. "I'm always right."

Sydney put on the dress and the shoes and the diamond studs and garnet bracelet. Then she stood at the full-length mirror in her dressing area and scowled at herself. "I don't know…" She touched her brown hair, which she'd swept up into a twist. "Should I take my hair down?"

"No. It's great like that." Lani tugged a few curls loose at her temples and her nape. Then she eased the wide neckline of the dress off her shoulders. "There. Perfect. You look so hot."

"I am not the hot type."

"Yeah, you are. You just don't see yourself that way. You're tall and slim and striking."

"Striking. Right. Still, it would be nice if I had breasts, don't you think? I had breasts once, remember? When I was pregnant with Trevor?"

"Stop. You have breasts."

"Hah."

"And you have green eyes to die for."

"To die for. Who came up with that expression, anyway?"

Lani took her by the shoulders and turned her around so they faced each other. "You look gorgeous. Go. Have a fabulous time."

"Now I'm getting nervous."

"*Getting?* Syd. You look wonderful and you are going."

"What if he doesn't show up?"

"Stop it." Lani squeezed her shoulders. "Go."

Rosewood Mansion at Turtle Creek was a Dallas landmark. Once a spectacular private residence, the Mansion was now a five-star hotel and restaurant, a place of meticulous elegance, of marble floors and stained-glass windows and hand-carved fireplaces.

Her heart racing in mingled excitement and trepidation, Sydney entered the restaurant foyer, with its curving iron-railed staircases and black-and-white marble floor. She marched right up to the reservation desk and told the smiling host waiting there, "I'm meeting someone. Rule Bravo-Calabretti?"

The host nodded smartly. "Right this way."

And off she went to a curtained private corner on the

terrace. The curtains were pulled back and she saw that Rule was waiting, wearing a gorgeous dark suit, his black eyes lighting up when their gazes locked. He rose as she approached.

"Sydney." He said her name with honest pleasure, his expression as open and happy as her little boy's had been when she'd tucked him into bed that night. "You came." He sounded so pleased. And maybe a little relieved.

How surprising was that? He didn't look like a person who would ever worry that a woman might not show up for a date.

She liked him even more then—if that was possible. Because he had allowed her to see he was vulnerable.

"Wouldn't have missed it for the world," she said softly, her gaze locked with his.

Champagne was waiting in a silver bucket. The host served them.

Rule said, "I took the liberty of conferring with the chef ahead of time, choosing a menu I thought you might enjoy. But if you would prefer making your own choices…"

She loved that he'd planned ahead, that he'd taken that kind of care over the meal. *And* that he'd asked for her preference in the matter. "The food is always good here. Whatever you've planned will be perfect."

"No…dietary rules or foods you hate?" His midnight gaze scanned her face as though committing it to memory.

"None. I trust you."

Something flared in his eyes. "Fair enough, then." His voice wrapped around her, warm and deep and so sweet. He nodded at the host. "Thank you, Neil."

"Very good, then, your—" Neil paused almost imperceptibly, and then continued "—waiter will be with you shortly." With a slight bow, he turned to go.

"Neil seems a little nervous," she whispered, when the host had left them.

"I have no idea why," Rule said lightly. And then his tone acquired a certain huskiness. "You should wear red all the time."

"That might become boring."

"You could never be boring. And what is that old song, the one about the lady in red?"

"That's it. 'Lady in Red.'"

"You bring that song to mind. You make me want to dance with you."

How did he do it? He poured on the flattery—and yet, somehow, coming from him, the sweet talk sounded sincere. "Thank you for the flowers."

He waved a lean hand. "I know I went overboard."

"It was a beautiful gesture. And I hope you don't mind, but I shared them—with the data entry girls and the paralegals and the crew down in Human Resources."

"Why would I mind? They were yours, to do with as you wished. And sharing is good. You're not only the most compelling woman I've ever met, you are kind. And generous, too."

She shook her head. "You amaze me, Rule."

He arched a raven-black eyebrow. "In a good way, I hope?"

"Oh, yeah. In a good way. You make me want to believe all the beautiful things that you say to me."

He took her hand. Enchantment settled over her, at the warmth of his touch, at the lovely, lazy pulse of pleasure that seemed to move through her with every beat of her heart, just to be with him, to have her hand in his, flesh to flesh. "Would you prefer if I were cruel?"

The question shocked her a little. "No. Never. Why would you ask that?"

He turned her hand over, raised it to his lips, pressed a kiss in the heart of her palm. The pulse of pleasure within her went lower, grew hotter. "You fascinate me." His breath fanned her palm. And then, tenderly, he lowered their hands to the snowy tablecloth and wove his fingers with hers. "I want to know all about you. And truthfully, some women like a little more spice from a man. They want to be kept guessing. 'Does he care or not, will he call or not?' They might say they're looking for a good man who appreciates them. But they like...the dance of love, they revel in the uncertainty of it all."

She leaned closer to him, because she wanted to. Because she could. "I like you as you are. Don't pretend to be someone else. Please."

"I wouldn't. But I *can* be cruel." He said it so casually, so easily. And she realized she believed him. She saw the shining blade of his intention beneath the velvet sheath that was his considerable charm.

"Please don't. I've had enough of mean men. I..." She let the words trail off. The waiter was approaching their table. Perfect timing. The subject was one that desperately needed dropping.

But a flick of a glance from Rule and the waiter turned around and walked away. "Continue, please," Rule prompted softly. "What men have been cruel to you?"

Way to ruin a beautiful evening, Syd. "Seriously. You don't need to hear it."

"But I *want* to hear it. I meant what I said. I want to know about you, Sydney. I want to know everything." His eyes were so dark. She could get lost in them, lost forever, never to be found. And the really scary thing was that she almost felt okay with being lost forever—as long as he was lost right along with her.

"What can I say? There's just something about me..."

Lord. She did not want to go there. She tried to wrap it up with a generalized explanation. "I seem to attract men who say they like me because I'm strong and intelligent and capable. And then they get to work trying to tear me down."

Something flared in his eyes. Something…dangerous. "*Who* has tried to tear you down?"

"Do we have to get into this?"

"No. We don't. But sometimes it's better, I think, to go ahead and speak frankly of the past." Now his eyes were tender again. Tender and somehow completely accepting.

She let out a slow, surrendering sigh. "I lived with a guy when I was in law school. His name was Ryan. He was fun and a little bit wild. On the day we moved in together, he quit his job. He would lie on the sofa drinking those great big cans of malt liquor, watching ESPN. When I tried to talk to him about showing a little motivation, things got ugly fast. He said that I had enough ambition and drive for both of us and next to me he felt like a failure, that I had as good as emasculated him—and would I get out of the damn way, I was blocking his view of the TV?"

Rule gave one of those so-European shrugs of his. "So you got rid of him."

"Yes, I did. When I kicked him out, he told me he'd been screwing around on me. He'd had to, he said. In order to try and feel at least a little like a man again. So he was a cheater and a liar, too. After Ryan, I took a break from men. I stayed away from serious entanglements for the next five years. Then I met Peter. He was an attorney, like me. Worked for a different firm, a smaller one. We started going out. I thought he was nothing like Ryan, not a user or runaround or a slacker in any way. He never formally moved in with me. But he was…with me, at my house, most nights. And then he started pressuring me to get him

in at Teale, Gayle and Prosser." She said the name of her
firm with another long sigh.

"You weren't comfortable with that?"

"No, I wasn't. And I told him so. I believe in network-
ing, in helping the other guy out. But I didn't want my
boyfriend working at the same firm with me, especially
not if he was hired on my say-so. There are just too many
ways that could spell trouble. He said he understood."

Rule still had his fingers laced with hers. He gave her
a reassuring squeeze. "But he didn't understand."

"Not in the least. He was angry that I wouldn't give
him 'a hand up,' as he put it. Things kind of devolved from
there. He said a lot of brutal things to me. I was still an
associate at the firm then. At a party, Peter got drunk and
complained about me to one of the partners. By the time
he and I were over, I…" She sought the right way to say
it.

He said it for her. "You decided you were through with
men." She glanced away. He caught her chin, lightly,
gently, and guided it back around so that she met his eyes
again. "Are you all right?" He sounded honestly concerned. She realized that her answer really mattered to
him.

She swallowed, nodded. "I'm okay. It's just…when I
talk about all that, I feel like such a loser, you know?"

"Those men. Ryan and Peter. *They* are the losers."
He held her gaze. "I notice you haven't told me their last
names."

"And I'm not going to. As I said, it's long over for me,
with both of them."

He gave her his beautiful smile. "There. That's what I
was waiting to hear." He let go of her hand—but only to
touch her in another way. With his index finger, he traced
the line of her jaw, stirring shivers as he went. He caught

one of the loose curls of hair that Lani had pulled free of her French twist, and rubbed it between his fingers. "Soft," he whispered. "Like your skin. Like your tender heart..."

"Don't be too sure about that. I'm not only prickly, I can be a raving bitch," she whispered back. "Just ask Ryan and Peter."

"Give me their last names. Ryan and Peter and I will have a long talk."

"Hah. I don't think so."

He touched her cheek then, a brushing caress of such clear erotic intent that her toes curled inside her Jimmy Choos. "As long as you're willing to give men another chance."

"I could be. If the *right* man ever came along."

He took her untouched champagne flute and handed it to her. Then he picked up his own. "To the right man."

She touched her glass to his, echoed, "The right man." It was excellent champagne, each tiny bubble like a burst of magic on her tongue. And when she set the glass down again, she said, "I always wanted to have children."

He answered teasingly, "However, not nine of them."

Suddenly, it came to her. She realized where she'd been going with her grim little tale of disappointed love. It hadn't really been a case of total over-sharing, after all.

"Actually," she said. "This is serious."

"All right."

"There's something I really do need to tell you."

His expression changed, became...so still. Waiting. Listening. He tipped his head to the side in that strangely familiar way he had. "Tell me."

She wanted—needed—for him to know about Trevor. If learning about Trev turned him off, well, she absolutely *had* to know that now, tonight. Before she got in any deeper with him. Before she let herself drown in those beautiful black eyes. "I…" Her mouth had gone desert-dry. She swallowed, hard.

This shouldn't be so difficult, shouldn't matter so very much. She hardly knew this man. Holding his interest and his high regard shouldn't be this important to her.

Yet it *was* important. Already. She cared. A lot. Way, way too much.

He seemed too perfect. He *was* too perfect. He was her dream man come to vivid, vibrant, tempting life. The first minute she saw him, she'd felt as though she already knew him.

Yes, she should be more wary. It wasn't like her to be so easily drawn in.

And yet she was. She couldn't stop herself.

She thought of her grandmother, who had been a true believer in love at first sight. Grandma Ellen claimed she had fallen for Sydney's grandfather the first time she met him. She'd also insisted that Sydney's father had fallen in love with her mother at first sight.

Could falling in love at first sight be a genetic trait? Sydney almost smiled at the thought. She'd believed herself to be in love before—and been wrong, wrong, wrong.

But with Ryan, it hadn't been like this. Or with Peter. Nothing like this, with either of them.

Both of those relationships had developed in the logical, sensible way. She'd come to believe that she loved those men over a reasonable period of time, after getting to know them well—or so she had thought.

And look what had happened. She learned in the end that she hadn't really known either Ryan or Peter. Not well enough, she hadn't. With both men, it had ended in heartbreak. Those failures should have made her more wary. Those failures *had* made her more wary.

Until today. Until she met Rule.

With Rule, her heart seemed to have a will of its own. With him, she wanted to just go for it. To take the leap, take a chance. She didn't want to be wary with him. With him, she could almost become a believer in love at first sight.

If only he wasn't put off by learning that she already had a child....

"It's all right," he said so gently. "Go on."

And she did. "I was almost thirty, when it ended with Peter. I wanted to make partner in my firm and I wanted a family. I knew I could do both."

He gave a slow nod. "But the men were not cooperating."

"Exactly. So I decided...to have a family anyway. A family without a man. I went to a top cryobank—a sperm bank, at a fertility clinic?"

"Yes," he said in a way that could only be called cautious. "I know what a cryobank is."

"Well, all right." Her hands were shaking. She lowered them to her lap so he wouldn't see. "I went to a sperm bank. I had artificial insemination. The procedure was successful. I got pregnant. And now I have a beautiful, healthy two-year-old son."

"You have a child," he repeated, carefully. "A boy."

She folded her hands good and tight in her lap to still the shaking. And her heart seemed to have stopped dead in her chest—and then commenced beating way too hard and too fast. It hurt, her own heart, the way it pounded away in there. Because she *knew,* absolutely, that it was over, between her and Rule, over before it had even really begun. And it didn't matter *how* perfect he was for her. It didn't matter if he just happened to be her dream-come-true. It didn't matter that he made her want to believe in love at first sight. She was absolutely certain at that moment that he wouldn't accept Trevor. And if he didn't accept her son, she wanted nothing to do with him.

In a moment, she would be rising, saying good-night. Walking away from him and refusing to look back.

She drew her shoulders tall. Her hands weren't shaking anymore. "Yes, Rule. I have a son, a son who's everything to me."

Chapter Three

And then, just as she was dead certain that it was finished between them, Rule smiled.

A *real* smile. He laid his warm, lean hand along the side of her face. "How wonderful. I love children, Sydney— but I already said that, didn't I? When can I meet him? Tomorrow, I hope."

She blinked, swallowed. Almost sick with emotion, she put her hand against her churning stomach. "I… You what?"

He laughed, a beautiful, low, sexy sound. "You thought I wouldn't want to meet your son?" And then he frowned. "You don't know me very well."

"I… You're right. I don't know you." She took slow, deep breaths, ordering her stomach to settle down, stunned at how much it mattered, that he wasn't rejecting Trevor. That it wasn't over after all, that she didn't have to rise and walk away and not look back. She could stay right here, in this beautiful restaurant, at this private table, with this incredible man. She chided, "I have to keep reminding myself that I don't know you well, that we only met this afternoon."

"Unbelievable." His frown had faded. "I had forgotten. Somehow, it seems that I've known you forever."

She confessed, "I have that feeling, too." And then she laughed, a laugh that felt as light and bubbly as the excellent champagne. "I had it the first moment I saw you."

"You did?" He wore that boyish look, the one that made her think of Trev.

"Yes. I thought how you couldn't be looking at me. And then I thought how familiar you looked, that I must have met you before...."

"Of course I was looking at you," he said it with a definite note of reproach. "But you were very busy reminding yourself that you were through with men."

"I was. I admit it. How dumb was that?"

"It's all right. Now that you've told me why you gave up men, I thoroughly understand. And I'm not complaining. If you hadn't decided to stay away from the male sex, you might have found someone else by now and I wouldn't have a chance with you."

"And that would have been a tragedy," she teased.

"Yes, it would. A true catastrophe. But you did give up men. Now all I have to do is convince you to give one more man a chance." He raised his glass again. She clinked hers against it. "Are you ready for the first course?"

Suddenly, she was starving. "I am, yes."

He cast a glance beyond the open curtain. That was all. Just a glance. The waiter appeared again and made straight for their table.

Two hours later, Rule walked her out to the valet stand and had her car brought around. He tipped the valet generously and then took her hand and led her away from her waiting Mercedes. "Just for a moment…"

She went with him, down the sloping front entrance, to a shadowed area next to a large brick planter thick with greenery, beneath a beautiful old oak. The spring night felt warm and close around them.

He turned to face her. His eyes gleamed like polished stones through the darkness and his fingers trailed up her bare arm, a long, slow, dancing caress that left her strangely weak and slightly breathless. "Sydney…" He clasped her shoulders, and then framed her face between both wonderful hands. "Sydney O'Shea. I was becoming frightened."

His words confused her. She scanned his shadowed features. "But why?"

"That I would never find you. Never meet you…"

"Oh. That." She felt a glad smile curve her lips.

"Yes. That." His sweet breath stirred the loose curls at her temples as he bent his head closer to her.

A kiss. *His* kiss. Their first kiss. She tipped her face up to him, offering her mouth.

He held her eyes as he lowered his lips to hers.

Warm. Soft. Easy…

Her eyes drifted shut as his mouth touched hers, lightly, cherishingly. And she trembled, the moment was so exactly as she'd imagined it might be during their lunch that afternoon, during the long, glorious meal just past.

"Sydney…" He whispered her name against her mouth and she opened for him.

Instantly, she wanted more, wanted to be closer. *Had* to be closer.

Surging up, she wrapped her arms around him. A tiny, hungry cry escaped her at the sheer glory of such a perfect moment.

He took her cue and deepened the kiss, gathering her into him, cradling her against his body, so that she felt his warmth and solidity all along the length of her. He tasted of coffee and the heavenly pistachio mascarpone cake they'd shared for dessert. And the way he kissed her, the way his warm, rough-tender tongue caressed her…oh, there was nothing, ever, in her experience, to compare to it.

Nothing to compare.

To his kiss…

She wished it would never end.

But of course, it had to end. He took her shoulders again and reluctantly lifted his mouth from hers.

"Tomorrow," he said, gazing down at her, his eyes heavy-lidded, holding her a willing captive with his light touch at her shoulders, with his tender glance.

"Yes," she vowed, though she didn't even know yet what he planned for tomorrow.

He brushed the backs of his fingers against her cheek, and then up to her temple, causing those lovely shivers to course across her skin. "In the morning? I could come and collect you and your little boy. We could…visit a park, maybe. A park with swings and slides, so he'll have a chance to play. My little niece and nephew love nothing so much as a few hours in the sunshine, with a sandbox and a slide."

"You didn't tell me you had a niece and a nephew."

He nodded. "My older brother, Max, has two children—say yes to tomorrow."

"But I already did, didn't I?"

"Say it again."

"Yes—and why don't you come for breakfast first? You can meet my best friend, Lani, who has a degree in English literature, is a fabulous cook and takes care of Trevor while I'm at work."

"I would love breakfast. And to meet your friend, Lani."

"I have to warn you. Breakfast comes early at my house."

"Early it is."

"Seven-thirty, then." She took his hand, automatically threading her fingers with his, feeling the thrill of touching him—and also a certain rightness. Her hand fit perfectly in his. "Come on." She pulled him back toward her car. "I'll give you my address and phone number."

"Where's Michael?" Sydney asked, when she let herself in the house at quarter of eleven and found Lani sitting on the sofa alone, wearing Tweety Bird flannel pajama bottoms and a yellow cami top.

"How was the big date?" Lani asked, with a too-bright smile.

Sydney slipped off her red shoes and dropped to the sofa beside her friend. "It was better than...anything. Wonderful. I'm crazy about him. He's coming for breakfast at seven-thirty."

"Good. I can check him out. See if he's good enough for you."

"He's good enough. You'll see. I thought maybe one of your fabulous frittatas..."

"You got it." Lani took off her glasses and set them on the side table.

"Hey." Sydney waited until her friend looked at her again. Then she guided a thick swatch of Lani's dark, curly hair behind her ear. "You didn't answer my question about Michael."

Lani's big eyes were a little sad, and her full mouth curved slightly down. "Tonight, when I watched you getting ready to meet this new guy, putting on your makeup, fixing your hair, waffling over that perfect red dress..."

"Yeah? Tonight, what?"

"I thought, '*That*. What Syd's feeling. I want *that*.'"

"Oh, sweetheart..."

Lani's shoulders drooped. "And then you left and Michael came over and I thought what a nice guy he is...but I couldn't go on with him. Because he's not *the* guy." She laughed a little, shaking her head. "Do you know what I mean?"

Sydney reached out. Lani sagged against her and they held each other. "Yeah," Sydney whispered into her friend's thick, fragrant hair. "Yeah, I know exactly what you mean."

The next morning, the doorbell rang at seven-thirty on the nose.

"I get it!" Trevor fisted his plump hand and tapped the table twice. "Knock, knock!" he shouted. "Who's there?"

Sydney kissed his milk-smeared cheek. "Eat your cereal, Bosco."

"Banana!" Trev giggled. "Banana who?"

Lani said, "The coffee's ready and the frittata's in the oven. Answer the door, Syd."

"Orange. Banana." Trevor was totally entranced with his never-quite-right knock-knock joke. He banged his spoon gleefully against the tabletop. "Orange your... banana..."

Lani took his spoon from him. "Well, I guess I'll have to feed you, since you're not doing it."

"Lani, no! I eat. I do it myself."

"You sure?"

"Yes!"

She handed him back the spoon. "Go," she said to

Sydney, canting her head in the general direction of the front door.

Her heart doing somersaults inside her chest, Sydney went to let Rule in.

"Hi." She said it in the most ridiculous, breathy little voice.

"Sydney," he replied in wonderful melted-caramel tones. Could a man get more handsome every time a woman saw him? Rule did. The bright April sunshine made his hair gleam black as a crow's wing, and his smile had her heart performing a forward roll. He had a big yellow Tonka dump truck in one hand and a red ball in the other.

"I see you've come armed for battle," she said.

He shrugged. "In my experience, little boys like trucks. And balls."

"They do. Both. A lot." She stared at him. And he stared back at her. Time stopped. The walls of her foyer seemed to disappear. There was only the man on the other side of the open door. He filled up the world.

Then, from back in the kitchen, she heard her son calling out gleefully, "Orange. Banana. Banana. Orange…"

Lani said something. Probably, "Eat your cereal."

"It's the never-ending knock-knock joke," she said, and then wondered if they even had knock-knock jokes in his country. "Come in, come in…"

He did. She shut the door behind him. "This way…"

He caught her elbow. Somehow he had managed to shift the toy truck to the arm with the ball in it. "Wait." He said it softly.

She turned back to him and he looked down at her and…

Was there anything like this feeling she had with him?

So fine and shining and full of possibility. He pulled her to him.

She went willingly, eagerly. Close to him was where she wanted to be. She moved right up, snug and cozy against his broad chest, sharing his strong arms with the red ball and the yellow truck. "What?"

"This." And he kissed her. A brushing kiss, tender and teasing. Just right for early on a sunny Saturday morning. She felt his smile against her own.

When he lifted his mouth from hers, his eyes were soft as black velvet and full of promise. "May I meet your son now?"

"Right this way."

Trevor was shy with Rule at first.

Her little boy stared with big, solemn dark eyes as Sydney introduced Rule to Lani.

"And this is Trevor," Sydney said.

"Hello, Trevor. My name is Rule."

Trevor only stared some more and stuck a big spoonful of cereal in his mouth.

"Say hello," Sydney instructed him.

But Trevor turned his head away.

Rule sent her an oblique glance and a slight smile that said he knew about kids, and also knew how to be patient. He put the ball and the truck under the side table against the wall and accepted coffee, taking the empty chair between Lani and Sydney.

Lani served the frittata and they ate. Rule praised the food and said how much he liked the coffee, which Lani prepared to her own exacting tastes, grinding the beans with a top-quality grinder and brewing only with a French press.

He asked Lani about her degree in literature. The two

of them seemed to hit it off, Sydney thought. Lani was easy with him, and friendly, from the first. She told him her favorite Shakespeare play was *The Tempest*. He confessed to a fondness for *King Lear,* which had Lani groaning that she might love *Lear,* too. But she had no patience for thickheaded, foolish kings. Sydney didn't know a lot about Shakespeare, but it did kind of please her, that Rule seemed well-read, that he could carry on a conversation about something other than the Mavericks and the Cowboys.

He turned to her. "And what about you, Sydney? Do you have a favorite Shakespeare play?"

She shrugged. "I saw *A Midsummer Night's Dream* once. And I enjoyed it. Everybody falling in love with the wrong person, but then it all worked out in the end."

"You prefer a happy ending?"

"Absolutely," she told him. "I like it when it all works out. That doesn't happen often enough in real life."

"I like trucks!" Suddenly, Trev was over his shyness and back in the game.

Rule turned to him. "And do you like balls?"

"Red balls! Yes!"

"Good. Because that truck and that ball over there beneath the table? They're for you."

Trevor looked away again—too much attention, apparently, from this intriguing stranger.

Sydney said, "Tell Rule 'thank you.'"

"Thank you, Roo," Trev parroted obediently, still looking away, the soft curve of his round cheek turned down.

But Rule wasn't looking away. He seemed honestly taken with her little boy. Her heart did more wild and lovely acrobatics, just to look at the two of them, Rule watching Trev, Trev not quite able to meet this new guy's eyes.

Then Rule said, "Knock, knock."

Trev didn't look, but he did say, "Who's there?"

"Wanda."

Trev peeked, looked away, peeked again. "Wanda who?"

"Wanda cookie?"

Slowly, Trev turned and looked straight at Rule. "Cookie! Yes! Please!"

Rule actually produced an animal cracker from the pocket of his beautifully made lightweight jacket. He slid a questioning glance at Sydney. At her nod, he handed the cookie over.

"Grrr. Lion!" announced Trev and popped the lion-shaped cookie in his mouth. "Yum." He chewed and swallowed. "Thank you very much—Orange! Banana! Knock, knock."

Rule gamely went through the whole joke with him twice. Trev never got the punch line right, but that didn't have any effect on his delight in the process.

"It never ends," Lani said with a sigh. But then she grinned. "And you know we wouldn't have it any other way."

"All done," Trev told them. "Get down, Mama. Play trucks!"

So Sydney wiped his hands and face with a damp cloth and swung him down from his booster seat. He went straight for Rule. "Roo. Come. We play trucks!"

"It appears you have been summoned," Sydney said.

"Nothing could please me more—or *almost* nothing." The teasing heat in his glance hinted that whatever it was that pleased him more had something to do with her. Very likely with kissing her, an activity that pleased her a bunch, too.

He tossed his jacket across the family room sofa and went over and got down on the floor with Trev, who gathered all his trucks together so they could roll them around making *vrooming* noises and crash them into each other. Sydney and Lani cleared the table and loaded the dishwasher. And soon enough, it was time to head for the neighborhood park. Lani begged off, so it was just the three of them. Since the small park was only a couple of blocks away, they walked, Trev between Sydney and Rule, holding both their hands.

Trev was an outgoing child, although he was usually pretty reserved around new people. It took him a while to get comfortable with someone. But apparently, with Rule, he was over his shyness after those first few moments at the breakfast table.

Trev chattered away at him as they strolled past the pretty, gracious homes and the wide, inviting lawns. "I walk fast, Roo. I strong! I happy!"

Rule agreed that he was very fast, and so strong—and wasn't it great that he was happy? "I'm happy, too," Rule said, and shared a speaking glance with Sydney.

Trev looked up at them, at Rule, then at Sydney, then back at Rule again. "Mama's happy, too!" he crowed. "Knock, knock!"

"Who's there?" asked Rule. And then he went through the endless loop of the joke two more times.

They stayed at the park for three hours. Sydney watched for a sign that Rule might be getting tired of pushing Trev on the swings, of sitting with him on the spinner, of playing seesaw—Trev and Sydney on one end, Rule on the other.

But Rule seemed to love every minute of it. He got down and crawled through the concrete tunnels with Trev, heedless of his designer trousers, laughing as Trev scuttled ahead of him calling out, "You can't catch me, I too fast!" Trev popped out of the tunnel.

Rule was right behind him. Rule growled, playing it scary. Trev let out a shriek of fear and delight.

Finally, at a little after eleven, Trev announced, "Okay. All done." And he was. All the fun had worn him out.

The walk back to the house took a little longer than the stroll over there. When Trevor was tired, he dragged his feet and kept trying to sit down instead of moving forward.

But they got him there, eventually. Lani took over, hustling him to the bathroom to change him out of the diaper she'd put on him for the park and back into the lighter-weight training pants he wore most of the time now.

Alone with Rule for the first time since their kiss at the front door, Sydney said, "You were wonderful with him."

His gaze held hers. She did love the way he looked at her—as though he couldn't get enough of just staring into her eyes. He said, "It wasn't difficult, not in the least. I enjoyed every minute of it." And then he added in that charming, formal way of his, "Thank you for inviting me, Sydney."

"It was my pleasure—and clearly, Trev's, too. Had enough?"

He frowned. "Are you saying you would like for me to go now?"

She laughed. "No way. I'm just giving you an out, in case you've had enough of crashing trucks and knock-knock jokes for one day."

"I want to stay, if you don't mind."

"Of course I don't mind." Now her heart was doing cartwheels. "Not in the least."

Yes, all right. Maybe she should be more cautious. Put the brakes on a little. But she didn't *want* to put the brakes on. She was having a great time and if he didn't want to go, well, why should she feel she should send him away?

He could stay for lunch if he wanted, stay for dinner.

Stay…indefinitely. That would be just fine with her. Every moment she was with him only convinced her that she wanted the *next* moment with him. And the one after that. Something about him had her throwing all her usual caution to the winds.

Was she in for a rude awakening? She just didn't think so. Every moment she was with Rule only made her more certain that he was the real deal: a great guy who liked her—a lot. A great guy who liked children, too, a guy who actually enjoyed spending the morning playing in the park with her and her little boy.

As long as he gave her no reason to doubt her confidence in him, well, she *wouldn't* doubt him. It was as simple as that.

He said, "Perhaps we could take Trevor and Lani to lunch?"

"I wish. But no. Trev's going to need to eat right away, and since he's been on the go since early this morning, he's probably going to be fussy. So we'll get some food down him and then put him to bed. His nap will last at least a couple of hours. You sure you won't mind just hanging around here for the afternoon?"

"There's nothing I would rather do than hang around here with you and your son." He said it so matter-of-factly, and she knew he was sincere.

"I'm glad." They shared a nod of perfect understanding.

As Sydney had predicted, Trev was cranky during lunch, but he did pack away a big bowl of chicken and rice. He went right to sleep when Sydney put him in bed.

Then she and Rule raided the refrigerator and carried their lunch of cheese, crackers and grapes out to the backyard. They sat under an oak not far from the pool and he told her more about his family, about how his older brother

Max's wife had tragically drowned in a water-skiing accident two years before, leaving Max with a broken heart and two little children to raise on his own.

"They were so happy together, Max and Sophia," Rule said, his eyes full of shadows right then. "They found each other very young, and knew they would marry when they were both hardly more than children. It's been terrible for him, learning to live without her."

"I can't even imagine how that must be for him. I've always envied people who find true love early and only want a chance to have a family, to grow old side by side. It's just completely wrong that your brother and his wife didn't get a whole lifetime of happiness together."

They were sitting in a pair of cushioned chaises, the platter of cheese and fruit on the low teak table between them. He held out his hand to her. She took it without hesitation and let him pull her over to his chaise.

He wrapped an arm around her, using his other hand to tip her chin up. They shared a slow, sweet kiss. And then he spoke against her softly parted lips. "I love the taste of your lips, the feel of your body pressed close to mine...."

She reached up, touched the silky black hair at his temple. A miracle, to be here with him, like this. To be free to touch him at will, to be the one *he* wanted to touch. "Oh, Rule. What's happening with us?"

He kissed her again, a possessive kiss, hard and quick. "You don't know?"

"I...think I do. But I've waited so long to meet someone like you. It almost seems too good to be true."

"You're trembling." He held her closer.

She laughed, a torn little sound. "Not so prickly now, huh?"

"Come here, relax..." He stretched out in the chaise and pulled her with him, so she lay facing him, tucked against his side, his big arms around her, his cheek touching her hair. A lovely breeze came up, stirring the warm afternoon air, making it feel cool and comfortable beneath the oak tree. "Don't be afraid. I would never hurt you. I'm only grateful that I've found you, at last."

"So, then," she teased, "you lied yesterday when you said you weren't looking for me."

"Can you forgive me?"

She took a moment, pretended to think it over and finally whispered, "I'll try."

"Good. Because I've been looking for you all my life. And now that I have you in my arms, I never want to let you go."

"I want to be with you, too." She laid her hand against his chest, felt the steady, strong beating of his heart. "And I'm not afraid," she added. And then she sighed. "Well, okay. That's not so. I *am* afraid—at least a little."

"Because of those fools Ryan and Peter?"

She nodded. "I haven't had good luck with men."

He kissed her hair. "Maybe not."

"Definitely not."

"Until now," he corrected her.

She tipped her head back and met those shining dark eyes and…well, she believed him. She honestly did. "Until now," she repeated, softly, but firmly, too.

"Come out with me tonight. Let me come for you. We'll have dinner, go dancing."

It was Lani's night out. But Sydney had more than one sitter she could call. "I would love to."

Trev woke at a little before three, completely refreshed and ready to play some more.

Rule was only too happy to oblige him. Together, they built a wobbly Duplo castle—which Trev took great delight in toppling to the floor the moment it was finished.

Then the three of them took the red ball outside to Trev's fenced play area and rolled the ball around. Finally, inside again, Rule and Trev played more trucks until Lani announced it was time for Trev's dinner.

The man amazed Sydney. He seemed completely content to spend hours entertaining her toddler. He honestly did seem to love children and Sydney couldn't help thinking that he would make a wonderful father.

Rule called his driver at five-twenty-five.

"Bye, Roo. Come back. See me soon!" Trev called, pausing to wave as Lani herded him toward the stairs for his bath.

"Goodbye Trevor."

"We play trucks!" Trev started up the stairs in his usual way, using both hands and feet.

"Yes." Rule nodded, watching his progress upward. "Trucks. Absolutely."

Trev turned to Lani and started his knock-knock joke as he and Lani disappeared on the upper landing. The moment they were out of sight, Sydney moved into Rule's open arms.

They shared a kiss and then he took her hand and brushed his lips across the back of it. "Your son is amazing. So smart. Just like his mom."

She answered playfully, "And don't forget strong. Trev is very strong. Just ask him."

"Yes, I remember. Very strong and very loud when he wants to be—and I'm honored that you shared the story of his birth so honestly with me. And that you've trusted me enough to tell me about those idiots Ryan and Peter."

"I think it's better," she said, "to be honest and forthright."

"So do I." Something happened in his eyes—a shadow of something. Uneasiness? Concern?

Her pulse beat faster. "Rule. What is it? What's the matter?"

"I'm afraid I have a confession to make."

Now her pulse was racing dizzyingly fast. And she felt sick, her stomach churning. So, then. He really *was* too good to be true. "Tell me," she said softly, but not gently. She couldn't hide the thread of steel that connected the two simple words.

"Remember how I told you I admired my mother?"

She wasn't getting it. "This confession is about your mother?"

He touched her cheek, a light touch that made her heart ache. She really liked him. So very much. And now she just knew it was all going wrong. He said, "No, it's not about my mother. Not essentially."

"What do you mean? It is, or it isn't."

"Sydney, I admire my mother for any number of reasons. And I revere her as the ruler of my country."

She was sure she must have misunderstood him. "Excuse me? Your mother rules your country?"

"My mother is Adrienne II, Sovereign Princess of Montedoro. And my father is His Serene Highness Evan, Prince Consort of Montedoro."

"Okay. You'll have to say that again. I'm sure I misunderstood. Sovereign Princess, you said?"

"Yes. My mother holds the throne. My father is Prince Consort and my brother Maximilian is the heir apparent. Before Max had his son and daughter, I was second in line to the throne."

Chapter Four

Sydney gaped up at him. "A prince. You're telling me that you're a prince? And not just as in, 'a prince of a guy,' but a *real* prince? A…royal prince?"

He chuckled. "My darling, yes. That is, more or less, what I'm telling you."

"Um. More or less?"

"The truth is that Montedoro is ruled by a prince, not a king. And, in terms of his or her title, a ruling prince is said to have a throne, but not a crown. And only those who are the children or grandchildren of ruling kings or queens, or are the spouses of royalty, are given the honorific of royal. However, in the sense that 'royal' means 'ruling,' yes. I am of the royal family of Montedoro, or more correctly, the princely family. And even though we are not addressed as royal, both our family coat of arms and our individual monograms contain the image of a crown."

She was still gaping. "I don't think I understood a word you just said."

He frowned. "I see your point. Perhaps that was more information than you require at the moment."

A prince. A prince of Montedoro. Should she have known this? "Wait. Evan Bravo. I remember now. Your dad was in the movies, right?"

He nodded. "It was a big story in all the newspapers and tabloids of the day. My mother married a film actor and he returned with her to Montedoro, where they had many children and lived happily ever after." He gave a wry smile. "Sydney, you look pale. Would you like to sit down?"

"No. No, really. I'm fine. Just fine."

"Perhaps you would like to see my diplomatic passport...."

"Ohmigod. No. Really. I believe you. I do." Still, she couldn't help looking around nervously, half expecting Ashton Kutcher and the *Punk'd* camera crew to be making their appearance any second now. She turned her gaze up to him again and tried to look stern. "You should have told me."

"I know." He did seem honestly contrite. "But the moment never seemed right. I wanted you to know me, at least a little, before we got into all of that."

"Last night. At the Mansion. The nervous host..."

"Yes. I'm staying there. He knows who I am." He took her chin, tipped it up to him. "But none of that matters."

"Rule. Of course it matters."

"Only if you let it. To me, what matters most of all, more than anything, is this..." And he lowered his dark head and claimed her lips.

And by the time that kiss was through, she was inclined

to agree with him. "Oh, Rule..." She clung to him, feeling light-headed and slightly weak in the knees.

"I'll leave you now," he said ruefully, stroking her hair, his eyes full of tenderness and understanding. She thought how crazy she was for him—and how she would look him up on Google the minute he was out the door. One side of his mouth curled up in the gorgeous half smile that totally enchanted her. He said, "You'll have time to look me up on the internet before I come to collect you for the evening."

She shook her head. "You know me too well. How is that possible? We only met yesterday."

"Forgive me. For taking so long to tell you..."

"I'll consider forgiving you as soon as my head stops spinning."

"One last kiss..."

She gave it. She simply could not resist him—and beyond that, she didn't *want* to resist him.

When he lifted his head that time, he released her. She opened the door and watched him jog down the front walk to his waiting limousine.

As soon as the long, black car disappeared from sight, she shut the front door and went upstairs to get with Lani about her plans for the evening.

She found her friend on her knees filling the tub. Trev sat on the bathroom floor in his training pants, putting a new face on his Mr. Potato Head.

"Lani..."

"Hmm?" Lani tested the water, turned the hot water tap up a little.

"Just wondering if you were going out tonight?"

"Nope, I'm staying in. And yes, I'd be happy to watch Trev."

"Wonderful." So that was settled.

"Mama, see?" Trev held up Mr. Potato Head, whose

big, red lips were now above his moustache and who had only one eye in the middle of his forehead. She bent down and kissed him. He asked, "Mama read a story?"

"After your bath, I promise."

"O-*kay!*" He removed Mr. Potato Head's red hat and reached for a blue plastic ear.

Sydney kissed him again and then ran back downstairs to her office off the foyer. She kept a PC in there and she figured she had maybe twenty minutes before Trev finished his bath and would come looking for her.

Sydney was good at research, and she knew how to get a lot of information quickly. By the time Trev came bouncing down the stairs and demanded her attention again, she intended to know a whole lot more about Rule.

She found pages and pages of references to the courtship and marriage of Rule's father and mother.

Evan Bravo was born in San Antonio, second of seven sons, to James and Elizabeth Bravo. Several sources cited early estrangement from his overbearing father. Determined to make his mark in Hollywood, Evan Bravo moved West at the age of eighteen. Talent and luck were on his side. He was never a big star, but at twenty-five, he won a Golden Globe and a Best Supporting Actor Oscar for his portrayal of a charming but crooked L.A. detective in a big-budget box office hit called *L.A. Undercover.* Then he met Princess Adrienne of Montedoro. There ensued a whirlwind courtship, a fabulous palace wedding—and celebrating in the streets of the whole of Montedoro when their first child, Maximilian, was born. Princess Adrienne, as the last of her line, was expected to provide her country with an heir and a spare and then some. She did exactly that, bearing eight more children in the succeeding eleven years.

Sydney read the story of the tragic death of Maximilian's wife, Sophia—drowning while water-skiing, just as Rule had already told her. Also, she learned that third-born Alexander had been captured by terrorists in Afghanistan and held prisoner for four years, until somehow engineering a miraculous and daring escape only a few months ago.

Prince Rule, she learned, had obtained his degree in America, from Princeton. He was the businessman of the family, the glamorous bachelor, big in international trade, and was known to champion and generously contribute to several worthy causes. Over the years, his name had been linked with any number of gorgeous models and actresses, but those relationships had never seemed to last very long. Some sources claimed that he was "expected" to marry his longtime friend from childhood, HRH Liliana, aka Princess Lili, heir presumptive to the throne of the island state of Alagonia. However, no actual announcement of an engagement had so far been made.

Sydney went looking for images of the princess in question and found several. Liliana of Alagonia was blonde, blue-eyed and as beautiful as a princess in a fairy tale.

Sudden apprehension had Sydney catching her lower lip between her teeth and shifting in her swivel chair. Princess Lili, huh? Rule had never mentioned this supposed "childhood friend." Tonight, she would definitely have a few questions for him.

"Mama, read me books!"

Sydney looked up from the computer to find her little boy and Lani standing in the open doorway to the front hall.

Lani said, "Sorry to interrupt, but he hasn't forgotten that you said you would read to him."

"And I will, absolutely."

Trev, all pink and sweet from his bath, wearing his Captain America pajamas, marched over and tugged on her arm. "Come *on,* Mama."

Further research on Princess Liliana would have to wait. Sydney swung him into her arms and carried him upstairs where he'd already picked out the books he wanted her to read to him.

Later, after he was in bed, as she hurried to get ready for the evening, she told Lani that Rule was a Montedoran prince.

"Whoa. And I didn't even curtsy when you introduced me to him."

"It's a little late to worry about protocol." Sydney leaned close to the mirror as she put on her makeup. "Which is fine with me."

"What would it be like to marry a prince?" Lani wondered out loud.

"Did I mention marriage? We've only just met."

"But it's already serious between you two, I can tell. Isn't it?"

Sydney set down her powder brush and turned to her friend. "Yeah. I think it is—and I may be late coming home tonight." Unless Rule confessed that he intended to marry the lovely Princess Lili. In that case, she would be coming home early, crying on Lani's shoulder and swearing off men for the next decade, at least.

"Oh, Syd…" Lani grabbed her and gave her a hug. And then she took Sydney by the shoulders and held her away. "You look wonderful. I love that dress. It brings out the color of your eyes." Lani sighed. "Enjoy every moment."

"I will." Sydney smoothed her hair and tried to banish any thought of pretty Princess Lili from her mind.

Rule arrived in his limousine at eight.

Once on the inside of the tinted-glass windows, Sidney

saw there were two men in the front seat: the driver in his dark livery and chauffeur's cap and also a thick-necked military-looking guy with a crew cut, who had a Bluetooth device in his ear and wore sunglasses even though it was nearly dark.

Sydney leaned close to Rule, drawn to his strength and his warmth and the fine, subtle scent of the aftershave he wore. She whispered, "Don't tell me. You keep the Secret Service on retainer."

He gave a shrug. "Effective security is something of a necessity. It's a sad fact of life in this modern age."

They went to another really wonderful restaurant, where they were once again ushered into a private room.

She waited until they were served the main course before she brought up the subject that had been bothering her. "So tell me about Princess Liliana of Alagonia."

He sent her a wry sort of smile. "I see you've been checking up on me."

"Did you think I wouldn't?"

"I absolutely knew that you would."

She told him exactly what she'd learned. "Rumor has it that you and the princess are 'expected' to marry."

He held her gaze. "You should know better than to put your faith in rumors."

"You're hedging, Rule." She sat back in her chair and took a drink from her water goblet.

"Lili's eight years younger than I am. She's like one of my little sisters."

"But she's *not* your sister—little or otherwise."

"All right, enough." He said it flatly. "I am not going to marry Liliana, Sydney. We are not affianced. I have never proposed marriage to her."

She took a wild guess. "But *she* wants to marry *you*. It's *assumed* that you will marry her."

He didn't look away. But his eyes were definitely guarded now. "She...looks up to me."

Did he imagine she would wimp out and leave it at that? Hah. "Just say it. She *does* want to marry you."

He sat back in his chair, too. And he looked at her so strangely, so distantly. When he spoke, his voice was cold. "I would not presume to speak for Liliana. She's a sweet and lovely person. And yes, if I married Lili, it would be considered a brilliant match, one that would strengthen the bonds between our two countries."

She said sharply, "So, then you *should* marry her."

"Not only that." His eyes were so dark right then, dark and full of secrets, it seemed to her. Suddenly, she was thinking that she didn't know him at all, that this brief, magical time she'd shared with him had truly been just that: magic, not reality. Nothing more than a beautiful, impossible fantasy. That the truth was coming out now and the fantasy was over.

So soon. Way too soon...

He spoke again. "Do you recall how I told you I had to marry by my thirty-third birthday?"

"Yes."

"Did you think I was only teasing you?"

"Well, I thought you meant that there was pressure in your family, as there is in a lot of families, for you to settle down, start providing your parents with grandchildren, all that."

"It's considerably more than just pressure. It's the law."

She looked at him sideways. "Now you really are kidding."

"On the contrary, I'm completely serious. My country was once a French protectorate. And France...casts a long shadow, as they say. We have signed any number of treaties with France, treaties wherein the French promise to guarantee Montedoro's sovereignty."

As a lawyer, she knew what he was getting at. "And the simple fact that another country is in a position to guarantee your sovereignty is…problematic?"

"Precisely. Although my family is officially in charge of succession, the French government must approve the next ruling prince or princess. There is even a stipulation that, should the throne go vacant, Montedoro will revert to a French protectorate. That is why we have a law designed to ensure that no prince will shirk his—or her—obligation to produce potential heirs to the throne. Montedoran princes and princesses are required to marry before their thirty-third birthday or be stripped of all titles and income. I will be thirty-three on June twenty-fourth."

"Two and a half months from now."

"Yes," he said softly.

Sydney was certain of it then. No matter what he'd said a few moments ago, he did intend to marry the lovely Lili. This thing between the two of them was only…what? A last fling before his ingrained sense of duty finally kicked in, before he went back to Montedoro and tied the knot with the pretty blonde princess he'd known since childhood—and then got to work having a bunch of little princes with her.

And why, oh, why, if he just *had* to have a final fling, couldn't he have chosen someone else? Sydney was a hard-driving, overworked single mom and the last thing she needed was a whirlwind romance with a man who was planning to marry someone else. Plus, she'd already suffered through more than her share of disappointments when it came to the male gender, thank you very much.

Bottom line? She really did not have time for this crap.

And she wanted desperately to be furious with him.

But she wasn't. The whole situation only made her miserable. She longed to put her face in her hands and burst into tears.

But no—in fact, *hell* no. She was an O'Shea and an O'Shea was tougher than that. No way was she letting him see her break down and cry. Instead, coolly, she advised, "Don't you think you're cutting it a little close?"

"More than a little. And the truth is I *have* considered asking Liliana to be my wife."

Surprise, surprise. "So what's stopped you?"

"No man wants to marry a woman he thinks of as a sister. Not even if she is a fine person, not even to keep his inheritance, not even for the good of his country. And so I've hesitated. I've put off making my move."

"Rule. I have to say it. You need to stop dithering and get with the program."

That slow smile curved his beautiful mouth. "A prince does not *dither.*"

"Call it what you want. Looks like dithering to me."

"If I *was* dithering, Sydney—and I'm not admitting that I was—I'm not dithering anymore."

She cast a pained glance toward the ceiling. "Okay. You lost me there."

"I'm absolutely certain now that Liliana will never be my bride. In one split second, everything changed for me."

She didn't get where this was going. She really didn't. And she told herself firmly that she didn't care. What mattered was that it was over between them. It had to be, she saw that now. Over and done before it even really got started. "In one split second," she parroted with a heavy dose of sarcasm. "So...the realization that you're definitely not marrying dear Princess Lili hit you like a lightning bolt, huh?"

"No."

"I'm not following you."

"It's quite simple. While everything changed for me in an instant, it took a little longer than that for me to accept that marriage to Lili had become impossible."

"I have no idea what you're telling me."

"*That* happened after lunch yesterday."

"*What* happened?"

"You said goodbye and got into your car and drove away. I stood and watched you leave and tried to consider the concept of never seeing you again. And I couldn't do that. Right then, marrying Lili became impossible."

"So there was no lightning bolt, after all."

"Of course there was a lightning bolt. It struck the moment I saw you, striding into Macy's, indomitable. Unyielding. Ready to take on the world. At that moment, Liliana was the last thing on my mind. Right then, all I could think of was you."

Sydney reached for her untouched glass of wine and took an extra-large gulp of it. She set the glass down with care. "Well, I…" Her voice had a definite wobble to it. She drew in a slow, steadying breath. "You're not marrying the princess. You're sure about that?"

"Yes. Absolutely certain."

"You mean that? You really mean that?"

"I do, Sydney. With all my heart."

"Don't mess with me, Rule."

"I promise you, I'm not."

Her throat felt tight, so tight it ached. She gulped to relax it a little. "Okay," she said softly, at last. "You're not marrying the princess, after all."

"I'm so glad we're finally clear on that." His voice was gentle, indulgent. "You've hardly touched your food. Is it unsatisfactory?"

"Oh, no. It's fine. Really. Delicious." She picked up her fork again.

They ate in silence for a while.

Finally, he spoke. "I like you in that emerald-green satin. Almost as much as I like you in red."

"Thank you."

"I still want to take you dancing."

She sipped her wine again, suddenly as certain as he seemed to be. About the two of them. About…everything. Whatever happened in the end, she wanted this night with him. She wanted it so much. She wanted *him*. "I have a suggestion."

"And I am always open to suggestion. Especially if the suggestion is coming from you."

"Take me back to the Mansion, Rule. Take me to your room. We can dance there."

Chapter Five

His room was one of the two Terrace Suites on the Mansion's top floor. It was over thirteen hundred square feet of pure luxury.

There was champagne waiting for them in the sitting room—champagne and a crystal bowl full of Montedoran oranges. He took off his jacket and tie and they sat on the sofa, sipping the champagne. She slipped off her shoes as he peeled an orange for her.

"Oh, this so good," she said, savoring the ruby-red sections, one by one. They tasted like no orange she'd ever had before.

He bent close and kissed her then, a slow kiss that started out light and so tender and deepened until she was slightly breathless—scratch that. More than slightly. A lot more than slightly. "Very sweet," he said when he lifted his mouth from hers. He wasn't talking about the orange.

She only gazed at him, her heart beating in a slow, deep,

exciting way, her body warm and lazy, her eyelids suddenly heavy.

The sofa was nice and fat and comfortable. She considered stretching out on the cushions, reaching for him as she went down, pulling him with her, so they were stretched out together.

But he set his half-full flute aside and picked up the remote on the coffee table. The large flat screen above a bow-fronted cabinet flared to life. Before she could ask him why he suddenly wanted to watch *Lockup,* he changed the channel to a music station. A slow romantic song was playing.

"Come." He offered his hand and they rose together. They went out to the terrace, where the lights of downtown Dallas glittered in the balmy darkness of the April night.

They danced. It was like a dream, a dream come to life, just the two of them, holding each other, swaying to the music, not saying anything.

Not needing to speak.

Then he put a finger under her chin and she looked up into his eyes, into the light shining within that velvet darkness. She tried to remind herself that she still wasn't sure about the whole love at first sight thing, didn't really believe that you could meet someone and know instantly that here was the person you wanted to spend the rest of your life with. It took time to know another person, time to learn his ways, time to discover if there really was any chance for the relationship in the long-term.

But when Rule looked at her, well, she believed that *he* believed. And his belief was powerful. His belief made her want to believe, too.

"I see you," he whispered, and she couldn't help smiling. He reminded her of Trev again, Trev playing peekaboo: *I see you, Mama. I see you, I do.* "I know," he said. "It sounds silly when I say it. It sounds self-evident. And not important in the least."

"I didn't say that. It was only, for a moment, you reminded me of Trev."

"Ah." He searched her eyes some more. "Well, good, then. I'm pleased if I make you think of him. And it *is* important that I see you. I see in you all that I've been looking for, though I didn't even realize I *was* looking until yesterday. I see in you the best things, Sydney. The things that matter. I see that with you I can be a better man, and a happier man. I see that you will always interest me. That you will challenge me. I want to…give you everything. I want to spend my life making sure you have it all, whatever makes you happy, whatever your heart desires."

She searched his astonishingly gorgeous face. "You are tempting me, you know that?"

"I hope so." He brushed one soft, warm kiss against her lips, a kiss that lingered like a tender brand on her skin even after he had lifted his head to gaze down at her once more. "I want to tempt you, Sydney. Because I've never met anyone like you. You amaze me. I want to be with you. I never want to let you go." He kissed her again, an endless kiss, as they danced. His mouth was so soft, not like the rest of him at all. His mouth was hot and supple and his tongue eased past the trembling barrier of her lips, sliding hot and knowing, over the edges of her teeth, across the top of her tongue, and then beneath it.

She felt…lost. Lost in a lovely, delicious kind of way. She didn't know where she was going. And Sydney Gabrielle O'Shea *always* knew where she was going. She'd always kept her focus, because she had to. Who would keep her on track if she didn't? Her parents were gone without her even knowing them. And then, too soon, so was her strong, steady grandmother. The men to whom she gave her trust were not dependable.

There was only Lani, her true, forever friend. And then there was Trevor to light up her days.

And now this. Now Rule.

At last. Long after she'd been sure there would never be a man for her. Her doubts, her hesitations were falling away. *He* was peeling them away. With his tenderness and his understanding, with his honesty and his frank desire for her.

Who had she been kidding? She *could* believe in love at first sight. Like her beloved grandmother before her, she *did* believe in love at first sight.

As long as it was love at first sight with a certain man. With the *right* man. The one she could trust. The one she could count on to be there when she needed someone to lean on. The one who honestly seemed to like everything about her, even her prickly nature and her sometimes sharp tongue.

Maybe that wasn't so surprising, that he had no issues with her strength and determination, with her ambition and her drive. After all, she had no issues with him— or whenever she did have issues, he would patiently and calmly put them to rest.

And she certainly liked the feelings he roused in her. The excitement, the desire. And the unaccustomed trust. Every time she felt her doubts rising—about him, about the impossibility of this thing between them—he stepped right up and banished them. He kept proving to her that he was exactly the man he seemed to be, exactly the man she'd never dared to dream she might someday find.

They danced some more, still kissing. She wrapped her arms around his neck, threaded her fingers up into the warm silk of his dark, dark hair. He lifted his head, but only to slant his mouth the other way and continue to kiss her, endlessly, perfectly. She sighed and lifted closer to him, loving the feel of her breasts against his hard chest, of her body and his body, touching so lightly, striking off sparks.

Sparks of promise, sparks of building desire.

He broke the kiss. She sighed at the loss. But then he only lowered his mouth again and kissed her cheek and then her temple. He caught her earlobe between his teeth, worried it so gently.

She made a soft, pleasured sound and pressed her body even closer to him, wanting to melt right into him, wanting to become a part of him, somehow—his body, her body, one and the same. He went on kissing her—his wonderful lips gliding over the curve of her jaw, down the side of her neck.

Her green dress had spaghetti straps. With a lazy finger, he pushed the left strap out of his way and kissed her shoulder, a long, lingering kiss. She felt his tongue, licking her, sending hot shards of pleasure radiating out along her skin. And then his teeth...oh, those teeth. He nipped her, but carefully, tenderly.

They had stopped dancing. They stood in the shadow of a potted palm, in a corner of the terrace. He eased the side of her dress down. She felt the sultry night air touch her breast.

And then he kissed her there. He took her nipple into his mouth and sucked it, rhythmically. He whispered her name against her skin.

She cradled his head, close—closer, her fingers buried in his hair. The heat of him was all around her, and down low, she was already liquid, weak, yearning. A silver thread of pure delight drew down through the core of her, into the womanly heart of her, from her breast, where he kissed her endlessly. He drew on her eager flesh in a slow, tempting rhythm, making her bare toes curl on the terrace flagstones. She moaned, held him closer, murmured his name on a slow, surrendering sigh.

And then he lifted his head. She blinked, dazed, and gazed up at him, feeling like a sleepwalker, wakened from the sweetest dream.

"Inside." He bent close again, caught her lower lip between his teeth, licked it, let it go. "Let's go in..."

She trembled, yearning. Her nipple was drawn so tight and hard, it ached. It ached in such a lovely, thrilling way. "Yes. Oh, yes..." And she tried to pull her strap back up, to cover herself.

"Don't." He caught her hand, stilled it, then brought her fingers to his lips and kissed them. "Leave it." His voice was rough and infinitely tender, both at once. "Leave it bare..." He bent, kissed her breast again, but only briefly that time. "So beautiful..."

And then he swept her up as though she weighed nothing and carried her through the open door into the sitting room, pausing only to turn and slide the door shut. A new song began.

He stopped in midstride. Their gazes locked. "'Lady in Red,'" he whispered.

"Not tonight," she whispered.

"It doesn't matter, whether you happen to be wearing red or not. To me, this song is you. This song is *yours*. You're my lady in red..."

"Oh, Rule." She touched his cheek with the back of her hand. His fine tanned skin was slightly rough with the beginnings of his dark beard, slightly rough and so very warm.

He took her mouth again, in a hard, hot kiss. She surrendered to that kiss. She let him sweep her away with the heat of it. She was seduced by the carnal need in it.

And he was moving again, carrying her through the door that led to his bedroom. The bed was turned back. He bent to put her down on the soft white sheets, so carefully, as though she might break, as though she was infinitely precious to him.

He laid her down and he rose to his height again. Swiftly, without ceremony, he took off his shirt, undid his belt, took down his trousers and his briefs. He sat and removed his shoes and socks. And then he rose once more to toss everything carelessly onto the bedside chair. The view of his magnificent body from behind stole every last wisp of breath from her body.

And then he turned to face her again. His eyes were molten.

Naked. He was naked and he was as beautiful—*more* so—than she had even imagined, the muscles of his chest and arms and belly so sharply defined. His legs were strong and straight and powerful, dusted with black hair, black hair that grew dense and curly where his big thighs joined.

The proof that he wanted her jutted out hard and proud. She dragged in a ragged breath and let it out with care.

And then he came down to her.

More kisses. Long, deep kisses, until she was pliant and more eager than ever. Until she whimpered with need. He took down the other strap of her dress and he kissed her right breast so slowly and deliciously, with the same erotic care he had lavished on the left.

By the time he eased her to her side facing away from him and took the zipper of her dress down, she was ready.

For him. For the two of them. For whatever he might

do to her, do *with* her. Ready for tonight. And tomorrow night. And all the nights to come.

With him. Beside him. Always.

Was this a dream? If it was, she prayed she might never wake up.

Tucked close behind her, his front to her back, he eased the dress down, gently, carefully, making the simple act of peeling the fabric away from her body into a caress. A long, perfect thrilling caress.

She lifted enough that he could take the dress down over her thighs and off. She wore no bra. She didn't need one.

He cupped her breasts, one and then the other, his hand engulfing them. He whispered that they were beautiful. "Delicate," he said. "Perfect."

She believed him. Seduced by the magic of his knowing touch, she had relinquished everything, even the wisdom of a little healthy skepticism. She believed all the things he whispered to her. She believed every last rough-tender, arousing word. Every knowing, skilled caress. He touched her face and she smelled the tart sweetness of blood oranges on his fingers. And it seemed to her that the scent was his scent—sweet, tempting, ruby-red.

His hand moved downward, over her breasts again and lower, along her belly. She gasped as his fingers eased under the elastic of her panties.

He found the feminine heart of her. He whispered that she felt like heaven there, so wet and hot and slick for him. He stroked her, a touch that quickly set every last nerve she possessed ablaze. Her whole body seemed to be humming with excitement, with electricity, with heat. She was liquid and burning and close to the brink.

She wanted it to last, wanted the climb to the top to go on forever, wanted to hold off on completion until she had him within her. But in no time, she was shuddering, going over the edge, moaning his name, working her hips against his fingers—oh, those fingers of his: magic, just…magic. She cried out.

He whispered, "Yes, like that. Just like that."

And then she was sailing out from the peak, into the wide open, drifting slowly, slowly down into her body again, her body that had his body wrapped around it.

"You feel…so good," she murmured, lazy. And she took his hand and tucked it tenderly close to her heart.

But he wasn't through yet.

Which was totally fine with her. She could go on like this, touching him, *being* touched by him, forever.

He was moving, shifting her onto her back, resettling himself close against her side. She sighed and let him do as he wished with her. She was drifting, satisfied, deeply content, on the borderline of sleep.

"Sydney…"

Reluctantly, still lost in the echoes of so many beautiful sensations, she opened her eyes. He was up an elbow, gazing down at her, his eyes liquid, black as the middle of a very dark night.

She reached up, touched his mouth. "So soft. You're such a good kisser…"

He bent near again, kissed her with that mouth of his, her fingers still on his lips, so he kissed them, too. "Sydney…" He kissed her name against her mouth, against her fingers.

"Mmm." She eased her hand away, parted her lips, took his tongue inside. "Mmm…" Maybe she wasn't so sleepy after all. She clasped his hard shoulder, loving the rock-like contour of it, and then she let her hand glide around to his strong nape. She caressed the amazing musculature of his broad back. "I just want to touch you…"

He didn't object. He went on kissing her, as she indulged herself. She wanted to touch every inch of him—his back, his powerful arms, his fine, strong chest. He had a perfect little happy trail and she did what a woman tends to do—she followed it downward.

And when her fingers closed around him, she took great satisfaction in the low groan he let out. She drank in that groan like wine.

Was there ever a guy like this? She doubted it. Every part of him was beautiful, her fairy-tale prince made flesh.

She closed her eyes again and reveled in the feel of him. She wanted...everything from him. All of him. Now.

She whispered in a shattered sort of wonder, against his beautiful lips. "Oh, Rule. Now. Please, now..." And she urged him to come even closer, all the way closer, opening her thighs for him, pulling him onto her, so eager, so hungry.

More than ready.

"Wait..." He breathed the word against her parted lips.

"What?" She moaned in frustration. "No. I don't want to wait."

"Sydney..." He took his mouth from hers.

And again, she lifted her heavy eyelids and gazed up at him, impatient. Questioning. "What?"

He gave her one of those beautiful, wry, perfect smiles of his. And he tipped his dark head toward his raised hand. She tore her gaze away from all that manly beauty to see what he held.

A condom.

"Oops." She felt her cheeks flush even redder than they already were. She let out a ragged sigh. "I can't believe it. I didn't even think about that. How could I not think of that? I'm never that foolish, that irresponsible."

His shining midnight gaze adored her—and indulged

her. "It's all right. There are two of us, after all. Only one of us had to remember. And I haven't minded at all seeing you so carried away that you didn't even think about using protection."

"I *should* have thought of it."

He shook his head, slowly, lazily, that tempting smile of his a seduction in itself. "You are so beautiful when you're carried away." His smile, his tender words, the hot-candy sound of his voice. She was seduced by every aspect of him.

Seduced and loving it.

Still, she tried to hold out against him. "I'm not beautiful, Rule. We both know that."

"You *are* beautiful. And please give me your hand and stop arguing with me."

Really, the guy was irresistible. She held out her hand.

He put the little pouch in the center of her palm. "Do the honors?"

She laughed, a soft, husky laugh, a laugh that spoke so clearly of her desire. "Now you're talkin'."

He lay back on the pillows and watched her, his eyes so hot now, molten, as she removed the wrapper and set it aside.

She bent over him, kissed him, in the center of his chest, on that silky trail of hair, not far from his heart. His skin was hot. He smelled so good. She rained a flood of kisses on him, to each side of his big chest, over his rib cage, on his ridged, amazing belly, all the way to her goal.

When she got there, she kissed him once more, a light, feathery breath of a kiss. He moaned. The sound pleased her. She stuck out her tongue and she licked him, concentrating first on the flare, then centering on the sensitive tip. And then, at last, taking him inside—then slowly, by agonizing degrees, lifting once more to release him.

A strangled sound escaped him. And he touched her hair, threading his fingers through it, lifting himself toward her, begging wordlessly, on another groan, for more.

She gave him what he asked for. She took him in again slowly, all the way, relaxing her throat to accommodate him, and then, just as slowly, let him out. She used her tongue on him, licking, stroking, swirling, teasing.

His moans and his rough, ragged breathing told her that he couldn't take much more. Good. She wanted to lead him all the way to the brink. She wanted to make him go over, into a perfect satisfaction, as he'd done to her.

But then he caught her face between his hands and he guided her up his body again, until she was looking right into those beautiful eyes.

"Put it on," he commanded in a rough, hungry growl. "Put it on now."

And she realized she was fine with that. More than fine. She rolled on the condom carefully. Once it was on, she rose onto her knees, intending to take the top position.

But then he reached for her, and he lifted up from the pillows and she happily surrendered as he guided her so gently down onto her back again. He eased her thighs wide and settled between them, his arms against the mattress to either side of her head, his fingers in her hair.

"Sydney…" His mouth swooped down to claim another kiss. Deep and hot and perfect, that kiss.

And she felt him, nudging against her, so slick and hard and wonderfully insistent. He pressed in slowly, filling her. She opened for him eagerly, her mouth fused to his as he came into her.

Oh, it was glorious, thrilling, nothing like it.

Not ever.

Not ever in her life before.

He began to move, rocking into her, his hips meeting hers, retreating—and returning. Always, returning.

She lifted herself up to him, wrapped her legs around his waist, her arms around his shoulders, clasping his strong neck, her fingers clutching his hair.

She was lost, flying, burning, free. There was nothing, just this. This beauty. This magic. The two of them: her body, his body—together. One.

Retreating. Returning. Over and over. Wet and hot and exactly as she'd never realized she'd always wished it might be.

Nothing like it.

Not ever.

Not ever in her life before.

"Sydney…" His voice in her ear. His breath against her skin. "Sydney…"

She sighed, turned her head away, so luxuriously comfortable, only wanting to sleep a little more.

"Sydney…" He nuzzled her temple, caught the curling strands of hair there between his lips, gave them a light, teasing tug.

She kept her eyes stubbornly shut, grumbled, "I was sleeping…"

His mouth on her cheek. Warm. Tempting. His words against her skin. "But you have to wake up now."

Wake up. Of course. She knew he was right. She turned her head to him, opened her eyes, asked him groggily, "What time is it?"

"After three." He was on his side, braced up on an elbow, the sheet down around his lean waist, clinging like an adoring lover to the hard curve of his left hip.

With a low groan, she sat up, raked her hair back off her forehead, stretched and yawned. Then she let her arms drop to the sheets. "Ugh. You're right. I do have to get home." She started to push back the covers.

He caught her hand. "Wait."

She smiled at him, searched his wonderful face. "What?"

"Sydney..." His mouth was softer than ever and his eyes gleamed and he looked so young right then. Young and hopeful and...nervous.

He did. He actually looked nervous. Prince Rule of Montedoro. Nervous. How could that be? He really wasn't the nervous type.

"Rule?" She laid her palm against his beard-roughened cheek. "Are you okay?"

He took her wrist, turned his head until her hand covered those soft lips of his. And he kissed her, the most tender, sweetest kiss, right in the heart of her palm, the way he had done the night before when he asked her if she would prefer him to be cruel.

A shiver went through her, a premonition of...

What? She had no idea. And already the strange, anxious feeling had passed.

There was only his mouth, so soft against her palm. Only the beauty of the night they had shared, only the wonder that he was here with her and he was looking at her like she hung the moon, as though she ruled the stars.

He lowered her hand so it no longer covered his lips. And then, raising his other hand, he put something in her palm, after which he closed her fingers tenderly over it.

And then he said the impossible, incredible, this-must-be-a-dream-and-can't-really-be-happening words, "Marry me, Sydney. Be my bride."

Chapter Six

Still trying to believe what she thought he'd just said, Sydney uncurled her fingers and stared down in what could only be called shock and awe at the ring waiting there.

The brilliant emerald-cut diamond was huge. And so icily, perfectly beautiful. Flanking it to either side on the platinum band were two large, equally perfect baguettes.

She looked up from the amazing ring and into his dark eyes. "Just tell me…"

"Anything."

"Is this really happening?"

He laughed, low, and he brushed the hair at her temple with a tender hand. "Yes, my darling. It's really happening. I know it's crazy. I know it's fast. But I don't care about any of that. In my heart, I knew the moment I saw you. And every moment since then has only made me more certain. Until there is nothing left. Nothing but absolute certainty that you are the woman for me."

"But you... I... We can't just—"

"Yes. We can. Today. We can fly to Las Vegas and be married today. I don't want to wait. I want you for my wife now. I have to return to Montedoro on Tuesday. I want you and Trevor with me."

"I don't... I can't... Oh, Rule. Wait."

He shook his head. "My darling, I don't want to wait. Don't make me wait."

"But, I mean, I have a c-career," she sputtered. "I have a house. I live in Texas. Can you even marry someone from Texas?"

"Of course I can. As long as that someone will have me."

"But you can't possibly... I mean, now that I think about it, well, don't you have to marry someone with at least a title? A duchess. A countess. A Lady Someone-or-Other?"

"My mother married an American actor and it's worked out quite well, I think. Times change. And I'm glad. I can marry whomever I choose, Sydney. I choose you—and I hope with all my heart that you choose *me*."

"I can't... I don't..."

"My love, slow down."

"Slow down? You're telling *me* to slow down? You just asked me to marry you and you meant today!"

He laughed then. "You're right. I'm no position to talk about slowing down. But I do think it wouldn't hurt if you took a breath. A nice, deep one." It was pretty good advice, actually. She drew in a slow breath and let it out with care. "Better?" he asked so tenderly.

She looked down at the ring again. "I think I might faint."

"No." He chuckled. "You are not a woman who faints." Still, he pulled her against him. She went, leaning her head on the hard bulge of his shoulder, loving the warmth and solidness of him, the scent of him that was so fine, yet at the same time so undeniably male. Loving everything about him.

Love. Was it possible? She knew that *he* thought it was.

And yet, still. Even given the possibility that it really was love at first sight between the two of them, well, she'd thought she would have a little more time than this before he asked her to commit to forever...

She pulled away, enough that she could meet his eyes. "It's so fast, Rule. I mean, so soon to jump into marriage. It's just...really, really fast."

"I know. I don't care." His gaze was steady on hers. He spoke with absolute certainty. "I know what I want now. At last. I told you, I've waited my whole life for this, for *you.*"

"Yes. I know. We've...spoken of that. But still. Marriage. That's a lot more than talk as far as I'm concerned. For me, marriage would be a lifetime thing."

"Yes. I know. We agree on that, on what it is to be married, that it's forever."

She searched his face. "It's the marriage law, right? You have to choose a wife and you have to do it soon."

"I do, yes."

"But not until June. You have until then. We could... have more time together, a few weeks, anyway. We could get to know each other better."

"I don't need more time, Sydney. You're the one. I know it. More time isn't going to change that—except to make me even more certain that you are the woman for me. I don't need to be more certain. I need...you. With me. I need at last to begin the life I've always wanted. The life my parents have. The life Max had with Sophia before he lost her. I want you to be mine. I want to be yours. I want every moment that God will grant us, together. Because fate can be cruel. Look what happened to Max. He thought he had a whole life ahead of him with Sophia. And now he's alone. Every day they did have is precious to him. I don't want to waste a day, an hour, a moment now, Sydney. I want us to begin our lives together today."

"Oh, Rule..."

"Say yes. Just say yes."

She wanted to. So much. But her inner skeptic just had to ask, "But...for a lifetime? I mean, come on. I looked you up on Google. You're the sexy bachelor prince. I'm pretty certain you've never dated a woman like me before. A really smart, really capable, average-looking, success-driven career woman."

His eyes flashed fire. "You are not average-looking."

"Oh, fine. I'm not average. I'm attractive enough. But I'm no international beauty."

"You are to me. And that's all that matters. Plus, you're brilliant. You're charming. People notice you, they want to...follow you. I don't think you realize your own power. I don't think you truly see yourself as you appear to others. I don't think you understand that strength and determination and focus in a woman—in the right woman—can be everything to a man. You're not the only one who knows how to use a search engine, Sydney. I looked you up. I read of how you graduated college at twenty. I read about the cases you've won for your law firm. And with all that ambition and drive, you have a good heart. And a deep, honest, ingrained sensuality. And last but in no way least, you're a wonderful mother—and you *chose* motherhood. Even with all your accomplishments, you also wanted a family. And when the men around you refused to be worthy of you, you found a way to be a mother, to make your own family. Of course I want you for my wife. You're everything I've been looking for." He brushed a hand, so lightly, along the curve of her cheek and he whispered, "Marry me, Sydney."

"I..." Her throat felt tight. She had to gulp to relax it. "You make me sound so amazing."

"Because you *are* amazing." He pulled her into his arms again.

She went without resisting. "Oh, Rule..."

"Say yes."

She tried to order her thoughts. "Can you move here, to Texas?"

His lips touched her hair. "That, I can't do. I have obligations to my country, obligations I couldn't bring myself to set aside."

She puffed out her cheeks with another big breath. "Just like a man. I knew you were going to say that."

"We can return often. My business dealings bring me to the States several times a year. Would it be so terrible, to live in Montedoro?"

"No. Not terrible. Just...huge. I would have to leave Teale, Gayle and Prosser..."

He rubbed her arm, a soothing, gentle caress. "I seem to recall that you said you were ready for a change in your work, that you would like a chance to help people who really needed your help."

"Yes. I said that. And I meant it."

"As my wife, there would be any number of important causes you might tackle. You would have many opportunities to make a difference."

"But what causes? What opportunities?"

He tipped up her chin, kissed the tip of her nose. "My darling, I think that would be for you to discover." She knew he was right on that score. And she was strong and smart and she learned fast. There wasn't a lot she couldn't do, once she set her mind and heart to doing it.

What about Trevor? He was young enough that the move probably wouldn't be as big a deal for him as it might have been—if he were already in school, if he had to leave close friends behind.

She thought of Lani then. "My God. Lani…"

"What about your friend?"

"I would lose Lani."

"You wouldn't *lose* her. A friend is a friend, no matter the miles between you—and who knows? If you asked her to come with us, she might say yes."

"So, Lani could come, too? If that worked for her. You wouldn't mind?"

"Of course not. What I know of her, I like very much. And I want you to be happy. I want you to have your dear friend with you."

"She might find it interesting. She writes, did I tell you?"

"No, I don't believe you did."

"She does. Right now she's working on a novel. She might find lots to write about in Montedoro. She might enjoy the experience of living somewhere she's never been before. Maybe she *will* want to come…."

"So, then. You will ask her." He kissed her again, on the cheek.

And she wanted more than that. So she turned her head enough that their lips met.

Heaven. Just heaven, kissing Rule. He guided her back onto the pillows and kissed her some more. She could have gone on like that indefinitely. But it was after three in the morning—on what she was actually starting to let herself think of as her wedding day.

She had a thousand things to do before they left for Las Vegas. She pushed at his chest.

He leaned back then, enough to capture her gaze. "What is it?"

"You really want to fly to Vegas today?"

"Yes. That's exactly what I want. Be my wife, Sydney. Make me the happiest man in the world. Bring your beautiful child and your excellent friend and we'll be married today. And after that, come live with me in Montedoro."

She reached up, touched that soft mouth of his. Oh, she did love touching him. Lightly, she smoothed the dark hair at his temples. She loved everything about him. And she was ready, to make a change.

To take a chance on love.

He spoke again, those black eyes shining. "I think Trevor would thrive if we married. I know you already have so much to offer him, that you're giving him an excellent start in life. But if we're together, he can have even more. For one thing, you would be able to spend more time with him. You could plan the work you choose to do specifically around him, during these years when he needs his mother most of all. And I would hope that, in time, we can speak of my adopting him."

Was there a more fabulous man in the whole world? She doubted it. "You would want to adopt him?"

"I would. So much. And I would hope that we also might have more children—I know, I know. I promise not to expect *eight* more. But maybe one or two...?"

"Oh, Rule..."

"Say yes."

She still had her hand on his chest, where she could feel the sure, steady beat of his heart. "I would need more time, here, in Dallas, before I could move to Montedoro. I have to give my partners reasonable notice. I can't leave them scrambling when I go. *I* may be ready to move on, but it would be wrong to leave *them* high and dry."

"Is it possible that you could be ready to go in two weeks?"

She gasped. "No way. Cases have to be shuffled, clients reassigned. I was thinking three months, if I really pushed it."

"What if you brought them more clients, big clients, as a…compensation for making a quick exit?" He named a couple of big oil companies, a major health food and vitamin distributor and a European bank that had branches in the U.S.

Sydney realized her mouth was hanging open. She shut it—and then she asked, "You're serious? You can deliver those?"

"Yes. I have a number of excellent connections worldwide. And if it doesn't work out with one or two of those particular companies, I'm sure I can offer others just as good."

"Well, I could possibly get away in a month or so, if my partners were grateful enough for what I brought them before I left."

"I'll get to work on that potential client list in the next few days. And I'll arrange the introductions, of course. I think you might be surprised at how quickly you can wrap things up with Teale, Gayle and Prosser, once they know exactly how much business you'll be bringing in before you go."

He was right. It would make all the difference, if she brought in some big clients. "I can't do it in two weeks. But if you bring the right clients, I'll give it my best shot. I could manage it in a month. Maybe."

His whole fabulous face seemed to light up from within. "I believe that you just said yes."

"Yes." She said the beautiful word out loud. "I did. Yes, Rule. Yes." And she threw her arms around his neck and let her kisses say the rest.

"Wow, Syd. When you finally go for it with a guy, you *really* go for it." Lani, in her pj's, still groggy from sleep, was shaking her head as she reached for her glasses. But at least she was smiling.

It was ten of five on Sunday morning. Sydney had headed for Lani's room the moment she walked in the front door and they were sitting on Lani's bed. Rule had said he would return at eight and Sydney had promised to be ready to go. He'd told her that he would have a private jet waiting at the airport. It helped to be a rich prince when you wanted to elope to Vegas at a moment's notice.

"So...you don't think I'm crazy?" Sydney asked, apprehensions rising.

"No way. I knew he was the one for you the moment I saw him."

"Uh, you did?"

"Oh, yeah. I mean seriously, Syd. The guy is your type."

"Well, yeah. In my wildest fantasies."

"Which have now become reality. He's intelligent, smooth and sophisticated. He's tall, dark, killer handsome—and I really think he's a good man. It's quite the major bonus that he happens to be a prince. And seeing him with Trevor, well, he's terrific with Trev. And have you noticed they look enough alike to be father and son?"

Sydney chuckled. "I have, actually."

"I go a lot on instinct," Lani said. "You know that. And my instinct with Rule is you've made the right choice."

Sydney beamed. "You are the best friend any woman ever had."

"Likewise."

"Say you'll come to Vegas with us." Sydney put on her most pitiful, pleading expression.

"Are you kidding? Like I would miss that? No way. I'm going."

"Oh, I'm so glad!" Sydney grabbed her friend and hugged her hard.

"How long am I packing for?" Lani asked when Sydney released her.

"Just overnight. I'll take tomorrow off. But Tuesday, I've got to get back to the office and start wrapping things up for the move to Montedoro."

"Oh. My. God. You're marrying a prince and moving to Europe. I don't believe it—or, I *do* believe it. But still. It's beyond wild."

"Yep. I think I need to pinch myself." Sydney let out a joyous laugh. "Is this really real?"

"Oh, yes, it is!" Lani replied. "Let me see the ring again." She grabbed Sydney's hand. "Just gorgeous. Absolutely gorgeous." And then she stuck out her lower lip and made out a small, sad puppy-dog sound. "But you know I will be sulking. I'll miss you way too much. And Trev, oh, how will I get along without him?" She put her hand on her chest and pantomimed a heartbeat.

Sydney had the answer to that one ready. "You don't have to miss us, not if you come with us."

"Come with you? You mean, permanently?"

"Oh, yeah. I would love that."

Lani blinked. "You're serious."

"You bet I am. I've already discussed it with Rule. He's good with it. More than good. And I would love it if you were there—I mean, if that could work for you."

"Me. Living in Montedoro with my best friend, the prince's bride. Interesting."

"I was hoping you might think that. But don't decide now. Take your time. No pressure. I mean that."

Lani bumped her shoulder affectionately. "I'll give it serious consideration—and thank you."

"Hey. Don't thank me. I'll miss you like crazy if you decide you don't want to do it. If you come, *I'll* be the grateful one."

"I'll think about it," Lani promised. "And we'd better get cracking if we're going to be ready to head for Vegas at eight."

As it turned out, Rule had Bravo relatives in Las Vegas. Aaron and Fletcher Bravo ran a pair of Las Vegas casino/hotels. Rule was a second cousin to both men. His grandfather James and their grandfather Jonas had been brothers.

"Fletcher and Aaron are half brothers," Rule told Sydney during the flight to Nevada. "They have different mothers, but both are sons of Blake Bravo."

"I have to ask. You don't mean *the* Blake Bravo?"

"Ah. You've heard of the infamous Blake?"

She nodded. "He died in Oklahoma about a decade ago, and at the time, the story made the front page of every paper in Texas. He *was* pretty notorious."

Rule nodded. "Yes, he was. Kidnapping his own brother's son for a fortune in diamonds, marrying all those women…" Beyond the whole kidnapping thing, Blake Bravo had been a world-class polygamist. He'd married any number of women all over the country and he'd never divorced a single one of them. Each woman had believed she was the only one.

Sydney said, "A very busy man, that Blake."

"*Busy* is not the word I would have chosen," Rule said dryly. "But yes, both Aaron and Fletcher are his sons."

The flight took a little under three hours, but they

gained two hours because of changing time zones, so they touched down at McCarran International Airport at ten after ten in the morning.

There was a limo waiting. The driver loaded the trunk with their luggage, the security guy who had flown from Dallas with them got in front on the passenger side and off they went to High Sierra Resort and Casino.

Aaron Bravo was CEO of High Sierra. The resort was directly across Las Vegas Boulevard from Impresario Resort and Casino, which Fletcher ran. The two giant complexes were joined by a glass breezeway five stories up, above the Strip.

Aaron greeted them at the entrance to his resort. Tall and lean with brown hair, Aaron wasn't classically handsome. But he was attractive, very much so, with a strong nose, sharp cheekbones and a square jaw. He said how pleased he was to meet Sydney and Lani—and Trevor, too. Then he introduced them to his wife, Celia, who was cute and friendly, a redhead with big hazel eyes.

Celia led the way to their suite, which had its own kitchen, a large living area and four bedrooms branching off of it. The security guy, whose name was Joseph, had the room next door.

The first order of business was to get the marriage license. Lani stayed behind with Trevor. Sydney, Rule and Joseph headed for the Las Vegas Marriage Bureau. An hour later, they were back in the suite, where Trev was playing with his trucks and Lani was stretched out on the sofa with her laptop.

"Ready for pampering?" she asked. "Celia says the spa is called Touch of Gold and it's full service...."

"Go," said Rule. "Both of you. The wedding's not until four." The short ceremony would be held in the wedding chapel right there at High Sierra. "I'll watch Trevor."

Sydney hesitated to let him do that. How strange. Here she was about to marry this wonderful man, and she felt reluctant to leave him alone with her son.

But no. Her reaction was only natural. It was one thing to trust her own heart. Another to leave her child alone with someone for the first time—even someone like Rule, who was so good with Trevor.

Lani spoke up. "Uh-uh. I'm onto something with this chapter and I'm not giving it up now. You go, Syd. I'm staying."

"Roo!" called Trev from under the table. "Come. We play trucks!"

So Rule and Lani both stayed in the suite with Trevor. Sydney went by herself to the spa. On the way, she stopped in at the resort's florist and ordered a bouquet of yellow roses, which she told them she would pick up personally in a few hours. She also asked to have a yellow rose boutonniere sent up to the suite for Rule.

At Touch of Gold, she decided to start with a hot rock massage. After the massage, she had it all, mani-pedi, haircut and blow dry and the expert attention of the spa's cosmetician, too.

And then, when she was perfectly manicured, with her hair smooth and shiny and softly curling to her shoulders and her makeup just right, Celia appeared with a tall, stunning brunette, Cleo, who was Fletcher's wife. The two women took Sydney to the bridal boutique not far from the spa.

Sydney chose a simple sleeveless fitted sheath dress of white silk and a short veil. Her shoes were ivory satin platform high heels, with side bows and peep toes. Celia had Sydney's street clothes sent back to the suite and Sidney left the boutique dressed for her wedding. After that, they stopped off at the florist to pick up her bouquet.

And then the two women led her straight to the High Sierra wedding chapel. Sydney waited in the chapel's vestibule for the "Wedding March" to begin. Staying to the side, out of sight, she peeked around the open door.

The rest of the small wedding party was already there: Lani, holding Trev, and Aaron and another dark-haired man who was obviously Cleo's husband, Fletcher Bravo. She saw him in profile and noted the family resemblance between him and Aaron—and Rule, too, she realized.

Her groom was waiting for her, standing down in front with the justice of the peace, looking fabulous as always in a black silk suit with a lustrous cobalt-blue tie and a shirt the color of a summer sky. In his lapel, he wore the yellow rose she'd sent him.

Sydney's pulse beat faster, just at the sight of him. And she smiled to herself, thinking of all the years she'd been so sure she would never find him—the right man, a good man, solid, smart and funny and true. The fact that he'd turned out to be a real-life prince who was total eye candy and had a voice that turned her insides to jelly, well, that was just the icing on the cake.

He was exactly the man for her. He made her feel beautiful and bold and exciting—or maybe he simply saw her beauty and made her see it, too. It didn't matter. With him, she could have it all. She could not wait to start their life together.

The only thing that could have made this day more perfect was if her Grandma Ellen could have been here, too.

Cleo helped Sydney pin the short veil in place.

And then the "Wedding March" began.

With a smile of pure happiness curving her lips and the glow of new love in her heart, Sydney walked down the aisle toward her waiting groom. She was absolutely certain she was making the right choice, marrying a man who saw beyond the walls she had erected to protect her injured heart. A man who had loved her the first moment he saw her, a man who wanted to be a real father to her son. A man who had been charmingly reluctant to reveal his princely heritage. A man of honor, who spoke the truth.

A man who did not have a deceptive bone in his body.

Chapter Seven

The justice of the peace said, "I now pronounce you husband and wife. You may kiss the bride."

His eyes only for her, Rule raised the short veil and guided it back over her head.

And then he drew her closer to him and he kissed her, a tender, perfect kiss. A kiss that promised everything: his love and his devotion, the bright future they would share. Sydney closed her eyes and wished the special moment might last forever.

After the ceremony, they all went to dinner in a private dining room in High Sierra's nicest restaurant. More children joined them there, six of them. Celia and Aaron had three, as did Fletcher and Cleo. The food was great and the company even better.

Aaron and Fletcher proposed a series of excellent toasts and when the kids were done eating, they were all allowed to get down and play together. There was much childish laughter. Trev loved every minute of it. He seemed quite taken with Fletcher and Cleo's oldest child, Ashlyn. He followed her around the private dining room, offering her dazzling smiles whenever she glanced his way. Ashlyn didn't seem to mind. And she knew several knock-knock jokes. She patiently tried to teach them to Trev, who inevitably got carried away and started playing both parts.

"Knock, knock," Ashlyn would say gamely.

And Trev would crow, "Who's there? Bill! Orange! Wanda!"

There was a cake, three tiers tall, a yellow cake with white fondant icing and edible pearls, crowned with a circle of yellow rosebuds. Celia took pictures as Sydney and Rule fed each other too-big bites of the sweet confection.

Trev tore himself away from his adoration of Ashlyn to join them at the cake table. "Roo, Mama, cake! Now!" He reached up his chubby arms.

So Rule swept him up against his chest and Trev laughed in delight. "Roo!" he cried. "Kiss," and puckered up his little mouth.

Rule puckered up as well and kissed him with a loud, smacking sound, which made Trev laugh even harder. A second later, he demanded, "Cake, Mama!"

"Cake, *please?*" she suggested.

And he shouted, "Cake! Please!"

So Sydney fed him a few bites of cake while Celia snapped more pictures. Then they served everyone else. The kids were silent—for a few minutes anyway—as they devoured their dessert.

After that, everyone lingered, reluctant to call an end to an enjoyable event. The adults chatted, the children went back to running in and out under the table, laughing, playing tag.

Eventually though, the little ones started getting fussy. Lani said she would take Trev up to the suite. Sydney offered to go, but Lani said she wanted to get back to her writing anyway. She could handle Trevor and work on her book at the same time, and often did. She would keep her laptop handy and sneak in a sentence or two whenever Trevor gave her a moment to herself.

So Lani took him up. Soon after, Celia and Cleo gathered their respective broods and left for the onsite apartments each family kept in the resort complex.

That left Fletcher and Aaron playing dual hosts to the newlyweds. The men talked a little business. The Bravo CEOs agreed that Montedoran oranges would be a perfect addition to the complimentary fruit baskets they offered in their luxury suites.

Rule invited his two second cousins and their families to Montedoro. Both said they would love to come. They would stay at the Prince's Palace and visit the fabulous casino in Montedoro's resort ward of Colline d'Ambre.

Finally, after more good wishes for a long and happy life together, the half brothers went to join their families. Rule and Sydney were left alone in the private dining room.

He drew her close to him, tipped up her chin and kissed her slowly and so sweetly. "My wife…" he whispered against her lips. "My own princess."

She chuckled. "Just like that? I only have to marry you and I get to be a princess?"

He took her hand, laid it against his chest. "And you will always rule my heart."

She laughed then. "Oh, you are so smooth." And then she frowned.

He kissed her furrowed brow. "What?"

"Your mother, the princess. Your family. This will be quite a surprise to them."

"A happy surprise," he said.

"So...you haven't told them anything about me yet?"

"Only my father. He knows...everything. And by now he will have told my mother that I've married the only woman for me."

She searched his face. "The way you say that. *Everything*. It sounds mysterious somehow."

He touched her cheek, smoothed a few strands of hair behind her ear. "Not mysterious at all. I spoke with my father this morning, before I came to take you to the airport. He wished us much happiness and he looks forward to meeting his new daughter-in-law and grandson."

"So he's not overly disappointed that you're not marrying Princess Lili?"

He traced the neckline of her wedding dress, striking sparks of excitement. "My father is a great believer in marrying for love. So he wants me to be happy. And he understands that I *will* be happy—with you."

"And your mother?"

"I know that she will be happy for me, as well." He kissed her again, slowly. A kiss that deepened, went from tender to scorching-hot. Her mind went hazy and her body went loose.

When he lifted his mouth from hers that time and the small dining room swam into focus again, a busman stood at the door. "Excuse me. I'll come back...."

Rule shook his head. "No. We're just leaving." He stood and pulled back her chair for her. "Shall we try our luck in the casino?"

"I'm terrible at games of chance."

"Never admit that. Lady Luck will hear you."

Her bouquet and her short veil, which she'd removed a while ago, lay on the table. Rule signaled the busman over, tipped him hugely and asked him to have both items delivered to their suite.

The busman promised it would be done.

Sydney took the rose from Rule's lapel, feeling wonderfully wifely and possessive of him as she did it. "This, too," she told the busman. "And the cake. I want the rest of the cake."

The busman promised he'd have the cake boxed and sent to their suite with the veil, the bouquet and the boutonniere.

They took the wide glass breezeway across the Strip to Impresario, which was all in blacks and reds and golds, a Moulin Rouge theme. They played roulette for over two hours. Sydney surprised herself by winning steadily. When they left the roulette table she was up more than a thousand dollars.

She caught sight of Joseph a few feet away and leaned close to her new husband to whisper, "Joseph is following us."

He brushed a kiss against her hair. "Joseph is always following us. That's his job."

"You're kidding. You mean every time I've been out with you...?"

"That's right. Joseph has been somewhere nearby."

"I swear I never noticed before."

"You're not supposed to notice. He's paid to be invisible until he's needed."

"Well, he's very good at it."

"He'll be pleased to hear that. Joseph takes great pride in his work—and what would you like to play next?"

"I was kind of thinking it would be fun to try my luck at blackjack."

"Blackjack it is, then." They found a table and played for another hour. Sydney won some more.

When they left the blackjack table it was after ten.

He leaned close. "I think you're lucky, after all."

"I think it's you," she whispered back. "You bring me luck."

He had his arm around her and pulled her closer, right there in the aisle, on their way toward the elevators that led up to the fifth floor and the breezeway back to High Sierra. Their lips met.

And a flash went off.

She laughed. "I think I'm seeing stars."

But he wasn't smiling. "The jackals are onto us."

"Ahem. Excuse me….?"

"Paparazzi. We have to go." He already had her hand and was moving fast toward the elevators. She hurried to keep up. More flashes went off.

A balding guy in tight pants and a black shirt with a big gold chain around his neck stepped in front of them. He stuck a microphone in Rule's face and started firing questions at him, racing backward to keep up with them. "Enjoying your visit to America, Your Highness? Who is the woman in white? Is that a wedding ring I see on the lady's finger?"

Rule only said, "Excuse me, no comment," and kept walking fast.

That was when Joseph appeared. He must have grabbed the guy with the microphone, because the man stumbled and fell back, out of their path.

Rule forged on. They reached the elevators and one rolled open as if on cue. He pulled her in there, pushed the button for the fifth floor and the doors slid shut.

"Whew," she said, laughing a little. "Looks like we're safe."

He just looked grim. "I should have known they would spot us." A moment later, the doors slid open wide. They got off and a group of men in business suits got on. Rule had her hand again. They were headed for the breezeway. Halfway across it, Joseph caught up with them. "Is it handled?" Rule asked low.

"Too many cameras." Joseph spoke softly, but his face looked carved in stone. "And they refused to deal, anyway. They got away with the shots they took."

Rule swore under his breath and pulled her onward.

On the High Sierra side, they took an elevator up to their floor. When the elevator stopped and the door opened, Joseph stuck his head out first. "We're clear," he said and signaled them out.

They walked at a brisk clip down the hallway to their suite. Rule had the key ready. He swiped it through the slot and they were in as Joseph entered the room next door.

The suite was silent. Trev had been put to bed hours ago and Lani must have retreated to her room. She'd left the light in the suite's granite-tiled foyer on for them.

Sydney sagged against the door. "Wow. That was exciting."

Rule braced a hand by her head and bent to kiss her—a hard, passionate kiss that slowly turned tender. When he pulled away, he whispered, "I'm sorry…"

"Whatever for? I had a great time."

"I knew it was unwise, to take you out on the casino floor and then stay there for hours. We were bound to be spotted."

She touched the side of his face, brushed the backs of her fingers along the silky, beautifully trimmed hair at his temples. "It's not the end of the world, is it, if our pictures end up in some tabloid somewhere?"

"In my family, we prefer to control the message."

"Meaning?"

"I was hoping we could keep our marriage private for the next few weeks, until I had you with me in Montedoro. From there, a discreet and carefully worded announcement could be made. And pictures could be taken by the palace photographer to send to the press, pictures of our choosing."

"What? A candid shot of you and me racing down a hallway with our mouths hanging open in surprise isn't discreet enough for you?"

He laughed then. But his eyes were troubled. "No, it's not."

She smoothed his lapel, straightened his collar. "Well, no matter how bad it is, just remember how much fun we had. As far as I'm concerned, I had so much fun, it's worth a few ugly pictures in some scandal sheet. Plus, I won almost two thousand dollars, about which I am beyond thrilled. I never win anything. But all I have to do is marry you, and suddenly it's like I've got a four-leaf clover tattooed on my forehead."

He was looking at her in *that* way again. The lovely, sexy way. The way that set small fluttery creatures loose in her stomach and had her feeling distinctly sultry lower down. "There is no four-leaf clover on your forehead." He kissed the spot where it might have been.

"Oh, it's there," she said softly, breathlessly. "You just can't see it. I was clever that way. I insisted on an invisible tattoo."

"Wait. I think I see it, after all." He breathed the words against her skin. And then he kissed his way down between her brows, trailing that wonderful mouth along the top of her nose. He nipped her lips once and then kissed her chin. "And I'm glad you enjoyed yourself."

"Oh, I did." Her voice was now more breath than sound. "I really did...."

He covered her mouth with his again. Luckily, she had the door at her back to lean against. She stayed upright even though her knees had gone deliciously wobbly. And as it turned out, she didn't need to hold herself upright much longer anyway. Still kissing her, he scooped her up in his arms carried her through the open archway to the central room of the suite.

The busman had kept his promise. On the dining table, she saw the large cake box, her veil and bouquet and also Rule's boutonniere. She smiled against his lips as he turned and carried her through the open door to their room, where the lamp by the bed had been left on low. Also, on a long table against the wall, a pair of crystal flutes flanked an ice bucket holding a bottle of champagne. The covers on the king-size bed were turned invitingly down.

She stretched out an arm to push the door shut behind them. Rule carried her to the side of the wide bed and set her down on her feet. They shared another kiss, one that went on for a lovely, endless space of time.

When he lifted his head, he guided her around so her back was to him. She read his intention and smoothed her hair to the side. He lowered the zipper at the back of her dress.

She took it from there, easing her arms free, pushing the dress down. Stepping out of it, she bent and picked it up and carried it to the bedside chair, where she took time to lay it down gently, to smooth the white folds.

"Come back here," he said, his voice rough with wanting.

"In a moment..." She sent him a teasing glance over her shoulder as she returned to the door long enough to engage the privacy lock. From there, she went to the dressing table on the far side of the room. She took off her shoes, her bra, her white lace panties and pearl earrings. And after that, she removed the single strand of pearls her grand-mother had given her and the blue lace garter provided by the bridal boutique. Finally, wearing nothing but a tender smile, she faced him again. "Your turn."

He made a low sound in his throat, his gaze moving over her, hot and possessive. "Don't move. I'll be right back."

The room had a walk-in closet. He entered it and came back out a moment later. Returning to the side of the bed, he laid two wrapped condoms on the nightstand.

She told him softly, "We won't need those."

Something flared in his eyes—triumph? Joy? But then he stood very still. "Are you sure?"

She nodded. "We both want more children. I'm think-ing there's no time like the present to get going on that."

"Sydney O'Shea Bravo-Calabretti," he said. "You amaze me."

She did like the sound of her name, her new name, on his lips. And she had no doubts. None whatsoever. She told him so. "I know what I want now, Rule. I want you. I want a family, with you and Trev. And I'm greedy. I want more babies. I honestly do."

He took a step toward her.

She put up a hand. "Your clothes. All of them. Please."

He didn't argue. He undressed. He did it swiftly, with no wasted motion, tossing the beautifully tailored arti-cles of clothing carelessly aside as he removed them. His body was so fine and strong. Just looking at him stole her breath.

When he had everything off, she went to him. She lifted her arms to him and he drew her close. Nothing so fine as that, to be held in his powerful arms, to feel the heat and hardness of him all around her.

He smoothed her hair, caressed her back with a long stroke of his tender hand. "I think I'm the happiest man in the world tonight."

She tipped her head up to him. "I'm glad. So glad..."

He kissed her and she thought how she would never, ever get enough of his kisses. That with him, she'd finally found everything she'd almost let herself forget that she'd been looking for.

She pulled him down onto the bed with her and gave herself up to his touch, to the magic of his lips on her skin.

He kissed her everywhere, each secret hollow, each curve, even the backs of her knees and the crooks of her elbows. He kissed her breasts, slowly and thoroughly, and then he moved lower. He kissed all her secret places, until she cried out and went over the edge, clutching his dark head, moaning his name.

She was still sighing in sweet satisfaction when he slid up her body again. All at once, he was there, right where she wanted him most. She wrapped her arms around him, so tightly. And he came into her, gliding smoothly home. Her body was as open to him as her mind and her heart. She accepted him eagerly, the aftershocks of her climax still pulsing through her. And when he filled her, she let out a soft cry of joyous abandon.

Did it get any better than this?

She didn't see how it could. Somehow, she'd finally found the man she wanted for a lifetime—or rather, *he* had found *her*.

There was nothing, ever, that could tear them apart.

Rule wasn't sure what woke him.

A general sense of unease, he supposed. He turned to

look at the woman sleeping beside him. The lamp was off
and the room in darkness. Still, he could hear her shallow,
even breathing. So peaceful. Content. He could make out
her shadowed features, just barely. A soft smile curved her
mouth.

She pleased him. Greatly. In so many ways.

No, she wasn't going to be happy with him when she
found out the truth. But she was a very intelligent woman.
And there was real chemistry between them. Surely, when
the time came, she would forgive him for his deception.
He would rationally explain why he'd done what he had
done. She would see that, even if he hadn't been strictly
honest with her, it had all worked out perfectly anyway.
She wanted to be with him and he wanted her *and* the boy.
They could work through it and move on.

He wanted to touch her. To kiss her. To make love to
her again. When he was touching her, he could forget that
he'd married her without telling her everything.

But no. He wouldn't disturb her. Let her have a few
hours of uninterrupted sleep.

Settling onto his back, he stared into the darkness, not
happy with himself, wondering why he had become so ob-
sessive over this problem. His obsession served no one. It
was going to be a long time before he told her the truth,
anyway. Maybe he never would.

In the past twenty-four hours or so, he'd found himself thinking that there was no real reason she ever had to
know....

Except that he'd always considered himself an honest
man. And it gnawed at his idea of his own character and
his firm belief in fair play, to have this lie between them.

Which was thoroughly ironic, the more he considered
it. He'd chosen the lie when he realized he wanted her for
his wife. He'd seen it as the only sure way to his goal. So

he supposed that meant his idea of himself as an honest man was only another lie.

And damned if he wasn't giving himself a headache, going around and around about this in his mind, when he was set on his course and there was no going back now.

He heard a faint buzzing sound: the cell phone in his trouser pocket, flung across that nearby chair.

Slowly, carefully, so as not to wake her, he eased back the covers and brought his feet to the floor. By then, the phone had stopped buzzing. He collected it from the trousers and tiptoed to the room's bath, where he checked to see who had called.

His father.

The voice mail signal beeped. He called to pick up the message.

His father's voice said "Rule. Call me on this line as soon as you get this. We need to touch base on the subject of Liliana."

Lili. What now?

With the nine-hour time difference, it would be around noon in Montedoro, which made it as good a time to call as any.

But not from the bathroom, where Sydney might wake up and walk in on him.

So he returned to the dark bedroom, where his bride was still sleeping the untroubled slumber of the blameless. He found his briefs and his trousers and put them back on. He tiptoed to the door and pulled it slowly open. The hinges played along and didn't squeak. He slipped through and closed it soundlessly behind him.

The suite had a balcony. He went out there, into the warm desert night, and closed the slider behind him.

His father answered on the first ring. "I understand congratulations are in order?"

The balcony had a café table and a couple of chairs. He dropped into one of them. "Thank you. I'm a very happy man."

"How is the boy?"

"Trevor is…a revelation to me. More than I ever might have wished for. Wait till you see him."

"I'm looking forward to that. When will you bring them home to us?"

"Sydney needs a month, she says. I'll come home ahead for a week or so and take care of my commitments there, and then return to help her through the transition."

"I heard that you had a little run-in with the press."

Rule didn't ask how his father knew. Joseph could have turned in a report—or the information could have come from any number of other sources. "Yes. They got away with pictures. And they put it together—Sydney's white dress, her engagement diamond and wedding band."

"So I understand. It won't take the story long to end up in the tabloids."

"I know." Rule felt infinitely weary thinking of that.

"Liliana is still here, still our guest at the palace. She has no idea that you've already married someone else."

"I know," Rule said again. He got up, stood at the iron railing, stared down at the resort pool, at the eerie glow the pool lights made, shining up through the water, at the rows of empty lounge chairs.

"Your mother is waiting to hear from you. She's always thought of you as the most considerate and dependable of her children."

"I've disappointed her."

"She'll get over it." His father's voice was gentler now.

"I'm trusting you to keep my secret," he reminded his father.

"I haven't told anyone, not even your mother." His father sighed.

"I should have spoken to Lili first, I know, for the sake of our long friendship—and in consideration of Montedoro's sometimes strained relationship with Leo." King Leo was Lili's hot-tempered, doting father. "But it was awkward, since I had made no proposal to her. How exactly was I to go about telling her that I *wouldn't* be proposing? Also there was the timing of it. As soon as I finally met Sydney and made my decision, I felt it was imperative to move forward, to attain my goal before leaving the States."

"You are so certain about this woman you have married, this woman you have only just met?"

"Yes," Rule said firmly. "I am."

"You *wanted* to marry her, for herself? Not simply for the child. You feel she is…right for you?"

"Yes. I did. I do."

"Yet you don't feel confident enough of her trust in you to tell her the basic truth of the situation?"

Rule winced. His father had cut a little too close to the bone with that one. He said, "I made a choice. I'm willing to live with the consequences."

His father was silent. Rule braced himself for criticism, for a very much deserved lecture on the price a man pays for tempting fate, for doing foolish, thoughtless, irresponsible things and telling himself he's breaking free, that he's trying to help others.

More than three years ago, Rule had let his hunger for something he didn't even understand win out over his good sense. And now, when he'd finally found what he was looking for, he'd lied to secure the prize he sought. And he was continuing to lie….

But then his father only said, "Fair enough, then. I see

your dilemma. And I sympathize. But still, it's only right that you explain yourself to Liliana, face-to-face, as soon as possible. She should hear it from you first. She's an innocent in all this."

"I agree. I was planning to return on Tuesday, but I'll try to get away Monday…I mean, today."

"Do your best."

Rule promised he would and they said goodbye.

He turned to go inside and saw Sydney, her hair tangled from sleep, her green eyes shadowed, full of questions. Wearing one of the white terrycloth robes provided by the resort, she stood watching him through the sliding glass door.

Chapter Eight

He'd been facing away from the suite, he reminded himself. And speaking in low tones. She couldn't have heard the conversation through the thick glass of the door.

Tamping down his anxiety that she might have overheard something incriminating after all, he pulled the door open and murmured regretfully, "I woke you...."

"No. The *absence* of you. That's what woke me." She took his hand, pulled him into the suite and slid the door shut. After that, she stood gazing up at him, and he had that feeling he so often had with her, the feeling he'd just described to his father. The feeling of rightness, that he was with her, that he had finally dared to approach her, to claim her. Too bad the sense of rightness was liberally mixed with dread at the way-too-possible negative outcome of the dangerous game he played. "Is there something wrong?" She searched his face.

He still had her hand in his, so he pulled her back to

their room. Once he had her inside, he shut and locked the door.

"Rule, what?"

He framed her sweet, proud face between his hands. He loved her wide mouth, her nose that was perhaps a little too large for her face. A nose that made her look interesting and commanding, a nose that demanded a man take her seriously. One lie, he had already told her. A huge lie of omission. All else must be the absolute truth. "You're going to be angry with me...."

"You're scaring me. Just tell me what's going on. Please."

He caught her hand again, took her to the bed, sat her down and then sat beside her. "That was my father, on the phone. He asked me to come back to Montedoro today. He thinks I should talk to Liliana, that I owe her an explanation, that I should be the one to tell her that any proposal she might have been expecting is not forthcoming, that I'm already married."

She pulled her hand from his and drove right to the point. "And what do *you* think, Rule?"

"I think my father is right."

She speared her fingers through her night-mussed hair, scraping it back off her forehead. He wanted to reach for her, but he didn't dare. "Princess Lili is still waiting, I take it, for you to ask her to marry you?"

"That's the general assumption. She's a guest at the palace. It would be pretty unforgivable of me to let her find out in the tabloids that I'm already married."

"*Pretty* unforgivable?"

"All right. Simply unforgivable. As I said before, she's like a sister to me. While a man doesn't want to marry his sister—he doesn't want to see her hurt, either."

"I understand that."

"Sydney..." He tried to wrap his arm around her.

She dodged away from his touch. "Why, exactly, is she expecting you to marry her?" She looked at him then. Those green eyes that could be so soft and full of desire for him, were cool now, emerald-bright.

"I told you, she's always believed herself to be in love with me, ever since we were children. She's looked up to me, she's...waited for me. And as the years have gone by and I never married, it has been spoken of, between our two families, that I would need to marry soon due to the laws that control my inheritance. That Lili would be a fine choice in any number of ways."

"What ways?"

He suppressed an impatient sigh. "Ways of state, you might say. Over the years, there has been conflict, off and on, between Montedoro and Alagonia."

"Wars, you mean?"

"No. Small states such as ours rarely engage in wars. In Montedoro, we don't even have a standing army. But there has been discord—bad feelings, you could say—between our two countries. The most recent rift occurred because King Leo, Lili's father, wanted to marry my mother. My mother didn't want to marry him. She wanted to rule Montedoro and she wanted, as much as possible, to protect our sovereignty. If she'd married a king, he could so easily have encroached on her control of the throne. Plus, while she's always been fond of King Leo, she didn't feel she could love him as a husband. And she wanted that, wanted love in her marriage. She managed to avoid a situation where Leo might have had a chance to propose to her. And then she met my father."

"Don't tell me." At least there was some humor in her voice now. "It was love at first sight."

"So my mother claims. And my father, as well. They

married. King Leo is known for his hot temper. He was angry and even went so far as to put in place certain trade sanctions as something of a revenge against my mother and Montedoro for the injury to his pride. But then he met and married Lili's mother, an Englishwoman, Lady Evelyn DunLyle. The king loved his new wife and found happiness with her. He gave up his vendetta against my mother and Montedoro. Leo's queen and my mother became fast friends. Though Queen Evelyn died a few years ago, relations between our countries have been cordial for nearly three decades and we all think of Lili as one of our family."

"You're saying that if you'd married the princess, it would have bolstered relations between your countries. But now that you've essentially dumped her, if she goes crying to her father, your country and her country could end up on the outs again."

"I have not dumped her." He felt his temper rising, and quickly restrained it. "A man cannot dump a woman he's never been with in any way. I swear to you, Sydney, I have never so much as kissed Liliana, except as a brother would, chastely, on the cheek."

"But she thinks you're *going* to kiss her for real. She thinks you're going to *be* with her. She thinks that she'll be married to you before the twenty-fourth of June."

"Yes." He said it resignedly. "I believe she does."

"You realize that's kind of pitiful, don't you? I mean, if you've never given her any sort of encouragement, why would she think that you'll end up proposing marriage—unless she's a total idiot?"

"Lili is not an idiot. She's a romantic. She's more than a little...fanciful."

"You're saying she's weak-minded?"

"Of course not. She's a good person. She's…kind at heart."

Sydney shook her head. "You strung her along, didn't you?"

"No. I did no such thing. I simply…failed to disabuse her."

"Come on, Rule. She was your ace in the hole." Those green eyes were on him. He had the rather startling intuition that she could see inside his head, see the cogs turning as he tried to make excuses for what he had to admit was less than admirable behavior. "You never encouraged her. But you didn't *need* to encourage her. Because she'd decided you were her true love and she's a romantic person. You figured if you never met anyone who…worked for you, as a partner in life, you could always marry Lili when your thirty-third birthday got too close for comfort."

"All right." He threw up both hands. "Yes. That's what I did. That is exactly what I did."

She gave him a look that seared him where he sat. "And it was crappy what you did, Rule. It was really crappy."

"Yes, Sydney. It was…crappy. And I feel accountable and I want to apologize to her in person."

"I should hope so." She huffed out a disgusted breath.

And then there was silence. He stared straight ahead and hated that she was angry with him.

And by God, if she was angry over Lili, what was he in for when she found out about Trevor?

He couldn't stop himself from pondering his own dishonesty. About Trevor. About Lili. He was beginning to see that he wasn't the man he'd believed himself to be. That he was only an honest man when it suited him.

Such thoughts did not make him proud.

Plus, he found himself almost wishing he'd told her another lie just now, given her some other excuse as to why he had to go back right away to Montedoro. He hated this—the two of them, so late on their wedding night it was already the next morning, sitting side by side on the edge of their marriage bed, not looking at each other.

"We'll leave right after breakfast," she said. "You can go straight to Montedoro. I'll get a commercial flight for Lani and Trevor and me."

"I will take you to Dallas," he said.

"Really. It's fine. I'll—"

"No." He cut her off in a voice that brooked no argument. "I will take you to Texas. And then I'll go straight on from there."

A half an hour later, they lay in bed in the darkness together, but not touching, facing away from each other. Sydney knew it was the right thing, for him to go, to make his peace with the woman he'd kept on a string.

She knew it was the right thing...

But she didn't like it one bit. She was disappointed in Rule. And more than a little angry that because of him, their wedding night had ended in such a rotten, awful way.

Here she'd married her prince, literally. She'd been so sure he was the perfect man for her—and the day after their wedding, he had to leave her to fly back to his country and apologize to the woman everyone had *thought* he would marry. A woman Rule said was like a sister to him, a woman who was pretty and delicate and romantic at heart. Sydney was none of those things. Not pretty. Not the least delicate.

Okay, maybe she *was* a bit of a romantic. But she'd never had the luxury of indulging her romantic streak—not until her own personal prince came along.

Maybe her prince wasn't such a fine man, after all. Maybe she should have slowed things down between them, at least a little, given herself more time to make sure that marrying him was really right for her. She'd been hurt before, and badly. She should have kept those past heartaches more firmly in mind. Ryan and Peter had proved that she didn't have the best judgment when it came to giving her heart. And yet, after knowing Rule for—*oh, dear God,* under forty-eight hours—she'd run off to Vegas and married him.

Sydney closed her eyes tightly. Was she a total fool, after all? She'd followed her heart yet again. And look at her now, hugging the edge of the bed on her wedding night, curled into a tight ball of pure misery.

And then the truth came to her, cool and sweet as clean water poured on a wound. Rule wasn't Ryan or Peter. He hadn't lied to her or manipulated her.

He'd told her the truth about Princess Lili on Saturday night *before* he'd asked her to marry him. And when his father had called him home to make peace with Lili, Rule hadn't lied to her about what was going on. Even though he so easily could have, he hadn't taken the easy way, hadn't made up some story for why he needed to get back. After all, she knew he had responsibilities in Montedoro and she would have most likely accepted any credible story he'd told her about the sudden necessity for him to go.

But he *hadn't* lied. He'd taken the hard way, the way that proved his basic integrity. He'd told her what was really going on, and told her honestly. Told the truth, even when the truth didn't show him in the greatest light.

All at once, her stomach didn't feel quite so tight anymore. And her heart didn't ache quite so much.

Carefully, slowly, she relaxed from the tight little ball she'd curled herself into. She stretched out her legs and then, with a sigh, she eased over onto her back.

She could feel him beside her, feel his stillness. A concentrated sort of stillness. She couldn't hear his breathing. He must be awake, too. Lying there in misery, hating this situation as much as she did.

No, she didn't forgive him, exactly. Not yet, anyway. She couldn't just melt into his arms, just send him off to Princess Lili with a big, brave smile and a tender kiss goodbye.

But she could…understand the position he was in. She could sympathize.

The sheet between them was cool. She flattened her hand on it, and then moved her fingers, ever so slowly, toward his unmoving form.

He moved, too. Only his hand. His fingers touched hers and she didn't pull back.

She lay very still. No way was she going to let him wrap those big, warm arms around her.

But when his fingers eased between hers, she let them. And when he clasped her hand, she held on.

She didn't let go and neither did he. In time, sleep claimed her.

Rule had a car waiting for them in Dallas. He exited the jet to say goodbye to them as their bags were loaded into the trunk and airport personnel bustled about, preparing the jet for the flight to Montedoro.

Trev went eagerly into his arms. "Bye, Roo! Kiss!" And he kissed Rule's cheek, making a loud, happy smacking sound.

Rule kissed him back. "I will see you very soon."

"Soon. Good. Come see me soon."

"You be good for your Mama and Lani."

"I good, yes!"

Rule handed Trev over to Lani and turned to Sydney. "A moment?" he asked carefully. Lani left them, carrying Trev to the open backseat door where the driver had already hooked in his car seat. Rule brushed a hand down Sydney's arm—and then instantly withdrew it. She felt his touch like a bittersweet echo on her skin, even through the fabric of her sleeve. He said, "You haven't forgiven me." It wasn't a question.

"Have a safe trip." She met his eyes, made her lips turn up in a fair approximation of a smile.

He muttered, low, "Damn it, Sydney." And then he reached for her.

She stiffened, put her hands to his chest, started to push him away. But then he was kissing her. And he tasted so good and he smelled like heaven and…

Well, somehow, she was letting her hands slide up to link around his neck. She melted into him and kissed him back. A little moan of frustrated confusion escaped her, a moan distinctly flavored with unwilling desire.

And when he finally lifted his head, she couldn't make up her mind whether to slap him or grab him around the neck, pull him down and kiss him again.

"Kisses don't solve anything," she told him tightly, her hands against his chest again, keeping him at a safer distance. She should have jerked free of his hold completely. But he would be gone in a minute or two. And she'd already kissed him. She might as well go all the way, remain in the warm circle of his arms until he left her.

"I know they don't. But damned if I can leave you without a goodbye kiss."

Okay, he was right. She was glad he had kissed her. Sometimes a kiss said more than words could. She lifted a hand and laid it cherishingly against his lean cheek. "Tell the princess I…look forward to meeting her."

He turned his lips into her palm, kissed her there, the way he had that first night, in their private alcove at the

Mansion restaurant, his breath so warm and lovely across her skin. "I'll return for you. Within the week."

A week wasn't going to cut it. He should know that. She reminded him, "I told you I would need a month, at least, to tie up loose ends at the firm—and that's with you giving my partners a few rich clients as a going-away present."

"I will do what I said I would. And I'm still hoping you can be finished faster."

"Well, that's not going to happen. Get used to it."

"I'll try. And when I return, you're going to have to make room for me at your house." He added, so tenderly, "Because I can't live without you."

His words softened her heart and she wasn't sure she wanted that. She was all turned around inside, wanting him so very much, *not* wanting to be vulnerable to him. She rolled her eyes. "Can't live without me. Oh, right. Kissing up much?"

He took her by the arms. "Correction. I don't *want* to live without you. I'm wild for you. And you know that I am."

Well, yeah. She did, actually. She relented a little. "Of course you'll be staying at my house. I don't want to live without you, either, no matter how angry I happen to be with you."

"Good."

"After all, we're only just married—we only just *met,* if you want to get right down to it."

"Don't." He said it softly. But his eyes weren't soft. His eyes were as black and stormy as a turbulent sea. "Please." He took her hand and kissed the back of it and the simple touch of his mouth on her skin worked its way down inside her, into the deepest part of her. It warmed her and thrilled her—and reassured her, too. "One week," he said fervently. "At the most. I will miss you every day

I'm away from you. I will call you, constantly. You'll be sick and tired of hearing the phone ring."

"I won't mind running to answer the phone. I'll answer and answer gladly," she confessed in a near-whisper. "As long as it's you on the other end of the line."

"Sydney…" He kissed her again, a quick, hard press of his lips against hers. "A week."

And he let her go. She watched him mount the steps to the plane. And she waited to wave to him, when he paused to glance back at her one more time before going in.

Finally, too soon, he was gone.

Rule arrived at Nice Airport at five in the morning. From there, it was only a short drive to Montedoro. He was in his private apartments at the Prince's Palace before six.

At eight, Caroline deStahl, his private secretary, brought him the five newspapers he read daily—*and* the three tabloids that contained stories about him and Sydney. All three tabloids ran the same pictures, one of the two of them kissing, and another of them fleeing down an Impresario hallway. And all three had similar headlines: The Prince Takes a Bride and Wedding Bells for Calabretti Royal and Prince Rule Elopes with Dallas Legal Eagle.

It was a little after 1:00 a.m. in Dallas. Sydney would be in bed. He hated to wake her.

But he did it anyway.

She answered his call on the second ring. "It's after one in the morning, in case you didn't notice," she grumbled sleepily.

"I miss you. I wish I was there with you."

"Is this an obscene phone call?"

He laughed. "It could become one so easily."

"Are you there yet?"

"In my palace apartment, yes. My secretary just delivered the tabloids. We are the main story."

"Which tabloids?"

He named them. "I'm sure we're all over the internet, as well. You are referred to by name. And also as my bride, the 'Dallas Legal Eagle.'"

"Ugh. I was hoping to explain things to my partners at the firm before the word got out. Have you spoken with Princess Liliana yet?"

"No. But I will right away, this morning."

"What can I say? Good luck—and call me the minute it's over."

He pictured her, eyes puffy, hair wild from sleep. It made an ache within him, a sensation that some large part of himself was missing. He said ruefully, "I'll only wake you again if I call...."

"Yeah, well. It's not like I'll be able to go back to sleep now. At least, not without knowing how it went."

He felt thoroughly reprehensible. On any number of levels. "I shouldn't have called."

"Oh, yeah. You should have. And call me right away when it's over. I mean it."

"Fair enough. Sydney, I..." He sought the words. He didn't find them.

She whispered, "Call me."

"I will," he vowed. And then he heard the faint click on the line, leaving him alone, half a world away from her, with just his guilty conscience to keep him company.

Two hours later, he sat in the small drawing room of the suite Liliana always took whenever she visited the palace. He'd been waiting for half an hour for her to appear and he didn't know yet whether she had heard about his marriage or not. Her attendant, one of Lili's Alagonian cousins,

Lady Solange Moltano, had seemed welcoming enough, so he had hopes that he'd arrived in time to be the first to tell her what she didn't want to know.

The door to the private area of the suite opened. He stood.

Lili emerged wearing all white, a pair of wide-legged trousers and a tunic-length jacket, her long blond hair loose, her Delft-blue eyes shining, her cheeks pink with excitement. She was absolutely beautiful, as always. And he really was so fond of her. He didn't want to see her hurt.

He'd never wanted to see Lili hurt.

"Rule." She came toward him, arms outstretched.

They shared an embrace. He looked down at the golden crown of her head and wished he were anywhere but there, in her sitting room, about to tell her that a brilliant, opinionated and fascinating brunette from Texas had laid claim to his heart.

She caught his hands in her slender ones, stepped back and beamed up at him. "You're here. At last…"

So. She didn't know.

"Lili, I came to see you right away, as soon as I got in. I have something important to tell you."

She became even more radiant than a moment before—if that was possible. "Oh." She sounded breathless. "Do you? Really? At last…"

What if she fainted? She'd always been so delicate. "Let's…sit down, shall we?"

"Oh, absolutely. Let's." She pulled him over to a blue velvet sofa. They sat. "Now. What is it you'd like to say to me?"

He had no idea where to begin. His tongue felt like a useless slab of leather in his mouth. "I… Lili. I'm so sorry about this."

Her radiance dimmed, marginally. "Ahem. You're... sorry?"

"I know you've always had an expectation that you and I would eventually marry. I realize I've been wrong, very wrong, to have let things go on like this, to have—"

She cut him off. "Rule."

He coughed into his hand. "Yes?"

Her perfect face was now scarily composed. "All right. So, then. You're not here to propose marriage to me."

"No, Lili. I'm not. I'm here to tell you that I'm already married."

Lili gasped. Her face went dead-white.

He got ready to catch her as she collapsed.

Chapter Nine

But Lili remained upright on the sofa. She asked in a voice barely louder than a whisper, "Would you mind telling me her name, please?"

"Sydney. Sydney O'Shea."

"Not Montedoran?"

"No. I met her in America. In Texas."

Lili swallowed, her smooth white throat working convulsively. "Sydney O'Shea. From Texas."

"Yes. Lili, I—"

She waved a hand at him. "No. Please. I... Fair enough, then. You've told me. And I hope you'll be very happy together, you and this Sydney O'Shea." Her huge blue eyes regarded him, stricken. Yet she remained so calm-seeming. She even forced a tight smile. "I hope you will have a lovely, perfect life." She shot to her feet. "And now, if you don't mind, I think I would like you to go."

"Lili..." He rose. He wanted to reach out to her. But that

would be wrong. He would only be adding insult to injury. What good could he do for her now? None. There was no way he could help her through this, nothing he could do to make things better.

He *was* the problem. And he really needed to leave, now, before she broke down in front of him and despised him even more for bearing witness to her misery.

"Go," she said again. "Please just go."

So he did go. With a quick dip of his head, he turned on his heel and he left her alone.

He called Sydney again the moment he reached his own rooms.

"How did it go?" she asked.

"Not well. She sent me away as soon as I told her."

"Is there someone with her? Someone she can talk to?"

"She has a cousin with her. But I don't think that they're close."

"Who *is* she close to?"

"My God, Sydney. What does it matter? What business is it of mine or yours?"

"Men are so thickheaded. She needs someone to talk to, someone to comfort her, someone who understands what she's going through."

He needed a stiff drink. But then again, it was barely eleven in the morning. "You don't know her, Sydney. How can you possibly know what she needs?"

"Rule. She's a woman. I *know* what she needs. She needs a true friend with a shoulder she can cry on. She needs that friend now."

"Sydney. I adore you," he said in his coolest, most dangerous tones. "You know that. And I'm very sorry to have made such a balls-up of all this. But you don't know Liliana and you have no idea what she needs. And I'll thank you to stop imagining that you do."

"I'm getting seriously pissed off at you. You know that, right?"

"Yes. I realize that. And we're even. Because I am becoming pretty damn brassed off at *you*."

Dead silence on the line. And then, very flatly, "I think I should hang up before I say something I'm bound to regret."

"Yes. I agree. Go back to sleep, Sydney."

"Hah. Fat chance of that." *Click.* And silence.

"Goodbye," he said furiously, though it wasn't in any way necessary, as she had already hung up.

He put down the phone and then he just stood there, staring blindly at an oil painting of a pastoral scene that hung over the sofa, wanting to strangle someone. Preferably his bride.

A tap on the outer door interrupted his fuming. "Enter."

His secretary, Caroline, appeared to inform him that Her Sovereign Highness and Prince Evan wished to speak with him in the Blue Sitting Room of their private apartment.

In his parents' private rooms, they didn't stand on ceremony.

His mother embraced him and told him she forgave him for running off and marrying his Texas bride without a word to the family beforehand. His father congratulated him as well and said he was looking forward to meeting Sydney and her son. Prince Evan said nothing about the secret Rule had finally shared with him a few weeks before. Rule was grateful to see that his father, at least at this point, was keeping his word and telling Her Sovereign Highness nothing about how Rule had come to meet his bride in the first place.

And when his mother asked him about that, about how he and Sydney had met, he told her the truth, as far as it went. "I saw her going into a shopping mall. One look, and I knew I wanted to know her. So I followed her. I convinced her that she should have lunch with me and after that, I pursued her relentlessly until she gave in and married me. I knew from that first sight of her, getting out of her car, settling her bag on her shoulder so resolutely, that she was one of a kind."

His mother approved. She'd more or less chosen his father that way, after seeing him across a room at a Hollywood party during a visit to the States. "You did have us worried," she chided. "We feared you would fail to make your choice before your birthday. Or that you would marry our darling Lili and the marriage would not suit in the end."

Rule had to keep from gaping. "If you thought that Liliana and I were a bad match, you might have mentioned that to me."

His mother gave a supremely elegant shrug. "And what possible good would that have done? Until you met the *right* woman, you were hardly likely to listen to your mother telling you that the perfectly lovely Lili, of whom you've always been so fond, was all wrong for you."

Rule had no idea how to reply to that. He wanted to say something angry and provoking. Because he felt angry and provoked. But that had more to do with his recent conversation with Sydney than anything else. So he settled for saying nothing.

And then his mother and father shared a look. And his mother nodded. And his father said, "I hope you'll be having a private word with Liliana soon."

At which point he went ahead and confessed, "As it happens, I've already spoken with her."

His mother rose abruptly. Rule and his father followed suit. She demanded, "Why ever didn't you say so?"

Yes. No doubt about it. To strangle someone or put his fist through a wall about now would be extremely satisfying. "I *did* tell you. I told you just now."

"When did you speak with her?" his mother asked.

He glanced at his wristwatch. "Forty-five minutes ago."

"You told her of your marriage?"

"Yes." His parents shared a speaking glance. "What? I *shouldn't* have told her?"

"Well, of course you needed to tell her."

"Then I don't understand what—"

"Is she alone now?"

"I have no idea. Solange Moltano answered the door to me. I'm assuming she's still there, in Lili's apartment."

"The Moltano woman will never do. Lili will need someone to *talk* with, someone to comfort her."

It was exactly what Sydney had said. And that made him angrier than ever. He gritted his teeth and apologized, though he was sick to death of saying how sorry he was. "It's all my fault. I can see now I've handled everything wrong."

His mother put her cool hand against his cheek. "No, darling. You did what you had to do—except for not telling me the moment you left her. Lili will need me now. I'll go to her right away." And with that, she swept from the room.

Into the echoing silence after her departure, Rule said, "I think I would like to hit someone."

His father nodded. "I know the feeling."

"I've broken Lili's heart. And my wife is furious at me."

"Lili will get over this, Rule. Leave it to your mother.

She loves Lili like one of our own and she will know just what to say to comfort her—and why is your bride angry with you?" His father frowned. "You've *told* her already, about the boy?"

Rule swore. "No. Not yet. And I won't. Not...for a while, in any case. Sydney's upset about Lili. She sympathizes with Lili. She says I used Lili as my 'ace in the hole,' as a way to hedge my bet in case I didn't find someone I really wanted to marry before Montedoran law took my title and my fortune."

"She sounds like a rare person, your new wife. Not many brides have sympathy for the 'other' woman."

"Sydney is like no one I've ever known," he said miserably.

"That's good, don't you think?"

"I don't know what to think. She has me spinning in circles. I don't know which end is up."

"A good woman will do that, turn your world upside down."

"I've mucked everything up." Rule sank to the sofa again, shaking his head. "Sydney believes absolutely in honesty and truth and integrity. She's disappointed in me because I wasn't honest with Lili, because I didn't make my true feelings—or lack of them—clear to Lili long ago. I keep thinking, if Sydney can hardly forgive me for not being totally honest with Lili, how can I ever tell her the truth about Trevor?"

His father sat down beside him. He said gently, "You have a real problem."

"I used to see myself as a good man, a man who did what was right...."

"Do you want my advice?"

"You'll only tell me to tell her, and to tell her now."

His father's lips curved in a wry smile. "So that would be a no, then. You don't want my advice?"

"I can't tell her. Honesty is everything for her. If I was going to tell her, I should have done it at the beginning, that first day I met her, before I pushed for marriage..."

"Why didn't you?"

"She confided in me concerning her past romantic relationships. I knew she had very good reasons not to put her trust in men. If I'd told her before I married her, she might never have allowed me to get close to her. Certainly she wouldn't have let me near her in the time allotted before the twenty-fourth of June. It's as I said to you on the phone. There was no good choice. I made the choice that gave me a fighting chance. Or at least, so I thought at the time."

"What do you have on your calendar?"

Rule arched a brow. "And what has my schedule got to do with my complete failure to behave as a decent human being?"

"I think you should clear it."

"My calendar?"

"Yes. Fulfill whatever obligations you can't put off here and do it as quickly as possible. Reschedule everything else. And then return to Texas. Make it up with Sydney, get through this rough patch, spend time with Trevor, strengthen your bonds with both of them. And return to Montedoro when your wife is ready to come with you."

That morning, Sydney actually had two reporters lurking on her front lawn. When she backed out of her garage on the way to the office, she stopped in the driveway, rolled her window down and let them snap away with their cameras for a good sixty seconds.

They fired questions at her while they took the pictures.

She told them that yes, she had married her prince and she was very happy, thank you. No, she wasn't willing to share any of their plans with the press.

One asked snidely if she'd met the Alagonian princess yet. She said no, but she was looking forward to making Princess Liliana's acquaintance—and in case they hadn't noticed, hers was a gated community. She would be calling neighborhood security the next time she found them on her property. That said, she drove away.

At the firm, she met with three of her partners. They already knew about her marriage.

And they weren't surprised when she told them she would be leaving Teale, Gayle and Prosser. They weren't happy with her, either. She was a valued and very much counted-on member of the team, after all. And they were going to be scrambling to fill the void that would be created by her absence.

When she told them she hoped to leave for her new home within the month, an icy silence descended. After which there was talk of her obligations, of the contract she had with the firm.

Then she told them about the potential clients she would be bringing in before she left. She named the ones Rule had mentioned the night before their wedding. And she explained that His Highness, her husband, had excellent business connections worldwide—connections he was willing to share with Teale, Gayle and Prosser.

By the time the meeting was over, her partners were smiling again. Of course, they would be waiting to see if she delivered on her promises. But at least she had a chance of getting out quickly with her reputation intact and zero bridges burned.

She went to work with a vengeance, getting her office and workload in order.

Rule hadn't called since the second time she'd talked to him the night before, when she'd gotten all up in his face. Had she been too hard on him?

Oh, maybe. A little.

But she couldn't believe he'd just dropped the bomb of his elopement on the poor, lovesick princess and then left her all on her own because she'd *asked* him to. Sydney hoped her harsh words had put a serious bug up his butt— as her Grandma Ellen might have said—and that he'd found a way to make sure Liliana had the confidant she needed at a time like this.

At five that afternoon, Sydney was called into the main conference room, which was packed with her partners, the associates, the paralegals, the secretarial staff and even the HR people. There was champagne and a pile of wedding gifts and a cake.

Sydney couldn't believe it. It was really happening. She was getting the office wedding shower she'd been so certain she'd never have.

She thanked them and made a little speech about how much they all meant to her and how she would miss them. And then she ate two pieces of cake, sipped one glass of champagne and did the rounds of the room, her spirits lifted that her colleagues had made a party just for her.

It was nine at night when she left the office. She was seriously dragging by then. Sleep had been in short supply for five days now—since last Friday, when her whole life had changed in an instant, because she'd gone into Macy's to buy a wedding gift for Calista Dwyer.

At home, Lani helped her carry in the gifts from the party. "You look exhausted," Lani said. "Just leave everything on the table. I'll deal with it tomorrow."

Sydney dropped the last box on the stack and sank into a chair. "How was your day?"

"Fabulous. Trevor took a three-hour nap and I got ten pages done. And then later, we went to the park. He seems to have slacked off on the endless knock-knock jokes."

"That's a relief."

"I so agree—he asked twice about 'Roo.' He wanted to know when Rule was coming to see him again so they could play trucks."

Sydney was happy that her son was so taken with his stepfather. She only wished she didn't feel edgy and unsure about everything. But it had all happened so fast between them, and now he was gone. A sense of unreality had set in.

She told Lani, "He said he'd be back in a week."

"Well, all right. Good to know—and is everything okay with you two?"

Sydney let her shoulders slump. "There are some issues."

Lani knew her so well. "And you're too wiped out to talk about them now." At Sydney's weary nod, she asked, "Hungry?"

"Naw. I had takeout at the office—and two pieces of cake at the party. I think I'll go upstairs and kiss my sleeping son and then take a long, hot bath."

Forty-five minutes later, Sydney climbed into bed. She set the alarm for six-thirty, turned off the light and was sound asleep almost as soon as her head hit the pillow.

Rule didn't call that night. Or the next morning.

Apparently, he really was "brassed off" at her. She thought it was rather childish of him, to cut off communication because she'd pissed him off. Then again, nothing was stopping her from picking up the phone and calling *him*.

She felt reluctant to do that, which probably proved that she was being every bit as childish as he was. And she did wonder how things had worked out with Liliana, if he'd done what she'd asked him to do and found someone for the poor woman to talk to.

And okay, she hadn't *asked*. She'd more like *commanded*. And he hadn't appreciated her ordering him around.

Maybe she shouldn't have been so hard on him. Maybe she should have...

Who knew what she should have done? She was totally out of her depth with him. She'd only known him since Friday and now they were married and already he was halfway around the world from her. No wonder they were having "issues."

She hardly knew him. And how would she *get* to know him, with him there and her here?

All she knew for certain was that she ached with missing him. The lack of him was like a hole in her heart, a vacancy. She needed him with her, to fill that lack. She wanted him there, with her, touching her. She wanted it so bad. She wanted to grab him in her arms and curl herself into him, to hold on so tight, to press herself so close. She wanted to...somehow be inside his skin.

She wanted the scent of him, the sound of his voice, the sweet, slow laugh, the feel of his hands on her, the touch of his mouth...

She was totally gone on him. And he'd better return to her in a week, as he'd promised, or she would do something totally unconstructive. Track him down and shoot him, maybe. Not fatally, of course. Just wing him.

At the office the next day, she got calls from a couple of oil company executives, representatives of two of the companies Rule had said he could deliver to her firm. The calls eased her mind a little.

Okay, he hadn't been in touch the way he'd promised

that he would. But he was moving ahead with his plans to help her get away from Texas gracefully. That was something. A good sign.

Before the end of the day, she'd set up the first getting-to-know-you meetings between her partners and the reps from the oil companies.

Thursday morning at six-thirty, at the exact moment that her alarm went off, the phone rang. Jarred awake, she groped for the alarm first and hit the switch to shut it off.

Then she grabbed the phone. "Hello, what?" she grumbled.

"I woke you."

Even half-asleep, gladness filled her. "Hello."

"Are you still angry with me?"

She rolled over onto her back, and raked her sleep-scrambled hair back off her face. "I could ask you the same question."

"I know I said I'd call every day…" God. His voice. How could it be better, smoother, deeper, just plain sexier than she remembered?

She corrected him. "You said you would call *constantly*. That's *more* than every day."

"Will you ever forgive me?"

She chuckled, a low, husky sound. She just couldn't help it. All he had to do was call and her world was rosy again. "I would say forgiveness is a distinct possibility."

"I'm so glad to hear that." He said it tenderly. And as if he really, really meant it.

"I miss you, Rule. I miss you so much."

"I miss you, too."

"How can I feel this way? I've only known you for, what, five days?"

"Four days, nineteen hours and…three minutes—and

you'd better miss me. You're my wife. It's your job to miss me when we're apart."

"Well, I'm doing my job, then."

"Good."

"And I'm sorry," she said, "that we argued."

"I am, too."

"Those two oil men called yesterday. I set them up with my partners."

"Excellent."

She hesitated to ruin the conciliatory mood by bringing up a certain princess. But she really did want to know what had happened. "Did everything work out then, with Liliana?"

"You were right," he said quietly. "I should have sent someone to be with her."

"Oh, no. What *happened?*"

"When I told my mother that Lili hadn't seemed to take the news of our marriage well, she rushed off to comfort her. Lili wasn't in her rooms. Lili's attendant said that she'd fled in tears."

"Omigod. She's missing, then?"

"No. They found her shortly thereafter. She simply turned up, looking somewhat disheveled, or so I was told, and insisting she was perfectly fine."

"Turned up?"

"One of the servants found her in the hallway between Maximilian's apartments and Alexander's. She claimed she'd simply gone for a stroll."

"A *stroll?*"

"That's what she said."

"Is she friends with your brothers? Did she talk it out with one of them?"

"Not possible."

"Why not?"

"Max is with his children, at his villa. And Alex and Lili have never gotten on, not since childhood."

"That doesn't mean he might not have been kind to her, if he saw that she was upset."

"Sydney, he's hardly come out of his rooms since he returned from Afghanistan. But you're right, of course. Anything is possible. Perhaps she talked to him, though no one told me that she did."

"But…she's all right, then?"

"Yes. She did end up confiding in my mother. And in the end, Lili promised my mother that she is perfectly all right and that no one is to worry that her father's famous temper will be roused. Lili said she had finally realized that she and I were not right for each other, after all. She told my mother to wish me and my bride a lifetime of happiness. My mother believes that Lili was sincere in what she said."

"Okay. Well. Good news, huh?"

"I believe so, yes. Lili departed yesterday morning for Alagonia. King Leo has not appeared brandishing a sword or insisting on pistols at dawn, so I'm going to venture a guess that renewed animosity between our two countries has been safely averted."

"I'm so glad. I have to admit, I was worrying—that Liliana might have done something crazy, that her father might have taken offense. And then, when you never called, I only worried more."

"I'm a complete ass."

"Do you hear me arguing? Just tell me you're coming back here to me by Tuesday or Wednesday, as promised."

"Sorry. I can't do that." He said it teasingly.

Still, her heart sank. She tried to think of what to say, how to frame her disappointment in words that wouldn't get them started fighting all over again.

And then he said, "I'll be there tomorrow."

She felt deliciously breathless. "Oh, Rule. Say that again."

"You *do* miss me." The way he said that made her heart beat faster.

"Oh, yes, I do," she fervently agreed. "I want to have *time* with you. I want you near me. Here we are, married. We're going to spend our lives together, yet in many ways we hardly know each other."

"Tomorrow," he said. "It'll be late, around ten at night, by the time I reach your house."

"Tomorrow. Oh, I can't believe it—and late is fine. I'm lucky to get home by nine-thirty, anyway. I'll be here. Waiting."

"I have work to do there, too, you know. I have to introduce your partners to any number of excellent potential clients, so they'll realize they owe it to you to let you go right away."

She beamed, even though he wasn't there to see it. "I can't tell you how glad I am that you're coming back now. It will be so good, to be with you every day—even if I do spend way too much of every day at work. But I'm going to change that. When I'm through at the firm, I'm going to make sure I never again take a job where I hardly see my son, where I'm rarely with my husband."

"I do like the sound of that."

"Good— Oh, and I forgot to tell you. Trevor will be so pleased to see you. He's been asking for you."

"Tell him I'm on my way."

Chapter Ten

Sydney was waiting at the picture window in the living room Friday night when the long, black limo pulled in at the curb. The sight of his car had her heart racing and her pulse pounding so hard, it made a roaring sound in her ears.

With a glad cry, she spun on her heel and took off for the door. Flinging it wide, she ran down the front steps and along the walk. He emerged from the car and she threw herself into his arms.

He kissed her, right there beneath the streetlight. A hard, hot kiss, one that started out desperate and ended so sweet and lazy and slow.

When he lifted his head, he said, "I thought I'd never get here."

She laughed, held so close and safe in his arms. "But you *are* here. And I may never let you go away from me again." She took his hand. "Come inside…"

The driver was already unloading Rule's bags. He followed them up the front walk. Joseph followed, too.

In the house, the driver carried the bags up to the master suite and then, with a tip of his cap, took his leave.

Joseph remained. For once, he wasn't wearing those dark glasses. But he still had the Bluetooth device in his ear. And he carried a black duffel bag.

Rule looked slightly embarrassed. "I'm afraid Joseph goes where I go."

Sydney spoke to the bodyguard. "I hope you don't mind sleeping in a separate room from His Highness."

The severe-looking Joseph almost cracked a smile. "Ma'am, if you have a spare room, that would be appreciated. If not, the sofa will do well enough."

"I have a guest room." She indicated the doorway at the end of the hall. "The kitchen is through there. While you're here, make yourself at home. You're welcome to anything you find in the pantry or the fridge."

"Thank you, ma'am."

She turned to Rule. "Are you hungry?"

His dark eyes said, *Not for food,* and she felt the loveliest warmth low in her belly, and a definite wobbliness in her knees. He told her, "I ate on the plane."

So she led the way up the stairs and showed Joseph to his room, indicating Trevor's bathroom across the hall. "I'm afraid you'll have to share the bathroom with my son."

"Thank you. This will suit me very well."

Before joining Rule in her room, she tapped on Lani's door and told her friend that Rule's bodyguard was staying in the guest room.

Lani, reading in bed, looked up from her eReader, over the top rims of her glasses. "Thanks for the warning—and don't stay up all night."

"Yes, Mother."

"Say hi to Rule."

"Will do."

She went to her own room and found Rule standing in the bow window, staring out at the quiet street. "Lani says hi."

He turned to her. "I like your house. It's comfortable, and the rooms are large. Lots of windows…"

She hovered in the open doorway, her stomach suddenly all fluttery. "We've been happy here. It will be strange, to live in a palace."

"I have other properties. Villas. Town houses. You might prefer one of them."

All at once, the life that lay before her seemed alien, not her own. "We'll see." The two words came out on a breath.

He held out his hand to her. "Are you shy of me now, Sydney?"

Her throat clutched. She spoke through the tightness. "A little, I guess." A nervous laugh escaped her. "That's silly, isn't it?"

He shook his dark head. "Come here. Let me ease your fears."

Pausing only to shut the door and engage the lock, she went to him and took the hand he offered. His touch burned her and soothed her at once.

He reached out with the hand not holding hers and shut the blinds. "I put my suitcases in your closet…."

She moved in closer. He framed her face. She said, "It seems like forever, since you left…."

"I'm here now."

"I'm so glad about that."

He kissed her. And the throat-tight nervousness faded. There was only his mouth on her mouth, his hands against her cheeks, brushing down the sides of her throat, tracing the collar of her cotton shirt, and then going to work on the buttons down the front of it.

She was breathless and sighing, pulling him closer. He took away her shirt and her bra. He pushed down the leggings she had pulled on after work. She kicked away her little black flats and wiggled the rest of the way out of the leggings.

And then he went to work on his own clothes, kissing her senseless as he ripped off his jacket, his shirt, his trousers…everything. She had only her panties on and he was completely naked when he started walking her backward toward the bed.

"Wait," she breathed against his lips.

He only went on kissing her—until she gave a gentle shove against his chest. With an impatient growl, he lifted his mouth from hers. "You know you're killing me…."

She put her finger to those amazing lips of his. "Only a moment…"

"A moment is too long." But he did let her go.

She turned around and pulled the covers down, smoothing them. "There."

"Sydney…" He clasped her by the hips and drew her back against him.

"I'm here. Right here…" She lifted her arms and reached for him, clasping his neck, turning her head to him so their mouths could fuse once again.

His tongue plundered her mouth and his hands covered her breasts. And she could feel him, all along her body, feel the power of him, the heat. Feel the proof of how much he wanted her, silky and hard, pressing into her back.

And then he was turning her and guiding her down onto the sheets and right then, at that moment on that night, she was the happiest woman in Texas. There was only the feel of his big body settling against hers, only his kiss, only his skilled touch, on her breasts, her belly and lower.

He took away her panties and those wonderful fingers of his found the womanly core of her and she moaned into his mouth. He kissed her some more as he caressed her, bringing her higher, making her clutch his hard shoulders and press herself closer.

Closer...

And then she couldn't wait. Not one second longer. She eased her hand between them and she wrapped her fingers around him and she guided him into place.

When he came into her, she let out a soft cry at the sheer beauty of it, at the feel of him filling her. So perfectly. So right.

He kissed her throat, and then scraped the willing flesh there with his teeth. And then he licked her. And then he blew on her wet skin and she moaned and pulled him closer again, lifting her legs to wrap around his waist, pushing herself harder against him, demanding everything of him, wanting it all.

When he held her like this, when he worked his special magic on her skin, she had no doubts at all. She would follow him anywhere, and she would be happy.

Just the two of them and Trevor. And maybe, if they were lucky, more children. Three or four. Nine or ten...

She'd forgotten how many she wanted, how many they had finally agreed on. And what did it matter how many? She would love them all, every one.

And by then, she'd forgotten everything—everything but this, but the man who held her, the man who filled her. The pleasure was building, spinning fast, and then gathering tight.

Only to open outward, a sudden blooming, so hot and

perfect. She cried out again, loud enough that he had to cover her mouth with his hand.

She laughed against his fingers, a wild sound. And then he was laughing with her. And still the pleasure bloomed and grew. And all at once, they were silent, serious, concentrated, eyes wide open, falling into each other.

Falling and spinning, set gloriously free: the two of them, locked together. She was lost in his eyes. And more than happy to be so.

She whispered his name.

With a low groan, he gave hers back to her.

She must have slept for a time.

When she woke, he was braced up on an elbow, looking down at her, his eyes black velvet, his mouth an invitation to sin.

She reached up, curved her fingers around the back of his head, pulled him closer. They shared a quick, gentle kiss. "It's so good, to wake up and find you here. I want to do that for the rest of my life."

"And my darling, you shall. Now go back to sleep."

"Soon. Tell me about your parents. Are they angry, that you married me?"

"No. They're pleased. Very pleased."

She wasn't buying that. "They don't even know me. You met me and married me in like, ten minutes or less. How can they be pleased with that? I mean, I could understand if you said they were…accepting. But *pleased*?"

"They know me. They know that I'm happy, that I've found the woman I want to be with for a lifetime. They're relieved and they're grateful."

"Well, okay." She traced the shape of his ear. It was such a good-looking ear. "I get that. I mean, they were probably getting pretty concerned, right, that you wouldn't marry in time?"

"They were, yes." He caught her hand, kissed the tips of her fingers.

"But if you'd married the Princess of Alagonia, wouldn't that have made them a lot happier?"

"No. Evidently not. They told me they didn't think Lili and I would have been a good match."

"You'd think they might have said that earlier."

"My response exactly."

"Someone should change that ridiculous law."

"My mother's great-grandfather, who ruled Montedoro for fifty years, *did* change it. He abolished the law. And then my mother's father put the law in place once again."

"But why?"

"My mother's *grand*father didn't marry until late in life. He had eight children, but only one was legitimate, my mother's father, *my* grandfather. Then my grandfather had just one child, a daughter, legitimate, my mother. The family was dying out. My grandfather took action. He put the law back in place."

She laughed. "And then your mother obeyed it. She married young, brought in fresh blood and took her reproductive duties to heart."

"Yes, she did. And look at us now."

"Heirs and spares all over the place."

"That's right. So you see, the law has its uses."

She frowned, considering. "There must be any number of ways around it. You could marry someone in time to keep your inheritance, and then divorce her as soon as your thirty-third birthday has passed."

He nuzzled her neck. "Already planning how you'll get rid of me, eh?"

She laughed, and caught his face and kissed him, hard,

on the mouth. "Never. But you know what I'm saying, right?"

"We are Catholic. The heir to the throne always marries in the church. Divorce is not an option in the church. There is annulment, but there are specific grounds for that, none of them pretty. And you have to understand. In my family, we are raised to respect the Prince's Marriage Law. We believe it is a good law, good for Montedoro—especially after we saw what happened when my great-great-grandfather abolished it. And we grow up committed to the spirit of that law, to finding a proper marriage partner by the required date. My parents were good parents, parents who spent time with their children, what you would call in America 'hands-on' parents. My mother considers each of her nine children to be every bit as important as her throne."

"Well, all right," she said. "I guess I can't argue with success. But I do have a couple more questions."

"Ask."

"Do *we* have to marry in the church in order for you to keep your inheritance?"

"No. The heir must marry in the church. The rest of us are only required to be legally wed before the age of thirty-three. But, should I become the heir—which is most unlikely at this point—you and I would have to take steps for a church-sanctioned marriage. That would not be complicated, as neither of us has been married before."

"Do you want us to be married in the church?"

He kissed the tip of her nose. "I do, yes."

"Good answer." She slid her hands up his chest and wrapped them around his neck. "I want that, too."

"Then we shall take the necessary steps to make it happen as soon as we're settled in Montedoro."

"Agreed. I think we should seal it with a kiss."

"Beyond a doubt, we should."

So they kissed. A long, slow one. The kiss led to more kisses and then to the usual stimulating conclusion.

Rule told her again to go sleep.

She said, "Soon."

And then they talked for another hour about everything from the success of his plan to sell Montedoran oranges to a number of exclusive outlets in the U.S., to why his brother Alex and Princess Lili had never gotten along. Alex, Rule said, had always thought Lili was silly and shallow; Lili considered Alex to be overly brooding and grim, with a definite tendency toward overbearing self-importance.

Sydney learned that his brother Max's son was named Nicholas and Max's little girl was Constance. And Rule told her that in his great-grandfather's day, the economy of Montedoro was almost solely dependent on gambling revenues. His grandfather and his mother had made a point to expand the principality's economic interests beyond its traditional gambling base.

"Now," he said, "gambling accounts for only four percent of our nation's annual revenues."

She reminded him that he knew all about Ryan and Peter. But other than Liliana, she knew nothing of the women who had mattered in his life.

"You already know that I admire my mother," he said with a gleam in his eye.

"Your mother and your sisters don't count. I'm talking love affairs, Rule. You know that I am."

So he told her about the Greek heiress he'd loved when he was fourteen. "She had an absolutely adorable space between her two front teeth and she spoke with a slight lisp and she intended to run away to America and become a musical theater star."

"Did she?"

"Unfortunately, she was tone deaf. I heard her sing once. Once was enough."

"Destroyed your undying love for her, did it?"

"I was young and easily distracted. Especially when it came to love." He spoke of the girl he'd met in a Paris café when he was eighteen. And of an Irish girl he'd met in London. "Black hair, blue eyes. And a temper. A hot one. At first, I found her temper exciting. But in time it grew tiresome."

"Luckily there were any number of actresses and models just waiting for their chance with you."

"You make me sound like a Casanova."

"Weren't you?"

"No. I was not. Yes, I've spent time with a number of women, but seduction for its own sake has never interested me. I was…looking for someone. The *right* someone." He lowered his head until their noses touched. "You."

Her heart did that melty thing. "Oh, Rule…"

He kissed her forehead, her cheeks, and finally her lips—sweet, brushing kisses. "Will you please go to sleep now?" He tucked the covers closer around her. "Close your eyes…"

And she did.

The next day was Saturday. Sydney left Rule having breakfast with Trevor and Lani and spent the morning at the office, where things were pretty quiet and she got a lot done.

She returned home at lunchtime and spent the rest of the day with Rule and her son and her best friend. She and Rule went out to dinner that night and then, at home, made slow, wonderful love. They fell asleep with their arms wrapped around each other. Her last thought before she drifted off was that she had it all now. Her life was exactly as she'd once dreamed it might be.

Sunday she stayed home, too. She and Rule took Trevor to the park in the morning. She watched Rule pushing Trev on the swings and thought how already they seemed like father and son. Trev adored him. It was "Roo" this and "Roo" that. The feeling was clearly mutual. Rule seemed to dote on Trev. He never tired of listening to Trev babble on about the things that mattered to a curious two-year-old.

And an older lady, a woman there with her grandson, leaned close to Sydney when they sat on the bench together. "Your boy looks just like his daddy."

Sydney smiled at the woman. "He does, doesn't he?"

Later, at lunch, Trev was back into his knock-knock jokes. He and Rule played a never-ending game of them until Sydney put her hands over her ears and begged them to stop.

Trev laughed. "Mama says, 'No more knock-knock!'"

Rule piped up with, "Mama says, 'Touch your nose.'" He touched his nose and then Trev, delighted, touched his. And Rule said, "Mama says, 'Rub your tummy.'" They both rubbed their tummies.

Trev caught on about then and they were off on the "Mama" version of Simon Says. Sydney laughed along with them.

The woman at the park had been right. And Lani had noticed the resemblance, too. They were so much alike, really. They even had mannerisms in common—the way they each tipped their head, a little to the left, when thoughtful. Even the way they smiled was similar—slow and dazzling.

Sydney supposed it wasn't all that surprising, how much Trev resembled his new stepdad. The sperm donor she'd chosen had a lot of characteristics in common with Rule—hair and eye color, height and build. And the similarities weren't only physical. The donor had an advanced degree in business and enjoyed travel and sports. And the description of him compiled by the staff at the cryobank? All about how charming and handsome and bright and dynamic he was. How well-spoken and articulate, a born leader *and* a good listener. His profile also said that family was important to him and he believed in marriage, that he felt it could and should last a lifetime.

She'd selected that particular donor mostly because he sounded like the kind of man she'd given up on finding. After all, a woman hopes her child might inherit traits that she admires.

A little shiver skittered up her spine as she watched her son and Rule together and compared her husband with the man who had supplied half of her child's DNA. Life could be so strange and amazing. Really, she'd chosen her own personal fantasy man as her sperm donor, not even realizing that he was destined to materialize in the flesh and promptly sweep her off her feet into their very own happy-ever-after—let alone that he would so quickly become a doting father to her son.

That Sunday was sunny and clear, with a high in the mid-eighties, a little warm for mid-April. It was a great day for splashing around in the pool—which they did as soon as Trevor woke up from his nap. Later, Lani made dinner, a fabulous Greek-style shrimp scampi.

Monday it was off to work again. Rule showed up at a little after eleven. Sydney introduced him around the office and two of the partners were only too happy to join them for lunch at the Mansion.

It was a working lunch, and a very productive one. By the end of it, Rule had set up three dinner dates where he would introduce her colleagues to more potential clients. After lunch, he returned to the house and she went back to work.

Their days fell into a certain rhythm. The office owned her during the long weekdays, but she spent her nights with her new husband and managed to get most of the weekend free to be with Trevor, too. Rule spent a lot of time with her son and the growing bond between the man and the boy was something special to see. Rule would play with him for hours during the day and read him his bedtime stories most nights.

Sydney worked and worked some more. Rule often appeared to take her to lunch—and he moved forward on the goal he'd set for himself of giving her partners enough new business that they wouldn't consider themselves cheated when she moved on.

There were more tabloid stories. Sydney didn't read them, but evidently a few of her coworkers did. She found more than one discarded scandal rag on the lunch table in the break room. Somehow, they'd gotten her high school and college graduation pictures, and there were pictures of Rule, bare-chested on a sailboat with a blonde, and also wearing a tux at some gala event, a gorgeous redhead on his arm. Sydney hardly glanced at them. Rule said that when they got to Montedoro, a press conference would be arranged. They would answer questions for a roomful of reporters and let them take a lot of pictures. That should satisfy them if they hadn't already moved on to the next big story by then.

Twice during the weeks it took her to finish up at the firm, Rule had to travel. He had business in New York and spent four days in Manhattan. And he also returned briefly to Montedoro to meet with a certain luxury car manufacturer who was considering giving one of his new designs, a sleek high-end sports car, the name "Montedoro."

Sydney missed him when he was gone. Her bed seemed so empty without him there to keep her warm in the middle of the night. Trev missed him, too. "I sad, Mama. I want Roo," he would say. And she would remind him that Rule would return soon.

On the last Friday in April, Sydney came home late as usual. Rule was back from Montedoro. He and Lani had waited to have dinner with her. They'd even invited the ever-present but usually silent Joseph to join them. Lani had outdone herself with a crown roast of lamb. Rule opened a lovely bottle of Syrah. And Lani announced that she'd decided to take them up on their offer and come with them to Montedoro.

Sydney jumped from her chair and ran around the table and hugged her friend good and hard. "Whew. I didn't want to pressure you, but I really was hoping you would come with us."

Lani laughed. "Are you kidding? Miss the chance to live on the Mediterranean in the Prince's Palace? I couldn't pass it up."

Even Joseph was smiling. "Good news," he said and raised the glass of wine he'd hardly touched.

Lani said, "Life experience is everything for a novelist. Plus, well, what would I do without you?"

"Exactly." Sydney hugged her again. "And how could we possibly get along without *you?*"

Deep in the night, Sydney woke suddenly from a sound sleep. It was after three and she had no idea what had wakened her.

And then she heard Trev crying. "Mama...Mama..."

Beside her, Rule woke, too. He sat up. "I'll go..."

She kissed his beard-scratchy cheek and pushed him back down to the pillow. "No. I'll do it." She threw on a robe and went to see what was wrong.

Trev was fussy and feverish, his dark hair wet with sweat. He kept putting his hands to his cheeks and crying, "Hurt, Mama. Hurt…"

Lani came in, her hair every which way, a sleep mark on her cheek, belting her robe. "Can I do something?"

"It's all right. I think he's teething. Go back to bed. I've got him."

"Come get me if you need me."

"Will do."

Yawning, Lani returned to her room.

Sydney took Trev's temperature. It was marginally elevated. She gave him some children's acetaminophen and took him downstairs to get one of the teething rings she kept in the freezer. She was back in his room, sitting in the rocker with him as he fussed and chewed on the teething ring when Rule appeared in the doorway to the upstairs hall, bare-chested in a pair of blue pajama bottoms.

"He's not a happy camper," she said. "I think it's his teeth. I gave him a painkiller. It should take effect soon."

Trev pushed away from Sydney. "Roo! Hurt. I have hurt…" He held out his chubby little arms.

Rule came for him, scooping him up out of Sydney's lap without a word or a second's hesitation. Trev wrapped his arms around his stepfather's neck and held on, sticking the ring back in his mouth and burrowing his dark head against Rule's chest. Rule began walking him, back and forth across the bedroom floor.

Sydney, still in the rocker, stared up at the man and the little boy, at their two dark heads so close together, and tried to get a grip on exactly what she was feeling.

Jealousy?

Maybe a little. Rule had become nothing short of proprietary about Trev—and Trev about him. In recent weeks, with Rule around day in and day out, Trev had grown to count on him, to expect him to be there, to demand his attention. Since Rule was only too happy to spend lots of time with Trev, and did, it was natural that a powerful bond had swiftly developed between them.

And wasn't that bond a *good* thing? As a father figure, Rule had so far proved himself to be pretty much the ideal. So what was bothering her?

Did she want Rule to defer to her when it came to Trev, was that it? When he'd grabbed her son from her arms without so much as a do-you-mind, had that somehow threatened her, made her feel that her status as Trev's parent was in jeopardy? Lani and Trev had a close relationship, but Lani always remembered that Sydney was the mom, that her claim on him came first.

Rule, though...

He didn't defer to her anymore, if he ever had. He seemed to consider himself as much Trev's dad as Sydney was his mom.

And what was wrong with that?

Wasn't that what she'd been hoping for all along?

Ugh. Maybe it was guilt—scratch the "maybe." *Probably* it was guilt. *Her* guilt, because she knew she'd never been around enough. She worked killer hours and a lot of days she didn't see her son awake except early in the morning, when she kissed him goodbye on her way out the door.

No wonder he chose Rule over her when he needed comforting. Rule was more a consistent presence in his life than she was.

But that was going to change. Very soon. And it would change *because* of Rule, because of what he offered her and Trev, because of the kind of husband and father he was. Not only deeply committed to his family, but also an excellent provider.

As soon as she was finished at the firm, *she* would be available to Trev more consistently—constantly, in fact, at least at first. And even when she found interesting work in Montedoro, it was going to be work with reasonable hours for a change. She would truly have it all. Time to be a mom, time to be a wife, time to do good work that mattered.

It was all going to be fine and she needed to get over her guilt and her jealousy. Trev had a dad now, that was all that was happening here. Sometimes a child wanted his dad over his mom. And there was nothing at all wrong with that.

She leaned her head back in the rocker and closed her eyes.

The next moment—or so it seemed to her—Rule was whispering in her ear. "Come back to bed, sleepyhead."

She forced her heavy eyes to open, asked, "Trev?"

He put a finger to his lips, tipped his head toward the toddler bed across the room, where Trev was curled up under the blankets, his arm around his favorite stuffed dinosaur.

She gave Rule her hand and he pulled her out of the chair. He drew her close and she leaned against him as they returned to the master bedroom.

In bed, he gathered her close to him. "You work too hard." He stroked her hair.

"Not for long. Another week or so, the way I figure it, and I'm so outta there."

"I can't wait to take you home with me—you and Trevor both."

She traced his dark brows, one and then the other, by

feel more than sight. They had turned off the lamp. "I have a secret to tell you."

"I love secrets." He bent closer, kissed her temple. "Especially *your* secrets."

"Don't laugh."

"I promise, I won't." He stroked her hair.

"You and Trev look a lot alike."

He kissed her lips, a brushing kiss, his breath so warm across her cheek. "We do, a little, don't we—and is that your secret?"

"No. I'm getting to it, though. And it starts with the resemblance between you and Trev, which is pretty striking, really. Beyond the dark hair and eyes, you both tip your heads at the same angle when you're thinking. And when you smile...you make me think of him. In fact, that first day we met, remember how I've said I kept thinking how you looked familiar? Remember, I even asked you if we'd met before?"

"Yes. I remember."

"I've been thinking about that a lot lately, kind of marveling over it. And then I realized it's not surprising in the least."

"Why not?"

"Simple. The sperm donor I chose was a lot like you— and yes, that would be my big secret." She traced the so-manly strong line of his jaw. "I chose him because he was just like you—I mean, the you I didn't even know then. He had your same height and build, dark eyes and dark hair. I chose him because he seemed like the man I always hoped to meet someday. The man I had by then decided I would *never* meet."

He withdrew from her then, turning over onto his back beside her.

She wondered at that. "Rule? Are you okay? Did I say something that upset you?"

"Of course you didn't." He sounded…distant. And a little strange. "I'm perfectly all right."

"You don't *seem* all right."

He found her hand under the covers, twined his fingers with hers. "I'm fine."

"Good." She smiled into the darkness. "You sure you were never a sperm donor?"

"You're joking."

"Well, yeah. I guess I am. But sometimes, it's almost eerie, the resemblance between you and Trev."

He didn't say anything.

She went on, "I always kind of hoped to meet him. But he was a confidential donor. I left permission that he could contact me if he ever changed his mind. He didn't. Not so far, anyway—and that reminds me. I need to change my contact information with Secure Choice—that's the clinic I used, Secure Choice Cryobank." She waited for his response, thinking of his possessiveness concerning Trev—and also a little worried about the dreamy way she'd spoken of a man she'd never met.

Was he jealous? Would he try to talk her out of keeping her information current, want her to make it more difficult for the donor to get in touch should he ever decide he wanted to?

But then Rule only reached for her again. He eased his arm under her nape and drew her into him, bringing her to rest against his warm, hard chest. "Go to sleep."

She closed her eyes and let the steady, even sound of his heartbeat lull her.

Of course he'd never been a sperm donor. She knew what a donor went through. She'd researched the whole process when she decided on artificial insemination. It wasn't just a matter of doing the happy hand in a cup.

A man went through all kinds of testing before he could become a donor. Only a small percentage of applicants were accepted. A man had to donate weekly, at least, and he couldn't have sex for two days before each donation. He also couldn't go more than five days *without* ejaculating, because not often enough was as bad for sperm production as too often. Most sperm donors signed contracts for six months to a year of donations—six months to a year of having sex in a cup on a strict schedule. The money wasn't even all that much, averaging under a hundred dollars per viable donation.

To have been her donor, Rule would have had to sign on for all of the above with the fertility clinic she had used, or an affiliate. What were the odds of that?

He was a hardworking man who traveled the world doing business for his country. Not only would being a donor be unprofitable, time-consuming and a logistical nightmare for Rule, it just…wasn't like him. He felt so strongly about family and fatherhood. He wasn't a man who could help to give a child life and not want to be there while that child was growing up.

Still, she didn't get the way he'd pulled away from her when she talked about how much alike he and Trevor were, when she'd confessed that he, Rule, was pretty much her dream man come to life. He'd turned onto his back before she said anything about how she'd given permission to be contacted, so his original withdrawal really couldn't be chalked up to apprehension that the donor might show up someday.

She didn't like the way he'd said, *You're joking,* when she'd asked him if he'd ever been a donor. He could so easily have given her a simple, direct denial.

It wasn't that she actually suspected he might be Trevor's biological father. She only wondered why he'd seemed so defensive and why he'd pulled away from her when she'd only been trying to tell him that he was everything she'd ever wanted in a man.

Chapter Eleven

But by the next morning, in the bright light of day, as Sydney hurried to get ready to head to the office, her vague suspicions about Rule...

Well, they seemed downright ridiculous.

He hadn't really pulled away from her last night, had he? He'd only rolled over to his back. And when she'd asked if anything was wrong, he'd told her there was nothing.

And his seeming evasiveness when she teased him about being a sperm donor? It just didn't strike her as all that odd now that she'd had a little time to think it over. He was very attached to Trevor. He didn't want to dwell on the stranger who had fathered her child. She could understand that.

She decided that she would put the whole issue from her mind. She had so much work to do and not all that much time to do it in. The last thing she needed was to waste her energy stewing about stuff she'd made up in her head.

Plus, if she wanted to dwell on something, why not choose something real? Something important. Something potentially quite wonderful.

As of that morning, her period was one week late. It was beginning to look as though she and her new husband were already getting their start on that larger family they both hoped for.

But she shouldn't get ahead of herself. She *had* been under a lot of stress lately—meeting and marrying Rule in the space of forty-eight hours, and then having to send him away to make his apologies to the "other woman" in his life. And then there was the way she was working like crazy to finish up at the firm, planning a move halfway around the world.

Yes. Her life was especially stressful right now. And stress could really mess up a woman's cycle.

She decided she would wait a few weeks before she said anything to Rule. No reason to get his expectations up unnecessarily—or her own, for that matter. She would let that question rest for a while, not allow herself to get too excited about it until more time had passed.

Trev was much better that morning. He seemed to be over the bout of teething pain. His temperature was normal and he was eating his breakfast cereal, chattering away, when she left for work.

He gave her a big kiss. "Come back soon, Mama!"

"Don't you worry, I will."

And that evening, she managed to get away from the officer earlier than usual. She was even in time to give Trev his bath before bed. Once he was in bed, Rule said he wanted to take her out to dinner.

They went to the Mansion. Sydney loved the food and

service there and Rule liked it, too. The staff knew him and protected his privacy.

He made a toast. "To us. To our family. To our whole lives together."

She clinked her wineglass with his, aglow with happiness, knowing that she had to be the most fortunate woman in all of Texas. After a couple of sips, she set her glass down and didn't pick it up again. Might as well be cautious. Just in case she really was pregnant.

Not that she thought she was. Uh-uh. She wasn't going there. Not yet.

Four days later, on the first Friday in May, Sydney said goodbye to Teale, Gayle and Prosser.

She left her desk clean and neat and her clients effectively shifted to other attorneys in the firm. She also departed on good terms with her former partners, all thanks to her strict dedication to doing things right—and her new husband's willingness to share his connections.

The next week was all about packing for the move. Lani, one of the most organized human beings on the planet, had already gotten a good head start on that. But there was more to do. Sydney got to work on the rest of the job with her usual enthusiasm. They were leaving the house furnished and in the hands of an excellent Realtor.

Their passports were current. Even Trevor's. Sydney had gotten his for him months before, when she'd been thinking of taking a vacation in Ireland.

On the second Friday in May, they boarded the private jet for Montedoro. Lani's brother, Carlos, and her parents, Iris and Jorge, came to the airport to see them off. There were also reporters. They snapped lots of pictures and asked an endless number of way-too-personal questions.

Rule told them he had no comment at this time and Joseph herded them up the ramp and into the plane.

The flight was a long one and there was a seven-hour time difference between Dallas and their destination. They took off from Love Field at two in the afternoon and arrived at the airport in Nice at eight the next morning. A limo was waiting to whisk them to Montedoro and the Prince's Palace. So were more paparazzi. Again, they hurried to get into the car and away from the questions and cameras.

The first sight of the palace stole Sydney's breath. White as a dove's wing against the clear blue sky, it was a sprawling edifice of crenellated towers and paladin windows and balconies and arches. It stood on a rocky promontory overlooking the sapphire-colored sea.

The driver took them around to a private entrance. By a little after nine, they were filing into Rule's apartment.

After the grandeur of the arched, marble-floored hallways decorated in gorgeous mosaics, Sydney was relieved that Rule's private space was more low-key. The furniture was simple, plush and inviting, the walls were of stucco or something similar, with tall, curving ceilings and dark wood floors covered with beautiful old rugs woven in intricate patterns, most of them deep reds and vivid blues. Balconies in the large sitting room and in the master suite opened onto stunning views of the main courtyard and the crowns of the palms and mimosas, the olive and oak trees that covered the hillside below. Farther out, the Mediterranean, dotted here and there with pretty sailboats and giant cruise ships, shone in the afternoon sun.

The palace staff set right to work unpacking and putting everything away. In no time, that job was done and the soft-spoken, efficient maids had vanished. Lani retreated to her room at one end of the apartment, probably to work on her novel or jot down her first impressions of Montedoro in her journal. Trev sat on a glorious red rug in the sitting room playing with his plastic blocks, and Rule was off somewhere conferring with his private secretary, Caroline.

For a while, Sydney leaned on the carved stone balcony railing, the doors to the sitting room wide open behind her, and stared out at the boats floating on the impossibly blue sea. There was a soft breeze, like the lightest brush of silk against her skin. She felt tempted to pinch herself. It almost seemed like a dream that they were actually here, in Montedoro, at last.

And it got even better. Her period was now almost three weeks late. She had no morning sickness, but she'd had none with Trev, either. What she did have were breasts.

They weren't huge or anything, but they were definitely fuller, and more sensitive than usual. That was the same as with Trev, too.

Another baby. She put her hand against her flat stomach, the way mothers had been doing since the beginning of time. *Another baby.* When she'd had Trevor, she'd told herself to be grateful for one. And she had been. So very grateful.

But now, well, she was pretty much positive she would be having her second. Incredible. Talk about impossible dreams coming true.

She'd bought a home test the week before. And today, as she leaned on the stone railing and admired the sea, she was thinking it was about time to take the test.

And about time to tell Rule that their family was growing.

"Mama! Come. Play…"

She turned to smile at her son, who had stacked several brightly colored blocks into a rickety tower and waved two more at her, one in each chubby hand. "All right, sweetheart. Let's play." She went and sat on the rug with him.

"Here, Mama." He handed her a drool-covered block. Lately, as his back teeth came in, anything he got his little hands on ended up with drool on it.

"Thank you." She wiped the drool off on her jeans and hooked the block at the base of his tower. As long as she was helping, she might as well improve the stability a tad.

A few moments later, Rule appeared. Trev cried his name in sheer delight, "Roo!" And he came right over and scooped him high into his big arms. "Roo, we play blocks!"

"I can see that. Quite a fine tower you have there."

"Mama helps."

"Oh, yes, she does." Rule gave her a smile. Her heart did a couple of somersaults. "My parents are impatient to meet you."

"I'm eager to meet *them*." She gazed up at him from her cross-legged seat on the red rug and wondered if there was a woman alive as fortunate as she. At the same time, she was just a little nervous to be meeting his mom and dad, aka Their Highnesses, for the first time. "But maybe I need a few tips on palace protocol first...."

He shook his head as he kissed the fingers that Trev was trying to stick into his mouth. "We're invited to their private apartment at six. We'll visit, you'll get to know them a little. Then we'll have an early meal. There will be no ceremony, no protocol to observe. Just the family. Just us. Together."

"Perfect," she said.

"I knew you would think so." He asked Trev, "How about you, young man? Ready to meet your new grandpa and grandma?"

Trev beamed. "Yes!"

* * *

The sovereign's apartments were larger than Rule's, but even the private foyer had a welcoming quality about it. She got the sense that real people lived there. The floor was marble, inlaid with ebony and jade, and the chandelier was a fabulous creation of ironwork and crystal. But the hall table had a bowl filled with shells on it and a family photo taken outside, beneath the wide-spreading branches of a gnarled oak tree. Sydney barely had time to pick out a much-younger Rule from the nine children arrayed at the feet of the two handsome dark-haired parents, before the thin, severe-looking woman who had opened the door to them was leading them on, down a hallway lined with oil portraits of princely relatives, the men wearing uniforms loaded down with ribbons and medals and the women resplendent in fancy ball gowns and glittering tiaras.

Rule had hold of Sydney's hand. He carried Trev high against his chest on his other arm. As they approached the end of the hall, he squeezed her fingers. She sent him a smile and squeezed back, all too aware of the fluttery, anxious sensation in her stomach.

The hallway ended at a sitting room. The tall woman nodded and left them. The same dark-haired man and woman as in the picture in the foyer rose from a matched pair of gold-trimmed velvet chairs to greet them.

"At last," said the woman, who was tall, full-figured and quite beautiful. She seemed ageless to Sydney. She could have been anywhere from forty to sixty. She had the eyes of an Egyptian goddess and a wide, radiantly smiling mouth. "Come. Come to me." She held out slender arms.

Sydney might have stood there, gaping in admiration at Rule's mom forever. Luckily, he still had her hand. He started forward and she went with him.

Then, all at once, they were there.

Rule said, "Mother. Father. This is Sydney, my wife."

And then Rule's mom was reaching for her, gathering her into those slender arms. "Sydney," she said, with such warmth and fondness. "I'm so pleased you're here with us."

"Uh. Hello." *Smooth, Sydney. Very smooth.* Really, she should have insisted that Rule at least tell her what to call this amazing creature. Your Highness? Your Sovereign Highness? Your Total Magnificence? What?

And then Rule's mom took her by the shoulders. She gave her a conspirator's grin. "You shall call me Adrienne, of course—except during certain state functions, before which, I promise you will be thoroughly briefed."

"Adrienne," Sydney breathed in relief. "Rule speaks of you often, and with deep affection."

Those Egyptian eyes gleamed. "I am so pleased he has found what he was seeking—and just in time, too."

And then Rule was saying, "And this is Trevor."

Rule's mom turned to bestow that glowing smile on Trev. "Yes. Trevor, I…" HSH Adrienne's sentence died unfinished. She blinked and shot a speaking glance at Prince Evan. It only lasted a split second, and then she recovered and continued, "Lovely to meet you." Trevor, suddenly shy, buried his head against Rule's neck. Adrienne laughed. She had an alto laugh, a little husky, and compelling. "How are you, Trevor?"

"I fine," Trevor muttered, his head still pressed tight to Rule.

Rule rubbed his back. "Say, 'Hello, Grandmother. So nice to meet you.'"

It was a lot of words for a suddenly shy little boy. But he said them, "'Lo, Gamma. Nice to meet you," with his face still smashed into Rule's neck.

"And it's a delight to meet you, as well." Adrienne loosed that husky musical laugh again.

And then Trevor's dad was taking Sydney's hand. "A Texas girl," he said in a voice as smooth and rich and deep as his son's. "Always a good choice."

Sydney thanked him and thought that he was almost as good-looking as his wife. No wonder Rule was drop-dead gorgeous. How could he be otherwise with a mom and dad like these two?

They all sat down. The severe-looking woman reappeared and offered cocktails. They sipped their drinks and Evan wanted to know about her parents. So she told them that she had lost them very young and been raised by her grandmother. They were sympathetic and admiring, of her Grandma Ellen and of the successes Sydney had achieved in her life. They knew she was an attorney and asked about her work. She explained a little about her experiences at Teale, Gayle and Prosser.

The talk shifted to Rule and the progress on his various projects. It was a bit formal, Sydney thought. But in a nice, getting-to-know-you sort of way.

She was so proud of Trev. He sat quietly on Rule's lap for a while, watching the adults, big dark eyes tracking from one face to another. Both Adrienne and Evan seemed taken with him. They kept sending him warm looks and smiles.

Slowly, Trev was drawn in. After twenty minutes or so, during a slight lull in the conversation, he held out his arms to Adrienne. "Gamma. Hug, please."

Adrienne reached for him and Rule passed him over. She wore a gorgeous designer jacket and a silk dress underneath. Sydney worried a little that Trev would drool on Her Highness's lovely outfit.

But Adrienne didn't seem concerned. She hugged him and kissed his cheek and he allowed it, all shyness fled.

Lani appeared about half an hour into the visit, ushered in by the thin woman. After a brief introduction, she took Trevor with her back to their rooms.

The rest of them went in to dinner, where they were joined by two of Rule's brothers—Maximilian, the heir apparent, who'd come up from his villa to meet Rule's bride, and Alexander, the one who'd been a prisoner in Afghanistan.

Sydney liked Maximilian from the first. He was almost as handsome as Rule and he seemed to her to be a kind man, and very charismatic. He had sad eyes, though. She remembered what Rule had told her, about Max losing his wife in a water-skiing accident, and wondered if he was still grieving the loss.

It was difficult to like Alex. He was darkly handsome like the rest of the family, but more powerfully built and very quiet. He seemed…angry. Or perhaps sunk in some deep depression. Sydney supposed his attitude wasn't all that surprising. She imagined that being kept prisoner by terrorists would give anyone a bad attitude. But she could easily see why he and Princess Lili didn't get along. Sydney doubted that Alex got along with anyone.

Rule's other brother, Alex's twin, Damien, was something of a jet-setter. He was off on a friend's yacht. Two of his sisters, the youngest and second-youngest, Rory and Genevra, were away at school. Alice and Rhiannon were at an event in Luxembourg. And the oldest sister, Arabella, had gone to Paris. When they were home from school, Rory and Genevra still lived at the palace. The three older sisters had their own villas.

Dinner was several courses. The food was delicious. There was wine. Excellent French wine. As she'd done since she first suspected she might be pregnant, Sydney took care to drink very little of it.

Later, back in their own apartment, she and Rule celebrated her move to Montedoro by making love—twice. Once, while standing up against the tall, beautifully carved bedroom doors. Very well hung, those doors, she'd teased, as he was moving so deliciously inside her. Those doors didn't rattle once no matter how enthusiastic they became.

Eventually, they got into bed, where they made love the second time. It was after that second time, when she lay tucked close against him, that she told him, "Your mother says there's a large library here at the palace. A lot of books on Montedoran history. She also says the palace librarian can answer just about any question I might have about your country."

He stroked her arm in an idle, thoroughly distracting way. "Going to become a Montedoran scholar, are you?"

"I need to catch up, to understand how things work here, so I can begin to consider the kind of work I want to do, to discover where and how I can be most useful to my new country."

"So ambitious." He said it admiringly as he caressed her breast.

"You know I lose IQ points when you do that..."

He covered her breast with his warm hand. "I love your breasts."

"Good. You'll be seeing a lot of them as the years go by."

He caught her nipple between his fingers and squeezed. She sighed. He said, in a gentle, careful voice, "I believe they are fuller than they used to be."

It was the perfect opportunity to tell him that there was

a reason her breasts were bigger: she was having his baby. But instead, she elbowed him in the ribs. "Oh. You like them because they're *bigger*."

He nuzzled her hair. "*Are* they bigger?"

She got up on one elbow, where she could see his eyes. "Yes." She knew then. She could see it in his face, in the breathless way he looked at her. *He* knew already. She gave him a teasing smile. "My breasts are bigger. It's a miracle."

He asked, almost shyly, "Sydney…is it possible that you…?"

She smiled even wider. "That I *what,* Rule?"

"Don't tease me. Please." His eyes had gone dark as the middle of the night. It was a soft, yearning sort of darkness. He really, really wanted to know.

And her heart just…expanded. It felt suddenly twice as big as a moment before, as if it were pushing at her ribs, trying to make more room inside her chest. "I think so," she whispered. "I think we're going to have a baby."

He held her gaze, steadily, surely. "You *think?*"

"All the signs are there. The same ones I had with Trev. And my period is almost three weeks late. I haven't taken the home test I bought yet, though."

He touched her chin, brushed his thumb across her lips. "When will you take it?"

She smiled against his touch. "How about tomorrow morning?"

"Sydney…"

"What?"

"That's all. Just Sydney. Sydney, Sydney, Sydney…" He took her shoulders and pulled her close so he could kiss her. A long kiss, so tender. So thorough. So right.

She settled back onto his chest again, her chin on her arms. "So. You're happy?"

He stroked her hair. "I am. I can't tell you how happy."

"You're a good father. Trev is crazy about you."

He smoothed her hair, guided it behind her ear. "Trevor is everything I ever wanted in a son. And you are everything I ever dreamed of in a wife."

She remembered his mother's reaction at her first sight of Trev and smiled to herself. "Did you see how surprised your mother was when she met Trev? I'm guessing she noticed the uncanny resemblance between you two."

His hand stilled on her hair. "What makes you think that?"

Had something changed in his eyes?

She asked herself the question—and then decided it was nothing. He was stroking her hair again, regarding her so tenderly. She said, "I thought she looked pretty stunned when she saw him—you didn't notice the look on her face?"

"Hmm. Yes, I suppose…"

She asked, "Did you see it, or didn't you?" At his shrug, she frowned. "It was only there for a second and then gone. I guess I might have imagined it…."

He framed her face between his hands. "Come here. Kiss me."

She pretended to consider. "Well, now. That's a pretty tempting offer."

"Come here. Let me show you *how* tempting…."

She lifted up over him and then, with a happy sigh, settled her mouth on his. He was right. The kiss tempted her to kiss him some more.

Kisses led to more caresses and they made love again. Slowly. Beautifully.

She gazed up at his unforgettable face above her and thought how it just kept getting better between them. How there was nothing, ever, that could tear them apart.

* * *

An hour later, Rule lay in the dark staring up at the ceiling, listening to his wife's even, relaxed breathing beside him.

His pregnant wife...

He was sure of it. And so was she. The test in the morning was only a formality. She was having his baby.

His *second* baby.

And yes. He'd seen that look on his mother's face, too.

His mother had known that Trevor was his. One look at the boy and she'd had no doubt.

Very soon now, Her Sovereign Highness would be summoning him for a private talk. She was going to want to discuss the startling resemblance between him and his supposed stepson.

She would also be going after his father, working on the poor man. She would be insisting that her Prince Consort tell her the truth if he knew *anything* about what was really going on with Rule and his new wife and the child who was the mirror image of Rule at that age. One way or another, Adrienne would get to the bottom of it.

And as soon as she knew the truth, she was going to be after Rule to come clean with his wife. His mother was as much about integrity and truth in life and marriage as his wife was.

Rule felt the day of reckoning approaching. He had everything now: the woman he'd almost given up on finding; a healthy, happy, perfect son—and a second child on the way.

The only real question was how much he was going to lose when Sydney finally learned the truth.

Sydney's hands were shaking.

She turned her back to the test wand she'd left on the

corner of the serpentine marble counter and held both hands out in front of her. Yep. Her fingers trembled like leaves in the wind.

"Silly," she whispered. "So silly..." With a low moan, she lifted her hands and covered her face with them.

Really, there was no reason she should be such a bundle of nerves over this. She was either pregnant or not—and she just knew that she *was*. In a moment, the timer would go off and she would have proof.

No reason to be freaked out over it. No reason at all.

Rule tapped on the bathroom door. "Sydney? Are you all right in there?" As if in response to his question, the timer she'd set on the marble enclosure around the ginormous sunken tub started beeping. "Sydney! Are you all right?"

She went over and flipped the switch on the timer. It fell blessedly silent.

Rule didn't. "Sydney, my God!" He pounded on the door.

She whirled, stalked to the door, twisted the lock and flung it wide. He stood there looking fabulous, wearing nothing but a worried expression. Through clenched teeth she informed him, "I am *fine*. Get it? Fine."

He held out his arms.

With a cry, she threw herself into them, wrapped her arms around his lean bare waist and held on tight. She buried her face against his beautiful hard chest. "It's time," she said into that wonderful trail of hair that started between his perfect pectoral muscles and went on down, all the way to heaven. "I can't look."

"Sydney..." He said her name in that special way that only he could, so tenderly, so reassuringly. He stroked her back and then he took her chin and tipped it up. His dark eyes were waiting. "We both know what the test will say." He brushed a kiss across her lips.

Her mouth trembled. Sheesh. She was a trembling fool. She bit her lower lip to make it stop and then she said, "I *know* we both know. But what if we're wrong?"

He drew in a slow breath and dared to suggest, "Only one way to find out."

She shoved her face into his chest again, feeling like Trevor, the day before, clinging to his precious *Roo* upon meeting his new grandparents. "*You* look. I can't do it."

He chuckled. Oh, wasn't that just like a man? To chuckle at a time like this. He chuckled, and then he kissed the top of her head and then he gently took hold of her arms. "You will have to release me if you want me to be the one to look."

Reluctantly, with another soft cry, she let go of him and stepped out of his way. "Do it. Now."

He indicated the wand on the edge of the marble sink counter and slanted her a questioning glance.

She nodded.

He went to it, picked it up, frowned at it.

What? Suddenly, he couldn't read? She said, "The little window, it either says 'pregnant' or 'not pregnant.'"

He made a big show of squinting at the wand. "Well, now, let's see here..."

"I am going to grab that thing and hit you on the head with it. Just see if I don't."

He waved his free hand in a shushing kind of gesture. "All right, all right. It says... Well, what do you know? It says..."

"Rule. Stop it. I mean it. You stop it right now."

And then he dropped the wand in the sink, turned and grabbed her, lifting her high, spinning her around. She squealed and then she laughed. And then he was letting her down, slowly, the short silk nightie she wore catching, riding up, leaving her bare from the waist down. Her feet touched the floor toes-first.

Finally, he leaned close and whispered in her ear, "Pregnant."

Pregnant. The magic word.

She threw her arms around him. "Oh, I can't believe it. It's true. It's really true. We're having a baby. We really, really are. How amazing is that?"

"Extremely amazing," he agreed.

And then he scooped her high in his arms and carried her back to the bed where they celebrated the positive test result in their favorite way.

Later, Sydney asked Rule if he would mind keeping the news about the baby to themselves for a while. She was only a few weeks along, after all. No one else needed to know for another month or so, did they? She wanted a little time to have it be just between the two of them.

He kissed her. "However you want it."

"You're so easy."

"For you, anything," he told her. And he meant it.

He was feeling so good—about their life together, about the new baby, about everything—that he almost succeeded in forgetting his dread of the eventual moment of truth concerning Trevor.

And as that day went by and the one after that and his mother failed to invite him to a private audience, his dread diminished even further. For whatever reason, it appeared that his mother was not going to call him to task on the subject of his look-alike "stepson." Perhaps she'd decided that the similarity was merely a coincidence. Or perhaps she simply didn't wish to interfere.

Or possibly, she had come to the conclusion that when

Rule was ready to talk about it with her, he would. Whatever her rationale on the subject, she was staying out of it.

Rule was grateful. And relieved.

That first Tuesday, they got through the press conference where they formally announced their marriage to the press, though by then, their marriage was old news in the fast-moving world of the scandal sheets. Wednesday, they visited with the archbishop of Montedoro to request a wedding in the church. The archbishop was only too happy to help speed up the process. They took their expedited marriage classes on Thursday and Friday and then, quickly and quietly, on the Saturday after Rule moved his new family to Montedoro, he and Sydney were married in the church.

Rule had three days of meetings in Paris that next week. Sydney, Lani and Trevor stayed in Montedoro, where Sydney and his mother spent some time alone, getting to know each other a little. In bed the night of his return from France, Sydney said that his mother had asked her about Trevor's father.

Rule kept his voice light and easy. "And what did you tell her?"

"The truth, of course. That I wanted a family and I didn't have a man and so I went to a sperm bank. She took it well, I think. She smiled and said what a determined woman I am."

"And you are." He kissed her. She kissed him back. Nature took its course from there.

The next day, Liliana returned to Montedoro for a brief visit at HSH Adrienne's invitation. Sydney got to meet her. The two hit it off—the delicate Alagonian princess and Rule's tall, brilliant and determined American bride. Rule wasn't really all that surprised that they got along. They were both good women with tender hearts.

It was the same with his sisters. Sydney liked them all and the sentiment was mutual.

Rule and Sydney began to talk of a more private life. Sydney said she would prefer to live in their own house by the time the new baby came. So they engaged an architect to renovate Rule's nearby villa, modernizing and enlarging it to make it more comfortable for their growing family.

He and Sydney were so happy. He never wanted to do anything to hurt her, or to damage what they had together. In fact, sometimes he found himself wondering why, realistically, she even needed to know that he was actually Trevor's father.

Why *should* she know? What good could the truth possibly do her—or anyone—now? He had found her and his son and he had made things right for all of them. To tell her now would only upset her and drive a wedge between the two of them. It would threaten, and might even destroy, what they had as a family.

Rule's father would keep his secret, especially if his mother wasn't pushing to know more. And sometimes the wisest course was to do nothing, to leave a perfectly wonderful situation alone. He decided he would do just that.

And then he would realize how despicable that was. He should have told her at the first. It was information she had every right to know.

He should tell her now. Today.

But then, somehow, the moment was never right. Another day would go by.

Soon, he would promise himself.

He would tell her soon.

But he didn't tell her. And every day he said nothing, it only got harder to imagine being truthful. Every moment that went by in which he kept his silence, he was more and more deeply mired in the lie, more and more convinced that his silence was the best thing for everyone.

And then, on the last Wednesday in May, the truth finally caught up with him.

Chapter Twelve

It happened in the morning two weeks and five days after Rule brought his new family to Montedoro.

Caroline was waiting for him when he entered his office at the palace. She held a tabloid newspaper in her hand.

"Sir," said his secretary, her expression carefully neutral, "a particularly annoying article has appeared in *The International Sun*." *The Sun* was a London-based paper. A weekly, it claimed to deliver news. And it did. News on such burning issues of the day as which celebrity was heading for rehab again and which film star was having a torrid affair with His Grace, the very married Duke of So-and-So. "I thought I should bring it to your attention right away." It was one of Caroline's duties to keep up with both the legitimate news of the day and the scandal sheets. She made certain Rule knew of any and all information that appeared in print about him, his country, his business dealings and/or the people who mattered to him.

Usually, she simply left the various publications on the credenza, having red-flagged articles that she thought required particular attention. Her choosing to hand this one to him personally did not bode well.

"Thank you, Caroline."

With a nod and a murmured, "Sir," she left him, quietly closing the door behind her.

Circling around behind his desk, he dropped into his chair. Aware of a terrible, crushing sensation of dread, he spread the paper on the leather desk pad before him. For a time, he stared furiously down at it, as if by glaring at it long enough, he could somehow make the words and the pictures rearrange themselves into something else, something that had nothing to do with him or his family.

But no matter how long and hard he stared, what was printed on the front page didn't change.

The headline read, Stepchild—Or Love Child?

There were several pictures of him—by himself and holding Trevor, pictures of him holding Trevor with Sydney beside him, pictures of him at the same age as Trevor. Since the resemblance between Rule and Trevor really was so strong, the pictures themselves told a very clear story. Anyone glancing at them would say that Rule must be Trevor's biological father—or at the very least, a close relation.

The article itself was a total fabrication. It proposed that he and Sydney had earlier enjoyed a "torrid secret affair." When it ended, she was pregnant with his child. And he had walked out on her, left her to "have his baby alone," because he felt duty bound to marry in "the aristocracy of Europe."

But then, "as fate would have it," he'd been unable to forget the one woman who "held his heart." After more than two years had gone by, the "handsome prince" had at last realized that his child and his true love "mattered more than royal blood." He'd returned to claim the woman he'd "always loved" and the child he'd "left behind."

There was even a long explanation of how Sydney had "put it out" that her child was the result of artificial insemination. But *The International Sun* wasn't fooled and neither should its readership be.

"A picture is worth a thousand words." And the pictures showed clearly that the child in question was Prince Rule's. At least the prince had "done the right thing" in the end and married the mother of his child. Since "all was well that ended well," *The Sun* wished the prince and his newfound family a lifetime of happiness.

It was ugly, stupid, insulting and riddled with clichés. Not to mention mostly fiction. However, within the general ridiculousness lurked the all-important twin kernels of truth: that Trevor was in fact Rule's child. And that Sydney really had used a sperm bank.

And that was why deciding what to do in response to this absurd flight of pseudo-literary fantasy was of the utmost importance. Really, anything he did—from making no statement, to issuing an outraged denial, to suing the paper for slander—could make things worse. And no matter what he did next, some ambitious and resourceful reporter might decide to dig deeper. It was possible that someone, somehow, could unearth the fact that he'd been a donor at Secure Choice. If that happened, and he still hadn't told Sydney his secret…

No. He couldn't allow even the possibility that it might go that far.

He was going to have to tell her. Now. Today. And when he did, she was going to be angry with him. More than angry. She might never forgive him. But if she found out in the tabloids, the likelihood was exponentially greater that he would lose her forever.

Rule shoved the tabloid aside, braced his elbows on the desk pad and put his head in his hands. He should have told her by now, should have told her weeks ago. Should have told her at the first....

Should have told her...

How many times had he reminded himself of that? A hundred? Five hundred?

And any one of those times, he *could* have told her.

Yes, it would have been bad.

But not as bad as it was going to be now.

He'd made his choice—the wrong choice—a hundred, five hundred, a thousand times. He'd wagered their happiness on that choice. He should have known better than that. Wagers were not a good idea—not when it came to the things that mattered most.

Half an hour later, Rule and his father met in Evan's private office. Also in the meeting were Donahue Villiers, a family advocate, or legal advisor, and Leticia Sprague, Palace Press Secretary. Leticia had been a trusted member of the palace staff for over twenty years.

They discussed what their next move should be and decided that Donahue would be in contact with the paper's legal department to discuss the lawsuit the family intended to file. He would also demand that the paper print a full retraction which, he would assure them, would go a long way toward mollifying Prince Rule once a settlement for damages was under discussion. Leticia suggested that Rule release a statement wherein he refuted the story and made his outrage at such ridiculous allegations crystal clear.

Rule's father said, "Before we proceed with any of this,

there must be a *family* conference. Her Sovereign Highness must be brought up to speed and given the opportunity to make her wishes in the matter known. So, of course, must Sydney."

And that was it. The meeting ended. Leticia and Donahue left Rule and his father alone.

Rule and Evan exchanged a long, bleak glance.

And then Evan said, "It's not the end of the world, son."

Rule started to speak.

Evan put up a hand. "You will get through this—with your family intact. And you *could* look on the bright side."

Rule made a scoffing sound. "So unfortunate that there isn't one."

"Of course there is. The article is absurd. *The International Sun* is going to end up looking very bad."

"It's a tabloid. It's not as though they care if they look bad."

His father regarded him solemnly for a moment. "What you did, becoming a donor, you did in a good cause. With an honest heart."

"I was an idiot. It was an act of rebellion against everything I am, everything we stand for as Bravo-Calabrettis."

Patiently, his father continued, "You would never have found the wife you wanted if not for your 'act of rebellion.' There would be no Trevor. And that you finally arranged to meet Sydney, that you pursued her and convinced her to make a family with you, that you became a real father to your son...I find that not only admirable, but truly honorable."

Rule wanted to grab the crystal paperweight from the corner of his father's desk and smash it against the far wall. "You don't understand. Sydney still doesn't know. I still haven't told her."

"Then you *will* tell her. Right away."

"I could lose her over this."

"I don't think you will. She loves you. She will stick by you."

Rule said nothing to that. What was there to say? Evan had been for honesty with Sydney from the first. His father wouldn't rub it in. That wasn't Evan's way. But the knowledge that his father had been right all along made this unpleasant discussion doubly difficult.

Evan said, "I think it's time that you told your mother the truth."

Rule gave him a scowl. "Wonderful."

His father said gently, "You can't put it off any longer. One look at that child and your mother was certain he had to be yours. She asked me what *I* knew. I told her that you had taken me into your confidence and gotten my agreement that I would keep your secret. I said that if she demanded it, I would tell her everything, I would break my word to you."

Rule affected an American accent. "Gee, thanks, Dad."

His father's chuckle had little humor in it. "Once she saw Trevor, I couldn't have kept her in the dark if she needed to know. She rules my heart as she rules this land. Maybe that's beyond your understanding."

Rule thought of Sydney. "No. I understand. I do."

"As it turned out, I didn't have to break my word to you. Your mother said that I should keep your secret for you, that she preferred to respect your wishes in the matter."

"So she only knows that Trevor is mine."

"As I said, I never told her the truth outright. She has drawn her own conclusions and kept them to herself. It's time that you were honest with her."

"I have to tell Sydney first."

"Of course you do."

* * *

Sydney wasn't in their apartment when Rule entered a few minutes later, the offending tabloid rolled in his hand. Lani told him that she'd gone to the palace library and would return by eleven.

It was ten forty-five.

Trevor tugged on his trouser leg. "Roo. Come. Play..."

His heart like a large ball of lead in his chest, he got down on the floor with his son, set the rolled paper to the side and helped him build a fanciful machine with a set of connectable plastic wheels and gears.

Trevor glanced up, a plastic propeller in his hand. "See, Roo. 'Peller." He stuck the propeller on a bright-colored stick and blew on it. Then he chortled in delight as it spun. Rule tried to laugh with him, but didn't succeed. Trevor bent to fiddle with the wheels and cogs some more, leaving Rule to stare down longingly at his dark head. Rule wanted to grab him and hold him close and never, ever let him go, as if by clutching his son tight, he might somehow escape the impending moment of truth.

But there was no escape. He was done with this lie.

It wasn't long before he heard brisk footsteps approaching from the foyer. And then Sydney was there, laughing, asking Lani how many pages she'd written.

"Three paragraphs," Lani grumbled, pushing her glasses higher on her nose. "It's just not coming together."

"It will," Sydney reassured her friend. "It always does."

"Yeah, well. I hope you're right."

"Persistence is the key."

Lani grumbled something else. Rule didn't make out the words over the rushing of his own blood in his ears as Sydney's footsteps came closer.

She stood above them. "What kind of fantastical machine is this?"

For a moment, Rule stared at her pretty open-toed shoes, her trim ankles. Then, forcing his mouth to form a smile, he lifted his head to meet her eyes. "You'll have to ask your son."

Trev glanced up. "Hi, Mama. I make a machine, a machine with a 'peller."

"I see that and I…" Her glance had shifted. Rule followed her gaze. The paper beside him had opened halfway, revealing the outrageous headline and half of the pictures. "What in the…?"

He grabbed the paper and swiftly rolled it up again. "We need a few moments in private, I think."

Both of her eyebrows lifted. And then she nodded. "Well, I guess we do."

Trev sat looking from Rule to Sydney and back again, puzzled by whatever was going on between the grown-ups. "Mama? Roo?"

Rule laid a hand against his son's cheek. "Trevor," he said, with all the calm and gentleness he could muster. "Mama and I have to talk now."

Trev blinked. "Talk?" He frowned. And then he announced, "Okay. I build machine!"

Lani put her laptop aside. "C'mon, Trev." She jumped up from the sofa and came to stand over them. "How 'bout a snack?" She reached down and lifted him into her arms.

Trevor perked up. "I want graham crackers and milk. In the *big* kitchen." He loved going down to the palace kitchens where the chefs and prep staff doted on him.

"Graham crackers and milk in the big kitchen it shall be."

"Thank you." Rule forced a smile for Lani as he rose from the floor.

With a quick nod, Lani carried Trevor to the door. He heard it close behind her.

He and Sydney were alone in the apartment.

She said, "Well?"

He handed her the tabloid.

She opened it and let out a throaty sound of disbelief. "Please. They have got to be kidding."

"Sydney, I—"

She put up a hand. "Give me a minute. Let me read this garbage."

So they stood there, on either side of Trevor's pile of bright plastic wheels and cogs, as she read the damned thing through. She was a quick study. It didn't take her long.

Finally, in disgust, she tossed the paper to the floor again. "That is the most outrageous bunch of crap I've ever read. Do you believe it? The nerve of those people. We're suing, right?"

"I believe that is the plan."

"You *believe?* It's a pack of lies. Not a single shred of truth in the whole disgusting thing."

"Well, and that's the problem, actually. There *is* some truth in it. More than a shred."

"What are you talking about?" She regarded him sideways. "Rule, what's wrong?"

He gulped—like a guilty child caught stealing chocolates. "There's something I really must tell you."

"What?" She was starting to look frightened. "Rule. *What?*"

"You should...sit down, I think." He tried to take her arm.

She eased free of his grip. "Okay. You're scaring me. Whatever it is, you need to just go ahead and say it."

"I will, of course. It's important and I should have told you long ago, right at the first."

"Rule." Now she was the one reaching for him. She took

hold of both of his arms and she looked him squarely in the eye. "Tell me. Whatever it is, tell me right now."

Was there any way to do this gently? He couldn't think of one. So he went ahead and just said it outright. "I was a donor for Secure Choice Cryobank. It was my profile you chose. Trevor is my son."

Chapter Thirteen

She still clutched his arms, her fingers digging in. Her face had gone chalk-white. "No," she whispered.

"Sydney, I—"

She let go of him, jumped away as though she couldn't bear to touch him. "No." She put her hands to her mouth, shook her head slowly. "No, no, no. You never said. Ever. I asked you, I asked you directly…" She whispered the words. But to him, that whisper was as loud as a shout. As a scream.

"I know. I lied. Sydney, if we could just—"

"No." She shook her head some more. "No." And then she whirled on her heel and she marched over to the sofa where Lani had been sitting. Carefully, she picked up the laptop and set it on the low table in front of her. Then she sat down. "Here." She pointed at one of the wing chairs across from her. "Sit."

What else could he do? He went over there. He sat.

There was a silence.

They regarded each other across the low table, across a short distance that seemed to him endless. And absolutely uncrossable. He only had to look at her—the pale, locked-away face, the lightless eyes—to know the worst had happened.

He had lost her.

She asked in a carefully controlled voice, "So you did take my information from Secure Choice, after all?"

"I did, yes."

"Um. When?"

"Almost three years ago."

"When I was pregnant? You've known since then?"

"Yes. I knew from the first."

With another gasp, she put the back of her hand to her mouth. And then she seemed to catch herself. She let her hand drop to her lap. "All that time. You did nothing. And then, suddenly, out of nowhere, you were there. Lying to me, pretending it was all just a happy little accident, that you had happened to see me going into Macy's. That you were so very *intrigued* by my *determination*. But it wasn't an accident. Not an accident at all."

His throat clutched. He gulped to clear it. "No. It was no accident. I was following you that day." She pressed her fist to her stomach. *The baby.* He started to rise. "Sydney. Are you—?"

She stuck out her hand at him, palm flat. "No. Stay there. Don't you dare get up. Don't you come near me."

"But you—"

"I am not ill. I am...there are no words, Rule. You know that, don't you? No words. None."

He sank back to the chair, said the only thing he *could* say. "I know."

"Why now? I don't get it. After all the times you might

have said it, might have come clean about it, why now?" And then she blinked. He watched comprehension dawn in her eyes. "That stupid article. The pictures. You and Trevor, so much alike. It even mentions that I 'claim' to have used a sperm donor. You're afraid someone might do more digging, and reach the truth. You couldn't *afford* to keep me in the dark any longer."

What could he give her but shamefaced confirmation? "Yes. That's right."

"Oh, Rule. I thought it was bad, when you had to rush back here to Montedoro to explain yourself to Lili the morning after our wedding. I was…disappointed in you then. But I told myself that you had never lied to me. That you were a truly honest man, that you didn't have a lying bone in your body…" Though her eyes were dry, a sob escaped her. She covered her mouth again for a moment, hard, with her palm that time, as though she could stuff that sob back inside. When she had control of herself, she lowered her hand and said, "What a fool I was. How could I have *been* such a fool? All the signs were there. I saw them, *knew* them. And still you convinced me not to believe the evidence of my own eyes."

"I wanted to tell you," he heard himself say, and then cursed the words for their weakness.

Her sweet, wide mouth curved in a sneer. "Then why *didn't* you tell me?"

He said it right out. "At the first? Because I knew I wouldn't have a chance with you if I did."

"You couldn't know that."

"Of course I knew. After your wonderful grandmother who taught you that honesty was everything. After those bastards, Ryan and Peter…"

She waved her hand that time, dismissing his excuses.

"If not at the beginning, why not that night I asked you directly if you'd ever been a donor?"

"We've been so happy. I didn't want to lose that, our happiness. I didn't want to lose *you*."

"Were you *ever* going to tell me?" Her voice was furious and hopeful, both at the same time.

He longed to reassure her. To give her more lies. But he couldn't. Some…line had been crossed. All that was left to him now was the brutal truth. "I don't think so. I kept telling myself I would, but there was always an excuse, to wait a little longer, to put it off. I kept choosing the excuses over telling you what you had a right to know."

"So, then." The hope was gone. Only her cool fury remained. "You were never going to tell me."

He refused to look away. "No. I wasn't willing to risk losing you."

"And how's that worked out for you, Rule?" Her sarcasm cut a ragged hole in his heart.

He answered without inflection. "As of now, I would have to say not very well."

She sat very still. She…watched him. For the longest, most terrible stretch of time. And then she said, "I don't get it. It makes no sense to me, that you would become a donor. Why did you? It's…not like you. Not like you at all."

"Does it matter now?"

"It matters to me. I am trying very hard to understand."

"Sydney, I—"

"Tell me." It was a command.

He obeyed. "My reasons were… They seemed real to me, seemed valid, at the time." How could he make her see when he still didn't completely understand it himself? He gave it his best shot. "I wanted…something. I wanted my life to be more than the sum of its parts. I wanted what my parents have together. What Max and Sophia had. It seemed I went through the motions of living but it wasn't a rich life. Not a full life. I enjoyed my work, but when I came home I wanted someone to come home to." He shook his head. "It makes no sense, does it?"

She was implacable. "Go on."

He tried again. "There were women. They were... strangers to me. I enjoyed having sex with them, but I didn't want them beyond the brief moments of pleasure they gave me in bed. I looked into their eyes and I didn't feel I would ever truly know them. Or they, me. I was alone. I had business, in Dallas. I spent over a year there."

"When?"

"Starting a little more than four years ago. I would go down to San Antonio on occasion, to visit with my family there. But it was empty, my life. I had only casual friends at that time. Looking back, I can't remember a single connection I made that mattered to me other than in terms of my business. Except for one man. He turned up at a party I went to. We'd been at Princeton together. We...touched base. Talked about old times. He'd been a donor. He'd come from an American public school, was at Princeton on full scholarship. He became a donor partly for the money—which, he told me, laughing, wasn't really much at all. But also because he said it did his heart good. It felt right, he said. To help a couple who had everything but the child they wanted most. That struck a chord with me. It seemed that being a donor would be...something good, that I could do, something I could give—but you're right. It wasn't like me. I'm a Bravo-Calabretti all the way to the core. I just refused to see that until it was too late and my profile was available to clients. Until two women had chosen me as their donor."

Those lightless eyes widened. "*Two* women?"

"The other didn't become pregnant. By the time she ordered again, I'd had my profile taken down."

"Just two of us? But...I can't believe more women wouldn't have chosen you."

Under other circumstances, he might have laughed. "My profile was only available for a short period of time. I withdrew my samples when I realized what an idiot I'd been to become a donor in the first place. Secure Choice was not the least happy with me. Our agreement was for ten pregnancies resulting in births or nine months of availability. I made arrangements to reimburse them for the money they would have made if I'd fulfilled my commitment with them. In the end, I simply couldn't...let it go. And that's the basic job of a donor. To *donate* and let it go."

She continued for him. "But that was never going to work for you, was it? You realized that you *had* to know—if there were children, if they were all right..." She understood him so well.

He said softly, "Yes. And that was my plan, after I found out that you had become pregnant. That was all I ever intended to do, make certain that you and the child were provided for. I swear it to you. As long as you and Trevor were all right, I was never going to contact you or interfere in your life in any way. I had assured myself that you were a fine mother *and* an excellent provider. I knew Trevor was healthy. I knew you would do all in your considerable power to make certain he had a good start in life."

"Yes. I could give him everything—except a father."

It was her first misreading of his motives. He corrected her. "I didn't think of it that way. I swear that I didn't."

She crossed her long, slim legs, folded her hands tightly

in her lap and accused, "Oh, please. You are all about being a father. We both know that."

Her words hit him like blows.

They were much too true.

And they proved all over again what a hopeless idiot he'd been to become a donor in the first place, how little he'd understood his own mind and heart.

"All right," he said. "I'm guilty. Guilty in a hundred ways. It *is* important to me. That my child have a father."

"So you set out to see that he did."

He felt, somehow, like a bug on a pin under the cool regard of those watchful eyes of hers. And in the back of his mind a cruel voice would not stop whispering, *You have lost her. She will leave you. She will leave you now.* Somehow, no matter what happened, he had to make her see the most basic motivation for his actions concerning her. "No. I swear to you, Sydney. It wasn't...that way. It was *you.*"

"Oh, please."

He repeated, insisted, "*You.* It was you. Yes, Trevor mattered. He mattered more than I can say. But *you* were the starting point. I pursued *you,* not my son. I lied, yes, by omission. I never told you why I happened to be in that parking lot outside of Macy's that first day we met. That it was because of you that I was there, in the first place. Because you fascinated me. So bright and capable. So successful. And apparently, so determined to have a family, with or without a man at your side. I told myself I only wanted to see you in the flesh, just one time. That once I'd done that, I could let you go, let Trevor go. Return here to Montedoro, make my proposal to Lili..."

"You were lying to *yourself.*"

"Yes. The sight of you that first time, getting out of your car in the parking garage...the sight of you only made me realize I had to get closer, to see you face-to-face, to look in your eyes. To hear your voice, your laugh. I followed you into the store. And as soon as you granted me that adorable, disbelieving sideways glance while you pretended to read a price tag on a frying pan, I knew that there had to be more. Every word you spoke, every moment in your presence, it only got worse. Stronger. I swear to you, I didn't set out to seduce and marry you."

She made another of those low, scoffing sounds.

And he was the one putting up a hand. "Yes," he confessed, "it's what I did in the end. But it started with *you*. It was always about you. And by that first evening we spent together, when we had dinner at the Mansion, I knew I wanted you for my wife."

Her eyes were emerald-bright now. With tears.

The tears gave him new hope.

Hope she dashed by turning away and stealing a slow breath. When she faced him again, the tear-sheen was gone.

She said in the cold, logical voice of an accuser, "You had so many options. *Better* options than the ones you chose."

He didn't deny it. "I know. In hindsight, that's all so painfully clear."

"You could have asked to see me as soon as you managed to find out you'd been my donor. I *would* have seen you. I was as fascinated by the idea of you—of the man I had chosen as my donor—as you claim you were by me."

"As I *am* by you," he corrected. "And I had no reason to believe you would have been happy to see me. It seemed to me that the last thing a single mother really wants is a visit from a stranger who might try to lay a claim on her child."

"I had given permission for you to contact me. That should have been enough for you to have taken a chance."

"Yes. I see that, now that I know you. But I didn't know you then. I didn't know how you would react. And it seemed wrong for me to…interfere in your life."

"If you had sought me out at the beginning, you would have had more than two years until the marriage law went into effect. We would have had the time to get through all this garbage. *You* would have had time for the truth."

"Sydney, I know that. I see that now. But it's not what I did. Yes, I should have been braver. I should have been… truer. I should have taken a chance, arranged to meet with you early on. But I hesitated. I hesitated much too long. I see that. And by the time I acted, I was down to the wire."

"Wire or not," she said, refusing to give him an inch, as he'd known that she would, "you owed it to me to tell me the truth before you asked me to marry you. You owed that to me then, at the very least."

"I know that. We've already been through that. But by then there was all you had told me about how you valued honesty."

"So you should have been honest."

"And what about Ryan and Peter? What about your distrust of men? You would have assumed right away that I was only after Trevor."

She looked at him unwavering. "Telling me the truth was the right thing to do."

"Yes. And then I would have lost you. You were not about to give a third man the benefit of the doubt. It was too big a risk. We were getting along so beautifully. I couldn't stand to lose you when I'd only just found you. Are you going to deny that I *would* have lost you?"

"No. You're right. At that time, I…didn't know you well enough. I would have broken it off for a while, slowed things down between us. I would have needed more time to learn to trust you."

"You would have needed longer than I could afford."

She made a low sound. "Because of the Prince's Marriage Law."

"Yes."

"You're telling me you were trapped." She spoke with disdain.

"No. I'm telling you that I knew what I wanted, at last. After all the years of being so sure I would never find it, find *you*. I wanted you. I wanted our child. And I wanted my inheritance, too. I made choices to give myself— and us—the best chance that we could both get what we wanted."

"And you kept making choices. Kept making the *same* choice. To lie to me. Over and over and over again. Since our marriage, I can't even count the times when you could have made a different choice."

"I know it. And we're back to the beginning again. Back to where I remind you that we have been so happy, and that telling you the truth would have destroyed our happiness, back to where I say I did what I did because I couldn't bear to lose you."

She stood up. And then, looking down at him, she said, "In making the choice to lie to me, you stole *my* choices. You treated me like a child, someone not fully responsible, someone unable to deal with the facts and make reasonable decisions based on all the available information. For generations, men did that to women, treated them as incompetent, as unable to face reality and make rational choices. Treated them as possessions rather than thinking human beings. I will not be treated as your possession, Rule, no matter how prized. Do you understand?"

He did understand. And at that point, there was nothing left for him but to admit the wrong he'd done her—done them both—and pay the price for it. "Yes. I understand."

"It matters. That you believe in me. That you trust me. That you treat me as your equal."

"And I see that," he said. "I do."

"But given the same set of circumstances, you would lie to me all over again—don't you tell me that you wouldn't."

He wanted to deny it. But somehow, he couldn't. And his denial wouldn't matter anyway. He couldn't undo what he'd done. What mattered now was that, no matter what the circumstances, he wouldn't lie to her again. "I simply didn't want to lose you. That's all. I lied because I was certain the truth would cost me what we have together. And now, you can be assured I see that I made the wrong choice. I swear I'll never lie to you again." Her face was set against him. He shook his head. "But then, I look at you and I see that it doesn't matter what I promise you. I see in your eyes that I'm going to lose you anyway."

Her cold expression changed. She looked...puzzled. And also disbelieving. And then she actually rolled her eyes. "Of course you're not going to lose me, Rule."

He gaped at her, convinced he couldn't have heard her right. "What did you just say?"

"I said you're not going to lose me. I would never leave you. I'm your wife and I love you more than my life. But I am not the least happy with you. And I'm not going to hide how I feel about this, or pretend to get past it when I'm *not* past it. You may end up wishing that I *would* go."

"My God," he said, hope rekindled, catching fire. "I would never wish for you to go. You have to know that."

"We'll see."

He rose. His arms ached to reach for her. But her expression signaled all too clearly the reception he would get if he tried. "I want our marriage," he said, and longed to give her words back to her. *I love you more than my life.* But it seemed wrong to speak of his love now, wrong and cheap. So instead, he said, "I want only you, always. That isn't going to change, no matter what you do, no matter how angry you are at me."

"We'll see," she said again. And for a moment, he saw the sadness in her eyes. Men had disappointed her before. And now he was just like the others.

Except he wasn't. He refused to be.

Whatever it took, he would be more, better, than he had been until now. Whatever the cost, he would win back her trust again and reclaim his right to stand at her side.

She was watching him, assessing him. "How much do your parents know?"

"My father knows everything. I confided in him. But my mother knows nothing—beyond being certain that Trevor is my son as well as yours."

"You told her?"

"No. She guessed that he was mine the moment she saw him. She asked my father what he knew. He offered to betray my confidence and tell her everything. She didn't think that would be right, so she declined his offer to break his word to me."

"I do like your mother."

"Yes," he said dryly. "Like you, she is thoroughly admirable—and you remind me I need to speak with her."

She indicated the tabloid she'd tossed to the floor and asked him wearily, "About all this?"

He nodded. "By now, she'll have had her morning look at the newspapers, including *The Sun.* I have to go to her and explain."

Sydney said, "We'll go together."

It was more than he'd hoped for. Much more. "Are you sure?"

"I'll just leave a note for Lani."

They met with his mother in the apartments she shared with his father. It was just the four of them—Adrienne, Evan, Rule and Sydney.

Rule told the whole story all over again. His mother's face remained unreadable throughout.

When he was done at last, she turned to Sydney. "I am so sorry that my son misled you."

Sydney replied with a slow nod. "Yes. I am, too."

Rule stared straight ahead. He felt like the bad child in school, sent to the corner to sit on a stool facing the wall and contemplate the terrible extent of his transgressions.

His mother said, "All right. Where are we now in terms of dealing with *The International Sun* and their absurd pack of lies?"

His father outlined the brief earlier meeting with Leticia and Donahue, concluding with, "To start, at least, Donahue will demand a retraction."

His mother looked at Rule, at Sydney, and then at Rule again. "Would a retraction satisfy you two?"

Satisfy me? Rule thought. Hardly. What would satisfy him was to have his wife once again look at him with affection and desire, to have her forgiveness. "That would be fine," he said, not caring in the least anymore about the damned tabloid story.

"It's *not* fine with me," Sydney said.

He glanced at her, took in the tightness of her mouth, the spots of hectic color high on her cheeks. She was as furious at the tabloid as she was at him. It hurt him, to look at her. It made him yearn for the feel of her skin under his hand, for the pleasure of simply holding her. Despair dragged at him. She'd said she wouldn't leave him.

But how long would it be before she allowed him to hold her again?

Sydney went on, "The retraction, yes. Absolutely. They should *start* with a retraction. And then we should sue their asses off."

"Their asses," his mother repeated, exchanging a glance with his father. "I do admire your enthusiasm, Sydney."

"It's an outrage." Sydney pressed her lips more tightly together. She blew out a hard breath through her nose.

His mother said, "I agree. And we will have a retraction."

"It's not enough," Sydney insisted. "That article is a gross misrepresentation of Rule's integrity, of his character. Rule would never simply walk away and desert a woman who was pregnant with his child. Never."

Rule realized he was gaping at her again. He couldn't help it. She astonished him. As infuriated as she was at him, she still defended him. He reminded her gently, "Sydney. It's just a silly tabloid story. It doesn't matter."

Her eyes were green fire. "Of course it matters. It's a lie. And they deserve to have their noses rubbed in it. I think we should hold a press conference and tell the world what liars they are. I think we need to tell the world the truth."

Tell the world the truth. She couldn't be serious.

He said, with slow care, "You want me to tell the world that I was your sperm donor? That it took me more than two years to get up the nerve to approach you? That when I did, I didn't tell you I was your child's father, but instead seduced you and got you to marry me under false pretenses?"

"Yes," she said hotly. "That's what I want from you, Rule. I want you to tell the truth."

For the first time on that awful day, he felt his own anger rising. It was all coming much too clear. "You want to see me humiliated. And it's not enough for you that *The Sun* should make me look like a fool. You want to see me make a fool of *myself.*"

She sucked in a sharp breath and put her hand to her throat. "No. No, that's not it. That's not what I meant."

He told her icily, "Of course it's what you meant."

"Oh, Rule," she said softly after several seconds had passed. "You don't get it. You don't get it at all."

He said nothing. He had nothing to say.

Finally, his mother spoke softly. "Whatever action the two of you decide to take, you have our complete support. I can see this is something the two of you must work out between yourselves."

Chapter Fourteen

But Rule and Sydney didn't work it out. They returned to their apartment—together, but not speaking.

That night, Rule slept in the small bedroom off the master suite. He lay alone in bed in the darkness and realized he wasn't angry anymore.

He missed his anger.

It was a lot easier to be furious than it was to be ashamed.

Now his anger had left him, he could see that for Sydney it was as it had always been; it was about honesty. She saw that insane press conference of hers as a way to clear the air once and for all, to lay the truth bare for everyone to see. She saw it as a way to beat *The International Sun* at its own game. She was an American, an egalitarian to the core.

She didn't have generations of proud, aristocratic Calabretti ancestors behind her, staring down their formidable noses, appalled at the very idea that one of their own would even consider getting up in a public forum and explaining his shameful personal shortcomings to the world at large.

Such things were not done.

A Calabretti had more pride than that.

He had more pride than that. Too much pride. He could see that now.

He was not about to tell the world the unvarnished truth about his private life. Even if he'd behaved in an exemplary fashion, that would have been extraordinarily difficult for him.

But his behavior had not been exemplary. Far from it.

He'd been an imbecile. On any number of levels. And it just wasn't in him, to stand up and confess his own idiocy to the world.

The next day was as bad as the one before it. He and Sydney were polite with each other. Excruciatingly so. But they hardly spoke.

In his office, the phone rang off the hook. Every newspaper, every magazine, every radio and TV station wanted a few brief words with Prince Rule. He declined to speak with any of them.

And he stayed another night in the extra room. And then another after that.

The weekend went by. He spent time with his son. He and Sydney continued to speak to each other only when necessary.

Monday evening they had a meeting with Jacques Fournier, the architect they'd chosen, about the renovations at the villa. Sydney sent Rule an email about that on Monday afternoon.

An email. She was one room away, but she talked to him via email.

Do you want me to contact Fournier and tell him we won't be available tonight?

He zipped her off a one-word reply. Yes.

She didn't email back to update him on her conversation with Fournier. Just as well. He didn't really care if the architect was annoyed with them for backing out on him.

What he cared about was making things right with his wife. Unfortunately, he had no idea how to do that.

Or if he *did* have an idea, he had altogether too much pride to go through with it.

That evening, she surprised him.

She came and hovered in the doorway to his little room. Hope flared in him yet again, that this might mean she was ready to forgive him. But her face gave him nothing. She seemed a little nervous, maybe. But not like a woman on the verge of offering to mend a serious breach.

"I called Fournier," she said.

He set the book he'd been trying to read aside. "Thank you," he said stiffly.

"Fournier said it was fine, to call and reschedule when we were…ready." Her sweet mouth trembled.

He wanted to kiss the trembling away. But he stayed in the room's single chair, by the window. "All right."

"I'm sure he must know about that awful article…"

He shrugged. "He might."

"Not that it matters what the architect knows." She looked tired, he thought. There were dark smudges beneath her eyes. Was she having as much trouble sleeping as he was? "I… Oh, Rule…" She looked at him sadly. And pleadingly, too.

His heart beat faster. Hope, that thing that refused to die, rose up more strongly, tightening his throat, bringing him to his feet. "Sydney…"

And then she was flying at him and he was opening his

arms. She landed against his chest with a soft cry and he gathered her into him.

He held on tight.

And she was holding him, too, burying her face against his chest, sighing, whispering, "Rule. Oh, Rule…"

He lowered his lips to her fragrant hair, breathed in the longed-for scent of her. "Sydney. I'm so sorry. I can't tell you…"

"I know." She tipped her head back, met his waiting gaze.

Crying. She was crying, tears leaking from the corners of her eyes, leaving shining trails along her flushed cheeks.

"Don't cry." He caught her face between his hands, kissed the tear trails, tasted their salty wetness. "Don't cry…"

"I want…to make it right with us. But I don't know how to make it right."

He dared to kiss her lips—a quick kiss, and chaste. It felt wrong to do more. "You can't make it right. *I* have to do that."

She searched his face. "Please believe me. I didn't suggest that press conference to shame you. I swear that I didn't."

"I know. I see that now. Don't worry on that account. I understand."

"I'm…too proud, Rule. I know that I am. Too proud and too difficult. Too demanding."

He almost laughed. "Too prickly."

"Yes, that, too. A kinder, gentler woman would be over this by now."

He kissed the tip of her nose. "I have no interest in a kinder, gentler woman. And you are not *too* anything. You are just right. I wouldn't want you to change. I wouldn't want you to be anyone other than exactly who you are, any way other than *as* you are."

"Oh, Rule…"

He took her shoulders and he set her gently away from him. "Can you forgive me?"

She shut her eyes, drew herself taller. And when she looked at him again, she wasn't smiling. "I'm working on it."

Strangely, he understood exactly what she was telling him. "But you aren't succeeding. You can't forgive me."

She pressed her lips together, shook her head—and started to speak.

He touched his thumb to her mouth. "Never mind. You don't have to answer. Let it be for now."

"I miss you so. It hurts so much."

Gruffly, he confessed, "For me, as well."

She took his hand, placed it on her still-flat belly where their unborn baby slept. The feel of that, the *promise* of that, came very close to breaking his heart. "We have to… do something," she said in a torn little whisper. "We have to…get past this. For the baby's sake, for Trev. For the sake of our family. *I* have to get past this, put aside my hurt pride that you lied, that you didn't treat me as an equal. We have to move on. But then, just when I'm sure I'm ready to let it go, I think of all the times you might have told me, might have *trusted* me…."

"Shh," he said, and lifted his hand to touch her lips again with the pads of his fingers. "It's not your fault. I am to blame and I know that I am. Somehow, I have to make you believe that I do trust you in all ways, that no matter how hard the truth is, I will never lie to you again."

She let out a ragged breath. "I *want* to believe you. So much."

He lifted her chin and brushed one last kiss against her

tender lips. "Give it time," he said again. "It will be all right." Would it? *Yes.* Somehow, he would make it so.

She stepped back and turned. And then she walked away from him.

It was the hardest thing he'd ever done, to watch her go. To *let* her go. Not to call her back. Not to grab her close again and kiss her senseless. Not to promise them both that everything was all right now.

When it wasn't all right.

When something precious was shattered between them and he knew that, as the one who had done the shattering, it was up to him to mend a thousand ragged pieces into one strong, shining whole.

The answer came to him in the middle of the night.

Or rather, in the middle of the night, he accepted fully how far he was actually willing to go to make things right.

He saw at last that he was going to have to do the one thing he'd said he would never do, the thing he'd rejected out of hand because it was going to be difficult for him. More than difficult. Almost impossible.

But whatever it took, if it gave him a chance of healing the breach between him and Sydney, he was ready to do it. To move forward with it.

And to do so willingly.

Pride, she had told him. *"I'm...too proud, Rule."*

They were alike in that. Both of them prideful, unwilling to bend.

But he would bend, finally. He would do the hardest thing. And he would do it gladly.

If it meant he would have her trust once more. If it meant she would see and believe that he knew the extent of the damage he'd done and would never do such a thing again.

He turned over on his side and closed his eyes and was sound asleep in seconds.

When he woke, it was a little after seven. He rose, showered, shaved and dressed.

Then he went to his office where he got out the stack of messages he'd tossed in the second drawer of his desk—the stack he'd known somewhere in the back of his mind he shouldn't throw away.

Not yet. Not until he was willing to make his choice from among them.

He chose quickly. It wasn't difficult: Andrea Waters. She was a household name, with her own prime-time news and talk show in America, on NBC. She was highly respected as a television journalist. And women loved her warmth and personal charm.

He glanced at his watch.

It would be two in the morning in New York City. He would have to wait several hours until he could call her producer back himself.

He made the first call to New York at two that afternoon. By seven that evening, everything was arranged.

Now, to tell his wife. He rose from his desk to go and find her.

And there was a tap at his office door.

At seven in the evening? Caroline wasn't out there to screen visitors. He'd told her she could go more than an hour before.

He called, "It's open. Come in."

The door opened—and Sydney slipped through.

He stood there behind his desk and drank in the sight of her. His lady in red—a red skirt and silk blouse, wearing those pearls her grandmother had given her, her hair smooth on her shoulders, just as it had been that first day, when he saw her in the parking garage and couldn't stop himself from following her inside. She looked tired, though. There were still shadows under her eyes.

"I've been waiting to talk to you," she said. "I...couldn't wait any longer. I came to find you."

"It's been a busy day. I'm finished here now, though." He tried on a smile. "I was just coming to find *you*...."

Hesitantly, she returned his smile. "I hardly slept at all last night."

"I know how that goes." His voice sounded strange to his own ears—a little rusty, rougher than usual. "I haven't been getting a lot of sleep, either."

"I told you yesterday that I wasn't there yet, I...hadn't really forgiven you."

"And I said I understood. I meant what I said."

"Oh, but Rule..." Her smile widened. And all at once, her whole face had a glow about it. She hardly even seemed tired anymore. She had her hands folded in front of her. He thought she looked so young right then. A girl, an innocent. Looking at her now he would never have guessed that she'd given birth to his son, that she carried his second child under her heart. "Something happened," she said. "Something wonderful."

Something wonderful. His heart beat a swift tattoo beneath his ribs. "Tell me."

"I don't know. I...I was lying there, alone in our bed. It was almost one in the morning. I was thinking of how I missed you, beside me, in the dark. Thinking that I knew, I understood, why you had kept the truth from me. Objectively I could see how it must have been for you. Waiting too long to contact me, knowing you were up against the deadline of the marriage law. Telling yourself you were only waiting for the right moment to say the words. And then hearing about Ryan, about Peter. Fearing that if you

told me the truth, I would suspect that you only wanted
Trevor. And then, when you *didn't* tell me, I could see how
it only got harder for you, how every day the truth became
more and more impossible for you to reveal."

He shook his head. "None of which is any excuse."

She put her hands to her cheeks, as if to cool the hectic
color in them. "I just want you to know that I *did* understand...I *do* understand, intellectually." She let her left
hand drop to her side. Her right, she laid above her breast.
"But my heart...my heart wanted you to trust in me. My
heart wanted you to be bigger than your very realistic
fears. My heart wanted you to give me the truth no matter
the cost."

"And I should have trusted you," he said. "I was wrong.
Very wrong. And I want you to stop torturing yourself because you can't forgive me."

She laughed then. A happy laugh, young and so free.
And her eyes had that tear-shine, the same as the day
before. She sniffed, swiped the tears away. "But that's
just it. I was lying there, thinking about everything, how
wrong things had gotten between us, how I wanted to work
it out but my heart wouldn't let me. And all of a sudden,
just like that...I saw *you*. I saw you, Rule. I...felt you, as
though you were there, in our dark bedroom with me.
And I saw that you love me and I love you and that's what
matters, that's what makes it all worthwhile. And I didn't
even need to think about forgiveness anymore. It just...
happened. I let my anger and my hurt and my resentment
go. I realized I do believe in you. I believe in your good-
ness and your basic honesty. I believe that you love me as
I love you. I want...our family back. I want *us* back." She
was crying again, the tears dribbling down her cheeks,
over her chin.

"Sydney..." He was out from behind his desk and at her side in four long strides. "Sydney..."

She fell against him, sobbing. "Rule, oh, Rule..."

He wrapped his arms around her and held on tight. "Shh. Shh. It's all right. It's going to be all right..."

Finally, pressing herself close, she tipped her chin back and he met her shining, tear-wet eyes. "Rule. I love you, Rule."

"And I love you, Sydney. With all of my heart. You *are* my heart. I looked for you for far too long. I'm so glad I finally found you. I'm so glad what we have together is stronger than my lies." He lowered his head.

And he kissed her. A real kiss. A deep kiss. A kiss of love and tears and laughter. A kiss to reaffirm their life together. Again. At last...

That kiss went on forever. And still it wasn't long enough.

But finally, he lifted his head. He took her face between his hands and brushed away the tear tracks. "I think you're right. I think we're going to make it, after all."

"I know we will. I always knew—or at least, I kept promising myself that somehow, eventually, it would all work out."

"I was coming to find you when you knocked on the door."

She held his gaze, searching. "What? What is it?"

"You wanted me to call a press conference...."

"Yes. I see now that was probably a bad idea."

"At first, I though it was a bad idea, too. Mostly because of my pride."

"It's okay, Rule. Truly."

"But I reconsidered."

"You're kidding."

"No. I did reconsider—and I still decided against it."

"It's fine. I understand."

"Instead, I'm going to give Andrea Waters an exclusive interview."

She gasped. And then she made a sputtering sound.

He laughed then. "My darling, I believe you are speechless. I don't remember that ever happening before."

She groaned. "Oh, you…" And she gave him a teasing punch on the arm.

"Ouch!" He grinned.

"Really, Rule. You're not serious."

"Oh, yes I am. I'm going to tell the truth about you and me and our son. I'm going to tell it on *Andrea Waters Tonight.*"

"Um. *Everything?*"

"Well, I think it would be acceptable to *manage* the message, at least to a degree."

She reached up, laid her hand on the side of his face. That simple touch meant so much to him. It was everything. To have her in his arms again, to feel her cool palm against his cheek, to know they were together, and that they always would be. "It isn't necessary," she said in a whisper. "It was too much for me to ask of you."

"No. It wasn't."

She touched his lips with her thumb. "Shh. Hear me out." She waited for his nod before she spoke again. "Yes, when it comes to us, to you and me, I demand total honesty. But I certainly don't expect you to share all your secrets with the rest of the world."

He took her hand, opened it, kissed the soft heart of her palm the way he'd always loved to do. "I think it should be possible to do this with dignity. With integrity."

"You can cancel. I'll be completely accepting of that."

He only shook his head and kissed her palm again.

She said, "Okay. If you're determined to do this…"

"Yes?"

"I want to be there, beside you, when Andrea Waters starts asking the questions."

He turned her hand over, kissed the backs of her fingers, one by one. "I was hoping you would say that."

"Are we going to New York?"

"No. She will come here, to Montedoro. There will be a tour of the palace as part of the broadcast. And then we'll sit down, the three of us, and chat."

"Chat." Sydney shivered.

"Are you cold, my darling?"

"With your arms around me?" Her green gaze didn't waver. "Never. But I *am* a little scared."

"Don't be. It's going to go beautifully. I'm sure of it."

"Kiss me, Rule."

And he did, for a very long time.

Epilogue

Her Royal Highness Liliana, Princess of Alagonia, Duchess of Laille, Countess of Salamondo, sat alone in her bedroom in her father's palace.

She wore a very old, very large green The Little Mermaid T-shirt, bought on a trip to America years before—and nothing else. Perched cross-legged on her bed, she held a delicate black plate decorated with yellow poppies and piled high with almond cookies. Lili intended to eat every one of those cookies. It was her second plate of them. She'd finished the first plateful a few minutes before.

Also, close at hand, she had a big box of tissues. Already, she'd used several of those. The discards littered the bed around her.

She was watching the television in the armoire across the room. It was *Andrea Waters Tonight,* an American program. Andrea Waters was interviewing Rule and Sydney.

Lili thought the interview was absolutely wonderful. Such a romantic story. She'd had no idea. Rule, a sperm donor? She never would have imagined that, not in a hundred thousand years. And Sydney's little boy, Trevor—he was Rule's all along.

Of course, Lili should have guessed. The resemblance was nothing short of striking.

And didn't Sydney look adorable? She was such a handsome woman. And she sat so close to Rule, holding his hand. And the glances those two shared…

That. Yes. Exactly. Lili wanted that, what Rule and Sydney had. She wanted real love, strong love, true love, forever, with the right man.

Unfortunately, that she would ever find the right man was looking less and less likely. Especially after what had happened with Alex.

Really, how *could* she?

With Alex, of all people?

And now, just look at the mess she was in.

Lili ate another almond cookie, whipped out another tissue and blotted up tears. Unceremoniously, she blew her nose.

And then she sighed.

Rule and Sydney. They looked so happy. They *were* so happy. And Lili was happy *for* them.

Yes, it was true. She'd been something of a fool over Rule for all those years. He was so handsome and such a good man and he'd always treated her with warmth and affection. She'd let her vivid imagination carry her away. She'd dreamed of being Rule's bride.

She'd thought that she loved him. And she *did* love him. But now, at last, she understood that the love she felt for Rule wasn't the kind of love a woman feels for the man to whom she binds her life.

Again, Lili wondered if she would ever find that man.

It was beyond doubtful. Maybe even impossible, given her current condition.

Besides the cookies and the tissues, Lili also had her phone. It was on the bed beside her. She reached out and grabbed it and dialed the number she'd been putting off calling for too long now.

She waited, hardly daring to breathe, as the phone rang. And rang. Finally, an answering machine picked up.

Alex's recorded voice said, "I'm not available. Leave a message."

She waited for the beep and then she said, "Alexander. You are the most exasperating man." She wanted to blurt out the truth right then and there. But it wasn't a good idea. Not on the phone. "Read the letter I sent you," she said. "And then you'd better call me, Alex. We really do need to speak privately." She waited some more. Maybe he was there, listening. Maybe for once he'd behave like a reasonable person and pick up the phone.

But he didn't. She heard the click that meant the machine had disconnected her.

Very gently, she hung up.

And after that, she just sat there, not even crying anymore, not even wanting another almond cookie, feeling terrible about everything. Wondering what was going to happen when her father found out.

* * * * *

MILLS & BOON®

Why shop at millsandboon.co.uk?

Each year, thousands of romance readers
find their perfect read at millsandboon.co.uk.
That's because we're passionate about
bringing you the very best romantic fiction.
Here are some of the advantages of
shopping at www.millsandboon.co.uk:

* **Get new books first**—you'll be able to buy
  your favourite books one month before they
  hit the shops

* **Get exclusive discounts**—you'll also be
  able to buy our specially created monthly
  collections, with up to 50% off the RRP

* **Find your favourite authors**—latest news,
  interviews and new releases for all your
  favourite authors and series on our website,
  plus ideas for what to try next

* **Join in**—once you've bought your favourite
  books, don't forget to register with us to rate,
  review and join in the discussions

Visit **www.millsandboon.co.uk**
for all this and more today!